Christmas Cookies and Kissing Bridge

Holiday Romance Series

The Complete Set of Fabulous Feel Good Holidaz Romances!

BY

LINDA WEST

CHRISTMAS COOKIES
AND KISSING BRIDGE

Book 1 –

Christmas Kisses and Cookies

Book 2-

Holiday Kisses and Valentine Wishes

Book 3 –

Chocolate Kisses and Love Filled Wishes

Book 4 –

Firework Kisses and Summertime Wishes

This is the complete 4 book set
of holiday romance stories on Kissing
Bridge Mountain. We hope you enjoy
this series and we are proud to announce
that each of these stories
have become #1 Best Sellers in
Holiday Romance!

Linda West

Welcome to Kissing Bridge Mountain
the happiest place on Earth.

Next to Disneyland of course!

In this wonderful town you will find the most adorable and loving people. Holidays and traditions still matter, and dreams have a way of coming true.

Come along on this heart-warming and exciting adventure and enjoy the love stories of some of our favorite people on Kissing Bridge Mountain!

Each of the four stories contained in this set are stand-alone love stories. The series is based around the lovely town of Kissing Bridge Mountain, a sweet and traditional hometown.

In an effort to make it easier for you to understand, no matter which story you begin with, I made a simple key for you to refer to. Here is a list of Kissing Bridge Mountain shops and it's enchanting inhabitants.

Locations:

1. Kissing Bridge, Vermont.
2. Claim to fame: Highest ski peak in the East.
3. Location of the famous Eagle's Peak Lodge.
4. Home to the nicest people.
5. Holiday Crazy.

Important places:

1. Eagle's Peak Lodge and Ski Resort.
2. Eagle's Inn Hotel and Restaurant.
3. Lander's Bakery.
4. Aero Anderson Airlines.

Cast of Characters on Kissing Bridge Mountain:

Summer Landers – 29, Slender, tall, blonde blue-eyed Super-Model and Sport's Illustrated Cover Model.

Daughter of Ethel Landers and heir to the Blue Ribbon winning cookie recipe.

Ethel Landers – 72 – beautiful silver haired senior. Resident Kissing Bridge Queen of the Silver Bells Christmas Cookie Contest for 50 years.

Aunt Carol Landers – 78, precautious, bright red Bee –Hive hair do with a fake NY accent. Has an amazing ability to eavesdrop on conversations across the room.

Brad Anderson – Hometown hero and popular dude. Second youngest of the Anderson children. Dark haired, tall, Anderson signature grey flannel eyes. Works for United airlines as a commercial pilot.

Jason Anderson – Oldest of the Anderson Clan. Handsome, auburn wavy hair, grey eyes, ex- marine. Returned to Kissing Bridge when he came home from the war.

Kacey Anderson – the youngest Anderson and only girl. Strawberry blonde hair with grey eyes. Olympic Snowboarder.

Dodie Randall – Charity lover and activist. Recently moved to Kissing Bridge after horrible break up. Auburn hair and blue eyes with a face like a china doll. 36.

Murielle (Elle) Saunders -19 Runs the stable at Eagle's Peak Lodge and helps out at the Eagle's Peak Diner there as well. Granddaughter of Earl the Lodge owner. Dreams of a family of her own.

Earl Elkins – Popular old gent of 73, tall with dark hair flecked with grey. Lodge owner and keeper. All around popular good guy.

Old Man (Jackson) Jennings – 79, White hair, oil rich, quiet, and Earl the lodge keeper's best friend.

Dayton Lowry – American War Hero and recipient of the Purple Heart. Best friend of Jason Anderson. Comes to Kissing Bridge for healing and finds love and miracles. He is 22, dark haired, dark eyes, slender and muscled. Ex- marine.

All of the books on Kissing Bridge are also available on audible to listen to as well!

Welcome to Kissing Bridge Mountain :)

Table of Contents

A Fabulously Funny Feel Good Romance

Christmas Kisses and Cookies

A Fabulously Funny Feel Good Romance

BY
LINDA WEST

Morningmayan.com Publishing

What happy readers are saying about Christmas Kisses and Cookies

"A side-splittingly funny, heartwarming, and delightful read! I laughed so hard, my husband kept asking me what I was reading. The inhabitants of Kissing Bridge were adorable. ***If you want some perfect feel-good uplifting holiday fun this is the go-to book. I wish I could give it 10 stars!****"*

S. Stevens, Kindle Good Reads

"**Within a matter of pages, I was laughing my socks off** *and immediately fell in love with the slightly crazy Summer… Linda West has such a knack for the humorous side of characters… Her writing style is so upbeat and unique, I hope to see more of these characters I've come to love - can't wait to see what happens next in the cute town of Kissing Bridge!"*

M. Sinclair

"This is exactly the feel-good Christmas book I was looking for! Right from the start, I was absorbed in the magic of the season and had a smile on my face. **I laughed from the first page and finished it in one sitting! I'd love to see a movie made out of this."**

D. Dragna

Dedicated, with love
to
My Grandma Ethel

It's the Christmas season, the happiest time of the year!

Before we begin, let's get you settled in with a cup of cocoa and a comfy chair. Let's imagine a crackling fire is beside you casting a warmth and glow. Perhaps a light snow has begun to fall outside. When Christmas is upon us and joy fills the air, we remember that all good things are possible. So sit back, relax, and have a nice drink. You're about to take a wonderful fun-filled adventure with the adorable inhabitants of the Christmas-obsessed town of Kissing Bridge. Now on to the story. I hope you enjoy it. Sending you love and cheer and mistletoe wishes. May your days be filled with Christmas cookies and kisses…

With love,
Linda West

Make sure you turn
to the last page where we have
a free gift waiting for you!!

Chapter 1

It was a blistering hot December evening in Los Angeles.

The stereo blared the Beach Boys *Merry Christmas* as Summer Landers, a lovely long-legged blonde, strung a single Christmas light strand between her potted palm trees inside her Malibu mansion. She had tried to buy more festive lights at the market, but there were none left. You would think that it was because they had sold out, since Christmas was right around the corner. But no. They just didn't stock them. Lack of sales.

That was L.A. in a nutshell. Just forget finding a blow-up Santa anywhere.

Summer couldn't help but dislike

Christmas in Los Angeles. It went against every version of the holiday she had grown up with. The ever-sunny cloud-free skies were not compatible with her version of winter wonderland. She was a Vermont girl, brought up in a small mountain town, and Christmas meant snow. And snow meant skiing. And boy, how she *loved* to ski. It was her favorite sport—not that she'd had time to do it in years.

Summer finished hanging the lonely light strand. The blinking green and red lights seemed to mock her. They looked more 'downtown hooker row' than 'lovely holiday spirit.'

Summer sighed.

She had considered buying some of that fake snow in a bottle from Amazon, but decided it was probably full of toxic waste. She yearned for the smell of pine air. Amazon offered that in a can as well—probably also full of toxic waste.

What was an environmentally-friendly supermodel to do?

Her cat, Fluff, an overweight tabby, sauntered in with his too-bright holiday red collar and annoying tinkling bell. He hated the collar, but he put up with it every year—not that he had a choice.

He wanted to be fed, as usual. Summer went into the kitchen and opened a can of gluten-free cat food from Whole Foods. She should stop feeding him so often, people would say—but really he was fat because he didn't exercise. Summer couldn't let Fluff outside to play for fear he might get snagged up.

Her next-door neighbour had lost her peekaboo poodle, Mr. Peebles, just that way. One minute they were enjoying mimosas on the sun deck…the next minute, Mr. Peebles was flying across the yard via hawk. Ever since that upsetting episode, Fluff had been an indoor cat.

She poured him some milk into a bowl. He lapped away happily.

Summer glanced at the pile of mail on her table. She sighed and started sorting through the envelopes.

Boring, boring, boring.

Usually by now, one would think that people would be sending festive holiday cards. Back home, you received so many Christmas cards that you could decorate your house with strings of them! But no, not in La La land. Christmas was almost here and not one friend of hers in L.A. had seen fit to send a real holiday card. Sure, there had been e-cards and text emojis, but real handwritten Christmas cards seemed to be non-existent in L.A., and Summer assumed it must resemble *work* of some kind.

She gazed at the poor palm tree trying to support the twinkling lights. The palm fronds weren't meant to hold weight, so now they wilted like poor Charlie Brown's Christmas tree.

Summer sighed. This was the time of year when she missed home the most. She reminisced about Christmas back home and how very different it was from this shallow, shiny tinsel town, with no tinsel. The stores had been out of that too!

She glanced at the date. Twelve days before Christmas. By now, her mother's kitchen would be filled with the smells of baking sweets and roasted walnuts. Frank

Sinatra's Christmas music would be playing and mistletoe sprigs would be hung in all the archways. Her Aunt Carol and Mom would be decorating the tree, drinking hot cocoa, and making the famous Landers' Christmas cookies together.

Summer spotted a bright red envelope in the pile of regular boring white mail. She gleefully reached for it and opened it immediately.

Then she groaned.

It was the annual Mistletoe Ski Event invitation from her hometown, Kissing Bridge.

Summer shook her head.

Only people from Kissing Bridge Mountain threw their biggest galas in the midst of winter. Kissing Bridge was famous for its skiing and its snow, and the local mountain people embraced them both. It was also home to one of the most renowned ski resorts in all of Vermont, Eagle's Peak. Winter was always a happy event and the Christmas holiday season was the highlight of the year. In the winter fairyland of Kissing

Bridge Mountain, the 12 days before Christmas were filled with one merry celebration after another.

Summer didn't know why they kept sending her the invitation to that stupid Kissing Bridge Mistletoe Ski Event when she never replied. She hadn't gone in ten years.

It had been so long since she had gone home at all. One year had grown into two, then five, and now it was nearly ten years since she had been home for Christmas.

She frowned at it.

Still, the invitation to the event had continued to come every year at about this time. Summer couldn't help but smile as she looked at the old-time photo on the invitation. It showed the original vintage high school picture of her and her classmates on the very first Mistletoe Ski Event ever.

There she was with Brad Anderson. They were snuggled up together, arm in arm smiling. The picture of young love.

She and Brad Anderson had met in their freshman year and had dated all though high school. At one time she had thought they would be married and live happily ever after on Kissing Bridge Mountain. Who would ever have suspected that he would have done what he did to her, just hours after that picture was taken?

It had been the worst day of her life.

Chapter 2

Her iPhone rang out *Silver Bells*… Summer looked down to see her Aunt Carol's name on the screen.

"Hey, Aunt Carol. How are you?"

Her Aunt Carol was her mother's oldest sister and the oldest of all of Grandma Izzy's children. Aunt Carol had been engaged to a very wealthy New Yorker and lived there for a short bit, before he met an untimely demise—snakebite in Kathmandu. He died before he got off the mountain. Poor Aunt Carol was devastated. But not surprised.

It was a case of the Landers' curse.

Losing the men they loved was indeed the curse of the Landers Ladies. Due to this malady, the entire family had only ladies left in it. Yet, they weren't without their gifts.

Aunt Carol had swiftly moved back to Kissing Bridge Mountain after his death, but insisted on keeping her newly-adapted, heavy New York accent for show. She thought it made her seem regal. Who was anyone to tell her otherwise?

"Yes, I'm fine. Thanks, Aunt Carol. Busy as usual. I just got back from London last night…a letter from my mother? Oh, the cookie competition!"

Summer leafed through the rest of the boring white mail looking for her mother's signature Tiffany-blue-colored envelope.

"Here it is."

Summer opened up the envelope and took out a clipping of her mother's smiling face in the local *Kissing Bridge Gazette*. She was holding up the blue ribbon as winner of the Annual Silver Bells Cookie Competition.

Summer smiled. The Landers' clan had held claim to the reigning throne of the Silver Bells Christmas Eve Cookie

Competition Queen for the last 50 years. Long since before Summer was born, Grandma Izzy's famous cut-out cookie recipe had been winning blue ribbons for the Landers. The blue-ribbon-winning cookie recipe had been passed down from sister to sister, and now to Summer as well.

Every year the Landers made the cookies together, and every year they won. It was a Christmas tradition that the Landers ladies held proudly.

"I found it, Aunt Carol. I see it. She looks great! Looks like another blue-ribbon year for the Landers!"

A loud "HRMMPH" was her Aunt's only reply.

Summer looked at the phone.

"Obviously then, you're coming home for Christmas this year." Aunt Carol said it more as a fact than a question.

Summer was completely confused.

"I can't come home for Christmas, Aunt Carol. I'd love to, really…But, I'm flying out tomorrow to shoot a commercial for Gucci all week."

Another loud GRUNT from Aunt Carol's end.

It was not like Aunt Carol to be short on words.

Summer continued. "Then I have to fly right back to L.A. to do a shoot with Maxim."

Aunt Carol croaked out a curt, "fine." And with that, she hung up abruptly on her niece.

Summer looked at the phone oddly as she put it down. If she wasn't mistaken, she had just gotten hung up on.

It was Sunday, so as usual, Summer planned to watch her favorite movie, *Breakfast at Tiffany's*. The Landers women loved romance and one of the best romances of all time was *Breakfast at Tiffany's*. In fact, it was a weekly Landers' tradition back home, to all brunch together on Sundays and enjoy a sweet or two while they watched it together.

Summer cuddled up with Fluff on her big couch and hit the remote. Gosh, she loved Netflix. She smiled as the opening credits started, and soon she was mouthing all of the words she knew by heart.

Summer munched on a cookie, and

wondered if she'd be alone for the rest of her life.

Chapter 3

It had been another rough overnight flight.

She had to stop flying the red eye. Summer Landers stared at her reflection in the mirror with a sigh. She knew she was running late—*really* late. Her beautiful mane of golden hair reigned down over her shoulders, framing her beautiful face. She peered closer; she definitely wasn't going to be able to hide those circles under those stunning blue eyes from Jasper. Jasper—or as Summer referred to him—the 'Blue Monster,' was the lead photographer on the shoot. He was brilliant and keen-eyed and never missed a thing.

She snapped her compact closed and tossed it back in her purse.

Even when she didn't feel great, she still looked stunning. She was Summer Landers, after all. Just this month she had been named top supermodel and *Sports Illustrated* 'Babe of the Year.' Her time had finally come.

Since being scouted from her hometown, Summer had been flying around the world nonstop for years. The back and forth, late nights and different time zones were wearing. It was finally catching up with her. She got out of the cab and hurried toward the production trucks.

The place was humming with activity. A large crew, lights, and cameras were in place. Even a crowd had gathered to watch the Gucci commercial being filmed on Fifth Avenue.

Summer tried to sneak into the makeup truck, nodding to the skinny P.A. as she passed.

"Thank God you're here, Summer. Jasper is freaking out," she whispered conspiratorially. Just then an angry blue-haired Jasper came stampeding toward them.

"Really Summer, our biggest shoot? My career is hanging on this and you show up two hours late?"

"I'm sorry, Jasper. The red eye got in late. I didn't sleep great and the alarm—"

"Save it! You have more excuses than I have time for. I need you on set in 15 minutes!" He stuck his head in the makeup truck and yelled to the makeup crew inside. "15 minutes!"

Summer sat down in the makeup chair with a sullen look. The makeup and hair crew flocked around her and set to work. Within moments and swipes of the brushes she was transformed into a goddess.

The makeup artist studied her work. "You look gorgeous, Summer—if I do say so, myself."

Summer gazed at her reflection.

"Thanks, Marissa. You've worked your magic once again."

She felt horrible. Blue Monster was at his worst. Everyone thought modeling was so glamorous, and all she wanted was *out*.

Within moments, Summer was in front of the cameras, smiling as if she hadn't a care in the world. The camera lights kept popping—pop, pop, pop!

On the outside, she smiled like the professional model she had become. But inside, Summer was ready to explode.

Chapter 4

Thank goodness the shoot was over. Summer sat in her dressing room in front of the mirror, wiping off glitter makeup. The sun had been intolerable and Blue Monster had lived up to his ill-tempered self. Summer hated to make him angry. Of all the photographers she worked with, she enjoyed him the most, even if he did have a horrible temper. Her agency was not going to be happy. She'd been late again. Time is money, and all that.

Summer made her way toward the curb just as a new light snow had begun to fall. She thought how nice it was to be in Manhattan, where unlike L.A., there was festive holiday energy. She could almost feel the good will in the air in celebration of the happy holiday season.

Just then, a crowd of busy shoppers jostled by, knocking into her as they headed for the Macy's sale.

Summer tried to move out of the way to let them pass. "Oh owww, that was my foot! ... Oh excuse *me...* " She got pushed and shoved back and forth by the passing masses as they fought down the street.

One particularly rude man banged into her so hard, she fell down onto the cement ground and all the contents of her purse spilled out onto the sidewalk. She scrambled to pick up her things between the throngs of feet going by. The hurried crowd stampeded on, everyone nearly stepping on her. She grabbed up her phone and keys and finally snatched up her cat's favorite toy—a scary looking Gumby— just in time, before a dashhound nearly ate it.

Summer righted herself triumphantly, with her bag in one hand and Fluff's Gumby in the other. The mass of shoppers poured on by. So much for the holiday spirit!

Across the street, Summer spotted the

famous Tiffany's store from her favorite movie. She took a moment to take in the beauty of the storefront before she walked over to it.

Silent Night played over the speakers outside the store and the show windows were filled with beautiful diamond necklaces and rings. Summer peered at the pretty diamonds in the window lost in thought.

Tiffany.

Diamonds.

Christmas.

She sighed heavily.

Christmas was here again so soon. In the past, Christmas had been the highlight of her year. Now it just seemed to bring up all the painful memories she had tried to forget.

And what had that weird phone call from her Aunt Carol been all about?

Summer knew that it was only a matter of days now before her mother would call and ask her to come home for Christmas, *again*. First came the card with the clippings from the Kissing Bridge Gazette showing the picture of last year's cookie contest winners, and then came the phone call. It was always the same conversation. "Please come home. We love you. We miss you. We need your help with the cookies..."

Summer was running out of excuses.

A car honked and pulled Summer out of her reverie. Jerry, the uber rich executive producer from the shoot, stopped his expensive black Mercedes next to her.

"Looks like you could use a lift…" He accessed her, as if she were weak prey.

"No, thanks. I'm good."

"Sure?"

"Yes, I'm sure. I'm waiting for Drake."

That seemed to mollify him and he finally drove away.

She watched him leave, and then ducked into *Pinto* to call Drake.

Pinto was the trendiest new restaurant in town. There was a long wait for a table, even if you were rich and famous. It was decorated with all silver for Christmas. Silver lights, silver bells, silver plates. Lots of silver. Summer guessed silver must be in fashion this season.

"Chardonnay please," she smiled at the cute bartender with the deep dimples and the green eyes. He smiled back at her and filled her glass extra full.

Summer sat quietly sipping her drink and waited for Drake to join her. All around her, there were happy families dining and enjoying the Christmas spirit. Small children were dressed up in their finest outfits. Moms and dads were snapping pictures in front of the trendy Christmas tree and warning the young tots to, "*…Be good or Santa will bring you coal…*"

All of New York seemed to be joyous in anticipation of the coming holiday season. Summer sighed. She couldn't shake those *'mean reds'* as Audrey Hepburn called them in *Breakfast at Tiffany's*.

She knew she should be happy. She was grateful to have become a success. Growing up with a single mom had been financially difficult. Now, because of Summer's fame and fortune, they never had to worry about money again. Summer had been able to pay off the mortgage on their home back in Kissing Bridge Mountain the very first Christmas after she had started modeling.

Still, she hadn't been back home since she had left. It was just too hard for her. Going home just reminded her of the life she would never have. She had never intended to become a famous supermodel and end up with this fake life where only fame and money mattered and nannies raised the children.

It had been her dream to have five kids and be a stay-at-home mom. She was so far away from what her heart had always truly wanted.

She just had to have faith that God would work things out for her, despite the family curse.

Her mother had taught her that faith was very important, and Summer had cleaved on to that, and for good reason. She had known since childhood that strange things can happen in life and you have to be strong—and have faith. And sometimes due to the curse, you lost people you cared about.

Each of Summer's aunts had all lost

the men they loved— in various odd ways—due to the Landers' curse.

Aunt Carol had lost her fiancé with his untimely demise, and mom had lost Summer's dad as well.

Literally lost.

The story goes that her mom and dad were newly married and had wanted to start a family right away. When Mom got pregnant right off, they were so thrilled and excited, they had not even had time to change her name from Landers yet.

Mom started having some weird pregnancy cravings and one night had a special hankering for a Sloppy Joe from the local *Pup and Stuffs*, so dad had gone out to get one. Unfortunately, they had run out of Sloppy Joe's at the Kissing Bridge store, so they had suggested he go over to the *Pup and Stuffs* in the valley. So, off Dad had driven in search of that Sloppy Joe sandwich. Sadly, the *Pup and Stuff's* in the valley had also sold out of all their Sloppy Joes! So once again, Dad went out in the snow in search of a Sloppy Joe sandwich for Mom.

No one seems to know for sure

whether it was because of some mysterious unknown factor, or Dad just decided he wasn't coming back without that sandwich—but he was never heard from again. They never found his car and he never showed back up in Kissing Bridge Mountain.

When Summer was five and old enough for school, her mother registered her as 'Summer Landers.' No one ever brought up her missing ex-husband or that Sloppy Joe sandwich again.

It was another case of the dreaded Landers' curse.

Summer reasoned that she didn't need love anyway. It just broke your heart. She had a great life. She had lots of money. She had fame and excitement. She should be happy.

And yet…

Chapter 5

Drake Mason paced back and forth in front of the Tiffany's store on Fifth Avenue.

He glanced at his expensive gold Rolex watch. His driver, in his sleek black limousine, waited by the curb. A frown was beginning to form on his handsome face, when Summer finally came out of the restaurant. She was all long blonde hair and gangly legs like a young foal.

"Hey, I thought you wanted to have dinner? I finally got us a table. What's up?"

Drake Mason was a sight to behold. Tall, dark and with twinkly brown eyes, he was drop-dead gorgeous. Drake was considered quite the catch with his stunning good looks and playful personality. His family millions didn't hurt either—nor the fact he was a sought after A-list movie star. Drake Mason certainly had it all.

Still, Summer had not found herself falling in love with him, and for good reason. Drake was a perpetual Peter Pan type that refused to grow up and be serious. They had dated for six months and most of that time they had each been in different cities. From what the tabloids said, he hadn't been faithful to her either. She'd seen more than one photo of some starlet draped around him while he was away shooting a movie on set.

Drake interrupted her thoughts.

"Honey!"

He took off his blue Armani suit coat and wrapped it around her lovingly.

Summer pulled the coat closer and looked up at him with her liquid blue eyes. So much she wanted to say. I hate my life. I hate modeling. I don't know where I belong. I want to break up.

Instead she said, "Long day."

"Come on sweetheart, we'll get you some coffee. We can't have you half asleep for the most exciting night of your life!"

Summer wondered what he meant.

Chapter 6

That's how Summer found herself inside the prestigious blue-lined interior of the famous Tiffany store in New York for the first time in her life.

She was surrounded by rows of glistening diamond rings that the sales clerk had pulled out from the case.

Engagement rings.

So this was Drake's big surprise.

She had thought he had wanted to celebrate his recent movie deal with Donald Trump. Drake had just been cast to star as Donald in the story of his life on the big screen. He was due to start shooting *Donald—The Hair and The Story* as soon as he wrapped up his latest film about the life story of James Dean.

Summer held a steaming cup of coffee in one hand, as Drake pointed to another ring for the sales clerk to try on her finger.

The brilliant perfect diamonds sparkled around her, mimicking the snow that had begun falling outside the windows.

The classic Tiffany blue walls created a soothing effect against the piercing beauty of the rings. Summer thought how much her mother would have loved being there in person.

She looked at Drake. He had never mentioned getting married and having a family.

He was focused on the largest diamond in the case.

"Try this one on."

As if on cue, the salesperson slipped the six-carat, emerald-cut diamond ring on Summer's wedding finger.

It was stunning.

"We'll take this one."

Drake lifted Summer up with him as he rose. "We have dinner with Donald. We have to get moving." He led her out the door and called back to the clerk to, "Have it sent over to The Ritz after it's sized."

Summer felt like her world was spinning.

"Drake, I don't want to go to dinner. I don't feel well."

Drake laughed it off.

"A couple glasses of champagne and you'll be good as new. I need you there. Donald is bringing his wife."

Soon they were at *The Ritz* with Donald Trump and his beautiful wife. Drake and Donald were enmeshed in business talk and Summer chatted to Donald's model wife about the modeling business.

Suddenly, the lights dimmed, and a group of waiters appeared with a small delicate white cake. It was decorated with exquisite diamond chips that glistened in the candlelight. It said 'Congratulations Drake and Summer.'

A violinist appeared and began to play *Going to the Chapel.*

Drake turned to the restaurant diners, ecstatic.

"We wanted you to be the first to know...We're getting married!"

The whole restaurant began clapping and offered congratulations.

Champagne was brought and poured. Summer didn't even remember being asked. There had been no getting down on one knee and declaration of love forevermore ... No moment to remember... No story to tell the kids…

Still, it appeared the matter was settled.

Summer picked up one of the tiny diamond chips off the little white engagement cake and looked at it carefully.

A waiter leaned in and whispered, "They're edible!"

Summer's face brightened as she popped one of the diamond chips in her mouth and tasted it.

She rolled it around her tongue expertly. She couldn't make out the faint wonderful taste.

"Yum… Do you know what's in this?"

The waiter shook his head. "No miss,

that's Mr. Puck's proprietary recipe. His people dropped it off this morning."

"Ooooh ... Wolfgang Puck."

Summer was impressed. She knew he was the king of delicacies. Of course, they were superb.

Summer smiled her famous bi-coastal grin.

"They're delicious!"

Chapter 7

The skies over New York were clear, as the Boeing 757 got ready to make a landing.

Captain Brad Anderson finished the call sign to air traffic control. He was looking forward to a good time in New York tonight after the tough flight from Chicago. It had been the last flight out for the night because of the advancing storm system, and he was happy to be halfway home before it hit.

Eyes steady as he edged the bird onto the snowy runway, Brad was the perfect picture of a successful career guy at work.

He landed the plane smoothly, as usual.

After saying goodbye to the exiting passengers, he focused his attention on the beautiful flight attendant standing at the entrance. Not hiding the fact that she was attracted to him, she gave him a suggestive look before she wiggled her pretty behind out of the plane. Glancing behind her, she caught Brad admiring her.

She reached inside her uniform and rearranged her large boobs until her cleavage hung out almost over her collar.

Brad raised an eyebrow at her arranging ability.

She purred like silk, "Want to meet up tonight? I know a good place where we can go shake off the fatigue from the flight."

Brad was not one to let such an opportunity pass him by.

"Sounds good to me. I'll pick you up as soon as I get cleaned up."

It had become a habit for him to pick up pretty women on the layovers wherever he flew.

Whistling softly to himself, he flung his coat over his shoulders. Life had been good to him. He was one of the youngest Captains in the company, and his job was to fly the world. He was content to have it that way.

He was living the dream. No feelings. No commitments. No kids.

He should have been happy.

Chapter 8

Bright and early the next morning, Summer hurried through the TSA, listening to the beeping signal on her iPhone, indicating she had messages.

She didn't have time to answer it. She was trying to get her shoes on and the weird TSA agents always insisted on frisking her.

She knew it was her modeling agent again anyway—*not* happy. Summer knew she deserved her agent's ire but it would have to wait. The tongue lashing would be easier to take in a voicemail. She knew how it would go as usual…

"Summer, you were late. The producer complained. Summer, you didn't look your happy self. The client complained. Summer, Jasper doesn't like you calling him Blue Monster."

If she played it right, she could avoid dealing with anything until after the holidays. And by then, the whole fiasco might blow over.

Hopefully.

Thoughts of the upcoming Christmas planned for her this year brought up a new sadness in her.

Staying with Drake's parents in downtown L.A. was the worst Christmas holiday she could imagine. In winter she wanted to ski—*not* brunch at Wolfgang Puck's newest place—too many shallow elegant dinner parties with healthy trendy food. Winter was an excuse to eat cheese, darn it! What was wrong with these Californians?

And then also, the engagement well wishes.

She looked at the super huge diamond on her finger.

Ugh. She was losing it. She was just so unhappy lately, no matter how happy she *should* have been. She was the girl who had everything—except Prozac at the moment, which might have actually helped.

She had wanted nothing more than to marry a great guy and have a family. After the disaster with Brad, Summer had been too afraid to open up to love again. She had never given her heart to anyone since.

Of all the men she had dated over the years, Drake, at least, understood her the best.

Let her be her.

She wasn't getting any younger, Summer reasoned to herself. Maybe God had brought her Drake to give her the family she had always wanted? Maybe she was supposed to have faith?

He did get her a Tiffany ring. Surely *that* was a sign.

She thought back to Brad and that fateful night at the Christmas Mistletoe Ski Event.

At one time she had wanted to have five children and be a stay-at-home mom. Brad and she had planned to give their children all names that started with J's.

Summer almost laughed out loud thinking of the horror on her agent's face if she told her she was pregnant.

Ruin the body of the year? Gasp.

Perhaps that was the root of her sadness.

All she ever wanted was a big family, and instead she was flying around the world smiling for a living with not a child in sight.

Her Tiffany ring sparkled on her hand as the light bounced off the silver rails of the escalator.

She was engaged. Here was her chance to have the family she always wanted. Maybe she should just take what God had brought her and marry Drake?

She found her gate and sat down on an empty chair. She plopped Fluff down next to her in his Gucci carrying case and fished through her purse for his cat food and ugly Gumby toy.

An old lady with a nice face sat down next to her. She looked a lot like Summer's Grandma Izzy. Summer smiled at her.

The old lady smiled back. She looked

at Fluff in the carrying case. His little black nose was squished up to the net as his big yellow eyes peered out at them.

"It's so nice to be able to bring your pet nowadays."

Summer agreed. "And he's a joy to travel with."

She barely opened the top of Fluff's case and squished the Gumby in quickly before slamming it shut.

She had to keep Fluff in the case because he flipped out from too much airport stimulation. He was a chill Malibu cat. He didn't do crowds. They'd barely survived a bad stint in Singapore.

"Where are you spending Christmas this year?" Summer inquired, as she slid the cat food into Fluff's case carefully.

The lady said with a sigh, "Here, now. I just called my son to come back to the airport to pick me back up. I was supposed to fly out and visit my daughter this year in Denver. Oh well."

"I love Denver. Oh, I'm so sorry you can't go. What happened?"

She pointed at the TV screen above them showing the news channel with pictures of a large snowstorm coming in.

"They're saying it's the biggest snowstorm in decades. They're shutting down all the airports west of here. They just closed Chicago so that means no Denver for me."

Summer looked at the state of the weather on the TV screen in horror.

"Oh no! They closed O'Hare? And Houston? Shoot! That means I can't get back west to California either…"

She watched as the newscaster explained the extent of the storm.

Summer gasped. "Did that announcer just say that flights would be delayed for a week?! But that's all through Christmas!"

Summer put her head in her hands and moaned. This was turning out to be the second worst Christmas ever!

"I could have gone with my fiancé on the private jet last night, but Donald is allergic to cats."

She cast a blaming sideways look at Fluff.

The old woman fished in her bag for a minute and finally brought out some

Christmas cookies tied with a pretty bow.

She handed them to Summer.

"I was bringing them to my daughter, but you look like you need them more."

Summer did.

Over the loud speakers United announced, "Beginning boarding for Kissing Bridge, Vermont."

The nice lady that looked like Grandma Izzy motioned to the gate.

"Looks like that's the last flight out for the day and it's going north. Well, good luck, Sweetheart and Merry Christmas."

"Merry Christmas." Summer said.

The old lady walked away to meet her son.

Summer didn't know what to do.

She didn't have any close friends in Manhattan with whom she could spend Christmas. Christmas was the most special time of the year—the time you spent with your closest ties and family. Everyone was home with his or her family; everyone but *her*.

She gazed at the screen and was surprised to sees Earl, the lodge keeper up at Kissing Bridge Mountain on the TV.

He was being interviewed about the big snowstorm, "… Up here, we love snow! We have great snow! Now, if you like to ski, you should come on up to friendly Kissing Bridge Mountain!"

Summer smiled. "Hey Fluff, it's Earl, the lodge keeper. I know him."

Summer chomped on the nice lady's Christmas cookies in deep thought. She loved snow. She loved to ski. Snow and ski in Kissing Bridge.

The clerk at the United gate announced "Final boarding for Kissing Bridge, Vermont."

Chapter 9

Summer drank a hot cup of coffee and stared out of the plane window at the snow falling over the runway below. She pulled up her dark sunglasses and let the light hit her face.

Home.

She hoped she hadn't made the wrong choice—not that she had many options.

Fluff meowed in his carrying case; he hated flying, even in first class—especially the landings.

Summer reached into the case and pet him.

"Where'd your ugly Gumby squeaky toy go?"

Within minutes, they were on the

ground. Summer finished her coffee and avoided the stares of the deplaning passengers as they tried to recognize her behind her dark glasses. She fished around, looking for Fluff's ugly Gumby toy, as she dialed her mom's number. A smile came to Summer's face as she imagined her mother's surprise.

"Hey Mom, it's me. You'll never guess where I am! Mom, are you crying?"

Summer listened to her mother sniffling on the other end of the phone. She couldn't quite get out of her what was wrong.

"I'm going to grab a cab and I'll be right there, Mom. Don't worry!"

She grabbed her Gucci bag and Fluff's case and made her way off the plane.

A pretty flight attendant with short blonde hair and big breasts waved goodbye.

"Thanks for flying United," she chirped, in a fake sounding southern accent.

"Thanks. Hey, I lost my cat's squeaky toy. If you find it, can you please have it sent to where I'm staying?"

The flight attendant's pretty smile fell to a line.

"I have nothing better to do."

What the heck did that mean? Summer immediately disliked her, for some reason.

"Yeah? Well, thanks." Summer scribbled down her number on a piece of paper. "My cat loves that darn thing."

Summer turned to leave and bumped into the Captain exiting the cockpit.

Fluff's carrying case went flying with a resounding wail from the cat inside. Summer nearly fell over.

Brad Anderson grabbed her just as she lost her balance.

"Whoa there, little lady! Sorry about that. Are you all right?"

Summer collected herself, and spotted Fluff's case a couple of feet away. The cat was okay—albeit, glaring at her now through the mesh window.

"Yes, thank you." She looked up at him and almost fainted when she saw the familiar grey eyes.

"Brad?"

Brad looked confused. Then a scowl

formed on his handsome face. His eyes turned stormy. He thrust her back away from him.

"Summer."

Summer regained her composure and smiled, hoping he wouldn't notice how insecure she felt at that moment.

"Long time no see."

He looked her over with a hard stare.

"I forgot… you were blonde now, living in L.A."

Whoa that was icy. Summer's hope sank. How he managed to make L.A. and blonde sound so bad, she had no idea.

Darn that Brad Anderson. She didn't care what he thought.

She didn't *want* to care. Her heart beat loudly in her ears as she struggled to find something interesting to say.

"I am… I mean…I live back in L.A., but I travel all the time. Well, look at you; a big time pilot! No more flying crop dusters for your dad?"

The pretty flight attendant interrupted their conversation and slipped her arm through Brad's.

"We need to catch our crew car

Darling," she drawled in a sticky way.

Summer liked her even less now.

'Miss Big Boobs,' as Summer had now dubbed her, led Brad away down the ramp and far away from her.

Story of my life, Summer thought—Brad Anderson walking away from her. Some things never change.

Chapter 10

Summer found her mom busy in the kitchen making pies.

The house was decorated beautifully for Christmas. The smell of apples and cinnamon filled the air. A warm comforting heat rose from the oven. It felt like home.

"Hey honey! It's so great to see you!" her mom said, squishing her with a warm hug.

"Great to be home." Summer said—when she could breathe again.

They laughed together and hugged some more.

"It's so good to have you home, Honey. Thanks for coming."

She looked at her daughter seriously. She wiped a lone tear away.

Summer was concerned.

"Mom, what's going on?"

Her mother put the kettle on the stove to heat up.

"Honey, this is going to take some hot cocoa therapy."

Soon they were perched together on the couch in front of the decorated Christmas tree, hot cocoas in hand.

Mom's tree had dozens of strings of lights and barely a visible branch that wasn't loaded with ornaments.

A black and white newspaper article was lying on the table. It was open to the picture from the *Kissing Bridge Gazette* that Mom had sent her in the mail.

Her mother picked up the article and handed it to her.

"Look at it."

"It's a copy of the one you sent me?"

"Look again."

Summer peered closely again at the picture, and then her mouth fell open.

The clipping showed a picture of the cookie competition contenders that had been taken right after last year's judging. A proud smiling bunch of cotton tops (grey-haired ladies) stood together holding their ribbons up for show.

Her mom however, was not smiling in the picture.

Ethel Landers' unhappy face was clearly evident as she held up her *red ribbon* for second prize.

She held it far away from her, as if a skunk had sprayed it.

Summer pulled the *Gazette* closer to her face.

"Mom! Why is Mrs. Beaverton holding *your* first place blue ribbon? And why are you…."

Her voiced trailed off to a whisper as she looked at her mother in horror and realization.

"Because *she* won it!" shouted her mother.

Summer gasped out loud and brought her hand to her mouth in disbelief.

"But you sent me the annual picture of you winning? I don't understand?"

Ethel Landers looked at her daughter sheepishly.

"Photoshop."

Summer gasped again.

"Photoshop? When did you learn Photoshop?"

Her mother shrugged. "Your Aunt Carol and I took a senior class at the Y. I just switched out our heads. I also do the Facebook."

Summer didn't know which shocked her more.

"Mom, how could this happen? Nobody has ever beat Grannie Izzy's famous cut-out cookies!"

"You haven't been home in a long time, Darling. Things have changed."

Chapter 11

The next morning, bright and early, Summer and her mother got to work.

Frank Sinatra's Christmas Hits played in the backdrop. The kitchen was aglow with the crackling of the fireplace. The kitchen counter was completely filled with cookie ingredients. Flour, sugar, butter and a large, old recipe book lay open to a worn out page. A light snow was falling softly outside, and no one had any idea what the Landers ladies were up to.

Summer had decided that the recipe had been made wrong. Her mother assured her that she had done nothing different.

"I'm telling you, I made it the way we

always do. That Mrs. Beaverton has just gone and out-modernized me."

Summer looked puzzled.

Her mother shook her head. "She's had her grandson helping her on the internet, I'm pretty sure. I've seen him come up the walk at least once a week with that laptop holder thing."

This was getting serious.

Summer gazed out the window at the Beaverton's house next door.

Through the window, she spotted Mrs. Beaverton up early as well – making cookies! She pressed her nose to the window to get a better look. The requisite cookie ingredients were laid out in a mirror image to their own. Summer spotted an odd-looking spice jar. She squinted, trying to make out the words.

And with that, the window shade was suddenly rudely slammed down and blocked Summer's view.

"Well, I *never!*"

She turned to her mother.

"This is getting serious."

Her mother nodded in complete agreement.

Summer thought about it.

"We need a plan."

Mother was all ears. She waited for her to continue.

"I don't have a plan, mind you." Summer said.

Her mother threw up her hands.

"I'm going to be humiliated – *again!*"

Summer tried to calm her down.

"Let's think, Mom. Either we go standard all the way and hope they still appreciate the classic version we've always done, *or* we fight with fire and get on YouTube! You can learn anything you want on YouTube!"

Her mom considered that.

"I would like to see if they have any color videos. Although I can't imagine beating my colors from last year. The colors were impeccable, Summer. If you'd only seen them. They were truly magical. I really outdid myself."

Besides the fact that Grandma Izzy's cookie recipe was super and unbeatable, Mom had a special talent.

As I mentioned, the Landers had a curse, but they each also had a special unique one-of-a-kind gift.

Mom's unique talent was color healing. She was a legend for her coloring book pictures as a child, so it was only natural she ended up teaching water color painting to the high school kids as well. Mom was also the one who found the exact perfect red shade of hair color that set Aunt Carol apart from all other red heads.

Their house interior was painted a certain buttermilk cream ivory paint that was the envy of all the neighbors.

Many of them had asked over the years where to buy it, in an attempt to replicate the ethereal effect. Alas, there was no color to buy! Mother had created the color herself! She had bought a few gallons of paint and mixed them up, and magically came up with the envious hue that now graced their walls.

When Summer had been sick with grief after her break up with Brad, Mother had insisted they paint her room the subtlest of rose colors. Many a night, tears were dried staring at those lovely walls, and somehow solace was found and a career made.

There were many who believed it was her mother's gift with color that gave the Landers' Christmas cut-out cookies their extra edge.

After Grandma Izzy passed, the cookies taste changed ever so slightly. No one had been able to discern the subtle difference but the Landers themselves. However, their cookies were still far better than anyone else's, and so had continued to reign supreme.

Yes, they always won. But it was Mother's special gift for color that was the cherry on the cookie cake. Mother's joyful warm reds and vibrant tree greens shot out in contrast to the dull pastels of her competitors. Without a doubt, her mother had the gift with color.

Summer gazed at her mother's unhappy face in the picture, and her holding the red ribbon.

She felt filled with guilt.

She shouldn't have stayed away so long. Look what had happened.

Summer looked suspiciously toward the closed shades of the Beaverton's house across the way.

"Mom, do you think Mrs. Beaverton knows about YouTube yet?"

Mom sipped on her hot cocoa deep in thought.

"Her grandson is pretty wily—just like his father—the one that looks like a ferret." Wily. There's a chance he told her about *'The YouTube'*.

Summer considered this.

"Okay, then it's an even playing field. She has him, but you have *me*. And I have my computer. We'll have to think outside the box. In the meantime, let's make a batch of our originals and see if we can notice anything different. It could be oven temperature, or that the water had too much fluoride."

The two Landers ladies tied on their aprons and got down to business while *The Best of Bing Crosby's Christmas* tunes played in the background.

Chapter 12

Before long, they had a few dozen of their famous fresh-baked cookies lining the kitchen counters.

Mom was mixing up the frosting with the real vanilla maple syrup (one of the secret ingredients) when Aunt Carol walked in.

Aunt Carol was a sight to behold in person. She was a boisterous lady with a large red beehive that had somehow made it from the '50s straight on through to the 21st century. It had actually come back in style a couple of times during those decades—but in style or not, Aunt Carol bulldozed on.

Aunt Carol had also, upon returning home, turned into a notorious cat woman. At last count, she had over 20—and they were *all* black. It had gotten to be that anytime anyone in Kissing Bridge Mountain had a litter with a black cat, or just found an old stray black cat, they would just high-tail it over to Aunt Carol's and be done with it. Who knew how many she had now?

Aunt Carol also had a special talent. She had an unsurpassed amazing ability to eavesdrop.

Aunt Carol had the gift to be able to hear gossip drop a good 15 feet away, and in a ruckus crowd! One would never have expected that the loud, overly talkative senior could also *simultaneously overhear full conversations across the room*; even while she herself was in the midst of having one!

She was, in essence, a phenomenon.

The only liability with the talent was with the B's. She had a hard time hearing them for some reason. However, most of everything she overheard could still be pieced together with basic logic and substituting a 'B' now and then.

Of course, they had kept her special

talent a secret in the family so it could be best utilized.

Unbeknownst to the rest of the town, through Aunt Carol, they had been able to keep tabs on most of the goings-on in Kissing Bridge Mountain.

That's how, in fact, Summer had heard the truth about Brad that ruined her life.

Chapter 13

Before she had time to think further, Summer was swept up in everything that was Aunt Carol.

"Summer, what a wonderful surprise! Why Ethel, how dare you keep this from me," she chided her younger sister.

Summer laughed. "Don't blame Mom, Aunt Carol. It's my fault. I surprised her."

Aunt Carol looked at Mom trying to decide if that was, in fact, the truth. With a loud "Hrmmph," she gave up.

"Well then, I take it you have learned the state of things?"

Summer nodded in seriousness.

Mom and Aunt Carol went into the living room.

Mom put a log on the fire.

All three were soon seated around the Christmas tree, holding hot steaming mugs of cocoa in their hands.

Aunt Carol took on a serious look. "I don't want you getting upset… but I was walking by the GameStop at the mall and who did I see, but young Peter Beaverton!"

Summer looked at her mom for clarification.

"The wily one."

Summer nodded in understanding. "Oh, the grandson."

Aunt Carol waited for them to finish before continuing dramatically.

"He was bragging to another young man about his grandma and how she was going to win the Silver Bells Christmas cookie competition hands down this year - *again!*"

Summer looked at her mother.

"What, Aunt Carol… what did you overhear?"

Aunt Carol took a long swallow of her cocoa and looked her family in the eyes.

"She's getting private coaching…with a professional…*on Skype!*"

Mom looked confused.

"What—what's Skype???"

Aunt Carol shrugged.

Summer shot to attention.

"It means she's getting private coaching from someone that could be in *Ireland*, for all we know!"

Summer groaned.

"He is wily!"

Mom pulled herself together.

"Well then... I can't enter. I can't compete against Skype!"

Summer and Aunt Carol looked at each other. They wanted to console her.

They just couldn't.

The Beaverton's had a professional.

This was getting serious.

Chapter 14

Summer was thoroughly depressed. Here she had come home to get away from her sadness, and now her mother was ready to be committed. After Aunt Carol had left, her mother had taken to her room and refused to even come out for dinner.

Taking to the bed was a common expression of major depression for the Landers women. When one of them declared they were '*taking to the bed*' that meant lots of tears, lots of moping and generally little or no communication from the bed—other than for basic nourishment.

Depending on how bad the event to be dealt with was, nourishment could swing between pizzas—or juice-only cleanses.

By early evening, Summer was bored and decided to go to the corner café that was a walkable distance in the snow. She looked out the window at the snow banks blocking the road.

She pulled on her boots and hunted through the hall closet for a warm coat. She had left L.A. with just her leather coat on and that wouldn't hold up on Kissing Bridge Mountain. Up on the mountain, the winds whipped the snowfall into a blizzard in a blink and you had better be prepared with the correct gear.

Summer chose a parka and some fuzzy orange mittens. She donned her black sunglasses, even though it was night time. She didn't want to be recognized; she just wanted to get out of the house and possibly see what was going on at the Beaverton's house.

As she passed the driveway, she saw young 'Wily Junior'—as she had dubbed him now—trudging up the driveway with the dreaded laptop.

Ugh, she thought. Another Skype session with 'the professional'!

She focused on the falling snow. Getting stressed wasn't going to help anything.

The snow felt good on her face as she walked the short distance to the cafe. The neighbors all had their homes decorated with lights and ornaments and the pre- requisite blow up Santa dotted each snow-covered lawn; as they should be. She waved at an older Italian man who was outside shoveling his driveway. "Hey, Mr. Machelli," she called out gaily.

He waved to her, "Welcome home, Summer! It's been a long time! Merry Christmas!"

"Merry Christmas!"

Her spirits had lifted with the thought of some unhealthy cold weather fare. Back in L.A. it was kale salads and tofu everyday. When she was home, she wanted everything that came with gravy and lots of gluten.

The cafe was small and looked like an old cabin, but it had an inviting feel and gay holiday music spilling out from the door when it opened.

Summer took a seat at the bar.

The bartender came over quickly.

"Wow, you're gorgeous! What are you doing here?" Summer smiled. "I'm visiting, actually."

"Figures. No one wants to stay in Kissing Bridge."

"Actually, I never wanted to leave. But that's a story for another night…right now I'd like the most unhealthy dish you have."

A long slow smile spread over the bartender's face. "You got it, pretty lady!"

Soon Summer was drinking a glass of chardonnay accompanied by a side of french fries and gravy. She considered the events that had transpired in the last 24 hours.

Somehow, she had found herself engaged to Drake, who she had planned to break up with just the week prior.

Somehow, she had ended up running into Brad Anderson, who she'd been avoiding for ten years.

And now, her family's cookie legacy had been conquered without her even knowing!

She considered the possibilities before her, as she munched away.

It was all too much to think about. Suddenly, she was broken from her reverie.

"Summer? Summer Landers?! Welcome home! It's been a long time. You're all famous now!"

Summer focused on the smiling face in front of her. He was bald and slightly overweight and she had no idea who he was.

"Want to come on over and say hi to all the guys? They would be thrilled!"

Summer tried to remember him.

"Remember the time you barfed all over me in my car at Duff's? I had chicken wing sauce stains on that seat forever!"

A dazed memory came back of her throwing up in one of her friend's boyfriend's new Camaro.

"Jack Morgan. Hi Jack! Thanks, I was actually on my way out. I'm on west-coast time so I'm not sleepy yet. I thought gravy might help."

Jack laughed. "You're funny, Summer.

Okay then, we'll catch up at the Mistletoe Ski Event. You're going, right?"

"Uh, no. Probably not."

"Well, I hope you do. Make sure you bring your famous fiancé. My wife is crazy about him!"

Summer looked at him dazed.

"My what?"

Jack pointed at the huge diamond on her left finger.

"Been all over the tabloids. You and Drake Mason getting married. Pretty cool."

She held up the massive diamond ring like she had never seen it before.

"Oh yeah. It's really big, huh?" She couldn't help but giggle at the ridiculous size of it—even by Hollywood standards.

Jack laughed. "Yeah it sure is big!

He walked away and then turned back and said, "Hey, did you know Brad Anderson is back in town for Christmas too? He's going with his new girlfriend… guess she's super hot!"

"No, I didn't know that. Not that I care. Thanks."

Summer suddenly wanted to barf on Jack again.

Chapter 15

It was four days before Christmas and the official evening lighting ceremony of the Kissing Bridge Mountain Christmas tree.

All the inhabitants of Kissing Bridge were assembled for the special annual event.

Each year the captain of the high school ski team would ski up with the silver star that would grace the top of the tree. Behind him, the rest of the team would follow, carrying bags of lights and ornaments. The high school band would play.

A light snow had fallen overnight and it gave the whole event a holy glow. The school chorus was assembled as carolers.

They were dressed in happy red gowns with gold trim and the sounds of their merry voices singing *Holy Night* filled the air.

Summer had come with her mother and Aunt Carol. They had abandoned her and were both busy 'scouting,' as they called it. Summer had no idea what that meant, but they had taken off, as if on a very serious mission.

Summer thought about the upcoming competition. The fair was in three days and they still had not decided how to beat Mrs. Beaverton.

The sight of Wily Junior trudging up the walkway next door had become a daily sight at the Beaverton house, and a reminder of how dire the situation had become.

Surely, *'The Professional'* didn't have time to be Skyping with Mrs. Beaverton every day… Summer pondered. What could they be doing?

In the last few days the Landers ladies had scoured all of YouTube searching for the best hints and cookie recipes they could find.

They had made batch after batch of recipes that claimed to be *the best cookies in the world*, only to find that they failed miserably next to Grandma Izzy's original recipe.

Summer really didn't know what to do next.

Her phone rang and she picked it up.

Drake.

"Where was she? How come she hadn't picked up her phone? What about meeting his parents?"

The carolers were overly exuberant in their '*Here comes Santa Claus, Here Comes Santa Claus, Right Down Santa Claus Lane….*'

Summer could barely hear him over the loud singing. She looked around absently as he spoke, looking for a place to hear him better.

She spotted Brad, again with Miss Big Boobs. They were smiling and singing along with the carolers.

She spotted a tavern that looked open and made her way toward it.

"I know, I'm sorry Drake. I'm having trouble hearing you. There's a lot going on back here…"

She plopped down in the tavern at the counter bar and a young bartender sporting a Patriots football jersey handed her a menu.

She perused it, all the while holding the phone away from her head to dull the volume of Drake's yelling. He was angry, and Drake never got angry.

"I couldn't just abandon Fluff. Where was I supposed to put him?"

Her eyes widened at the sight of 'beef on weck' on the menu—a hometown specialty.

She pointed to it on the menu, and mouthed "…and a glass of chardonnay please."

Drake was still yelling on the phone.

"Well, maybe you should have asked Donald to take some allergy medicine and I'd be there…" Summer continued on the phone.

She finished one and a half beef on weck sandwiches and two chardonnays, before she gave up on coming to an understanding with Drake.

She just couldn't fight about it anymore. Exhausted from the argument and too much beef on weck, Summer was soon fast asleep on the bar counter.

Brad Anderson walked in and called out to the bartender.

"Billy, are you guys still selling beef on weck to go?"

"Sorry Brad. We just sold out."

He glanced over at Summer sleeping with half a beef on weck sandwich still on her plate.

"The Ponderosa is still serving."

Brad motioned to the blonde head asleep on the bar.

"What's going on there?"

Billy the bartender shrugged.

"Don't know. She was arguing on the phone with someone. Next thing I knew – snoring."

Brad scowled. He walked over to the sleeping figure and lifted up a tendril of blonde hair.

Summer.

"Billy, aren't you supposed to cut people off when they drink too much?"

The bartender threw his hands up in defence.

"Brad, she only had two glasses of

wine. How'd I know she was such a lightweight? She can sure eat like a man, though. Snores like one too. I've gotten a couple complaints from the other customers."

Brad rolled his eyes.

She certainly hadn't changed. How many times had she fallen asleep because she forgot to eat enough and had a half a glass of wine? She had to be the only person on Kissing Bridge Mountain that couldn't hold her liquor. It was a hard-drinking, beef- on-weck-eating town, and 'Little Miss Malibu' wasn't holding up very well.

He eyed the half-eaten sandwich still on the plate beside her sleeping head.

Summer started snoring again— *loudly.*

The bartender pleaded with Brad.

"Brad, you know her. Can you just take her home? Please?"

Brad shook his head. He popped the rest of her uneaten beef on weck in his mouth, and headed for the door.

"Not my problem anymore."

Chapter 16

Summer woke up in bed with a horrible hang over and her clothes on from the previous night.

She couldn't remember a thing. For a dreaded moment, she didn't recognize her old room.

She spotted her old high school photo on the wall and let out a sigh of relief.

She picked up her phone on the bedside table.

Ten voicemails. 15 Texts.

"Two Advil, please."

Summer rubbed her head and headed downstairs for a cup of coffee.

Her mother and Aunt Carol were already seated at the breakfast table in deep conversation. *Breakfast at Tiffany's* was playing on the TV in the living room.

They stopped talking abruptly as she entered the room.

They both stared at her.

"What's up?"

Her mother cleared her throat—something she always did before bringing up something serious.

"Your Aunt Carol and I went roaming last night to try and get some information about the Beaverton's cookies and we found out something very interesting."

Summer was wide-eyed and all ears, but her head was pounding.

She went over and poured herself a cup of coffee and sat down to hear what they had discovered.

"What's up?"

They looked at her seriously.

Another throat clearing by her mother, before Aunt Carol bursted out.

"You're an alcoholic!"

Summer rubbed her forehead and considered it.

"Alcoholic?"

Well, that would explain a lot. She was simply unhappy because she was an alcoholic. What a relief!

That actually solved a lot of issues in her life! Everyone knew you could blame all your problems from gaining weight to sagging jowls on substance abuse. After rehab, you popped out like a newborn babe with a clean slate with every transgression forgiven. It was the perfect system!

It had always been a dream of hers to go to rehab, but she had already been rejected—in fact, *twice.* Did you know you could get rejected by a rehab? Too healthy, they said. Too normal. Normie. How about going to rehab to get over the trauma from getting rejected by a rehab?

She was so envious the rehabs had all the best stuff. Talk about 'members only'! All of her famous friends had been to luxury vacation rehab centers and bragged about them; best masseurs, best private chefs, even the best tennis pros. Summer had just never been able to come up with a suitable reason.

Alcoholic! Bingo.

She looked down at the same outfit she still had on from the night before. She could only imagine the state of her hair. She touched it gingerly. It was matted and half-way to dread locks.

"So, I guess I need to go to rehab right away?"

Aunt Carol and Mom nodded in agreement.

"Of course, Darling but, since the whole town knows you have a problem, we thought it best you start right away—family name and all."

Mom slid an AA meeting schedule in front of her.

Summer considered for a moment defending herself. As if reading her thoughts, her mother continued.

"Brad Anderson brought you home last night. He had to carry you out of the tavern because customers were complaining about you snoring."

Summer turned bright red and winced.

Mom continued her point.

"He also carried you up the stairs and put you to bed."

Chapter 17

Summer found herself in a room full of recovering alcoholics later that day.

This was not the luxurious rehab she had been so jealous of her friends attending. This was Kissing Bridge Mountain AA.

Looking around, she felt uncomfortable about being there. She had donned a short brunette wig and her dark glasses and she hoped no one would be able to recognize her. It was anonymous, but there was no telling if that would really stick. More than likely, someone would call the Enquirer and a swarm of paparazzi would suddenly show up.

She looked around at the group. She made up her mind to leave and was just getting on her feet, when a young teenage girl walked over and sat down next to her.

"Hi, my name is Chelsea. Must be your first time here? I haven't seen you before." Summer noticed the girl's t-shirt sporting the moniker 'Life Sucks'.

Summer found herself liking her right away.

"Hi, I'm Summer."

Chelsea smiled a true smile.

There was something so darn likeable about this teenager.

That's how Summer ended up in a lucky seat, once again.

Now, as I mentioned, each of the Landers family had special talents. Aunt Carol had her eavesdropping. Mother had her color healing. And of course, Grandma Izzy had her cookie-making ability. She was the one that had created the famous Landers' blue-ribbon-winning recipe, after all.

Summer Landers had a lucky seating gift.

It was her lucky seating talent that got her seated next to ski instructor Joe, who had talked her into trying skiing for her very first time. It was her lucky seating talent that had happened to have her seated next to Brad as her lab partner in freshmen chemistry.

And it had ultimately been her lucky seating talent that gotten her the big modeling contract that had changed her life. A top Elite model scout had sat down next to her at Starbucks. That had occurred ten years ago right over on main street, just two blocks over.

Little did she know that she had once again landed just where she needed to be, thanks to her special gift.

After the meeting, Summer and Chelsea went outside to the corridor and helped themselves to a cup of coffee.

Chelsea turned to speak to Summer with a sombre expression on her face.

"Listen Summer, I really like you. Please don't take this personally ...but in all honesty… I looked over your intake sheet for a sponsor…and I'd love to do it but…"

Summer was quiet. Chelsea let out a hard breath.

"I just don't think you're an alcoholic."

Summer looked defeated.

"What do you mean? It kind of solved all my issues in one fell swoop! Can you check again?

Chelsea consoled her.

"I even checked your family history. There's never been a Landers ever that had alcohol issues."

Summer looked defeated.

"I knew it was too good to be true."

"Look, we would love to have you, but it wouldn't be ethical. You're a 'normie.' Just accept it."

Now Summer was left without a blanket excuse for her problems; she was back at square one.

"Oh well," Summer said defeated, "It was fun while it lasted."

Just then, Dolly Ferguson, the group coffee monitor, came bustling into the coffee room dressed in a festive elf outfit for the holidays. Dolly wore her elf outfit every year, every day, starting the first day of December. Dolly had a lot of Christmas spirit, and also obviously really liked that elf outfit.

In her hands was a tray of lovely cookies.

"Fresh cookies. Help yourselves, ladies."

Summer's eyes lit up at the beauty of the cut-out cookies. Such interesting and unique Christmas shapes! Not your usual tree and ornament cut out.

She raised a reindeer-shaped cookie to her mouth.

She brought it to her nose and smelled it. Fresh butter, a hint of…? She wasn't sure. She took a delicate bite and the taste assailed her senses like a breath of fresh air.

Delicate, light, perfect.

This was a winner! She had to have the recipe!

She turned to Dolly who was adjusting her elf hat.

"Dolly, where did you get these cookies? They're the best I've ever tasted!"

Dolly grinned.

"I know. Aren't they amazing?! They're the blue-ribbon winners from the fair, don't you know. Mrs. Beaverton donated them!"

Chapter 18

"Martha Stewart??!!"

Aunt Carol and Summer had to steady mother from falling over.

It was a devastating blow to the Landers' morale.

"It's a disaster!"

Summer and her Aunt Carol had to agree.

Who would have guessed the small-town Beavertons were keeping one of America's culinary giants up their sleeve?

The gig was up!

After luckily being seated next to Chelsea, who was best friends with the elf-dressed Dolly, Summer had been able to find out the dreaded truth by having her investigate on their behalf.

It seemed that the Beaverton's

youngest niece, Devora, had been caught shoplifting earrings, and actually been in jail with Martha Stewart for a time. Some chatter about being her prison b**** , that Summer didn't understand. But Devora had been the one that connected the Beavertons to Martha Stewart. The secret was out.

Mother paced back and forth in front of the twinkling Christmas tree. Even Fluff knew enough to run out of the room.

"Well, then. We can't enter. We can't compete against *Martha Stewart!*"

She stopped and through her arms up for emphasis.

"She's gosh darn *Martha Stewart*!"

Summer and Aunt Carol looked at each other. They wanted to console her.

They just couldn't.

She was gosh darn Martha Stewart.

Chapter 19

Summer was whipping up cookie dough in the kitchen the next day with a new determination.

Her mom and Aunt Carol had gone out shopping for ingredients for a new batch of cookies. Summer had been sure the secret spice she had tasted in the AA cookies Mrs. Beaverton had donated had been 'anise.'

They had decided to try out a new batch, and mother and Aunt Carol had run out to procure some anise to be sure.

Summer looked at the old recipe book spread out in front of her. Yes, Grandma Izzy's cookies had always reigned supreme but they had to come up with something unusual that would beat out Martha Stewart.

Summer was determined to find a way to beat Mrs. Beaverton, and re-throne her mother as rightly cookie queen of Kissing Bridge.

Summer had to think outside the box. Fluff wound around her legs purring loudly.

She bent down and pet him.

"Any ideas, Fluff? Don't hold back."

The cat was uncommunicative—as usual.

The doorbell rang. When Summer opened it, she nearly fell over.

It was Drake. He was dressed in a black cashmere sweater and matching pea coat. His scarf was a tasteful mix of deep grey tones, which set off his eyes perfectly. He looked exactly like the dazzling movie star he was.

"Darling!" He wrapped his arms around Summer and hugged her tight.

"Drake what, what are you doing here?'

"Well, you wouldn't come to me. So I came to you!"

Summer stammered, "I thought you were in Los Angeles with your parents?"

Drake took in the Christmas decorations all over the Landers home. It looked like a Norman Rockwell card. Holiday tablecloths, hanging rows of ribbon strung with Christmas cards, a rather large blow up Santa, a full ceramic set of Mary and the baby Jesus in the stable...

Drake pulled out a bottle of Crystal. His brown eyes were mischievous.

"Let's have a drink to celebrate my being here! I can't wait to meet my new Mother-in-Law!"

Summer wished she had remembered to mention to her mother about Drake…and that she had gotten engaged.

Drake looked at her naked finger.

"Darling, where is your ring?"

Summer had taken off the ring after the first night she arrived home. She had been making cookies and hadn't wanted to get cookie dough all over it. In the fury of the cookie battle, she had forgotten to put it back on.

"Oh, I didn't want to get dough on it." She explained.

"Dough?" Drake was confused.

Mom drove up outside. She looked at the long black sleek Mercedes parked in her driveway speckled with fresh snowflakes.

Young Wily Junior was walking up the Beaverton's driveway next door with that laptop thing on his shoulder and a smirk on his face.

Mom knitted her brow as she opened the door to find Drake Mason, the movie star, at her kitchen counter pouring champagne.

"Hello?" she said quizzically…wondering where Summer was.

Drake turned around in one graceful spin, making a gallant picture in his perfectness. Give it to Drake; he was a great dresser.

"Mother!" he sang out gaily.

Mother looked him over. She liked his color choices.

Just then, Summer came in with some logs from outside for the fire.

"Mom! This is Drake…my…fiancé!"

Mother opened her mouth but nothing came out... *thankfully*.

She looked back and forth between the two of them. She'd have to deal with this later.

"Nice to meet you, Drake," she said politely. Then she motioned to Summer to come talk to her in private.

They conferred by the fire. Mom whispered, "We've got a new problem."

Summer raised an eyebrow.

"Aunt Carol overheard Marybelle McGregor's mother say that a new star entry had been approved for the contest just this morning. She's a wild card entry with no prior cookie contest experience but, she's a *Hell's Kitchen* TV show winner!"

Summer sucked her breath in and considered this new threat to their throne.

Between Drake showing up, and this new entry information, Summer's head was swimming.

How could they beat 'Evil Martha Stewart,' as Summer now called her, and now a game show winner from *Hell's Kitchen* as well?

Things weren't looking good for the Landers' cookie future.

Chapter 20

The Christmas Eve Silver Bells Fair was one of the highlights of Kissing Bridge Mountain.

All of the local artisans and shops showed up to sell their special items for the holiday season and to cater to the last-minute gift buyers. All of the local restaurants had booths selling the best of cold winter foods, soothing warm drinks and toasty tasty treats. Everyone loved the Kissing Bridge Silver Bells Christmas Eve Fair.

The highlight of the fair was, of course, the cookie contest. The contest began each year after the gift booths closed down, at four o'clock sharp. It heralded the end of shopping, and the beginning of the full-out Christmas celebration. Afterwards, everyone would go to Christmas Eve mass and then home to prepare for Santa's arrival.

The Silver Bells Fair Cookie Contest was one of the most competitive sports in all of Vermont. Would-be bakers would travel for miles around to compete.

The various booth venders were readying and decorating their booths for the upcoming day. The fair was tomorrow and everyone was a-flurry, putting on last minute finishing touches.

Three young boys were erecting the scoreboard at the far end of the booths. It would show the odds of each of the contenders so the residents could place bets accordingly.

The Landers were gathered together in their corner booth. They still ranked a pivotal spot—despite last year's horrible loss.

Mrs. Beaverton and Wily Junior were across the way. Mr. Beaverton was there as well. Summer thought Mr. Beaverton looked just like Santa, with his fat belly and all natural white beard.

Summer frowned. That seemed an unfair advantage. She hoped they'd keep him under cover during the actual competition.

The whole Beaverton family was beginning to gather now. Hoards of them arriving en masse and all came bearing decorations, lights, ornaments and ... disco balls?

The Landers were still at odds on how best to outsmart Mrs. Beaverton and her professional ally, Evil Martha Stewart.

On top of that, they also seemed outnumbered in the decorating department.

Summer wasn't sure what distressed her more—the upcoming competition, or the fact Drake had talked her into going to the Mistletoe Ski Event that night. She really was dying to ski. She loved skiing and she was very good at it too. Still, the horrible memories from that fateful night so long ago... still haunted her.

Chapter 21

It was December 23rd and the night of the Kissing Bridge Mistletoe Ski Event.

The snow was falling hard and a large full moon filled the night sky.

The tradition was for everyone to meet at the high school parking lot and leave their cars. Together they would take a group bus up the mountain to Eagle's Peak Lodge.

They always hired a driver and the passengers started their pre-game activities in the back seats with flasks of hot cocoa laced with crème de menthe and Irish whiskey coffee.

Summer was not drinking, and Drake was drinking enough for both of them.

Before long, Drake had the entire bus singing Christmas carols.

Brad and his girlfriend, Miss Big Boobs, were seated near the front. She was even more annoying to Summer than ever, as she continually stroked Brad's face and stared all gooey-eyed at him.

At least he hadn't brought Marybelle McGregor, the girl he had cheated on her with—Summer mused; that would have been too much for her to handle.

Brad and Marybelle had started dating 'officially' right after Summer left to model in New York. Marybelle had been the head cheerleader at their high school and always wanted to date Brad, the varsity quarterback. She had always found a way to affix herself to Brad in spite of the fact that Summer and Brad had been together for years. Be it on the game bus, at the pep rallies or out of town games, you could be assured Marybelle McGregor had her hands all over Brad Anderson. Summer knew that Marybelle was always looking for a way to break them up and have Brad for herself, so it was no surprise to her when they later ended up together.

The lodge at Eagle's Peak ski resort was beautiful. The old redwood lodge was adorned with holly wreaths and bells and mistletoe. Large roaring fires blazed at each end.

In the center was the bar. That's where Summer found herself with Drake. Drake didn't ski, and Summer was beginning to regret that she had decided to come at all.

"Come on Drake, just try skiing. You'll love it. Won't you just *try*?!"

"I'm quite happy right here. I don't need to break any legs before I leave for Athens on that shoot. James Dean did not have a broken leg!"

Summer cajoled him. "We'll go easy down the bunny hill. You'll love it, Drake. You won't break anything…"

They were interrupted by a couple of older people who wanted Drake's autograph.

Summer wasn't giving up. She loved skiing. It was after all, the favorite pastime for the townspeople of Kissing Bridge. Everyone skied here. They down-hill skied for fun, and cross-country skied just to get around sometimes, depending if the roads were open or not.

"Drake, it means a lot to me. I've skied since I was four. I plan to teach our children some day and you—"

Drake laughed and cut her off.

"Oh Summer, you are so adorable. You're the only child I need to take care of."

Summer was confused.

"I'm not a child, Drake."

He smiled at her indulgently. "Of course you're not, Darling. It's just you need a lot of attention and I'm perfectly happy to be the one who gives it to you. I just don't see real kids in our future."

Summer's head began to swim.

Why had she assumed he wanted a big family like she did? He wasn't a guy from Kissing Bridge. He was Drake Mason, movie star Peter-Pan-Man, with his perfect clothes and his perfect penthouse! Of course there was no room for messy children in his life.

"But…but…" Summer stammered. "I want children very badly, Drake. I'd hoped you would want to start a family right away. I'm already 28. I assumed that's what you wanted too…"

Drake smoothed her hair and looked into her big blue eyes, and delivered the ultimate blow.

"Summer, you're not made to be a mom. You're made to be a model. That's why we're perfect for each other. I'll get you a dog."

Chapter 22

Summer was speechless.

"I'm going to go ski, Drake. I'll see you later."

She trudged out the large wooden door and avoided looking at Brad and Miss Big Boobs.

Soon she was outside in the snowy wonderland.

The cold breeze on her face felt good. The snow was coming down really hard. Summer could barely see in front of her as she made her way to the ski lift.

A group of old school friends were already waiting in line. She chatted amiably with Jodie Morrison, as they moved along in line beside each other. Their words made little frozen clouds as they spoke. Jodie's brood of boys kept running up and asking their mom for food and money for the games.

Summer noticed that Brad was also in line behind her. For a moment she thought she caught Brad looking at her.

The last time they had been here had been the end of her and Brad.

All the memories she had hoped to flee came flooding back to her as if the ten years had never passed.

She had been so happy that Christmas. That year Brad had helped the Landers decorate their booth and it had been the most beautiful booth they had ever had. Brad had become an expert on cookie competition decorating, as he had been dating Summer since Freshman year.

That night of the first Kissing Bridge Mistletoe Ski Event was magical. They had been on the lift headed for the top of the mountain. They both loved to ski and it was a stunning night for it. As the snow glistened below them and they were lifted up into the starry night, Brad had surprised her with a real Tiffany ring and proposed!

Of course, he knew the Landers women's penchant for Tiffany, and so this ring—albeit a chip of a diamond—meant all the more. They were truly made for each other. It had been the best day of her life.

By the time they had reached the top of the hill, they had planned their whole future together. They both wanted five kids. Brad was going to give up his dream of commercial flying and work for his dad's logging company. Summer was going to home school their children and teach them to ski—and make cookies, of course!

It was the happiest Christmas she could ever remember. That was, until Summer had learned the truth.

Then her whole world fell apart.

She thought back to that dreaded Christmas Eve morning. Summer had woken up to the sun glinting off her new engagement ring. She was over the moon in love.

In honor of the new engagement, Mom had put *Breakfast at Tiffany's* on the TV while they prepared the dough. They had been in the midst of last-minute cookie details, as usual this time of year, when Aunt Carol arrived.

Aunt Carol had run out to the *Super-Duper* to get more milk for the dough but had come back empty-handed. Summer had known there was something wrong right away.

Her usual gay face was solemn, and she was speechless for a long while. When Aunt Carol finally spoke, she apologized to be delivering sad news.

The Landers ladies gathered around the kitchen table and Aunt Carol had taken Summer's hand in support. She confessed that she had overheard in the apple section that Brad had kissed Marybelle McGregor under the Mistletoe.

She had heard it straight from the lodge keeper himself, Earl. Of course he hadn't been talking to *her*. He'd been talking to Mr. Jennings, but Aunt Carol had caught every word.

Apparently 'the kiss' had occurred just after Brad had given Summer the ring and proposed.

Brad's buddies had dragged him to the bar for a congratulatory beer, and Summer had wanted to take one more run down the hill before they left.

From what Aunt Carol heard, he had kissed Marybelle under the mistletoe to quite a crowd of onlookers.

For once, all the Landers ladies had been utterly speechless.

That had been the saddest Christmas Eve ever.

Summer had been so upset, that she had not even been able to attend the cookie competition; a first for the family.

After the tragic news, Summer had gone through all the stages of death. Shock, disbelief, depression. She wanted to believe it wasn't true, but she couldn't.

Aunt Carol's eavesdropping was never wrong.

Brad had kissed another woman while Summer had been blindly and blissfully skiing down the mountain and dreaming about their life together.

Brad, the cheater, denied everything. He hadn't kissed Marybelle, the head cheerleader. He hadn't cheated.

He lied.

Summer refused to take his calls, laden with lies.

That Christmas Day had passed with Summer staring blindly at her new rose-colored walls—courtesy of her mother—and trying not to die from a broken heart.

Of course, like all Landers ladies, she had taken to the bed. Her mom and Aunt Carol were so worried, they decided to take to the bed with her. They had hauled in the big screen TV into her bedroom, and climbed into bed along side her for the duration. The three of them had commenced to watch a *Breakfast at Tiffany's* marathon for an entire week. Many cookies and pastries had been consumed and tears dried.

When Summer finally emerged from the bed, it was to a new destiny. She went over to Main Street to get a coffee at Starbucks and unknowingly plunked herself down right next to a New York City model scout for the famous 'Elite' agency. He took one look at her sipping her peppermint latte, and signed her up on the spot.

She'd left Kissing Bridge Mountain the next day and was soon one of the highest paid models in the world.

Now all the memories she had hoped to flee came flooding back with a vengeance.

When she looked up, Brad was staring at her. She couldn't read his grey eyes. Nor could she turn away.

The snow continued to come down hard.

Jodie pulled Summer's attention away from Brad and motioned to the lift.

"Shoot. It looks like they're closing it down. There's a big storm coming in. I'm gonna get the boys home before they shut down the roads."

Summer looked at the walls of white snow beginning to pile up.

"Gosh darn it, I haven't skied in years!"

Jodi waved goodbye. "Merry Christmas, Summer!"

Summer waved back.

She wasn't giving up on her dream of skiing. If she had to deal with her feelings, at least she was going to get some satisfaction.

She approached the young man working at the ski lift. He was shutting down and putting up the CLOSED sign.

Summer looked at him with her big blue eyes.

"Is there anyway you'd let an old Kissing Bridge local have just one last ride before you close down? I've been in L.A. a long time and this snow is epic!" She smiled her famous smile.

The boy was overwhelmed. "Hey are you that *Sports Illustrated* girl?"

Summer smiled. "That's me."

"Oh, wow! Well, I can't let our hometown star go away without a ride on her home run. Sure, get on this last chair and then I'll shut it down. It's getting bad out there… You're an experienced skier, right?"

Summer made her way onto the lift. "Been doing it all my life. Believe me, I'll be safe."

The boy yelled out to the thinning crowd that still remained in line.

"Last ride. Sorry. We'll reopen after the snow clears. There's a bad storm coming in."

Summer settled into the lift and looked at the mountain ahead of her imagining a good ride down the mountain with perfect powder conditions. It was just what she needed to clear her head.

She pulled on her ski glasses and fixed her scarf. She considered her ugly orange mittens and wished she had bought proper gloves in Manhattan. Just as the lift started up, she felt a heavy thud land next to her.

She turned to discover none other than Brad Anderson!

The lift took off, and up the mountain they started. She looked back as the lift raised up higher and higher up. She would be stuck with him now for the next 15 minutes until they got to the top!

Summer was outraged.

"Really, of all people... You're the *last* person I want to see!"

Brad looked aghast. "I should say the same after what you did to me!"

Summer went red with anger.

"Me? Me? I'm not the one that kissed another girl in front of our entire graduating class."

Brad was equally incensed.

"I don't know what you're talking about! You left me. You broke all of our plans and you chose *modeling* over our life together!"

Summer was beside herself. How dare he accuse her of ruining their relationship?! She couldn't take one more moment of his lies.

With that, she just up and jumped off the lift. She fell with a loud yell and a dull thud onto the snowy drift below.

"OWWWWW!!!"

Brad swore beneath his breath.

He looked down at the precarious height, then jumped right off after her.

He recovered from the long fall and made his way over to her.

Summer's head was buried in the snow and both her boots were sticking out— but only one ski.

He pulled her out of the snow bank and dusted her off. He looked around for her other ski.

"Are you all right?"

"No. I think I broke my leg."

Brad reached to feel her leg.

"Let me help you."

"No!" She batted at him with her ugly orange mittens. "Just get away from me. I hate you."

Brad attempted to take off her boot to check her leg anyway.

"Summer, just let me help you."

"No! Get away from me, Brad Anderson!" She picked up a snowball and hurled it at him.

It bounced off his head.

A look of anger came over him.

"Gosh darn your stubbornness! I'm checking your leg, whether you like it or not!"

With that, he wrestled her to the ground.

"Just stay still!"

The mittens came off and Summer fought back pushing him away from her.

"Oww! You're taking advantage of a girl with a broken leg. I hate you, Brad *the cheater*, Anderson."

"Summer, stop, stop!"

Summer was exhausted, so she did stop—even though it wasn't because he asked her to.

He lightly felt her leg. "I think you just sprained it, thank goodness."

Summer sniffled. The anger left Brad's face and he actually looked like his old self—the one that really loved her.

"I never cheated on you, Summer. I don't know why you're saying that. It's a weak excuse for leaving me."

He shook his head. "I guess I'd hoped you'd have a real reason for ruining our life together."

Summer couldn't hold back the truth one more second.

"Brad, I found out! We kept it under wraps, but my Aunt Carol has a special gift. She overheard Earl saying how you had kissed Marybelle McGregor underneath the mistletoe in front of all our classmates! Right after you proposed to me! How *could* you?!"

Brad looked seriously confused.

I didn't kiss Marybelle McGregor that night!"

"Funny how you ended up dating her for five years as soon as I left."

Brad looked at her strangely.

Summer shrugged. "Facebook stalking."

"I never kissed Marybelle until you abandoned me to be Miss famous, star-dating bikini-blonde-L.A.-fake kale-eating supermodel…'

Summer stopped him.

"Don't you dare act innocent, Brad! And it counts as cheating even if you were under the mistletoe!"

Brad shook his head, and then an idea lit in his eyes. He glared at Summer.

"You're not referring to the little girl, *Murielle,* the granddaughter of Earl, the lodge keeper? The plump one that had a crush on me... the ten-year-old at the time?"

"My Aunt Carol overheard Earl plainly talking to Old Man Jennings and my Aunt Carol never hears wrong. Well, *except* her B's…."

Summer stammered off into a whisper….

Memories came flooding back to her of the cute, young freckled girl with the crush on Brad being held up by her grandpa Earl, for her first mistletoe kiss. It *had* been adorable. Their classmates had all clapped. She'd been right there clapping alongside them.

Murielle. The child. Not *Marybelle* the head cheerleader.

The limitation of Aunt Carol's gift minus the B's and her overcompensation had become perfectly clear.

Summer raised her hand to her mouth in horror.

"I'm so sorry, Brad. I completely forgot about her. I guess I went into shock when I heard it. I thought you were cheating on me...*That's* why I left!"

Her liquid blue eyes filled with tears. Her heart hurt and her leg hurt but maybe this moment was meant-to-be, all along. Maybe everything could be different now that the truth was out.

"I just thought the curse..."

He tore his eyes away from hers and scooped up her orange mittens. He helped her on with them lost in deep thought. The big diamond on her left hand was so outrageously large, he could barely get the mitten over it. He pulled and pulled and finally just gave up and tossed the mitten back down to the ground.

"The past is the past, Summer. I'm

glad we cleared it up. But our futures are in front of us now."

Brad shook his head.

"I have to get back to the lodge."

He pulled on his skis. Just then, a roar of an engine was heard and out of the white cloud of snow emerged a Ski-Do. The young guy from the lift was now on ski patrol. He helped Summer get on the back seat, being extra careful with her leg.

"I thought you said you had skied before?"

Brad flashed by them without looking back, as he jetted down the hill.

Once more, she watched the love of her life leave her.

Chapter 23

Back at the lodge, Brad was taking off his skis and shaking himself off.

The snow had not let up and most everyone had gone inside to wait out the storm. Summer came limping around the corner with some crutches from the first aid office. Her hair was still full of snow from being in the snow bank.

She ignored Brad and kicked open the front wooden door to the lodge with her good leg.

All she could focus on now was getting the heck off this mountain. Forget that bus ride back home with the gang! She would grab Drake and have him call a limo to come get them out of there— *pronto!*

She would leave tonight and fly far, far away with her movie star fiancé and they would start their new life anywhere but stupid Kissing Bridge Mountain with its Marybelles and Murielles and cookies.

She jostled in awkwardly with her crutches, trying not to grab anyone's attention.

She needn't have worried.

Everyone in the lodge already had their attention riveted to the archway near the main fireplace. She bumped through the crowd trying to get to the bar and retrieve Drake. But he wasn't there. She looked around, only to see Brad walk in. He didn't look happy.

Summer followed his gaze.

Through the crowd, she could make out a group of giggling women standing in a long line leading up to the fireplace.

Drake was under the mistletoe.

He couldn't have looked happier or more at home, as he motioned for the next woman in line to move along and get her Christmas kiss under the mistletoe.

Summer gasped.

The next woman in line was none other than Miss Big Boobs!

Summer turned to look at Brad, who now had a very angry look on his face.

Miss Big Boobs stepped forward and leaned in for a kiss.

It was a great big, sloppy, long smoochie kiss.

The crowd gaped, and then cheered when Drake came up for air and shot the group the thumbs up sign. Cell phones clicked pictures in rapid-fire click, click, click. Her hometown crew had been courteous to her, but a movie star was fair game.

Miss Big Boobs didn't move along though. She just grabbed Drake again and laid another big kiss on him.

And then another kiss.

And then another kiss.

And then it just got gross.

Finally, the lodge keeper, Earl, announced that the buses were leaving early to avoid the roads being shut down. It was time to go home. They had just gotten news that the storm was being upgraded to a blizzard.

The crowd dispersed as they realized that no one else was getting a turn with Drake Mason under the mistletoe tonight.

Summer watched as Drake continued to make out with Miss Big Boobs.

After all she'd been through…to have her same nightmare re-enacted almost identical to what had occurred ten years earlier. It was unthinkable.

It should have been devastating.

But somehow, it just wasn't.

The ride on the bus back home, however, was very uncomfortable—to say the least.

Chapter 24

Later that night, after the uncomfortable bus ride back, Drake took his Mercedes and drove away.

He had the good grace, and luck, to fly off of Kissing Bridge Mountain that very night. He said he wanted to give Summer some space.

Summer lay awake all night, unable to sleep.

Her sprained ankle weighed a ton because it had a dozen ace bandages wound around it. On top of that, for some reason, Fluff was obsessed with the bandages and he was draped across her lower leg, fast asleep.

She wiggled her toes, trying to get comfortable.

She knew she shouldn't have gone to that darn Mistletoe Ski Event. Another mistletoe disaster.

In all truth, she was relieved that she and Drake were over. She would deal with any residual relationship issues around that later. Maybe she would take to the bed for a week. Right now, she had to focus on the cookies.

Tomorrow was the Silver Bells Christmas Eve Fair and the cookie competition was fierce.

The pressure was on.

Try as she might, Summer had not managed to come up with a solution to beat Evil Martha Stewart, and now the *Hell's Kitchen* Goth child as well.

Finally, she managed to doze off. Summer slept fitfully that night, fraught with nightmares of Grandma Izzy and Mrs. Beaverton mud wrestling. Gosh, she had weird dreams. But, somehow out of the mud and screams had come a sparkling conclusion. The last thing she remembered was diamonds.

Big diamonds.

Big edible diamonds.

Big Tiffany diamonds.

Summer awoke with a fire in her belly and a new hope for the Landers' cookie future. She was a Landers, and she wasn't about to let her mother be de-throned on *her* watch.

She went downstairs to see her mother and Aunt Carol already up and awake, drinking Irish coffees. Aunt Carol got up when Summer came in and made her a cup of coffee. She picked up the whiskey and poured a big bit into it and handed it to her.

So, it was going to be *that* kind of day.

She looked at her mom and Aunt Carol.

Mom shrugged. "We've been up since sunrise." As if that explained it.

It was the morning of the competition and Summer doubted any of them had slept well either.

And so the Landers ladies began that fateful Christmas Eve morning with their heads held high—awaiting their cookie fate— while *Breakfast at Tiffany's* played in the background.

Little did they know, Summer had an idea up her sleeve.

Chapter 25

As you know, the Landers ladies all had talents to compensate for the curse.

And as you remember, Summer had the talent of lucky seating. So this next bit of news will come as no surprise…

It was early Christmas Eve morning still, and Summer Landers found herself down at the local *Puff and Stuff's* for a coffee and a donut. A sleepy man in a Santa hat plopped down next to her and wished her a merry Christmas.

Before Summer could reply, the man accidentally spilled his coffee all over Summer and the bench they shared.

Summer was a pretty easy-going girl, so this didn't upset her—although the man was totally embarrassed. He got up and started dabbing the coffee off of her and the seat with his newspaper.

"I'm so sorry." He dabbed away.

As the coffee seeped through the newspaper, Summer caught sight of a picture that indeed was a lucky catch.

It was a picture of Drake. He was brunching with his mother and father at the uber trendy new Wolfgang Puck's L.A. eatery, *Le Bon Cheri.*

Summer snatched up the wet paper and continued to read. The next line said…

"Drake Mason's mother is a close personal friend of Wolfgang Puck, rumored to have dated during nursery school…"

Summer smiled a smile so big her face hurt. Her lucky seating talent had paid off once again!

Chapter 26

The deal had gone smoothly. Drake was eager to keep his dirty laundry out of the tabloids.

And, of course, having Summer return her half-a-million-dollar ring would be wonderful.

Summer had asked only one small thing in return. She wanted his mother to text her Wolfgang Puck's private number.

It seemed a win-win certainly.

Drake's mother had been reluctant to give up Wolfgang's personal information at first, but the six-carat Tiffany perfect diamond ring had finally won her over.

A six-carat diamond from Tiffany was a hard thing to say 'no' to.

And so it was, that Summer found herself talking to the most amazing marvelous chef in the whole wide world; the gourmet extraordinaire, the incomparable, Wolfgang Puck!

She explained her situation to him. She was certain if her mom's cookies could just be adorned by his secret special diamond sugar chips that he had decorated her engagement cake with; that they would win the competition and beat Mrs. Beaverton and Evil Martha Stewart.

As luck would have it, Wolfgang also *abhorred* Evil Martha Stewart!

He immediately called his factory in Switzerland where he was spending Christmas with his family. He assured Summer that the diamond edible chips would be flown in special delivery especially for the contest, and arrive in Kissing Bridge by one o'clock.

The contest started promptly at four o'clock. It would be perfect.

Chapter 27

The Kissing Bridge Silver Bells Christmas Fair was one of the biggest events of the year.

The entire town turned out to purchase last-minute gifts and enjoy the holiday spirit together.

Santa Claus was taking final requests and a long line of excited children wound around the big town center and Christmas tree.

All sorts of special holiday foods and drinks were available. Old people drank hot cocoas and young people too. The teens toasted with warm apple cider spiced with cinnamon and clove.

All about the spirit of Christmas reigned pure and happy.

Only the cookie contest competitors felt the pressure.

There were ten competitors in this year's cookie bake-off. Nine were cotton tops and one was a Goth chick wild card entry *Hell's Kitchen* winner.

The competition was fierce.

Summer smoothed her apron. She had been delegated the early shift. Her job: show up and stare down the competition. Their strategy was to keep the cookies warm at home until the very last moment.

She would hold the booth down until Aunt Carol and Mom arrived with the newly-baked cookies at the last moment. Then she would get the secret ingredient from the Fed Ex post office at one o'clock, and proceed home to make the frosting so it was as fresh as possible.

Mom and Aunt Carol arrived and bustled into the booth with the cookies hidden mysteriously beneath a tin foil cover.

This year, part of the plan was to not unveil the cookies. They would spring a surprise on the crowd with a last-minute reveal, and so they planned to create quite a stir.

Part of the pre-game early activities offered at the Silver Bell Christmas Eve Fair entailed the *pre-viewing* of the cookies. Many townspeople arrived early just to dwell upon the cookie entries, and many placed bets solely based on the color quality of the cookies alone.

Today they would be betting blindly on the Landers' cookies based on past taste and winnings alone. Of course, that taste had won for the last 50 years.

The scorecard was alight now showing the betting odds ready for the big show.

The odds showed the top three contenders. Right now it was Mrs. Beaverton—40% Landers—30% and the *Hell's Kitchen* child— 20%.

Summer hopped into the car and threw her crutches in the back seat. She had to go get the special package at Fed Ex due in at one o'clock sharp.

By two o'clock, Summer was still staring at Stu, the mailman, at her wit's end. The very special package had still not come. This was disastrous. They needed the Wolfgang Puck diamond ice chips to pull off the new mysterious surprise Tiffany blue color her mother had created for the cookies this year! Without the diamond chips, they would just be the same old cookies with a different color.

Summer moaned. She stepped outside the mail centre to call Wolfgang's Swiss factory.

Brad pulled up just then in his big black truck, and leapt out of it in one manly motion.

He stopped for a moment when he saw her, then reached in the back and gathered a large amount of packages to mail, and then walked by without looking at her.

Summer turned her back on him, "Sorry, yes it's bad reception. I'm on a mountain. Could you please check on my package? It's very important. Of course, I know they *all* are…Yes, I'll hold. Thank you."

Skinny Stu, the mailman, helped Brad with his packages.

"Hey Stu, what's she upset about?"

Stu leaned in conspiratorially, "Waiting on a special delivery from Switzerland—from Wolfgang Puck. It's late."

Summer paced back and forth in front of the store trying to appear sexy with her limp, in case Brad was watching.

Brad looked out the window at Summer, who was hobbling back and forth sexily.

She still looked beautiful— *even* angry and wounded.

He knew the Lander ladies must have been sweating the cookie competition. He knew full well what this contest meant to them. He and Summer had dated for four years before she up and left for no good reason and never looked back. They hadn't held onto their men well, but they sure did hold on to that prestigious blue-ribbon cookie crown.

Some of his fondest memories had been scrambling to help them the night before the cookie contest; listening to Christmas music and wrapping gifts under the tree in anticipation of Christmas Day. He'd been the Landers ladies' resident guy and carried all their heavy groceries and made sure the home fire stayed lit and full of logs. He loved those times.

He almost felt bad for Summer. The whole town had heard about Mrs. Beaverton employing the help of Martha Stewart. The poor Landers didn't have a chance.

She was gosh darn Martha Stewart!

Chapter 28

By three o'clock, time had run out and Summer had no time left… so she lied.

"Of course I got the package, Mom no worries…ahh…traffic's bad." She looked around the empty streets while she talked on the phone. Of course, everyone was at the fair.

"I'm almost done with the frosting and I'll be right there."

"Drat!" She would just have to go home and make the frosting and hope that her mom's color gift and Tiffany blue chic would be enough—not that anyone ever heard of Christmas bell cookies without the bells.

"Drat!" She needed those Wolfgang Puck diamond chips for the bells!

Summer drove home and hopped quickly into the house. She flung her coat and scarf and crutches aside and pulled on her apron.

Fluff came walking in sleepily and hopped up on the counter to be pet.

Summer kissed his head, then shooed him away for the moment.

"I love you, Fluff, but I have to work!" She pulled out the ingredients for the frosting she had made so many times before. Grandma Izzy's trusty book lay open more in honor than for reference. Vanilla, milk, sugar, confectionary sugar, and the vial of the special Tiffany blue color her mother had spent the last few nights perfecting.

The kettle whistled and Summer made herself a cup of coffee and surveyed her work. The frosting was perfect. She tasted it. Exactly liked Grandma Izzy's—*almost.*

Now that she wasn't an alcoholic, Summer decided the coffee needed some whiskey if she was going to face the wrath of her mother. She found the bottle of whiskey, but the whiskey was all gone... it figures; *just* when she needed it most!

She had promised them a shoe-in winner with Wolfgang Puck's special delicious diamond-chip edibles, and now she had nothing!

She poured a bowl of milk for Fluff, and sipped her coffee. She went to close the cabinet door when she spotted an old bottle of vanilla liqueur that had been in the back of the cupboard, pretty much since she could remember. She pulled it out from the back of the cupboard. She poured a bit into her coffee. She tasted it. Mmmmm, delicious!

Her phone rang and she rushed to answer it.

"Yes, this is Summer...Yes, I'm waiting on a package...What do you mean 'They closed the mountain road down and they can't deliver it'?!"

Fluff was walking around the counter by the uncovered frosting. She hissed at him to get him away from the mixing bowl. With a dramatic leap, Fluff jumped off, and with a flick of the tail, he knocked the old vanilla liqueur over…

Summer was too involved with her phone call to pay attention.

"Any chance they can just go around the tree?"

The vanilla liqueur emptied into frosting bowl; drip, drip, drip…before it toppled over and off of the table onto the floor and landed with a big thud next to Fluff.

Fluff meowed loudly.

Summer closed her eyes.

"I see. Thank you anyway."

Summer threw her phone into her purse, defeated. In a daze, she covered the frosting with plastic wrap and hobbled out the door.

She never knew that in that magical miraculous moment of vanilla liqueur, and the swish of Fluff's tail, that the ghost of Grandma Izzy had come to the rescue.

As I mentioned, the Landers Ladies didn't lose easily.

Chapter 29

The judge was seated at his judging throne that had been erected especially for the event.

Mom was tending the booth and making sure the cookies were not tampered with. They were covered up still, mysteriously. Many of the onlookers had already tried to lift the tin foil off and peer underneath. But Mom shooed them away. This was a competition, after all!

Aunt Carol walked down the aisle of cookie competitor booths, casually perusing the competition. Aunt Carol's gift was a Godsend in these important pre-competition times. With her ears wide open, she listened to the town folks' commentary on the cookie viewings, trying to gage their odds of winning.

Mrs. Myers cookies looked, as usual, unprofessional. She had made Santa cookies, which were nice enough, but the red was a muddy hue, and goodness knows what they tasted like; if her colors were so mediocre. Each year she entered and each year she lost, but she still kept her spirits high, despite each defeat. The Goth chick from *Hell's Kitchen* had decorated her cookies *black*! They were supposed to be "*A representation of bad kids getting coal,*" Aunt Carol had overheard her say to Earl, the lodge keeper.

Aunt Carol didn't think they needed to worry about that. No matter how good those cookies tasted, the judge wouldn't be able to get past that gruesome black color.

The rest of the booths were filled with out-of-town contestants because most of the regulars in town had given up. There was no other cookie competition nearly as relevant as the Silver Bells Christmas Eve Fair Cookie Contest.

Most of the small town of Kissing Bridge Mountain had gathered for this most important annual event. Contestants had their fans, and of course the betting was a very popular part of the fair. The scoreboard was all lit up with Christmas lights.

Even though Mom and the Landers had won every past year—except last—she was coming out way below Mrs. Beaverton in the odds.

The news had leaked out around town that Martha Stewart had been coaching Mrs. Beaverton, so her odds had gone up!

The scoreboard currently showed the odds at Goth chick—whose name was Josephine Jamison, at 20%—Ethel Landers was next, with 30% and Mrs. Beaverton was sitting in first-place odds at 50%.

Summers hopped up to the back of the booth with the frosting. Her mother was a worried mess.

"Oh Summer, thank goodness you're here." She looked at the frosting and dipped a finger in.

"Oh, you outdid yourself, Honey. This is wonderful – and the color, I'm very happy with it! The diamond-chip Wolfgang Puck edibles are going to be exquisite—the feather in our cap—our blue-ribbon *winner's* cap!"

Summer smiled weakly. "Let's get started frosting the cookies, Mom, and then I'll grab the package out of the car so no one gets a peek."

Mom smiled broadly. "Great idea, Darling!"

Aunt Carol came bustling in. "I don't think we have any real contenders, except Mrs. Beaverton. I couldn't get through the crowd to even get a glimpse of her cookies, it's so crowded…"

Mother waved it away.

"No matter, Carol! We have the secret weapon!"

Summer realized that she was going to have to tell them the truth. Soon.

A tree had fallen and blocked the mail truck from coming. Wolfgang Puck was not showing up to save the day.

She couldn't bear to disappoint them both and tell them that the special diamond ice chips from Wolfgang Puck that were going to seal the win—just *weren't* going to show up.

It was 3:40 and the competition was about to begin at 4:00 sharp. Aunt Carol whispered in her ear. "I heard about the tree blocking off the road up the mountain…You did get the package, right?"

Summer looked at her sheepishly.

Aunt Carol groaned beneath her breath. Sometimes the gift of eavesdropping was a tough burden to bear.

Mom was exuberant. "Summer, go get the chips. We're ready!"

With that, the official Silver Bell Carrier, this year it was Dolly, still in the elf outfit, rang the bell to indicate the ten-minute mark. It sounded more like a death knell to Summer.

Summer stood planted in the booth not knowing what to do. Mom stared at her expectantly. "Summer, go get them, Honey. The competition is about to start!"

The look on Summer's face told her

everything. She looked back and forth at the blank faces of Aunt Carol and Summer. They had nothing to say.

It suddenly dawned on Mother that there were no Wolfgang Puck chips coming to save the day—no surprise super special diamond delicious chips to out-best Martha Stewart.

She glared over at the Beaverton booth.

"I can't tarnish the Landers Legacy, I'm going to throw in the cookie dough and drop out now."

Summer tried to encourage her, but what could she say? They were doomed.

It was going to be another humiliating loss and all because of a downed tree and the Evil Martha Stewart.

Mom collapsed into a chair and put her hands to her heads. "I'm going to have a nervous breakdown."

Summer patted her mother's back and tried to reassure her.

"Don't worry, Mom. The cookies are still the best tasting in all of Vermont, if not beyond. And that Tiffany color—so modern, yet *chic!*"

Aunt Carol took this moment to say something very profound.

"Ladies, no matter what happens, you're the most wonderful women I've ever known. I love you both. This will not reflect on how I feel about either one of you, or Christmas. I suggest we buckle our seatbelts and prepare for a bumpy cookie ride."

Mom continued to shake her head.

Summer added, "Come on, Mom. Aunt Carol is right. We're all here together! Christmas is all about love and we already have that."

She tried to get her mom to smile. "Right, Mom?"

Summer wished she could do something to cheer her up.

Just then, a large gust of wind stirred up the snow and sent snowflakes flying in many flurries like magical floating doves.

Dolly rang the bell, indicating five minutes until the official judging.

When the flurries cleared, Summer looked to see that the gust had come from a small plane that had just landed on the field beside the fairgrounds.

A moment later, Brad leapt out of the plane with a box under his arm and started to run in their direction.

The townspeople all stared at the commotion. And of course, everybody wondered what was in the box.

Chapter 30

The townspeople were enthralled by this extra excitement before the big competition.

It was obviously a very special gift that would cause Brad Anderson to have almost missed the cookie competition. By now, everyone knew that the roads had been blocked off leading up to Kissing Bridge Mountain.

What was so important that Brad had flown off the mountain to go get it in the middle of the Silver Bells Christmas Eve Fair?

Suddenly, a squealing scream sounded out of the crowd, and Miss Big Boobs burst from the crowd and came running toward Brad with her arms outstretched. Her big boobs bumped up and down and up and down and caused quite a stir in their own right.

This was turning out to be quite the Silver Bells Fair! Miss Big Boobs threw herself into Brad's arms, causing the box to fall. Brad dove to catch it before it hit the ground. The crowd *oohed and awed* in appreciation of the catch. Miss Big Boobs began to tug on the package with both hands.

"Oh Brad, is that my engagement ring? Let me see!"

A new murmur ran through the crowd. And then an expectant hush. Brad's mouth dropped from the big smile he had been grinning and he turned as red as Santa's coat.

"Ahh… no, actually." He bent over and whispered to her, "We broke up. I thought you left with Drake Mason."

Miss Big Boobs was enjoying all the attention. She decided to milk the moment; she feigned a horrified look and screamed as if she had been stabbed by the news. The entire town shook their heads. What was Brad Anderson up to now?

Brad caught site of the clock. It was

three minutes to the start of the competition.

Brad looked at Miss Big Boobs and said sincerely, “I'm so sorry. I thought I made it clear. We’re broken up. You mauled Drake Mason in front of the whole town. I have to go now.” With that, he left her standing there, and turned toward the competition booths.

Then he ran as fast as he could toward the Landers’ booth.

The whole town turned, as if one.

First, the Landers’ covered their cookies to keep them mysterious and so nobody could get a look—which was one of the most fabulous things about the cookie contest. And now Brad Anderson flying out of nowhere and bringing a mysterious box?

It was all too much excitement for one small town!

As Brad leapt over the Landers’ booth with the box, it was so quiet, you could hear the snowflakes hit the ground.

Ethel Landers cleared her throat and stepped forward and asked the question everybody wanted to know.

"What's in the box, Brad Anderson?"

Brad blushed when he realized the entire town was focused on him now. He cleared his throat.

"A package… for Summer."

A murmur went through the crowd at this new information. All eyes turned toward Summer.

Summer's mouth fell open. She looked at the box, and then her family.

"It's from Switzerland!"

Aunt Carol jumped up and down and screamed, "Wolfgang Puck! Suck it up, Beaverton!"

She stuck her tongue out at Wily Junior for effect. The entire crowd went wild. Everybody started talking at once.

The news that the Landers had pulled Wolfgang puck out of thin air at the last moment changed everything.

The odds keepers at the scoreboard began flipping the numbers— flip, flip, flip. The flippers couldn't flip quickly enough. Within seconds, new odds were posted.

Mrs. Beaverton had Evil Martha Stewart but the Landers had the ultra gourmet himself, Wolfgang Puck!

They now stood at equal odds.

Summer looked up at the board. 50% Landers, 50% Beavertons. The Goth chick from *Hell's Kitchen* had been pushed down into oblivion and no longer even showed on the board.

She screamed out in anger as her name fell in the ranks. "You're all getting coal. *Coal!*"

Never had the cookie competition been this exciting and this fierce.

People waved their money and quickly placed new bets as the clock ticked to one minute before the starting bell.

Mom watched the clock tick toward the last second, then threw off the tin foil cover dramatically and unveiled the cookies.

A gasp went up through the audience. They were stunningly beautiful!

So modern.

So chic.

So *Tiffany*.

A crowd gathered to gaze in appreciation. The Landers women had outdone themselves. They had chosen Christmas bells as their cut-out cookie shape, and mom had made up the softest loveliest Tiffany blue color that looked ever so enchanting on the bells.

The three Landers stepped back and looked at their friends admiring their cookies. They were beautiful.

Never had the Landers ventured from the traditional green and red combo. None of the contenders, in fact, had ever ventured from the standard red and green cookie combo—other than Goth chick who was just a random wild card.

A hush had come over the crowd in anticipation of what might come next.

All they needed was the coup de gras now, the Wolfgang Puck special diamond replica sweets for the bells.

Summer opened the box and undid the plastic tie to reveal the chips. But instead of the beautiful special diamond chips, there was only a sparkling shivering pool of melted liquid at the bottom of the box.

Alas, the magical diamond chips had melted away during transit.

Mom let out her breath so hard it sounded like a whale horn, and Aunt

Carol had to steady her from falling to the ground.

This was a game changer.

Summer looked at Brad. “I'm so sorry, Summer. I had no idea.” They stared at the melted diamond chips. Even melted, they were beautiful.

Summer shook her head and reached her hand out to touch Brad.

“It's okay, Brad. It doesn't matter. Thank you so much for doing this…it means so much to me, and my mom and Aunt Carol.”

Her mom was now being fanned by Aunt Carol, more to keep the stares away than cool her.

Behind them, the scoreboard boys were flipping again in frenzy. 60% Beaverton, 20% Landers, and now Goth chick, despite her upsetting threats, had pulled up again to rank at 20%.

Summer turned to Brad. “I’m so sorry, Brad. I was wrong. I should have trusted you. I was sure it was a case of the Landers’ curse. I should have had more faith in you.”

Brad looked at her with love. He

cupped her face in his hands and looked deeply into her eyes. "I've had a lot of time to think about this, Summer—ten years, in fact."

Her blue eyes gazed up into his grey orbs, and then he said, "It's only the Landers' curse if you stay a *Landers*. How about switching it up? What do you say about becoming 'Mrs. Brad Anderson'?"

A genuine smile of love and realization came over her beautiful face.

At that moment, a true Christmas miracle had occurred!

Summer realized that Aunt Carol and Mother had never given up their family name! Now, without a smidgen of doubt, Summer realized that's *all* she had *ever* wanted to do.

The curse could be lifted *after all.*

"I do!" Summer sang out loudly.

With that, Brad reached out and grabbed her and kissed her ardently. Summer let the box fall out of her hand and the liquid pool of diamond shimmers spilled out all over the ground.

The crowd erupted into clapping and hooting and cheers of "Go Brad, go Brad, go!"

When they stopped kissing and finally came up for air, Brad raised his arms up like he had scored a touchdown—just like in high school.

This whipped the crowd up into a new frenzy of clapping and congratulations only to be quieted by the ringing of the bell signaling the start of the competition.

Chapter 31

The portly judge was ensconced in a King outfit, complete with a large gold crown.

The outfit really did not have any connection to Christmas, but did lend emphasis to the supreme importance of his position.

Each year, the judge was chosen from a large number of culinary experts who had applied for the job. This year's judge was a professor from the *French School of Pastry* in Paris. This was not his first time as the chosen one.

'Mr. Frenchy', as Summer called him, had judged this contest many times before, and he was very experienced.

Jack, dressed as Santa, blew a horn, and then rolled out the official red carpet down the length of the booths. Mr. Frenchy strutted down the carpet in his King outfit.

Dolly followed behind him in her elf outfit with a silver tray holding a glass of milk and her bell.

He walked regally toward the first contender's table. He studied the colors and shapes. He then took a bite of a cookie, and motioned for Dolly to hand him a glass of milk to swallow and clear the pallet.

The crowd waited expectedly. He said nothing and moved on to the next booth, which was Goth chick from *Hell's Kitchen*.

Mr. Frenchy's eyes widened when he looked at the black cookies shaped as coal. He took a tentative bite then lifted a quizzical brow, and reached for the milk.

He slowly made his way down the corridor of contenders without a word.

The Beavertons' and the Landers' booths were at the very end. The end booths were the most coveted, and reserved for past winners to build excitement.

The judge continued on without a

word. Murmurs rose in the crowd as he sampled each of the cookies from the booths. The onlookers took side bets on what he might be thinking, based on the twitches of one eyebrow or another.

Sometimes the flexing of the nose held weight, although Summer thought it had more to do with his long nose hairs itching him—rather than an indication of what he thought about the cookies.

Now Mr. Frenchy was approaching the final two booths. The town's folk gathered around them. The gloves were off. Now that the crowd had been forced off the main drag walkway for the King, the final contenders were finally able to see each other.

Aunt Carol and mom glared across at Mrs. Beaverton's booth. The Beavertons glared back.

Now that the walkway had been cleared, they had a full view of each other's booths—and cookies.

It was a showdown. It may not have been the Wild West—but it was the Kissing Bridge cookie competition—and it was *fierce*!

Aunt Carol, Mom and Summer stared across the pass at the Beaverton's booth. They had chosen the traditional red and green combo colors. However, Mrs. Beaverton had changed up the usual shapes and gone for maroon sleighs and lime green elves. Indeed they were beautiful.

Mother stifled a gasp. "Those colors… they're mesmerizing! So…*Martha Stewart*!'

And with that, she went into a full throttle wail. There was no consoling her.

"I'm taking to the bed, I might as well go get in right now! Make sure you bring me water so I don't die. Sorry I'll miss Christmas. I loved you both…"

Summer looked at her Aunt Carol, who was shaking her head.

"Never saw that coming. Darn Martha Stewart!"

The Beavertons' cookies were truly a sight to behold. They were just sooo Martha Stewart, and of course that meant *amazing*.

Brad tried to reassure Mother. "Ms. Landers, you are the legendary *Cookie*

Queen! You're going to win. You're the Landers!"

Mom looked down at the Tiffany blue bells cookies—without the silver bell part now. She really had outdone herself with the color this time. She drew in her breath and gathered her courage. Certainly, with all three Landers helping this year, this batch of Christmas cookies had to be the best batch ever.

She nodded.

She hugged Aunt Carol and Summer.

So they weren't Martha Stewart coached, or Wolfgang Puck iced up with diamonds. They were *still* beautiful.

The judge approached the Landers' booth. He studied the Tiffany-blue perfect bells (missing the would-be diamond bells.)

It looked like he moved his left ear, which could or could not have been a good sign.

In any case, he took a bite of a cookie and a swallow of the milk, and without another word or expression, he turned to Mrs. Beaverton's booth.

The Landers looked at each other.

Brad grabbed a cookie and took a bite and said overly loudly, "Hmmm hmm! Mama, I really love these cookies! They're the *best ever*!"

Summer slapped her hand over his mouth and they all laughed.

Brad grabbed her and hugged her.

She realized that this was the best day in her entire life; with or *without* winning the blue ribbon.

The excitement of the crowd had grown to a fervor. Everyone gathered around Mrs. Beaverton's booth now. The crowd had pushed through onto the red carpet area and the Landers could barely see.

They huddled together in a little cookie prayer. Brad stood on his toes to see what was happening.

The judge picked up one of Mrs. Beaverton's cookies and took a bite.

There was a long pause.

He reached slowly for the milk, and took an extra long sip. Then he paused for a moment, before he reached over for the last swallow of milk and put the empty glass down with finality.

Dolly rang the bell, signaling the competition was officially over.

Everybody crowded in front of the judges' platform to await the results. Last-minute bets were still flying back and forth.

The King waddled back down the red carpet toward his judging throne.

The Landers waited expectantly holding hands.

Brad tried to keep their spirits up.

"I mean it. These are the best cookies I've ever had. You guys really outdid yourself this year!" He munched on another one. "HMMMM!" He held one out to Summer.

"Try one."

It was going to take a moment for the judge to squeeze his rotundness into the throne again.

Summer picked up a cookie and took a bite. A smile spread slowly across her face.

The flavor.

So fluttery perfect.

Heaven.

Summer took another bite.

"HMMMMM!" She looked at the cookie with a confused look.

Aunt Carol was studying her.

Summer shoved a cookie at her.

"Taste this."

Aunt Carol chewed. Her brows shot up. She smiled broadly. "What did you do different to the frosting?"

Summer looked confused. "I made it the same as we always did—straight out of Grandma's recipe book."

Aunt Carol chomped another bite of the cookie.

"It's so good! It tastes like ... like I remember when I was a little girl—when… when…"

Suddenly her excitement got the best of her.

"Ethel, try this!"

She pushed a Tiffany blue bell cookie into her sister's mouth. Ethel tore her gaze momentarily away from the judge who had finally gotten his butt into the throne.

Her eyes went wide as she chewed. She took another bite and a look of realization came over her face.

Aunt Carol and she both said at the same time, "Grandma Izzy's cookies!"

The Landers chewed on in amazement and joy. These certainly were the best batch of cookies ever! With, or without Wolfgang Puck, nobody surpassed Grandma Izzy!

Dolly rang her bell to signal the announcement of the winner.

The King cleared his throat.

He spoke French as Dolly translated, "It was a fabulous crowd this year. All the contenders did a wonderful job.... I want to thank Dolly for holding my milk tray... And also please pick up your trash on the way out, as tomorrow is Christmas and there will be no cleaning crew."

"Now, onto the results of the Silver Bells Christmas Eve Fair Cookie Competition.

"The winner is...

(in lieu of a drum roll, Santa blew his horn again).

"...In third place, for her unique contribution..."

A hush went over the group as they waited in anticipation.

"...Miss Josephine Jamison."

The crowd clapped. Goth chick ran out of the booth area cursing something very *un*-Christmas like.

The judge cleared his throat and the people turned their attention back to the podium.

"Second place, the red-ribbon winner... for her unique cut-out choice and excellent color combination...Mrs. Beaverton!"

The crowd clapped and hollered.

Mrs. Beaverton turned as red as her cookies.

Summer looked at her mother. A smile spread across their faces.

"...And first prize goes to... the best-tasting cookies I can ever remember tasting...*The Landers ladies*!"

The crowd went into an uproar.

Brad lifted Summer up into the air.

Aunt Carol and Mom hugged each other tightly.

They had won! The blue ribbon was coming home with the Landers tonight!

Brad went and lifted up Mom and carried her toward the platform, amidst cheers from the town folk. He carried her through the cheering crowd and up the stairs to where the King had just squeezed out of his throne, to turn over to this year's rightful Cookie Queen.

Aunt Carol followed behind their wake, thanking people along the way, as they reached out to shake her hand in congratulations.

She joined Mom on stage and soon they were taking bow after bow.

The townspeople cheered as they passed around the cookies and paid up on their bets. It had been a very exciting day for everyone.

Summer looked at the contestants lined up, holding their ribbons for the annual *Kissing Bridge Gazette* photo. Mom was beaming and Aunt Carol winked at her.

Summer was so happy with the way everything had turned out.

Whether it was the Tiffany blue, the magic of Christmas, or Grandma Izzy's ghost that managed to throw the vanilla liqueur (*her real secret ingredient*) into the frosting, it was the happiest Christmas

Summer could *ever* remember!

They had discovered how to break the Landers' curse, she and Brad were going to get married and have lots of kids, and Mom and Aunt Carol had regained their rightful place as Christmas Cookie Queens.

Everything was as it should be again, back on Kissing Bridge Mountain.

Against all odds, it had turned out to be a truly magical and wonderful blue ribbon Christmas after all.

If you enjoyed this book please follow your new friends on their new journey! The next two books in this series are currently available on amazon!

"Holiday Kisses and Valentine Wishes" and "Chocolate Kisses and Love Filled Wishes."

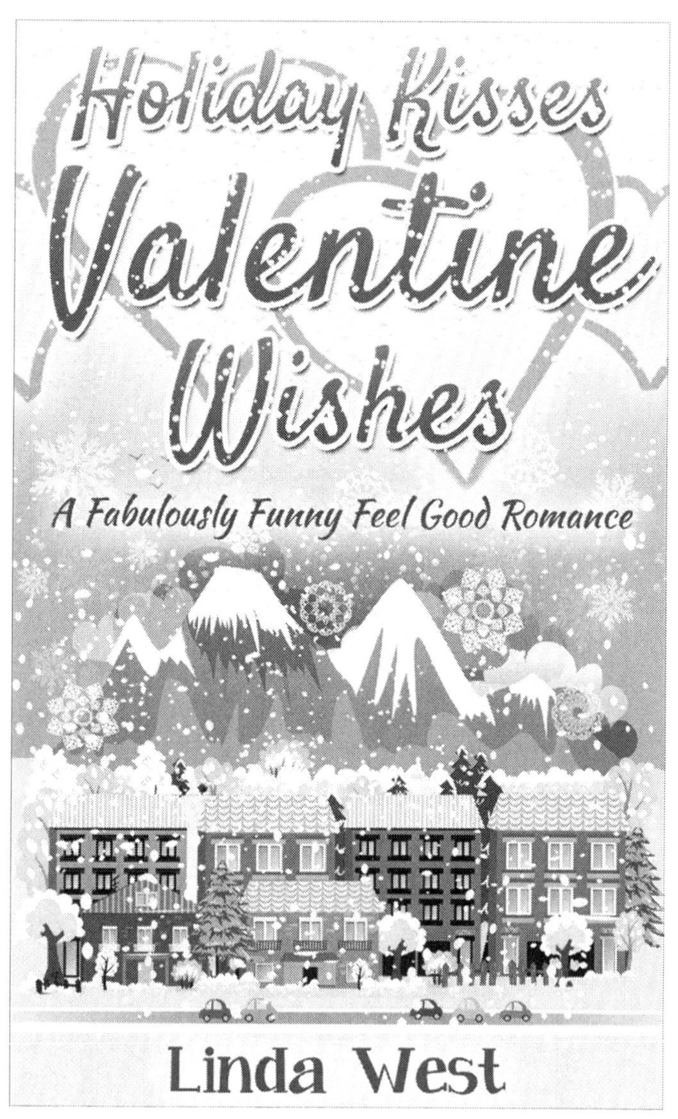
Holiday Kisses
Valentine
Wishes
A Fabulously Funny Feel Good Romance
Linda West

Holiday Kisses and Valentine Wishes

A Fabulously Funny Feel Good Romance

Continues on from where we left off in Kissing Bridge!

BY

LINDA WEST

If you haven't read the first two best-selling holiday books in the "Love on Kissing Bridge Mountain Series" please check them out!

#1
Best
Seller

Dedicated to,
My darling son Sebastian

Chapter 1

Christmas Eve

Summer Landers smiled as she looked up at Brad Anderson. Who would have ever thought that this Christmas would find her engaged to the man she had always loved? After being separated by a sad, eavesdropping mishap, the soulmates had found their way back together against all odds.

The full moon shone down upon the snowbanks. Christmas lights twinkled from the homes that dotted the streets of Kissing Bridge Mountain. The entire town had turned out for Christmas Eve Mass.

The old stone church was crammed

full of adults and excited children in their best holiday clothes, full of anticipation for Santa's arrival the next day. The vaulted roof swelled with the comforting notes of Christmas carols, while intricate layers of harmonies floated through the air.

Summer winked at her Aunt Carol, who stood squarely at the front of the choir, singing her heart out. Aunt Carol's signature red beehive was so large that it blocked out the ladies behind her. They had to keep popping their heads around its massive bundle, trying to smile at their loved ones in the pews.

A light snow had begun to fall outside, whispering on the stained windows bearing pictures of Mary and the Disciples and Apostles, and the warm, golden light of candles permeated the church. Their flames flickered with the music as if they were dancing. Summer thought to herself that life had never seemed so perfect.

What a difference a week could make.

The week previous she'd been sweating in the heat of Los Angeles, pining for a white Christmas, and trying to figure out how she'd managed to get engaged to a movie star she wasn't even in love with. *Drake Mason,* the whole world swooned. She didn't get the attraction anymore.

Now… well… she turned to look up again at Brad Anderson. His gray eyes shined in the candlelight as he smiled down at her in return. He hugged her close to him and she snuggled into his broad shoulder. Who ever would have thought that after breaking up ten years ago it would be Brad that she chose to spend her life with?

Summer was usually cautious about doing things too fast, but everything felt just right. Since coming back to Kissing Bridge she had been swept up in a whirlwind of activity. Against all odds and an evil Martha Stewart trained rival, the Landers ladies had reclaimed their cookie throne as the blue ribbon winners of the Silver Bells Fair.

Summer reached over and squeezed her mother's hand. They shared a warm smile. It was almost too good to be true.

Mother – Ethel Landers – stood with all the dignity and poise of royalty. Again crowned the cookie queen, she had steadfastly refused to remove her Blue Ribbon which was now pinned to the front of her dress for all to see.

Summer couldn't blame her.

It had been the toughest cookie competition in decades.

Churchgoers still streamed in, each face familiar. Every face that wasn't easily recognizable could be explained away with deduction. A young woman who walked in with Danae Truman – *probably her cousin.* A middle-aged man who accompanied old Mrs. Samworth – *must be her son-in-law.*

Summer spotted Earl, the lodgekeeper, as he made his way down the aisle. He was a seventy-something gent with an easy laugh and mischievous twinkling brown eyes. His eyes widened as he spotted Summer's mother.

He nodded at Summer and Brad, then leaned into Ethel. "That blue is a lovely color on you, if you don't mind me saying so."

Summer watched as her mom blushed. "Thank you, Earl," Ethel replied.

He winked and walked ahead to take a seat a few pews ahead of them. His best buddy, Old Mr. Jennings, tottered along after him. Old Mr. Jennings finally fit his name, Summer thought. He'd been called old since his hair had turned snowy white almost overnight in his mid thirties.

Earl tossed a cheeky glance back as he took his seat. Summer's heart sparkled as she watched her mom's cheeks blush a rosy shade of pink.

* * *

Dodie Randall dried the tears from her eyes and prepared to open the door to the church. It had been so long since she had ventured inside hallowed ground she wondered if they would reject her, or if God's thunderbolt would shoot down to put her out of her misery.

She had said, "I'm fine, just fine," to her uncle Earl as he held the door open for her. "I just want a moment more of fresh air, a moment to get my head together."

But there would never be enough fresh air for her to get her head around what had happened.

As she watched the gentle snowdrift, she wondered what the heck was wrong with her. Whenever life seemed to be going well, some evil, shadowy hand stuck into her life and rearranged everything into chaos. Her first marriage to a successful musician had ended suddenly when he died of an overdose, leaving her a young widow.

It had taken her a long time to open her heart again, but Peter had come along and changed that. He kept trying to win her heart and trust and love and he finally had succeeded in prying open the dusty doors of her feelings.

Peter had been perfect.

Life had been perfect.

Or at least she had thought so. He had two sweet grown sons that loved her. A big house in Chicago she'd spent years perfecting with just the right throw cushions, shades of paint and organizational systems for the laundry room. An engagement ring on the way.

As she'd gazed into Peter's green-flecked hazel eyes, she really believed she'd found her last resting place. It was simple, really, she'd started to think. Just love one another and be together, that was all. Their love was true and together they would grow more and more in love over the years. They'd be there for each other; sick, poor, whatever to the end. Nothing could break their rock-solid love.

Or so she thought.

When Peter had been so overjoyed at getting the tickets to *Lord of the Dance* that he'd jumped around the living room squealing, she had assumed he just enjoyed theatrical productions, perhaps to a fault, but she was prepared to let that slide. She didn't figure he was gay, but that little fact had been revealed a few weeks later in their own theatrical production that had started with a chat about their families and ended with a screaming match, insults, and hairbrushes flying across the room.

Dodie didn't have anything against gay men. She had just hoped her fiancé wasn't one of them.

She sighed deeply and then breathed in again, trying to draw some strength from inside herself.

The pine trees made her feel strong, the way they stood tall and steadfastly refused to let the wind sweep all their spikes away. You didn't get this kind of energy from the skyscrapers in Chicago.

Maybe that was one of the reasons that since moving to Kissing Bridge Mountain she had found a kind of solace. The air was so clean it felt like a totally different kind of breathing, too. The place felt safe, if that was even a possibility anymore. The townspeople had been more than welcoming to the strange outcast with the solemn eyes and the past she'd rather not talk about.

She had arrived a couple months before Christmas.

Unable to feel, let alone rejoice, Dodie had taken to helping at the local soup kitchen and assisting the older ladies write letters to the boys over in the war.

Somehow sending good wishes and happy holidays to the soldiers made her feel better. They, like her, were alone, afraid, and had no idea what the future held.

Chapter 2

Finally mustering enough strength, Dodie pushed the church's heavy door open. The first thing that caught her eye was the nativity scene arranged in the front, which was comforting in a way she couldn't quite put her finger on.

She lingered at the back for a moment, watching the smiling choir weave their melodies and fill the church with their warmth. Ms. Carol Landers stood out with her bright red hair and larger-than-life persona, and the eye was immediately drawn to her, even from way in the back. Dodie smiled. She had one friend. Carol was a fellow card-writer for the soldiers.

As she cast her eyes over the

congregation, Dodie caught sight of Summer Landers – supermodel come home. She'd seen her pictures plastered across magazines and billboards, so it was jarring to see her up close and personal.

Summer was standing next to a handsome man with dark hair and they looked very much in love. Dodie slipped into the pew behind them, her chest aching just a little. Maybe their love and happiness would rub off on her if she just managed to get close enough.

Dodie closed her eyes. *Please God, please make it all make sense.* Why had she wasted so many years pouring her heart out, all her love, for a man that could feel nothing for her? He'd broken up with her so matter-of-factly. Like he felt nothing. It was an eerie hole where once a dream had lived. One moment she was awaiting a proposal, the next he was gleefully helping her pack up everything she owned while saying, "This is such a relief, this is such a relief, Dodie, I can't tell you."

Four bags.

That's all her life amounted to.

She'd sold her house in Atlanta to build the one in Chicago with him. He'd offered her a ticket home but that was a cruel joke. She had no home now.

No one.

No heart, it felt like.

Her mom's only brother, Earl, ran the lodge up at Eagle's Peak ski resort and he had offered to let her stay at the lodge while she readjusted to single life. She'd headed to Kissing Bridge Mountain because it was as good as anywhere. A good place to start over again.

The choir began a rendition of *Glory* that made goose pimples rise and ripple along Dodie's arms. Ms. Carol caught sight of Dodie in the pew. She smiled her big smile and Dodie felt at least like she had a friend.

She just didn't relate to the younger people. They all wanted to get married, have kids, and at thirty-seven she was just hoping she didn't die alone.

Caught up in the music, she began to sing. She'd always had a lovely voice.

"Glory to God, glory to God, glory to God forever."

Summer turned around in front of her and gave her a mega-watt smile. Dodie managed a hint of a smile in return.

Maybe after Christmas things would be better.

Maybe her heart would mend.

Maybe she wouldn't feel like fading away as time went on.

Chapter 3

Christmas Day

Summer curled up in the window seat and watched the snowfall. It had gotten heavier overnight and now Kissing Bridge was buried under a thick, white blanket.

She breathed a sigh of perfect contentment and the pane misted up in a little circle. She was even glad of that – that would have never happened in LA.

She drew a heart in the condensation, marking it *S* on one side and *B* on the other. It was kind of childish, but she didn't care.

She was home.

She felt like a kid again, like the world was really full of possibilities. The beat-down, cynical feeling that had gripped her in LA had been left there. She'd even laid out an empty stocking for Santa to fill the night before, complete with cookies (the winning Tiffany-blue specimens, of course) and milk, and even carrots for his reindeer. The stocking was full on the mantelpiece and her heart was warm that her mother would humor her that way.

"Look, Santa's left you a cookie," Brad laughed as Aunt Carol let him in through the front door with a cold winter breeze.

Summer laughed and ran to him, desperate to feel the comfort of his arms once again. She couldn't get enough of it. "Merry Christmas, baby!"

He folded her in a tight embrace and kissed her on each cheek, then on her forehead, then on her lips, long and lingering. "Merry Christmas."

"My eyes, my eyes!" Aunt Carol pretended to scream as she headed back to the kitchen. "You'd better be careful, young lady, 'else Santa'll be bringing you a lump of coal next year."

Summer flapped at her and led Brad by the hand back to the window seat. She curled her feet under her and snuggled into his shoulder. "This is the best Christmas ever."

"I'll say," Brad replied. "It was like a Christmas card on the way over here. We must take a walk."

"I'd love that," she said.

There was nothing like bundling up and feeling the icy wind bite your face when you knew you were coming home to a roaring fire, gifts, the tree, and hot cocoa. "Why don't we go right away?"

"Well, okay," he said.

She jumped up from the window seat, taking off her robe, and piled on jumpers and fleeces and rainproof macs over her pajamas.

"We're going out, Mom," she said as she slipped her double-socked feet into knee-high boots. "See you in a while."

"Okay, don't be too long," her mom called out from the kitchen.

Delicious smells of warm apple-cinnamon punch, gingerbread, and apple pie wafted through into the living room, making Summer's mouth water. She grabbed the cookie Santa had left behind and broke off a piece.

"Open your mouth," she said to Brad, and she placed a piece on his tongue before feeding herself. "Let's go."

Brad was right.

It was just like a Christmas card. The whole of Kissing Bridge was covered in white, illuminated by the soft light of the morning. The sun had not yet fully risen, the sky still a shade that lingered between dusky rose and powder blue. Christmas lights twinkled, some from underneath thin snow drifts. No one else was out. They walked through the deserted streets, gloved hand in gloved hand.

"Wow," Summer said, feeling its beauty tug in her chest. "It's so, so beautiful."

Brad turned to her in the middle of the main street. She'd never been able to stand there before, but in that moment it felt like no traffic would ever come to ruin the moment.

"Not as beautiful as you," he said.

She smiled at him, her heart alight. So many men had called her beautiful, but when he did, it was different. He meant something deeper, something about her essence, her being, not just the way her facial features were arranged. He was her Brad and she was his Summer. She felt the warmth of his hands through his gloves, and the warmth of his heart through his loving eyes, and felt like the luckiest woman alive.

"I feel so honored that you're going to be my wife," he said. He turned one of his hands loose and plunged it in his pocket. "Last time I did this, there was something missing."

"Huh?"

He got down on one knee, right there in the snow.

Tiny snowflakes danced around them in the cool wind and the sky was finally beginning to find its light.

He withdrew his hand from his pocket, holding a ring box. Summer's heart swelled through her chest.

"Summer, will you marry me?"

"Yes," she said, before he even opened the box.

Brad's smile was as bright as the new sun when he opened the ring box and withdrew the ring.

She scrambled to take off her glove and he slid the ring onto her finger. She gasped.

There it was. The original Tiffany ring!

"Brad!" she said, overjoyed. "Our ring!"

He smiled shyly. "I kept it."

Then she dropped to her knees in the snow and kissed him again and again.

"Yes, yes, yes!"

* * *

Dodie blinked awake.

It was Christmas morning, but none of the fluttering carefree giddiness of the holiday danced in her chest. It hadn't since Peter.

She got up, her limbs feeling heavy, and went into the en-suite bathroom to wash her face.

Christmas music wafted up from

downstairs, punctuated by the laughter of small children. She guessed her cousin Jane's son and daughter were just discovering Santa's bounty and love for them.

She sighed deeply as she returned to her room to dress, not working out how she was going to find a smile for them, a happy word. She didn't want to be a downer, and the thought of staying cooped up in her room with a crossword puzzle flickered through her mind.

Gosh no. That was just like Peter and his incessant need to bury himself in a crossword and ignore her as she tried to converse with him from across the room. Love had inflated in her heart and shined in her eyes, while his brows knotted and he'd tried to figure out what down word mated with *Hamlet's love.*

Standing before the closet, Dodie dabbed at her eyes. They always seemed to be tear-filled these days. She wondered if she'd ever get back to the carefree woman she once had been.

She had every reason to be happy.

She was a lovely girl. Beautiful, some

even called her. With strawberry blonde hair that fell past her shoulders in thick waves and gleeful green eyes, she had always been popular and never had to worry about a date. Still, the years had rolled on and she'd never really found her partner. Her other. The one.

She'd thought Peter had been that. Solid, secure, and boring, he was the antithesis of the bad boys she'd chosen in her younger years. A perfect, safe, husband-to-be. Except for the gay thing of course.

Despite all of her attempts to fit into his cookie-cutter life, it just hadn't worked. Even if he weren't gay. With his penchant for meals wherever he had a coupon for and an obsessive need to watch YouTube golf videos all day, Dodie just couldn't relate. How could he do nothing all day but things for himself? People were homeless. Starving. Dying in wars. The oceans were being poisoned. How could a conscious person just do nothing?

Dodie's first, late husband had left her well taken care of. So Dodie spent her days donating her time to charity organizations with the grand hopes of saving the Amazon rainforest from deforestation and making a difference.

Giving back.

Helping the world because it needed love, just like she had.

She wished now that she had listened to her mom's advice and kept more of the money from the sale of her home instead of donating the bulk of it, but Dodie had true faith. Not so good a guy picker.

She selected a blue dress. Red was just too festive and so bright it assaulted her eyes. Besides, she was afraid it would accent the hollows under her eyes and the tear-wet lashes. She would have to do just as she was, for she knew that no amount of dabbing with makeup would improve the situation.

No, she didn't look her usual, pretty self, but she was moving.

She was alive.

She would go down and get coffee and put on her best happy face.

Chapter 4

"Your eyes better be closed," Summer teased. She held her hands over her mom's eyes while Brad closed his fingers over Aunt Carol's.

Summer glanced at Brad and grinned with anticipation.

She couldn't wait to see what they thought of her gift!

Unbeknownst to them, Summer had inquired on the empty store in the Kissing Bridge Mountain upscale shopping area and found it was for sale. So she snapped it up as an extra special surprise for her mom and Aunt Carol. She was sure she'd found the perfect Christmas gift! Though it was empty, devoid of personality and color, between

Aunt Carol's glittering persona and Ethel's gift for picking out just the right shade, Summer knew that they'd have the place looking perfect in no time.

"Okay, you can open your eyes," Summer said.

Both Summer and Brad took their hands away at the same time and stepped back.

"Taa daa!" Summer sang out.

Ethel and Carol both looked between the store and each other, confusion clouding their faces.

"It's a store," Ethel said.

"It's a bakery mom – YOUR BAKERY!" said Summer.

Aunt Carol smiled from ear to ear. "Looks like Summer bought us a job Ethel!"

They all laughed and hugged each other.

Mom was still beside herself. "Well this is quite a surprise. You shouldn't have spent so much money Summer!"

Summer hushed her mom. "Think of it as an investment in my kids cookies future!"

She pulled a plan book she'd prepared out of her purse, doing just like she saw designers doing. Swatches and colors and pictures of completed bakeries graced the pages of the book, a veritable treasure trove of ideas.

"Look, you could have it like this, or like this, or this."

Aunt Carol gasped in delight and Summer watched as her mom's eyes widened, and, as she turned the pages of the book, glazed over with tears.

"Oh, Summer," she said, her voice little more than a breath. "It's wonderful."

She imagined them baking cookies and cakes and offering cooking classes, filling the whole street with homely, delicious smells. Aunt Carol's cheeks and nose had turned the same color as her hair in the cold.

"You, Miss Summer Landers, are an absolute superstar." With that, she drew Summer into a tight hug. Soon Ethel piled in.

"Hey, Brad!" Carol called out, her voice muffled in Summer's shoulder. "Group hug!"

Brad laughed and joined them.

Summer guessed they must look quite a sight there, the four of them huddled in front of the store; a mass of padded coats and rubber boots ankle deep in the snow, but she didn't care. *These were her people.*

* * *

"Pleeeeease, Aunt Dodie?" Sophie wailed.

Though Dodie was really Sophie and Alex's first cousin once removed, their being Earl's grandchildren, they had always called her Aunt.

Sophie held a baking book she'd just unwrapped up to Dodie's face, pointing at a picture of brownies cut in a Christmas tree shape.

"Pleeeease can you make holiday brownies with us?"

Dodie had been sitting on the couch by the fire, nursing a large glass of eggnog and trying not to think about Peter.

She'd also been trying not to worry

about finances. Tallying up the cost of all the gifts she bought, as well as her over generous charity donations, her heart had started racing. She should get herself a job but couldn't think of what on earth she'd do or where she'd go.

Baking.

Not her specialty but she guessed it would be a welcome distraction.

"I'll try," she said, "though I'm not all that good at baking."

"Yes!" Alex said, jumping up from his crouched position and raising his fist in the air. He kept it raised and charged out of the living room into the kitchen like a superhero.

"Thanks," Earl's daughter Jane mouthed at Dodie. She had been run ragged by her children's antics all morning and sank into the couch with a huge sigh.

Dodie finished off the last of her eggnog and allowed herself to be led into the kitchen by Sophie's little hand clutching hers in a determined grip. Alex danced around the kitchen, hyped up on sugary drinks and cookies, sliding across the floor in his reindeer slippers and basically making a nuisance of himself.

"Okay, so what do we need?" Dodie said, taking the book from Sophie.

"I can read, I can read!"

Alex volunteered, skidding in their direction. He brought a pointed finger down on a random place on the page. "*Easy!*" he read.

Quick and Easy Brownie Recipe, the title read.

"Let's hope so," said Dodie. She'd never been one for baking – the cakes she baked with her kids never rose and the cookies burned all around the edges or were so irreversibly stuck to the sheet that they crumbled into smithereens with the first touch of the spatula.

She'd never even tried brownies before, but the directions looked simple enough and it was a kids' book.

"*Ingredients,*" she read aloud.

"Ineegients," Sophie said, placing herself in a position like she was ready to run a race. "I'll get 'em."

"Two cups white sugar," Dodie said.

Sophie clambered up onto the

counter. "Coming right up!" She opened the cupboard only to find a load of bowls and plates. Her face fell.

Dodie rushed to her and set her down on the floor, giving her a kiss. "Hey, Soph, I don't know where anything is in here."

"Me either." Sophie put her finger to her lip, thinking of a solution. "Let's open every cupboard?"

Dodie's eyes scanned the massive kitchen. This was going to take much longer than she thought. "Maybe we should ask Grandpa Earl?"

"Nuh uh," Alex chimed in. "He's sleeping and he said if we interrupt he's gonna give me something to remember."

Sophie and Dodie giggled. Earl always kept himself busy with the inn, stuffing it with guests who came to Kissing Bridge Mountain to escape their busy city lives. By the time he closed up for the holidays he was ready to collapse into a chair and sleep through Christmas. Jane fussed around him and cooked Christmas dinner.

So they ended up opening all the

cupboards, just as Sophie suggested, and the fridge. Before long they'd gathered the sugar, butter, cocoa powder, vanilla extract, baking powder, flour, cinnamon, walnuts and salt. Dodie flicked the oven onto medium heat and Sophie began to mix away with a wooden spoon, sending flour billowing up in white clouds.

They poured the batter into a pan and Dodie let Sophie take a lick of the bowl before she washed it up in the sink. They sat around playing Sophie and Alex's favorite card game, Alex finally settling down enough to concentrate, while the kitchen filled with the comforting smell of brownies.

"Mmmm… smells good," Sophie said, her eyes full of life.

They played a few more hands until Dodie got up, a burning smell curling into her nostrils. "Why hasn't the pinger gone off yet?" She hurried to the oven and looked up at the digital display to see how many minutes were left. Her heart sank as she realized she hadn't even set it.

She threw the oven open and a gust of

hot air rushed at her, carrying the smell of burned brownie with it. "Oh no!" She switched off the oven and snatched up the oven gloves, pulling the tray of brownies out and setting them on the side.

The sheet of brownie was totally black, burned so much that it was unrecognizable.

This was a true baking disaster.

Chapter 5

January

"We have to have a really large nice yard," said Summer, clasping her hands together.

"I want flowers all around it, and a fence of course so we don't have to worry about the kids running wild."

"I could build a playhouse," Brad offered.

"Perfect." Summer closed his hand in hers as they walked across town.

He squeezed her hand and she felt the pressure of the Tiffany engagement ring press up against her other fingers.

"The pictures looked good," he said.

"They sure did." She smiled up at him.

It was to be the third house they'd looked at. The first house was too big. Summer had said she couldn't imagine herself like a headless chicken trying to keep it clean. Besides, it was big enough for any kids to lose themselves in and needed some structural work on the roof.

The second was all right – clean and neat and strong enough. But it never captured their hearts. Summer had twisted her mouth and looked up at Brad to see him wearing the same expression.

"We'll try another one," Summer had said to the realtor.

So here they were, striding onto the third.

"Third time lucky?" Brad said hopefully.

"Let's hope." A giddy impatience had gripped her.

Summer wanted marriage, a house, babies, all at once. She guessed she'd buried those desires for so long, prancing about on catwalks and living the so-called high life with Drake Mason, that they all just came spilling out.

As they reached the corner, he turned to her, taking her hands in his and gazing deeply into her eyes. "Are you sure this is what you want to do?" he asked.

"Of course!"

"Summer," he said, his voice low and gentle. "Are you sure you want to stop modeling? To give up your career?

To come back out here in the middle of nowhere?"

"Yes," she said forcefully. "Definitely."

"You sure you don't want to buy somewhere in LA?"

"This is home, Brad. LA is no place to have a family."

She dropped his hand and turned the corner. He followed, taking her hand back up again.

"Why all these questions all of a sudden?" she asked, feeling like the wind had been taken out of her sails. "Are you having doubts?"

"No, babes," he said. "I just want to make sure you're happy."

"Well I am." She turned to him. "Happier than I've ever been in my life."

"I could say the same thing."

They walked on in amiable silence, swinging their hands together back and forth like little kids or love-struck teenagers.

A goofy grin stretched across Summer's face. She already knew the answer before she asked the question, she just wanted to hear it, feel the way it made her heart flutter.

"And you're sure you want to give up jetting all over the world?"

"Most definitely," he said, without a moment of hesitation. "I want to be here with you, with the kids when we have them. Not surrounded by a bunch of people who don't give a damn about me, away from you for weeks at a time. A pilot's life is not as glamorous as it sounds believe me."

Summer beamed. "I know your business will be a success. Eagle's Peak is such an amazing ski mountain and it's been virtually untapped. People are going to love it!"

He'd told her of his plans to start his own private carrier, to take rich folks who spent their vacations on the slopes of Kissing Bridge Mountain up to the top on private planes. The money would be good, the hours would be pretty flexible, and best of all, they would be together as often as possible. Now it was his turn to beam at her encouraging words.

"Hey, look," Summer said, pausing. "Isn't that Dolly's car down there?" Summer looked at the house as they approached it. It was everything she had hoped to find. With Brad by her side and the light snow falling on the rooftop, Summer thought it looked like the most beautiful house in the world.

Sure enough, it was Dolly. She stepped out of the car and waved to them. It was January now so Dolly had retired her December Elf outfit and was dressed in a lovely grey suit. Summer waved at her.

Dolly had turned out to be the best realtor either of them had ever dealt with, conjuring up a bunch of properties in tiny Kissing Bridge in the blink of an eye. Of course Dolly had lived in Kissing

Bridge her whole life and so it was to be expected she knew the best places!

Summer and Brad had both agreed to keep stoney faces no matter if they liked a home or not. Neither one of them was good at keeping secrets so they fought to keep on their poker faces. Now as they neared this perfect looking house Summer had to remind herself, and Brad that even if they liked it, they had to stay dead cool and casual so that they could go ahead and bid low. At the sight of the property, she almost lost her head, but instead of jumping around and squealing, she leaned into Brad. "I *want* it," she whispered.

It was two and a half stories with a third attic room peeping out of a window nestled into the brown roof. White shuttered frames were laid symmetrically on periwinkle wooden siding on the first floor, while the ground floor boasted a wrap-around porch and a beautiful stonework finish. Pristine white steps, ornate porch railings and details, and a front yard blooming with flowers perfected the home. The whole thing oozed country glamor.

"Let's buy it," Brad whispered back. "We'll set it up together while we plan the wedding! Building inspection, paperwork, transfer the money, it's wrapped up."

Summer grinned up at him. "Well you've just got all this figured out, haven't you?"

He winked back. "Just trying to work out what price we can get away with."

Dolly headed their way with a cell phone pressed to her ear talking rapidly and looking all business.

"I kinda miss the Elf outfit," Summer whispered.

They both tried not to giggle.

Chapter 6

"It's Ethel's new store," Earl said.

He had a twinkle in his eyes that brought a smile to Dodie's lips. "Ethel, huh? Who's that exactly?"

Earl couldn't help smiling either as he pulled his boots on and fumbled with the laces, though he kept his head ducked. "Nobody."

"Uh huh." Dodie placed her hands on her hips. "And pigs can fly too, right?"

She pulled her favorite scarlet coat around her. Red had always been the color she'd longed to wear but not always felt she could pull off. Some days it would boost her, making her feel like a powerful woman stepping out into the world, but other days she would feel so inadequate, so powerless, that she couldn't even bear to look at it, much less wear it. In those times she retreated into blacks and grays and safe, boring pastels. But as she slung her red coat over her shoulders that day, she felt good. There was hope for her future.

"Mind your own business," Earl said playfully, then stood up and stretched. "Ready to go?"

"I was born ready," Dodie said, her black stylish boots clicking against the floor as she crossed the hallway.

She loved that one could walk anywhere in Kissing Bridge, breathing in the cool air that was gently scented with pine. In Denver, she'd needed a car to go everywhere, with freeway after freeway lined with mini malls. So many people in the big city. She realized she didn't miss her home with Peter there. It had never suited her, it had suited him of course.

As she and Earl walked along the sidewalk, she turned her face up to the winter sun and felt the closest thing to contentment she had in a long time.

Things were already getting better.

When they got to the parade of stores, Earl stopped still and breathed out, gazing at a shop on the other side of the street. "Now isn't that something?"

She followed his gaze. "Landers Home Baking," she said, reading the store sign.

It was indeed something.

The whole storefront had been painted the most delicate shade of Tiffany-blue. The store name was in a modern, angular font and had a matching black awning with silver detailing. It was a perfect mix of edgy and sweet, of modern and traditional, and immediately caught the eye for all the right reasons.

"They've transformed it," Earl said, looking left and right before crossing.

Dodie crossed the street behind him and looked in the windows hungrily. She'd only had her customary coffee for breakfast and her stomach rumbled. The sight of freshly iced donuts, cupcakes piled high with frosting, and a selection of freshly baked breads made her mouth water. A piece of paper stuck in the window caught her eye.

Looking for a trainee baker, it read.

Apply inside.

Her heart beat a little faster.

Over the previous few days, she'd trawled the Internet for jobs in Kissing Bridge but the closest ones were miles away. She wasn't in any hurry to buy a car to start commuting. She'd asked around, too, but everyone shook their heads.

This was the first vacancy she'd seen.

If only she could bake.

She guessed since it was a trainee role they weren't looking for a master chef, but maybe someone with at least a pinch of natural aptitude.

Given her track record, she doubted she'd make the grade, but she headed into the store after Earl.

The smell was incredible and hunger clawed inside her stomach. She hadn't realized how famished she was.

"Good morning, Earl," a woman said from behind the counter, somewhat shyly. She kept her eyes firmly on the dough she kneaded.

"Good morning, Ethel," Earl replied.

He turned to Dodie and winked. "Dodie, this is Ethel Landers, the cookie queen of Kissing Bridge. Ethel, this is Dodie, my niece."

Ethel smiled, then held up her doughy fingers. "Maybe not the best idea to shake your hand," she said. "I think I saw you in church on Christmas Eve."

"Sure, I was there," said Dodie. "It's a great place you have here."

"Thank you," Ethel said. "My daughter gave it to me and we've been fixing it up for a couple of weeks."

Dodie was dying to ask if her daughter was Summer Landers, as she tried to remember if it had been Ethel who was standing beside Summer and her handsome beau, but she was too reserved.

"Big batcha donuts, coming right up," a loud, booming voice said, and Carol came in from the back room with a huge tray full of them.

Red wisps straggled down from her beehive and she pushed them back with the palm of her hand when she laid the tray on the counter. "Well, look at that," she said, looking at Dodie. "Come here, Miss Dodie."

She shimmied out from behind the counter and wiggled her way to Dodie, clutching her in the tightest hug Dodie had ever received.

"So good to see you," Carol said. "You want something to eat?"

"I'd *love* something," Dodie replied, scanning all the baked goods. "It's just so hard to choose."

"Tell me about it," Earl said. "These ladies are baking up a storm."

Dodie plumped for a piece of coffee cake. Carol placed a couple of Tiffany-blue cookies on the side and nodded at Ethel. "Her award-winning recipe, handed down from her mother."

Earl had a plate of shortbread and of course, a Tiffany-blue cookie.

They sat down at the only table and munched appreciatively, enjoying the softness of the warm light and lace tablecloth. The whole experience was just like Carol's hug.

Carol came over to them after a while and leaned against the table, her hand on her hip. "Enjoying it?

They nodded appreciatively, mouths full.

Carol cocked her beehive to one side. "You don't bake, do you, Dodie?"

Earl spluttered and sprayed a couple of crumbs. He'd seen her attempt at brownies.

"Oh, no, not really."

"Perfect!" said Carol.

She leaned back and hollered to Ethel, who was in the back room.

"We've got ourselves a trainee!"

Chapter 7

"Jason's coming home!" Brad hollered at the top of his lungs, running up the white steps and into their dream house.

He wove around the piles of cardboard boxes to find Summer in the kitchen unpacking dishes. He clutched the letter and practically threw himself at her. "Jason's coming home!"

Summer squeezed him tight, full of warm affection. She loved how Brad got when his big brother was around, all goofy and funny and humble, like the best little brother anyone could ask for. He never said all that much, but she knew he was worried about his brother's tours in the army, picking at his nails when he watched the news and pricking up his ears any time anyone mentioned war.

"He said those they didn't let go home for Christmas will be getting extra leave through January and February," Brad said. "Though…" His eyes scanned the letter, then lit up. "Though he's not sure he's even going to go back." He actually jumped up and punched the air. "Awesome!"

Summer had never seen him so excited and couldn't help but laugh a little.

Brad picked up the piece of toast that she'd just spread with peanut butter and jelly and took a bite into it.

"Hey!" Summer said, swatting at him.

He grinned, ripped it right down the middle and gave it back, licking the PB&J off his fingers. "I can't help it," he said. "It just tastes so much better when you make it."

She tucked into her toast half, rolling her eyes, while he strode up and down the room, pushing boxes to the edge with his elbow as he ate the toast.

"I can't wait until we're married and

we can move into this together. And you get to stay the whole night." Brad wiggled his brow at Summer. Summer hugged him again. She was so happy. They were building a life together bit by bit and she was loving every single thing about it.

"I should ask him to join my pilot business," he said. "That way he won't have to go back to war."

"That's not very patriotic," Summer laughed, tidying the kitchen area.

"I want another American citizen to stay alive and not die in some dubious war," Brad said. "That sounds pretty patriotic to me. He can fly well. Time for him to settle down, find a wife, have some kids. He's getting on a bit now."

"What happened to… what was that girl's name, the girl from Georgia?"

Brad grimaced.

"Becky. I'm only telling you this because I tell you everything, so don't tell anyone else. No one, right?"

"Sure."

"She cheated on him.

His buddy sent him pictures to prove it."

Summer brought her hands to her cheeks. “Oh my gosh. Poor guy.”

“You’re telling me.”

Brad sprawled out on the new sofa they bought online in the January sale, sinking into its soft beige pillows. “I think if we can get a deal with Earl going, we could do some really strong business.”

“That’s a good idea,” Summer said. “Hey, you could advertise the services together, that way you could draw in clients for the both of you.”

“I love it.” He propped himself up on his elbows and peered over at her. “Hey.”

She looked up to see his gray eyes dancing. “Yeah, baby?”

“I think we make a good team, don’t you?”

She smiled and leaned on the counter.

“Well, put it this way. There’s no one I’d rather be on a team with than you.”

Chapter 8

Dodie's hands just wouldn't stop shaking, no matter how many deep breaths she took or how she reassured herself in her mind. Today she was to instruct her first cooking class.

"But it's like the blind leading the blind!" she had protested to Ethel.

"More like the partially-sighted leading the blind," Carol corrected.

Ethel had put her arm around Dodie and told her in a gentle voice, "There's no better way to learn than to teach. We have faith in you."

Dodie tried to take heart in Ethel's words, but it wasn't all that easy. A hundred voices of doubt popped up in her mind and found her making stupid mistakes as she set up for the class that was due in at 10:00 AM.

There were six names on the list, which didn't sound like many at first but as the class had gotten closer had felt like a whole auditorium. In fact, she might have preferred an auditorium, where everything was dark and she couldn't watch people's facial expressions and where they couldn't ask questions. All she could hope was that these volunteers were novices in the most extreme sense of the word.

Miss Carol had taught her the key to baking was simply being precise. Follow the recipe. Don't guess. Measure. Preheat the oven. Don't over bake. Dodie knew that one.

She laid out the wooden spoons and the large mixing bowls and the bags of flour, then ran back into the main section of the bakery and tugged on Carol's arm as she kneaded bread dough. "Can't you take the class? Please?"

Carol shook her head. "You know I can't." She pointed back at the poster on the wall.

"The Valentine's Eve Sweetheart Bakeoff," Dodie read aloud. She'd heard them mention it but had been so wrapped up in her anxiety she hadn't had the chance or inclination to ask. Until now. "What is that, exactly?"

Both Carol and Ethel stopped their kneading. They leaned forward and stared. She felt all too keenly the discomfort that comes from being a newcomer in a small town. Dodie had quickly found that, as welcoming as the people of Kissing Bridge were, when she was ignorant to customs that had been ingrained into the fabric of their very lives, they looked at her like she didn't know her ABCs. Like she couldn't even count to ten.

"It's an auction," Ethel explained.

"Young women in town who are looking for a sweetheart create a baked good. These are then auctioned off anonymously on Valentine's Eve."

"Only eligible bachelors are allowed to bid," Carol cut in.

"Then each man is matched with the young woman who baked what he bought," Ethel continued. "They will be dates for the Valentine's Ball."

"Wow, what a great custom," said Dodie, momentarily relieved from her anxiety. "That's so fun."

"It sure is," said Carol.

Ethel shaped her pastry into a pie case. "And all the money goes to charity."

"Not only will we be baking everything for the Valentine's Ball, but we've got all those girls signed up for baking lessons to woo their beaus." Carol gestured at all the baking books piled up on the counter. "I've gotta flick through all of these at lightning speed to find recipes at all different skill levels."

Ethel looked at Dodie with sympathetic eyes. "We'll be here if you need us, no problem."

"And if there's anyone super advanced, you send them right back out here and we'll get them set up in a different group," said Carol. "We've tried to organize them already, but you never know."

"So I've got the beginners of

beginners of beginners, right?" Dodie said, twisting her red hair into a topknot and securing it with a clasp.

"Right." Carol nudged her playfully. "Now get in there and get ready."

Dodie took a deep breath and went back into the backroom. She scanned the *Jelly Heart Drops* recipe that Carol and Ethel had picked out for her, trying to tell herself it was easy. She recited the steps over and over in her head, lined up all the ingredients, and wiped the counters for the fourth time that morning. She glanced up at the clock. They were due any minute now.

Her hands jittered about, touching this and fixing that, when there was really nothing to do. In the end, she put them behind her back and rested against the counter.

She thought about the Valentine's Eve Sweetheart Bakeoff. *How ironic.* She'd be helping young women to bake cookies, which she couldn't do, and to kindle romance, which she didn't seem to be able to do either.

For a fleeting moment she considered

putting herself forward for the bakeoff, but figured that a plate of burned cookies wouldn't fetch much interest. If, by some miracle, she pulled off passable baked goods, the young man who bid on them might not be pleased when he saw that, instead of a perky peer, he'd landed himself with a mommy of young children. A yummy mommy, maybe, but still a mom of grown kids. She couldn't face the humiliation.

She wondered if she'd ever get another chance, if she'd ever be brave enough to take the first step out into the dating world.

Right then, romance felt a million miles away.

Chapter 9

Only four out of the six young women showed up, which Dodie was grateful for.

A cheerleader type named Tassy with a sleek mane of raven-black gloss was in first, pulling her hair up into a messy bun and making such polite and engaging conversation about her college plans that Dodie felt all her nervousness seep away.

Stephanie and Carina, obviously best friends who shared the same unusual style, came in together. Stephanie was abnormally tall with dark curls cut close to her head and striking features, while Carina was more rounded and pleasant with sandy coloring; the typical girl next door.

They both wore long-sleeved maxi dresses in thick cotton, Stephanie's in deep sea blue and Carina's in a dusky rose, with cinch belts around their waists. They chattered together.

Justine came in last, a sunny girl with a mass of springy curls in shades of cinnamon and caramel and a winning smile.

"Hey," she said as she came in. "I'm Justine. I know nothing about nothing about baking so I sure hope you have patience." She gave Dodie a hug.

"I was hoping you guys will have patience with *me*," Dodie said. She wondered why she had ever been nervous. The girls made her feel at ease. "So, you can all put on your aprons and we can get started."

They did.

"What are we making?" Carina asked.

"I wanted to make a special three-tier cake in the shape of a heart for the Sweetheart Bakeoff," Justine announced, giggling. "Though I guess I've got a long way to go!"

"Well, if you want heart-shaped,

you're in luck," Dodie said, grinning. "We're going for heart-shaped cookies today, with a jelly filling in the middle."

Everything seemed to go well, the girls sailing through the measuring, mixing, and shaping. Dodie was practically jumping for joy when everyone's cookies came out of the ovens perfectly. The cookies had to cool a little before adding the jelly, and they girls had already finished washing up while the cookies were baking, so they stood around and chatted.

"So are you entering the bakeoff, Dodie?" Justine asked.

Dodie laughed uncomfortably. "I don't think so."

"She probably has a husband already," Stephanie said.

"Not anymore," Dodie said with a grimace.

Justine took her apron off and began folding it into a tiny little square, just for the fun of it. "Oooh, so it's time for you to get back on the market."

Dodie looked around at them, at the genuine encouragement on their faces, and found herself confiding in them. "You don't think I'm too old?"

"No!" they all said at once.

"And you're so pretty it doesn't matter anyways, even if you were," said Tassy.

Dodie ducked her head. "You're all so sweet."

"Just telling the truth," Justine said, tipping her head on the side in a cute expression and sending her curls bouncing.

By the time the girls headed home with friendly waves and their cookies proudly tucked away into boxes, Dodie felt a warm glow all around her. Not only had she managed to pull off a delicious recipe, but she'd made four new friends. She bit into one of her cookies and smiled. Things were definitely looking up.

Dodie waltzed out of the backroom feeling like a million dollars. Ethel gave her a hug while Carol clapped her on the back and told her she was well on the way to being the Nigella Lawson of the south.

Dodie found a grin spreading over her face. "I can live with that." She took a deep breath. "I think I'm gonna enter the bakeoff myself."

"Great idea," Carol said, without so much as a raised eyebrow. She picked up a thick book of baking ideas and handed it to her. "Some bedtime reading."

That night, Dodie snuggled under the covers at Earl's and looked through the glossy pages by the soft, golden light of her bedside lamp. The rooms were so luxurious – the duvets and pillows thick and downy, the atmosphere warm and comforting – so much so that she looked forward to returning to her room at the end of the day.

She had soaked in a hot bubble bath, the room illuminated by candles, dreaming of the possibilities her new life could bring. The depression she had brought with her to Kissing Bridge was slowly fading and the last of it drained away with the water as it swirled down the plug. She had chosen a flannel nightgown, just to feel its softness against her warm, clean skin.

Though it all looked delicious, the passionfruit cake was the first thing to catch her eye. She imagined the combination of passionfruit's sweet tang and the creaminess of the filling and frosting and her stomach purred, even though she had eaten cookie after cookie, unable to quite believe they hadn't been burned or undercooked.

But a couple pages after, she was swayed to the pomegranate and chocolate torte. She deliberated on the raspberry and white chocolate cupcakes, a selection of shortbread hearts and a batternberg cake, but in the end decided on a cake that was red velvet on the inside, white and dark chocolate marble on the outside. Raspberry coulis was piped on in elaborate heart-shaped patterns and tiny gold detailing added.

It was perfect.

Page 43, she memorized.

The book was too nice to fold a page over and her bookmark was at the other side of the room.

That was what she was going to bake!

Chapter 10

Each of the Landers women was blessed with their own unique special gift. While Ethel had the gift of color, able to tune into its nuances and come up with just the right shade for any occasion or circumstance, Aunt Carol had the gift of eavesdropping.

She had ears like a bloodhound has a nose, primed to pick up the tiniest clue and deduce the truth before anyone else knew what had even hit them.

The only thing was that she couldn't hear B's, but that wasn't about to stop her.

"You can't have everything, but you can do the best with what you've got," she always said.

Besides, she could always work out where the B's went afterward.

Aunt Carol had long given up on love.

She was a firm believer in the Landers curse, the one that made the Landers women lose the men they adored.

For Summer's sake she hoped it wasn't true, or that Summer could break the curse and that the Landers women could finally move on and find romance in their lives without the fear of being cruelly cut loose by fate.

She sat at the table in the bakery, dawn's light streaming through the windows in a rosy haze.

She pulled the edges of the lace tablecloth until they were exactly equal all around, pondering over the list of their Valentine's Eve Sweetheart Bakeoff participants.

Beginners

Tassy

Justine

Stephanie

Carina

Plus Shayne and Faith, who didn't show up

Intermediate
Abigail
Tori
Naomi
Harley
Lenora
No show: Gina

Advanced
Addison
Hannah
Skylar

Some of them already had their eye on specific young men, and others were more interested in baking than love. She crossed these ones off the list, until she was left with the names of the young women who she knew *wanted* a man, but where not sure quite who.

She was left with Justine, Naomi (a sweet, shy scrap of a girl), a studious, willowy redhead named Harley, Addison (a young beautician with an edgy blonde haircut), and Hannah, a lithe girl who favored long sleeve basketball jerseys and miniskirts. After a rush of realization,

Carol scribbled *Dodie* at the bottom of the list.

She wondered who the heck would be a good match for Dodie. Though Carol had encouraged her to participate in the Bakeoff, she hadn't really thought it through. Who was single in the town, within a suitable age-range, eligible? Dodie was a good-looking woman and Carol wanted to find her an equal match but no one sprung to mind.

There was only one place to go.

That evening, Carol sidled into where all the young men and women of Kissing Bridge hung out, the old cabin café. Her plan was to cozy up at a table right in the middle of the café so that she could tune in and out to each conversation that happened around her. She wasn't one to drink but felt like a chardonnay. The bartender nodded and told her he'd bring it over.

She scoped the room like a criminal cases a joint, keeping her eyes open for every detail and her ears pricked up for any pertinent information. She took a loose piece of her hair from her massive beehive and twisted it around her finger, coaxing it back into its natural curl. She was trying to give off a relaxed, sociable vibe, like she wasn't here on business, on a secret eavesdropping mission. Only Ethel knew she was there, what she had come for.

There was a group of young skiers in the corner, a few hunks among them, but as their laughing and jokes got louder she could hear they were speaking in a language she didn't understand. Perhaps Dutch? Since they definitely weren't Amish, she figured they were tourists. She tuned them out so successfully it was like there was a brick wall between them.

She'd had many years of practice.

By the bar, a couple of young men threw back beer after beer after beer. For all their fervor they looked like they'd just turned twenty-one and would meet their end before twenty-two from alcohol poisoning. They blathered on about parties and hot actresses and how much liquor they thought they could drink before vomiting. Carol wasn't about to set them up with anyone. They got the brick wall treatment too.

The third group was more promising, and she was surprised her eye hadn't been drawn to them immediately. Though they were mostly in sweaters and jeans, she could tell by their heavy duty boots and a helmet rested on a free chair that they were firemen. *The jackpot!*

Already she was figuring that she'd check out the Kissing Bridge Mountain firefighters' website to find their names. Maybe they even had bios with pictures. *Perfect!*

There were a good mix of ages, too, and of course they were all fine physical specimens. Carol had to keep her wits about her to keep herself looking casual and not letting her eyes linger over them too long. She was almost beginning to wonder about baking for one of them herself, but remembered the Landers curse just in time.

"So, Hunter," she heard one of the young men say. "Found yourself a new girlfriend yet?"

They all nudged each other and laughed.

"Nah," the man who must be Hunter

replied somewhat defensively. "Have you?"

More laughing. "No. Everyone knows there aren't enough women in Kissing Bridge."

A slow smile crept over Carol's face.

"I can help with that," she whispered.

Chapter 11

Jason stood at the top of the stairs and took a deep breath. He pushed a strong, bronzed hand through his espresso-colored waves, finally growing out of their military stubble.

He stared at himself in the mirror, his gray eyes more steely than he ever remembered. He barely recognized himself and wanted to dive under the covers so no one else could see him either.

Although he was so glad to see his family, their joy was disconcerting. After all he had seen at war, it was all he could do to keep the horrific images his mind had collected flashing through them and sending him spiraling down into depression.

The house was still decorated with tinsel and baubles and lights, but he could find no comfort in it as he had before he had gone. It was as if all the joy in the world had seeped away and left a big empty hole.

It was only the letters that had kept him sane. There were times he had concluded he lived solely for those letters. Signed "Dodie," they had never given any personal details, but had been full of comfort, telling him that things would eventually get better and that sometimes things just had to be the way they had to be.

He couldn't get a finger on how he knew, but he got the sense that she was suffering a great deal more than she let on in her letters. He'd come to realize that happy people said the most infuriating things to people who were depressed, but she wrote things that cut right through the core of an issue and straight into his heart. He figured she couldn't have been all that happy.

"Jason? The food's getting cold!" his mother called out from downstairs. Her tone was caring and overly careful, as if he were made from the most delicate glass. He didn't want anyone to feel sorry for him.

He cleared his throat and walked down the stairs with his head high. His resolution would carry him through, he told himself. There was no need to break down or to fear he would crumble under the pressure. *Everything was all right.*

A Christmas feast was laid out in the kitchen, even though they were already into January. His father stood beaming next to Jason's mother. "Merry Christmas, son."

Jason surprised himself by bursting out laughing. "Christmas in January, who knew?"

His father laughed along. "You didn't think we were going to let you miss it, did you?"

At that moment, Brad led Summer into the kitchen by her hand, both of them laughing at some private lovers' joke. It was so strange to see them together, even though Brad had sent him a letter to let him know their romance was firmly back on.

"Merry Christmas!" they both said, rushing at him and enfolding him in a hug.

Hugs still felt strange.

For the past few months, his body had been an agent of destruction. Affection was so foreign and so welcome that it sent a strange tingle through his skin.

When they pulled away he found his eyes were wet with unfallen tears.

"Let's all sit down," his father said, rescuing him.

This gave him the chance to turn and wipe his eyes as they all sat down at the table. Hunger was mauling in his stomach and tears stopped threatening as he took in the magnificent spread. There was a generous portion of roast beef on the plate his father passed him and all his favorites were piled high in white ceramic dishes. Stuffing, mashed potatoes, squash, roasted vegetables. A gravy boat steamed. Pumpkin pie, marzipan, and his absolute favorite: chocolate pecan pie. All laid out on the kitchen counter.

He used to love apple pie but had

developed an allergy to every kind of apple in his teens and could never eat it since without breaking out in a rash and throwing up.

His mom picked up the stereo's remote and soon *Rocking Around the Christmas Tree* filled the room. Jason felt the heaviness of war lift a little as he looked around the smiling faces of his family, though it seemed like there would always be a hole in his heart.

He tucked in eagerly, spooning large helpings of just about everything into his mouth. Apart from the Pizza Hut van stationed in camp that he would occasionally go to, he had otherwise been stuck with his standard MRE packs, of which he could mostly only stomach the crackers, peanut butter, and M&Ms, chucking the rest of the foil-sealed packages right into the trash. A Christmas meal such as this was an unheard-of luxury.

"How does it feel to be back?" Brad asked him.

"Heaven," Jason replied through a thick mouthful, not thinking of much else other than the food.

"And you're not going back?"

Jason looked up to see Brad's eyes full of hope. Their mother glared across the table.

"Let your brother eat."

"It's okay, Mom," Jason said. "I don't mind talking about it." He gathered his strength to say the thing he had written but dared not speak aloud.

The Army had been his dream for so long it was terrifying to let it sail away into the past. "No, I'm not going back."

Brad smiled into his dinner.

Jason could tell he wanted to jump up and pound the air and hug him over his shoulder, but didn't want to upset Mom.

"I want to serve my country in a different way," Jason continued. "I want peace."

His father's expression radiated. He had never wanted him to go to war in the first place.

"I've just got to think about making some money."

Brad glanced at Summer, eyes bright, and she squeezed his hand.

"Join my pilot business," said Brad.

Summer sat up in her chair. "He's going to team up with Earl and take VIPs up the mountain."

It wasn't quite what he had in mind, but it would pay the bills.

Jason managed a smile. "All right then."

Chapter 12

It was a Breakfast at Tiffany's Sunday, as usual at the Landers' household. Summer pulled a warm quilt up to her neck and snuggled down, a breakfast tray on her lap. Cinnamon cake and a cup of strong coffee were the perfect accompaniment to Summer's favorite movie, and both Ethel and Aunt Carol seemed to agree as they chomped and sipped away at their own portions, tucked up on each side of her on the couch in the living room.

The snow fell steadily outside the window as they watched cozily inside by the fire. There was something about Holly Golightly and her escapades that could brighten up even the dreariest day.

As she watched the romance unfold on screen, she thought about her own love life.

"I don't want to speak too soon, but it looks like the Landers curse has been lifted just in time for the Valentine's Day Ball!" she said with a smile.

She looked from Aunt Carol's resigned expression to the smile her mom tried to keep off her lips but didn't manage.

It was pretty clear Ethel was thinking about someone, and to Summer, it was pretty clear who.

She elbowed her mom playfully.

"I think Earl likes you," she said, watching carefully for her mother's reaction.

Her mom blushed a little and tried to hide her cheeks with the coffee cup as she took a sip.

"You think so?"

"I know so," Summer said. "And I know you like him too."

Ethel shifted on the couch.

"Let's just watch the movie."

"You're changing the subject,"

Summer said in a sing-song voice, reaching over to pinch her mother's cheek.

Ethel jogged her arm away and gave her a warning look. "Stop it, Summer."

It was the same look that would have made an infant Summer drop the third cookie she had sneaked from the jar, her wide eyes full of guilt and mischief and feigned innocence. Summer knew when her mother meant business. She gave up picking on her mother and put another log on the fire. They settled into silence again as they watched the movie.

"I think you should enter," Aunt Carol said out of the blue.

At first Summer thought Aunt Carol was talking to her. "But why would I enter when—"

"Not you," Aunt Carol cut in, then reached over to pat Ethel's knee. "You. This curse business has gone on way too long."

"First Dodie, then me?" Ethel said.

Summer took a sip of coffee. "Looks like old ladies are starting a Kissing Bridge revolution!"

"Get out of here, you're not old ladies," said Summer. "You should get out there, start some fireworks!"

Ethel stared resolutely at the television. "Hmmm."

"No, really, Mom, you should," Summer said. She gasped with the brilliance of her own idea and turned to Aunt Carol. "And I'm sure if you put your ear to it you can use your eavesdropping skills to find out Earl's favorite food! That way we can be sure he'll choose what mom bakes and it'll all be so perfect!" She swooned. "Imagine dancing together at the Valentine's Day Ball. That's exactly what you need, Mom, some romance!"

Aunt Carol grinned. "I guess I could do just that! Count on me to find out what Earl likes!"

Ethel said nothing, but a smile danced at the corners of her lips, no matter how hard she tried to hide it.

Summer sat back on the couch, feeling like the world was finally coming into order. She finished her slice of cinnamon cake and snuggled back under the quilt, daring to believe that the Landers' curse was really coming to an end.

"You've found eligible men and all their favorites for everyone else, I take it?" Ethel asked.

Though Aunt Carol was quite happy to be single herself, her favorite pastime for Valentine's Day was matchmaking others. Every January would start her eagle eye a roaming and her ears a eavesdropping as she tallied the town singles. Many a marriage was due to her earnest endeavors to help others find love.

"I've got one for everyone but Dodie," said Aunt Carol. "I can't think of anyone who's the right age. Mid thirties would do just fine, but every single man in this town seems to be little more than a baby!"

Summer flipped through every man she knew like a virtual rolodex in her head, but came up with nothing. Everyone had a wife or girlfriend or had moved away to more exciting locales. Then an idea that made her feel stupid for not thinking of it earlier rushed through her head. "What about Jason? Brad's brother?"

Aunt Carol rocked forward to look at her squarely, her beehive tipping a little. "He's back in town?"

"Just came back," Summer said. "Didn't you know?"

"I can't keep up with what every young man in the army's doing," Aunt Carol said with a sniff. "He wasn't on my list of servicemen to write… I wonder who had him on their list and wrote to him. I can't remember."

"We'll ask Monday," Ethel said, a twinkle in her eye.

Chapter 13

"We're going to the Super Duper to get some supplies," Ethel said.

Dodie smoothed the back of her ponytail. "I'm really not sure I can do this."

Aunt Carol tugged at Dodie's apron and flashed her a winning smile. "Yes, you can. I taught you exactly what a new baker should know, and they say the best way to engrain what you know is to teach others. So you are the perfect person to teach other brand new bakers. Besides, we'll be back before the Intermediates are here."

"All right," said Dodie, trying to psych herself up. "I can do this, I can do this, I can do this." Who would have ever guessed that Dodie, who might as well have been called the burner as well as the baker, would be put in charge of the class of the whole bakery store, when it mattered most?

As she watched Carol and Ethel bustle out with their baskets, which they would return with full to the brim with Valentine Ball decorating and baking supplies, she imagined what she would wear to the Valentine Eve Sweetheart Bakeoff if she were asked.

The thought of starting a new romance both scared and excited her at this point in her life. She had lost all hope for love, or so she had thought. Then why did she have the butterflies in her stomach? Maybe she really could have a second chance at love in this sweet town. She stifled the thought and got back to work.

In the cold light of day she had begun to reconsider her cake idea, doubting she could pull it off or even if there'd be a suitable man there to buy it, but when Carol had caught her doubting expression that morning one side of her mouth had turned up in a mysterious smile and she'd winked.

"You just go out and buy yourself the prettiest dress you can find," she'd said. "That's all you have to worry about."

Ethel had leant over when Dodie had reluctantly opened the baking book. Her eyes had widened but her voice was kind.

"That's not the simplest of recipes, dear, in fact, it's so complicated I doubt I'd…"

"No, no, it's perfect," Carol had interrupted. "I hear a certain someone loves chocolate."

Dodie's heart had fluttered.

"A certain someone?" *Did they already have someone in mind?*

Carol had grinned and adjusted her beehive. "Never you mind."

So Dodie dreamed of dresses while she sat alone in the bakery, waiting for her final class with Tassy, Justine, Stephanie and Carina. The plan was that the Beginner group would come at 10am, the Intermediates at 1pm and the Advanced group at 4pm. Supposedly this would give them all enough time to finish their baked goods for the big day tomorrow, but Dodie wasn't sure, especially when the Beginners were under her watch.

Besides that, they expected a swarm of customers, especially men buying valentine's treats for their sweethearts. Carol and Ethel had been holed up in the bakery almost every hour of the day and night in the previous few days, baking up a storm of all kinds of pastries and cookies and cupcakes, cutting dough into hearts and adding strawberry jelly or red icing to just about everything.

Dodie saw herself dashing between the Beginners class in back and the storefront, juggling change and cookies and utensils until her arms dropped clean off. She was scheduled to work in the bakery the next day too.

Even if her cake was bought by some handsome young man that would become her date, she wasn't exactly in the primping mode. She imagined herself staggering into the Valentine Eve Sweetheart Bakeoff, exhausted, hair sprinkled with flour. Well, she'd stand out.

She didn't even know when she could squeeze enough time out of her schedule to actually bake the chocolate raspberry cake she'd picked anyway.

The only glimmer of hope was Carol's hint. Had she really found someone for her? Someone who would appreciate her chocolate cake? Someone who would appreciate her…? She sure wasn't ready for love, but a lovely date… why not?

Her chain of thought was disrupted by the sight of Justine waving madly outside the window, bouncing from foot to foot. She pushed open the door and swung in with a shoulder bag.

"Hey there Dodie!" she said, then squealed with excitement. "Got all my ingredients!"

Dodie just loved Justine's enthusiasm. It made her feel like maybe there really was hope in the world.

"Hey there, Justine."

"I got about a thousand apples in here," Justine continued, lugging her bag with exaggerated strain. "Apparently some guy likes apples. I don't even know who, but Carol's told me to trust her."

"Looks like we're in the same boat." Dodie smiled.

"I'll be in back?"

"Sure."

Carina and Stephanie and Tassy arrived soon after, clutching their bags of ingredients and grinning, the promise of new-found love sparkling in their eyes.

"Let's get baking!" Tassy said.

It was a surprising moment for Dodie when she realized that she wasn't needed.

All set to help them out, she'd rolled up her sleeves and got ready to dive in, but each of them read through their recipe and ploughed on. She smiled to herself.

Maybe she wasn't the greatest baker, but perhaps she was a little better at teaching. The way things were going, it looked like her Beginners group would be out well before the Intermediates arrived. Dodie dared to hope she might steal a sliver of time to get started on the sponge layers for her cake in between.

Hanging back and trying to picture her wardrobe, she decided on the red dress for the auction she'd passed over on Christmas Day. Things had felt too bleak then, the color way too bold for how weak and powerless she had felt, but now it seemed perfect. It was red, bright red, scarlet, even.

Though she still buzzed with anxiety, an underlying confidence shone through and she was set on breaking out of her heartbreak and setting herself free. Break ups happened. It didn't mean she was unlovable.

Dodie was determined to claim the life she wanted, even if she had to do it hands shaking, heart racing the whole way.

"Yes!" Justine said, pumping her fist in the air and grinning. "Ready to go in the oven!"

The rest of the girls clapped and whooped.

"Well done!" said Dodie.

These were such proud moments for her, watching these teens blossom under her care and feeling that she belonged finally. The kind people of Kissing Bridge Mountain had hugged her to their hearts and treated her like one of them.

They had embraced the broken person she was and helped make her whole. She felt happy for the first time in a very long while.

Once Justine had put her apple cake in to bake, she hoisted herself up on the counter next to Dodie. "So what are you baking for tomorrow?"

"I'm going to attempt a chocolate and raspberry cake," Dodie said. "I'm a little scared that it won't turn out so good."

"But you're great at baking," said Justine. "I couldn't bake a darn thing when I first came here and now look at me, baking a cake all by myself. You must be the best teacher I've ever had."

Dodie's heart swelled. It was so good, *so so* good, to hear that she'd helped someone, that her efforts had made a difference. After all those years of trying to reach out to Peter and being shut down cold, her heart was hungry for connection.

"Thanks," she said, trying not to let tears rise."

"I know you are new here Dodie, but we are all really happy to have you here in Kissing Bridge. I see you look sad sometimes and I don't know the whole story of what happened before you came here, but miracles happen you have to believe!" said Justine.

Dodie looked doubtful. "Hmmp haven't seen to many miracles in my life…"

With that the young girl jumped up and wrapped Dodie in a big bear hug. "Then I'll believe for you Dodie!"

Dodie couldn't help but laugh at her contagious faith.

Justine pulled away and looked at her with a big smile.

"I really hope some good guy buys what you make tomorrow Dodie, and I hope he knows just how lucky he is!"

Dodie thought of the odds of that happening, and guessed that might take a miracle after all. The tears welled up and she couldn't hold them back.

Chapter 14

Oh my gosh. She's beautiful.

Jason was caught totally off guard.

One moment he had been looking between the list he had offered to complete for his mother and the baked goods laid out under the glass, trying to work out what corresponded with what. The next moment he was standing face to face with possibly the most beautiful woman he'd ever seen.

There was something magnetic about her, mesmerizing. She looked at him expectantly, her green-gray eyes glassed over with tears.

"Hello welcome to Landers Home Baking what would you like, sir?"

"Are you okay?" he asked before he had even thought.

"I…" she began, her turn to be caught off guard. She struggled for words. "I…"

"Oh, sorry, sorry," he said, finally managing to break his gaze away from her, though it immediately begged him to raise his head again.

Her face was so gentle, peaceful, like she didn't have a hint of malice in her. Luckily he'd learned enough self-discipline in the military that he could keep his eyes firmly on his boots.

"Pardon me Miss…It's really none of my business."

"You don't have to be sorry," she said, her voice soft.

He had no doubt that voice, the soul behind it, could weave their way past all the blockades he'd erected in his heart, right to the very core of him. He'd never felt anything so strong on first sight.

"Did you come to pick up some cookies? Bread? Pastries?"

"Sure," he said, looking down at the list. "Hey, maybe you'd better take this. I don't know what half of these things are."

Her eyes widened as they scanned down the list he handed her.

"A lot of things, huh?"

"Yep. My mom likes to send Valentine gifts to all our family, all around the country, by special delivery. Cakes, flowers, plush toys, the whole lot. She's a sucker for holidays." He grinned.

Dolly couldn't help but smile, which made her even more beautiful to behold. "Seems like your mom is not the only sucker for holidays in this town!"

Now it was his turn to beam. He stifled a laugh. Since being back home it had seemed as if he entered a snow globe world of beauty and joy and love. It was so different from where he had been. He didn't recognize this alluring woman as a Kissing Bridge local, but she sure knew his town.

He went over and sat at the table, while the beautiful woman got to work picking things out and placing them in paper bags. "I like the sound of your mother already," she said.

"Yes, she's quite a lady" he said, laughing. His mind zoomed forward to marriage without his permission. He shook his head, wondering if he was going crazy.

She looked up at him and he felt a wave pulse through his body as they made eye contact. She looked right back down again and smiled at the paper bag she was folding over.

"You want something to eat while you wait?"

"You know, I'd just love that."

"You can have it on us, since you're buying so much," she said, then gestured across the entire counter. "Take your pick."

"Oooh," he said, getting up and looking over their offerings. "Got anything with chocolate in it?"

Her smile spread wider. "That's my favorite, too. We've got pain au chocolate, donut with pure chocolate filling and—"

"Whoa, you can stop right there!" he said. "Donut with pure chocolate filling. Wow."

Her eyes widened. "Tell me about it. I'm going to get so fat working here."

He opened his mouth to say that she had a gorgeous body but quickly caught ahold of himself and gave a little laugh. "You're far from fat."

She laughed along as she piled two donuts onto a plate for him and handed them across the counter. "Come back in a couple of months and see if that's still true then."

He sat back at the table and sank his teeth into the decadent doughiness. The chocolate in the center was nothing short of heavenly, but it didn't make him forget the angel across the room.

He didn't want to stare, but he couldn't help but cast glances at her from time to time, the way her strawberry blonde ponytail flipped back and forth as she worked, the way she pressed her lips together just slightly as she concentrated.

It was like he was falling in love.

Jason tried to pull himself together. He was getting it all, the butterflies in his stomach, the moisture on his palms, and the frantic rhythm of his heart. He couldn't believe it! He had been in the army too long.

He put his hand in his pocket to reach for the money to pay, but his fingertips rested on the folded letter he kept there.

He knew it was a little strange,

carrying around a letter from someone he knew nothing much about, but it felt like his lucky charm. Her encouraging words had bolstered him in his lowest moments and they felt almost like a talisman, protecting him from plunging back into that kind of depression again.

The wonderful woman named Dodie, that had poured her own heart and soul into the letters to a man she didn't even know and those letters had kept his hope alive. He owed her a debt of gratitude for helping him through some of the lowest moments in his life.

When his best friend had been blown up by a car bomb Jason had not wanted to live. The horrid sight of his dear friend's dead body had nearly driven him insane. It had been Dodie that broke through to him and the ice around his heart. It had been her he wrote to about his pain, and her that had given him a reason to keep going and make it back to safety after the ambush.

When he was on tour he'd vowed to go to the Kissing Bridge society that sent letters to the military, to find out who this mysterious Dodie was and thank her for all she had done, but once he'd got back the idea felt more and more daunting. What if she was nothing like the letter? What if she didn't want to talk to him? He had showed his true self to her and in a way that made it too vulnerable for him to present himself in person to thank her.

But he had made the vow to himself, and that meant he had to do it.

Jason was a man of his word.

The pretty girl put the last item into the last bag. There were a total of four bags full of baked goods now.

"So that's everything on the list?" he asked, nodding at the paper bags she'd piled up on the counter.

"Right." She smiled at him, and laid the paper bags carefully into a larger plastic one.

He paid and left ignoring the magnetic pull of her eyes and focusing his mind on the letter in his pocket. Love was dangerous but the letters were safe.

He had to find *Dodie.*

Chapter 15

The Valentine's Eve Sweetheart Bakeoff

Carina and Stephanie clutched each other and squealed.

"Wow, wow, wow!" Tassy said, gazing around the hall.

The Valentine Eve Sweetheart Bakeoff was always held in Kissing Bridge's function hall, but it had never looked so spectacular as it did now. The walls were covered with satin drapes in cream and crimson and antique gold, golden garlands strung horizontally across, dangling bells and hearts. The stalls set up on one side were dressed in carnelian cotton, white lace bows and edging setting off the look. Love songs crooned through a stereo. Dodie caught sight of supermodel Summer Landers stringing a garland of hanging hearts across one of the windows and apparently laughing at a joke her handsome fiancé had made.

And there he was, the handsome stranger from the bakery the day before! Dodie felt her heart leap.

He hung back a little from Summer and her man, drumming his fingers on his pocket. Even nervous, he still made her go weak at the knees. She had to avert her eyes right to the other side of the room to keep her cake steady. She had to concentrate.

It had come out so much better than she had expected. She'd always been bluntly honest with herself about her baking ability, so she didn't try to suppress the pleasant, self-satisfied glow that emanated from her smile as she carried it proudly across to the auction stall in its white box. Finally, she had done well. All she had to do was pipe on the raspberry and add the gold detailing.

She'd left that out on Carol and Ethel's advice, as apparently a cake should always be finished off as late as is humanly possible. Dodie had done so well with the sponge layers that she had no worries about the finishing touches. She approached the auction table with her cake.

Ethel had just arrived as well and laid a perfect specimen of Earl's favorite, Boston cream pie, on the auction table, beaming. She looked at Dodie's cake proudly. "I think we might just do all right tonight, dear!"

Dodie grinned. "Let's hope so. I adore your dress."

Ethel wore a lovely coral dress that set off the rosiness of her cheeks. Her grey hair was adorned with a lovely white rose bud and she looked radiant.

Carol fussed around the rest of the girls who bunched at the door, then bustled over to them and grinned. "It's looking great in here, huh? Summer's done a great job helping."

"She always had an eye for interior design," Ethel said proudly. "And a heart for celebrations."

It had been somewhat of a shock when Dodie had found out that Summer Landers, supermodel extraordinaire, was humble Ethel's daughter. She knew from the start they had the same name but assumed it was a small town with large, sprawling families who shared last names.

They all looked over at Summer and Dodie's eyes lingered on the handsome, gray-eyed stranger who still hung back. She tried to keep her voice casual. "Who's that?"

"Oh, that's Jason," Carol said with a wink.

"That's Brad's younger brother. He just got back from the war."

Carol planted her hands on her hips when an idea hit her. "Wasn't he on your list Dodie?"

Dodie looked blank.

Carol nudged her, "Jason Anderson do you remember writing him?"

It all came flooding back to Dodie.

Wow.

So the man she'd been writing to, spending ages curled up in her bed trying to think of the right words that would bring him comfort and strength in the face of so much atrocity, was *him.*

The man she had shared her own grief with and loss of hope with.

Jason.

The man she had dared let close to her through their writings because he was safe. Away. Not real.

But he was real.

He was real and he was here.

Dodie dared a quick look in his direction.

Jason, the stranger who'd waltzed into the bakery and made her heart jump. It was hard to wrap her head around.

She only realized she was staring at him when he looked in their direction and she jumped clean out of her skin. She looked away at anything, at her hands, at the wall, at the decorations.

She heard Carol giggle, very softly at first, then a little louder.

"I think you should tell her, Carol," Ethel said in a warning tone.

"Tell me what?" Dodie asked, careful not to turn around.

Carol beckoned her so she could whisper, and then leaned forward toward her ear. "That's who we figured could buy your cake at auction. He loves chocolate, you know."

Dodie's heart skipped a beat, and then sped up into a cadence so wild she could barely catch her breath. "Wow."

Carol nodded. "Uh *huh*. Now I've gotta go get these girlies sorted out. You'll come over once you've got your piping done, won't you, Dodie?"

"Sure, sure," Dodie said, still reeling. "Sure I will."

Carol winked at her and shuffled away with Ethel in tow, leaving Dodie alone to try and not look up. She felt so vulnerable when she looked into his eyes, as if he could see her naked soul, naked body, naked everything. The way her heart flooded with warm affection scared the heck out of her!

She rooted into the basket Ethel had carried in, where she'd packed the piping equipment and the jar of raspberry coulis. Dodie had spent ages boiling it down to just the right thickness that morning and after doing a test on a cupcake she was assured of its consistency.

After pouring it into the piping sleeve she took a deep breath and began to squeeze. She tried to remember the swirling pattern and apply it to the blank canvas of perfect chocolate sponge, but her hand shook and the pattern jutted out at odd angles. "Oh, goodness."

Eventually she managed a steady hand and sunk into a deep concentration, completing one side. It wasn't as good as the example in the book but it was good enough.

"Hi," a deep voice said.

It startled her so much she dropped the piping sleeve right on top of the cake, ruining the whole pattern and smudging coolie all over her hand. She looked up, stunned. "Jason."

"I'm *so* sorry," he said, attempting to pick the piping sleeve up out of the mess. "I didn't mean to startle you."

"It's okay." She stared at him, forgetting the cake altogether.

He smiled and she thought her knees

might give in. "Hey, how do you know my name?"

Somehow she managed to find her voice, though it sounded like it was coming from someplace far away and blood thundered through her ears. "Carol told me." She so badly wanted to tell him that she was the one who'd sent him so many letters, but the words caught in her throat.

"Is that a chocolate cake?" he asked.

"Yes."

"My all-time favorite."

They didn't break eye contact, even for a second.

"Yes."

He stood, admiring it, like he wanted to take a bite right then.

She felt like she was going to bust. Here she was acting as if they were strangers when they knew each other's deepest hopes and dreams. Knew each other better then she had ever known her ex fiancé even.

Safe Jason, her pen pal who was far away and never able to hurt the real her. Safe. She had thought he was a safe place to put her feelings because he wasn't really there. She couldn't let herself be hurt again by feeling anything real. He had been her safety net and now he wasn't safe at all. With those mysterious grey eyes and joyous grin he was far to real and far to able to hurt her. She couldn't bring herself to say anything. Suddenly, Summer appeared looking every bit her super model self.

Her long surfer blonde tresses fell about her beautiful face framing it perfectly. "Hey Dodie, mom was wondering if you had any extra vanilla she could borrow?"

Dodie was torn from her thoughts and started absently looking through one of the supply bags. She pulled out a bottle of vanilla and looked confused. "This looks to be an extra…"

Summer smiled at Jason.

"Hey Jason have you met Dodie yet? She's new in town. Earl's her uncle she's been living up at the lodge and working with mom and Aunt Carol at the new shop."

Jason was taken aback.

"Dodie…?"

Summer squeezed her tight like a best friend, "We adore her and were never letting her leave!"

Dodie smiled back at her and produced a small bottle of vanilla, "Flattery will get you everywhere."

Summer laughed back her way as she hurried off to meet her mom, "Oh won't it though!"

Jason and Dodie were alone now.

He looked deeply into her cat-like green eyes. Dodie looked away hoping he couldn't see how much she was drawn to him. He was her friend. She didn't need to complicate his life with feelings for him. Besides he was probably only home on leave for a while and then he would be gone. Not real again. For all she knew he had a girlfriend here in Kissing Bridge.

"Jason…I'm Dodie. You know, the letters… I was the one writing to you," she blurted out, "when… when you were away."

He glanced up at her, unresponsive for a moment. Then his eyes widened in shock and he drew his hand up to his pocket. "Dodie?" he whispered. He looked like he'd seen a ghost.

"Yes," she said, concern flooding her. "Is everything okay?"

"Wow, I can't believe it." He broke into the most joyful smile she'd ever seen. "Wow! Dodie, that's you?"

"Uh huh," she said, smiling right back.

"Oh my goodness." He sprung up on his toes, grinning from ear to ear. "Wow. Oh my goodness."

He instinctively reached out to hug her, but a squeal called their attention away from the moment.

"Dodie!" an urgent voice called from across the room.

Dodie glanced back to see Carina crestfallen and near tears.

A baking disaster must have ensued. She placed the piping sleeve down on the table. "Jason, I'm sorry, I've really got to go help her..."

She looked torn. The last place she wanted to leave was where she stood right now, next to him.

"No problem," he said, "We'll talk soon." And with that he walked away.

Chapter 16

"Oh no," Carol said, crossing her arms, her eyes darting nervously across the surface of Dodie's ruined cake. "It's a mess."

Ethel nodded in agreement. She glanced up at Dodie, who was across the hall attempting to attend to some cookie-related emergency, Carina and Stephanie and Tassy and all the other girls huddled around her. "It's such a shame," she said. "The sponge layers were so so good."

Carol slotted her hands into her waist and pursed her lips as she surveyed the cake once again. "This just won't do," she said, shaking her head.

After a moment or two of forlorn staring, both Ethel and Carol looked up at each other.

"Are you thinking what I'm thinking?" Ethel asked.

"The spare!" Carol said.

Whenever there was any kind of baking event, any discerning, reality-conscious baker would carry a spare!

It was just like a spare tire for the car. From time to time, it could be expected that something would go wrong or a baked good would fail for whatever reason, so Ethel kept a spare in her trusty basket, ready to be switched with the offending cake or cookies in record time.

It was *always* an apple pie, because, as Aunt Carol always said, "Who the heck doesn't like apple pie?"

Ethel scrambled under the table to find the basket while Aunt Carol packed the mess of a cake back in its white box. "Oh goodness," she said on closer inspection. "Poor Dodie. All that hard work."

"No matter," Ethel said, producing the perfect apple pie and placing it on the table. "She's sure to win Jason's heart with this one."

"Perfect," Aunt Carol said. "But what will we tell her?"

"I'm not sure," said Ethel. "I don't want to hurt her feelings. But I don't want to lie either."

After a few moments, Aunt Carol stuck her finger in the air, "Aha!" but didn't say anymore.

"What is it?" Ethel said, humoring her.

"Let's tell her that we found out Jason likes pies better than cakes."

"But it's not true."

Aunt Carol twisted her mouth. "You just wait there."

She marched over to where Summer and Brad were standing drinking hot cocoa and looking all googly eyed at each other. Jason leant against a table, gazing at the group across the hall.

"Hey Jason," Aunt Carol said. "Do you like cakes or pies better?"

"Huh?"

"Just answer the question, son."

He thought for a moment. "Well, pies, I guess.

With a loud confirming 'Hummf!" Aunt Carol strode away with her massive red beehive bobbing along as she went.

Jason looked confused. He had yet to realize the power of Aunt Carol when she was on a mission.

Summer laughed and warned him.

"Watch out! It appears Aunt Carol has you in her sights! I see lots of pies in your future Jason. Pecan pies, blueberry pies, apple pies…"

Brad wrapped his arms around Summer and gave her a kiss on the cheek. "No apples for my big bro honey. Jason's allergic to them."

Chapter 17

Carina screwed up her face in disgust as she bit into the cookie, tears welling in her eyes. "It's horrible, just horrible!"

Dodie took a tiny bite and it took all her strength not to spit it right out. It had a horrible sour, salty taste.

"What *is* that?"

"I don't know," said Carina.

"Mine are fine," Stephanie said. "Which is weird because we used exactly the same recipe. I even left out the vanilla and I worried about it but they still came out good." She put her arm around Carina. "Why don't you have mine?"

"No, no," Carina said. "You baked

your cookies especially for Tom and arranged them just the way you know he'd like them. I don't want to ruin that."

Dodie's heart was in her mouth. Once Stephanie had mentioned the vanilla she knew what her own mistake had been. That's why she had the extra one in her bag. "I am… Carina, I am so sorry."

"What?"

All the girls looked up at her with concern and she felt like sinking into the ground and never coming back out again. But she had to own her truth. She'd promised herself that much when she arrived here, that she'd say how she felt, admit her mistakes and stride out into creating a new life, no matter how hard it was. Admitting her mistakes was probably the hardest one.

"I…" She took a deep breath. "I think I poured out the wrong thing."

"Huh?" Carina looked up at her with her wet eyelashes and Dodie felt a surge of guilt.

"That wasn't vanilla essence you put in your cookies. It was soy sauce."

The girls gasped.

"And it was all my fault," she added.

She looked down at her feet, wondering how the heck she'd done it again. She'd already ruined a brownie experiment by pouring out the wrong black liquid into the batter. Aunt Carol had purchased the soy sauce for a citrus, brown sugar, soy sauce cake, which had come out a whole lot better than it sounded and had flown off the shelves, and had decanted it into the same type of robust plastic bottle that held the vanilla essence. Dodie's confidence drained out of her. How was she ever going to fix this?

A tiny, tinkling laugh made her look up. She saw a smile spread over Carina's face as her shoulders shook and she giggled. Soon the other girls joined in and they were all laughing.

"Yum, soy sauce cookies," Tassy said, licking her lips. "I'm sure Oliver will just love those."

Carina burst out into new peals of laughter. "How about tomato ketchup cookies, anyone?"

"Mustard cookies," Stephanie sugges-ted.

Addison threw her hands up in the air. "Or good old plain salt cookies."

"It's a classic!" Carina said.

"Mmmm, I know," said Justine, her whole face lighting up as if she were talking about the most delicious sweet treats in the world. "How about salt cupcakes with mayonnaise icing."

They all laughed.

"Can we stop talking about this now?" Stephanie asked, still laughing. "It's making me want to hurl."

Carina glanced over at Dodie, then touched her arm. "Seriously, don't look so guilty. It's fine. I don't mind. He might not have liked them in any case."

"No, no," said Dodie. "I made this mess, I'm going to fix it." She looked at the clock. "Let's run back to the bakery and whip up another batch. I think we just about have enough time."

"I can't run in this dress," said Carina, but two minutes later they were out the door, wiggling their way back to the bakery in their tight dresses.

"I am so sorry," Dodie kept saying.

* * *

Once back in the bakery, they tore into the back room. Dodie chucked Carina an apron and slipped one on herself, deciding that a dusting of white flour was probably not the best accessory for her vibrant red dress.

"Simple choc chip is okay?" Dodie asked, fumbling through the cupboards for ingredients.

Carina nodded. She headed over to the oven and turned the switch to the right heat.

"Let's do this."

Dodie had never baked so quickly or fluently in her life. They mixed everything up in lightning quick time but it was torture to wait for the oven to get hot enough to slide the cookie sheet in and get it baking.

"Thanks so much for helping me," said Carina.

Dodie hugged her. "It was me who messed up in the first place. I should be thanking you for forgiving me."

"I sure hope Oliver likes regular chocolate chip, but then who doesn't?"

"These are gonna be hot out of the oven," Dodie said. "By the time the auction's over they'll still be warm. No one else in this auction can lay claim to that!"

Carina smiled. "I guess you're right!"

There was no time to leave them to cool once they were done, so Dodie handed Carina a cooling rack and a spatula and picked up the oven mitts for herself.

They looked quite a sight hurrying down the street in their dressy auction clothes, Dodie with two oven mitts and a hot sheet full of cookies, Carina holding a spatula in one hand, the cooling rack in the other.

People were arriving in full force by this time, nodding at them and giggling a little at their expense.

"I just hope we get there in time," Dodie said. "I think by the time we get in there you could transfer them to the cooling rack."

"No problem," Carina replied.

They managed to weave their way through the crowd in the parking lot and lobby, pushing through to the function hall. Dodie laid the cookie sheet down on the table and chanced to touch it. It was just warm, perfectly comfortable to touch. She nodded at Carina, who began scooping up the cookies with the spatula.

Dodie glanced up at the clock.

It was nearly auction time.

The hall was heaving by now, so much so that she couldn't even get a glimpse of Jason as she looked around. She decided the best thing to do was to return to her place before all the bakers were sent out. Her eyes scanned all the auction stalls and tables, but she couldn't see her cake anywhere. She was so sure she'd left it next to the Boston cream pie Ethel had made hoping to lure Earl, but there was now an apple pie in its place?"

She hurried over, her brow creased. "Hi, Ethel, do you know where my cake is?"

Ethel looked uncomfortable and was about to open her mouth when Carol appeared. "We found that Jason prefers pies to cakes, so we made a substitution."

Dodie felt like all the wind had been knocked out of her sails.

"Oh." She couldn't find any more words than that. Maybe Jason did prefer pies, but if she won his date with something she didn't even make, it wasn't *real*. It was false representation. It almost felt like manipulation. But there, feeling tiny in the massive crowd, still feeling the burn of shame for substituting soy sauce for vanilla, in the presence of two seasoned bakers, she couldn't find a voice. "Okay," she said.

Dodie realized she felt relieved in an odd way as well. So Jason wouldn't pick her baked good and they wouldn't be paired as if by fate. She wasn't sure she could look him in the eyes on a full date anyway. He would see straight through her. To her feelings. She visibly shook now. She should have thought about this more. She wasn't ready for love or anything near love. She certainly wasn't ready for more disappointment and rejection. She wished she could just run away from the auction and that handsome man who knew her very soul, and never look back.

Instead, she took her place behind the

table and the crowd blurred over as tears formed a film over her eyes.

Snap out of it, she told herself. *You're being ridiculous.* She wiped her eyes furiously and pushed her chin up. Everything was going to be all right, she told herself. But she didn't quite believe it.

Just then, Justine crossed in front of them, proudly carrying her apple and cinnamon cake, grinning at them.

It was like it happened in slow motion.

Dodie saw every detail as Justine's high heeled shoe got caught in the hem of her dress and sent her flying, the cake dropping to the floor as quickly as she did. Justine lifted herself up, but couldn't do anything for the cake, which had splattered across the floor in pieces. She looked up at them in shock.

"Welcome, welcome everyone!" Dolly, the former elf outfit wearer, was now done up in her Valentine auction best for the Sweetheart bake off in a stunning gold dress that glimmered in the dimmed lights and the strings of fluffy hearts.

"We have a room full of sweets and sweethearts here on Kissing Bridge Mountain in celebration of the annual Valentine Eve Sweetheart Bakeoff!"

Everyone clapped and whooted.

"Tomorrow night will be the official Valentine's Day Ball right here in this room starting at seven o'clock. Many thanks to our sponsors, Landers Home Baking, who donated all the ingredients for tonight's Sweetheart bake off. Let's give them a big hand and let's celebrate love!"

The crowd was excited and clapped even more, except Dodie, Carol and Ethel, who rushed to Justine's assistance. Ethel scooped the cake off the floor as best she could while Dodie ran for the trashcan and Carol helped Justine to her feet.

"My cake's ruined!" Justine said.

Carol reached under the auction stall and picked up Dodie's cake to place on top. "This is all that's left. You'll have this."

Justine looked over it, her face downcast. She let out a deep sigh, and then remembered it was Dodie's cake and managed a small smile. "Okay," she squeaked.

Dolly looked regal in her gold gown as she spoke again. "We've had some last minute changes, so if all the bakers would like to file out, all the eligible men of Kissing Bridge can come forward and peruse this year's beautiful offerings again before bidding commences!"

Once the old apple cinnamon cake was safely in the trash, all the bakers filed out, looking gorgeous in their dresses.

"Wouldn't it make more sense if I just have my cake back and Justine takes the apple pie, since her guy likes apples?" Dodie hissed to Aunt Carol on the way out.

"Yes but Jason likes pies and Nathan likes chocolate, so there's no problem."

Justine whipped around. "Nathan?"

"Oh, darn," Aunt Carol said. She'd been trying to keep the names of their potential suitors a surprise.

Justine jumped up and down. "Nathan! He's perfect!"

Chapter 18

It turned out that Summer, a lifelong romantic, had volunteered in more ways than decorating. As the baking girls stepped into the small side room they were led into, she threw her arms open wide and greeted them.

"Hey ladies I have a surprise for you!" she said, her new Christmas diamond engagement ring sparkling in the light. "Thank you *so* much for making this event a success. Without you, none of this would be possible. This just goes to show that Kissing Bridge Mountain still believes in love!"

Though Dodie was still put out about the cake and apple pie business, she plastered a smile on her face and tried to lift her spirits. As long as Justine landed the man she liked it would be worth it.

Her Beginners class had so long looked forward to the event and she was determined that it would be just as special as they'd dreamed of.

Justine hooked her arm into Dodie's and they shared a smile. "Never mind," she whispered. "I sure hope Nathan likes chocolate cake."

"So, as you know, this year's auction was sponsored by my mom and Aunt Carol's new shop, Landers Home Bakery."

The girls applauded. "So in celebration for a change we decided to add a fun new twist to liven things up!" Summer continued.

A murmur went through the small group of girls.

"We thought it would be more fun to keep you guys out of the room so that your dates for the Valentine's Ball tomorrow will be a total surprise to both parties! Kind of like a mass blind date!"

The girls all started talking at once at this new development.

Dodie smiled wearily.

"So you've done all you have to do for this evening," said Summer.

A little groan went around the audience. They had all dressed up nicely and now the evening was over so much sooner than expected. But Summer had a great back up plan.

"We've decided to do something else a little different this year. Outside limousines are waiting to take you all to a secret destination for a very special girls only evening. We hope you have a great time, even though I'm super jealous!"

The girls erupted with squeals of joys. They hugged each other with excitement and and there was lots of jumping up and down as much as their dresses would allow. A stretch limousine was clearly not a regular feature of Kissing Bridge.

Summer's million-dollar smile spread across her face as she led the way out and all the young women followed her to the limousines. Each of the black stretch limousines were lit up with tiny heart light on all sides and gleamed in the dull dark of the parking lot.

A new round of squeals rang out from the girls.

Dodie squeezed in last. The seats were plush and each had a champagne bucket between them filled with chilling bottles of bubbly. The girls were all talking at once and Aunt Carol poured. Dodie accepted a glass of champagne and clinked it against Ethel's.

"I think you and my uncle Earl are a great match, Ms. Landers," she said shyly.

Ethel smiled back at her. "Thank you Dodie. That means a lot to me. I hope so darling. It's a big step for me with the…"

Aunt Carol stopped her.

"Not to worry Ethel! Here's to Summer for breaking the Landers curse!" Carol boomed and they all clinked their glasses.

"To breaking the Landers' curse!"

The champagne was the perfect antidote to the anxiety they were all feeling over the auction.

Ethel looked relieved. She shook her head.

"I used to think it was impossible to

break the curse, but Brad and Summer's love made the impossible possible again. I am so grateful."

Aunt Carol hugged her sister close. "I love you sis, you deserve happiness."

Ethel wiped away a happy tear and smiled. This was turning out to be the best Valentine celebration ever.

Dodie sank back into her seat, feeling like if there was a Landers' curse there must be a Dodie curse too.

She'd been so close to happiness yet it always eluded her. After the death of her first husband it had taken her years to open up her heart again. Then Peter. He had seemed so perfect, so kind, so loving she had let herself fall in love with him, only to have her heart torn out once more.

Now Jason threatened to make her feel what she had tried so hard to escape by coming here in the first place. The gorgeous stranger with the cloudy gray eyes had stood before her, so excited that she was the Dodie of his letters, declaring how much he loved chocolate cake.

And now her cake was an absolute mess that Justine had to endure, while hers was in the trash. She was a million miles away from Jason picking her baked good, she was sure about that. The apple pie was boring, safe, conventional, everything he was not.

She suddenly laughed at herself at how naive she was being.

She looked around her at the happy girls chatting and laughing and dreaming of love and Valentine dances. She really had fallen under the spell of this adorable holiday crazy town with its kind people and love of baked goods.

Dodie thought she must be losing her mind. This was still the real world and in the real world men did not fall in love with a woman because of her cooking talent!

Besides she wasn't ready for love. She had decided she just wouldn't care about the auction. Heck maybe it would be better if Old man Jennings picked her apple pie at least her heart wouldn't be jumping out of her dress.

Not that she would tell any of the girls that.

All the young women chattered away happily, talking about who would pick their cake, whether Oliver would pick Carina's choc chip cookies, and what they would do if someone they didn't like at all would pick their cake!

As they sped out of Kissing Bridge and onto the freeway, Dodie realized just how quickly this small town had become home. She still stayed in one of Earl's rooms at the lodge, not sure of her next move. She had heard Summer and Brad talking about setting up their new home in preparation for their marriage. They seemed so happy building a life together. Dodie pictured a small, cozy home with a little garden area where she could grow vegetables and flowers, though she couldn't help but feel she'd love someone else there, too.

Before she could stop herself she found herself picturing Jason in the kitchen, cooking up a storm. Jason in the garden, tending to the earth. Jason in the living room, eating her chocolate cake. She shook her head, trying to get the images out.

She of all people knew that Jason wasn't ready for love any more than she was!

His heart had been shattered by a betrayal just like hers had. That's what had bonded them so quickly through their letters. The understanding that some things hurt so much they shut you down for good. He had been cheated on and she had been left for another man. Love hurt. No feeling at all was better than risking being broken and unloved again.

Just then the limousine stopped outside a beautiful redbrick building. Justine pressed her face against the window. "It's a *spa!*"

Chapter 19

Valentine's Day

Dodie considered what to wear to the Valentine's Day Ball that night. She had changed her mind over and over again and was still unsure. She couldn't bring herself to rent out a puffy gown for the special occasion like the young women from her baking class. That would feel like dressing up like a cream puff, or a Disney princess.

She still marveled at this town's love of the holidays. She had never seen people go so far out to celebrate Valentine's Day!

She caught sight of her new pedicure

from the surprise spa visit last night. Dodie had opted for a soft pink shade with a red heart painted on each toenail. She wiggled her toes liking the effect.

All the women had been so excited to get pampered before the big event. The massage had been just what she needed to relax her last night, but today she found herself nervous and uptight all over again.

She wondered what kind of dress Jason might find her attractive in, and then berated herself for caring. She doubted Jason would even be there, having just come back from the war he most likely wasn't up for a frivolous evening, and she of all people knew the last thing he was looking for was a relationship. Why would he go? It looked like he was only there at the auction to help out Summer and Brad with the decorating.

She considered the night's possibilities before her. If Jason had opted to even buy a baked good, and by some chance had chosen her pie, then she would be his date for the entire event. Sit next to him. Dance with him. Be near him.

Once again she would fall for another unavailable guy.

Dodie wanted to explode.

The best thing she could do was hope that someone else, anyone else, but Jason had chosen her apple pie. Then she would be safe. Bored perhaps, but safe.

Dodie thought about the auction. All the young women were in a tizzy over who would be their date. She was too old for all of this and started bitterly regretting not doing like Carol and staying way out of it. She considered ways to back out and rejected them all as unbelievable. She was stuck.

Dodie looked through her wardrobe and finally pulled out a sleek black dress with a slit up the side. Black. Perfect for how she felt. While everyone else would be looking like a sparkle princess she would be Ursula, Queen of Darkness.

* * *

The Valentine's Day Ball

The hall from the night before had now been transformed into its final beauty for the Valentine's Day Ball, the booths were removed and a wooden dance floor was laid down. Small tables dotted the outskirts of the dance floor. They were decorated in pink with white rose bud centerpieces. Candlelight illuminated the room giving it a romantic feel.

The ballroom was full to the brim with well-dressed young people, beautiful and smiling and ready for love. From her seat at the sidelines, Dodie saw Summer and Brad intertwined as they danced to the soft music in the background, seemingly unable to wait for the official dancing portion to start.

Now that was love.

Aunt Carol was the host for the evening's gala. She was on a small stage in front of the auction hall. She wore a sequined red dress that flickered in the light and bounced off her brilliant red hair. A lovely gold necklace set off her outfit. Summer thought she had never seen her Aunt look so lovely. Aunt Carol thumped on the mic to make sure it worked.

Summer and Brad stopped dancing and moved to stand by mom, as the event was about to begin. Ethel Landers looked extra beautiful. She was wearing a floaty dress in her favorite Tiffany blue color and it was splashed with delicate little silver rose buds. The silver set her grey hair off just perfect and the blue mirrored the color of her eyes. Summer hugged her.

"You look beautiful mom, any guy would be lucky to have you."

Her mom blushed "I'm just a silly old fool for even entering what was I thinking?"

Brad pointed out Earl who was just entering. "Hey there's Earl." Brad called out to him. "Looking good Earl!

Earl was in a dark blue suit with a silver shirt that looked quite sharp. His hair was slicked back. He waved to them all from the door, and winked at Ethel.

Aunt Carol rallied the crowd. "Everyone please your attention!" She grinned and drum rolled on her knees.

"Let's announce the results!"

Aunt Carol continued, "The suitors have already taken their baked goods home to consume, and now they are to meet the woman who has either delighted or disappointed them!

No lawsuits, please." She flashed a smile and the audience laughed. "Okay, so will our beautiful bakers please come up to the stage."

Dodie's heart sank.

She hadn't dared to hope that Jason bought her pie, but somehow a little bit of hope had sunk in and now even that was dashed. She hadn't seen Jason in the crowd all night. Not that she was looking. Ethel took her hand and soon she was swept up in the swarm of young women that took to the stage. They arranged themselves in lines and some of them posed like they were in a pageant.

Aunt Carol held up a large golden envelope.

"Are you ladies ready to meet your dates?"

"Yeah!" the young women called out.

"I didn't hear you!" Aunt Carol called

out, grinning from ear to ear. "Are you ladies and gentlemen ready?!"

"Yeah!" The crowd burst into hoots and hollers.

"Perfect!"

Aunt Carol opened the envelope with a defiant rip.

"Right, first on the list is our very own royalty, our cookie queen extraordinaire, Ethel Landers! Step forward please."

Ethel, blushing the color of her lipstick now, stepped forward and clasped her hands behind her back. Dodie saw her wring them and fidget. She truly hoped that Earl had bought the perfect Boston cream pie that Ethel had worked so hard to prepare just for him.

The crowd awaited the name to be called. Aunt Carol announced triumphantly, "Your date is… Earl!"

Ethel turned and grinned at Dodie, bringing her hands to her face in disbelief.

Earl strode up the stairs, looking half the age he usually did, and held out his arm for Ethel. She slipped hers into his and everyone clapped and cheered wildly.

Earl beamed and pecked her on the cheek, sending the crowd into a gleeful uproar.

"Fabulous choice Earl, fabulous!" Aunt Carol said as they descended the steps and blended in with the crowd.

"Now next…Carina Marshall step forward!"

Dodie felt her spirit rise as she watched Carina get paired off with Oliver, who climbed up to the stage and declared her choc chip cookies even better than his grandma's. Carina was jubilant that everything had worked out so perfect after all. She shot Dodie the thumbs up as the she walked past her with Oliver.

Stephanie, Tassy, and all the other girls from their baking classes were magically paired up with exactly whom they wanted as well. One could say this was a mini miracle, but in all fairness with a talent such as Aunt Carol's on their side they couldn't lose! Aunt Carol's eavesdropping talent had come in handy once again managing to ferret out the perfect baked goods for each suitor!

Soon there was only Justine and Dodie left on the stage. Justine scooted over to her and clutched her hand. She leaned in and whispered, "I hope you get just who you want."

Dodie squeezed her hand and offered her an encouraging smile, though her stomach churned and she wondered what the heck she had gotten herself into.

"Now lovely lady, Justine Slater, please step forward!" Aunt Carol was really taking to this hosting gig.

Justine did so, turning loose Dodie's hand.

"Your date for tonight is…" she drum rolled on her knees again and the crowd joined in.

"Your date is… Jason Anderson!" Aunt Carol tried not to sound disappointed as she announced his name. She glanced over to see how Dodie was doing with this news.

Dodie felt a powerful drop in her gut, like she had an anchor in there. *Jason. He was there…*

A thousand thoughts shot through her

mind at once. So he *had* chosen her chocolate cake after all, only it was Justine's now!

Justine turned back to look at her, mouthing, "Sorry," her own sweet face crestfallen. She then turned and put on a show of excitement and gratitude, though Dodie could tell it was fake. Justine was just as disappointed as she was.

Dodie stared at her shoes as she heard Jason climb the stairs to the stage. She couldn't even look at him for fear he would see the feeling for him in her eyes and she'd make an even worse fool of herself. There was nothing she could do now. The letters had been just that, letters. Jason would spend a romantic Valentine's night with beautiful, vivacious Justine not her. Maybe Justine would open up his heart again where she could not. Why would he want a broken person like her anyway? Why would anyone?

Dodie was in a daze now as everyone clapped for the couple and they left the stage.

Aunt Carol bit her lip. She knew Dodie must be shook up and all because they had led her astray from her own instincts. She looked over at her sister Ethel who was happily seated with Earl at her side. She let our her breath in a big sigh. Well you win some and you lose some. She brightened up and put a big smile on her face for Dodie's behalf.

"Now, our last lady, is a newcomer in town, and a darn sweet addition if I might say so, our own Dodie Randall."

The crowd clapped for the lone standing baker on the stage.

She took a deep breath and stared right ahead of her, so intently that everything blurred. She plastered a smile on her face and waited.

"Your date, the final date is… Nathan Rose!"

Justine's intended. Figured. If it was possible for her stomach to sink any further, it did.

A young, hipster-looking guy swaggered up the steps and offered her a winning smile. They looked ridiculous together, like he was her teenaged son.

The audience cheered and laughed and Dodie felt heat rush to her cheeks.

He looped his arm into hers and made a play of romance and infatuation, batting his eyelids and swooning. The crowd laughed and laughed and she laughed right along, though humiliation burned in her heart. She was a punch line now. Nothing but a punch line.

Chapter 20

As soon as Nathan had led her into the crowd and they were out of the spotlight, Dodie excused herself.

"I have to go to the bathroom, sorry."

She dashed away, hoping against hope that she wouldn't burst into tears on the way. This was so unlike her, she thought to herself. Usually she was the first one up for a joke, for a laugh, but now it felt like every single giggle was a pin getting stuck in her. After the way the whole audience had laughed she felt like one certified voodoo doll.

When she got there, the main section of the bathroom was empty, but she heard the faint sound of muffled crying in one of the stalls. It made her strong and she managed to swallow the lump in her throat.

"Who's there?" she asked softly. "Is everything okay?"

"Dodie, is that you?" a voice thick with tears said.

"Yes, it's me."

The door opened and Justine flung herself at Dodie in a hug, a mess of tears. "It all went wrong," she wailed. "I dropped my cake and now this. Valentine's Day is ruined. I don't like Jason at all."

"And Nathan's not right for me," said Dodie. "He was just playing it up for the crowd."

"Now we're stuck all night with the wrong guy." Justine blubbered.

Dodie felt so bad for Justine. She was just seeing the other side of love. The lost side. She felt bad for her. Dodie wiped at Justine's tears with a tissue. "Come on Justine it will be all right…"

Justine just shook her head distraught. "I tried so hard Dodie."

"Hey, you know there's nothing in the rules to say we can't switch dates," Dodie said, though her heart pounded as she realized how presumptuous she was being. Who said that Jason really wanted a date with her? Maybe he just liked chocolate cake. But this wasn't about her and Jason right now, this was about a young girl's first love and that's all that mattered.

Justine straightened up. "You're right."

"You could go and tell Nathan what happened and straighten it all out," Dodie said.

"And you could go after Jason."

"I could?" Dodie's heartbeat pumped all the way up to her temples. "Could I?"

"Go, go, go!" Justine said, pushing her out of the bathroom. "He won't wait around forever!"

Before Dodie could change her mind she ran out of the bathroom, hurried along the lobby and out of the front door, the cold air of the evening rushing onto her face as she stepped out. She looked around but couldn't see Jason anywhere. One part of her wilted, urging her to go back into the party and enjoy everyone else's happiness, but another part propelled her pumps along the ground in the direction of the main street and the bakery.

"Jason?" she called out. She was being so bold that it almost felt like an out of body experience, but she wasn't going to stop now. "Jason?"

The town was the emptiest she'd ever seen, all of Kissing Bridge crowded into the Valentine's Day Ball.

"Jason?" she called out again as she turned the corner to the street where the bakery stood.

And there he was. Standing by the bakery. A soft snow was falling and it sparkled in the moonlight as it fell. Jason turned to look at her.

"Dodie?" he said, his voice soft with awe. "Is that you?"

She ran over to him. "Yes, it's me."

She was taken on how piercing his gray eyes were, how they made her feel he had so much kindness in him that he could see right through to the real her, through all the walls she had put up. All the letters between them had not prepared her for the actual living breathing man in front of her. Nor for the feelings he would awaken in her that she thought were dead forever.

Taking a deep breath, she looked at a spot behind his shoulder, determined to find the courage to speak. She'd come this far.

"I was just wondering if you bought the cake because you liked chocolate cake or because you wanted… because you wanted… you wanted me to be your date?"

"Both," he said immediately. "Both. And I'm allergic to apples."

She looked up at him, feeling a spark fly as they made eye contact. Now it was his turn to feel awkward. He thrust his hands into his pockets and stared at the cobblestone.

"I wanted to tell you how much your letters helped me," he said. "Sometimes they were my only reason for living."

"Really?" she said, her chest area sinking with awe. Sometimes writing letters to him was her only way of staying sane, of encouraging herself that she *would* get out of the rut she had somehow plunged into, that she *could* have a good life in the future. She told him these things, and she felt them herself. Both their hearts had been kindled by the words she had written. She had never known simple letter writing, simple words, sentences, could have so much power.

"Yes," he said. "And… and when I saw you at the bakery, I thought you were the most beautiful woman I had ever seen. But I didn't know who you were. Now I know that, if you're really Dodie and I'm not dreaming, that you're the most beautiful woman there ever was, on the inside and out."

Her heart soared, she suddenly she felt free from all the doubts and worries and fears that had plagued her. She felt as if she was being lifted up out of her darkness on the wings of angels, scooped up from her place on the cobblestone and taking off into the vast starry night. Suddenly love didn't feel scary at all. Suddenly it felt like a gift from God.

"If I may, can I hug you Dodie…" Jason said, leaning forward toward her.

"Yes," she whispered, with her whole heart.

Dodie lost all track of time as they clung to each other. When Jason pulled away and asked, "Do you want to go back to the ball?" She'd forgotten that there even was such a thing.

"Yes," she said, beaming from ear to ear.

Just like those on stage had done, he held out his arm for her to loop hers into it.

As they made their way back down the starlit streets, she swelled with a contentment that was so plentiful it spilled over from her heart and lit up her face.

When they reached the door of the hall, the moon streamed down upon them and romantic music wafted out from the Valentine's Ball. He paused on the threshold and looked into her eyes. She felt like the world was spinning in a whole new orbit.

"Dodie," he said. "It was really you who wrote me those letters?"

"Yes."

"Then you saved my life." He traced the contours of her face with his fingers, as if he were studying her face, trying to commit it to memory. His finger was gentle, tingling across her skin. "I know life is a lot different than letters, and we both said we intended to never let ourselves be hurt by love again…but, maybe this was our destiny. Maybe *we* were our destiny."

Jason held her chin and looked deeply into her eyes. Searchingly.

"I know we have both been hurt and I know it will be hard to trust again…but I hope you are willing to take a chance Dodie because I'm falling in love with you and I sure hope I'm not alone!"

Dodie looked at him with all the love she felt spilling out of her.

"I'm willing to try out love again if you are."

Jason wrapped her in his arms protectively and kissed the top of her head.

"It's going to be different this time Dodie. You and I were meant to be, you'll see."

Jason held out his strong, bronzed hand and she slid her own hand into his. It wouldn't be easy to be vulnerable again, but for this man she would risk anything. Even her heart.

"Will you dance with me?" he said, grinning.

"I would love to!" Dodie beamed back.

They entered the ballroom and the warmth of the room and the love enfolded them. As Dodie wound her arms around Jason's neck and swayed to the music, she looked around at all the couples at the ball. Justine was rocking to the music, pasted to Nathan. Carina was shining as she looked up into Oliver's face and Ethel and Earl were a sight to see, prancing around the dance floor like a couple of spring chickens!

Aunt Carol returned to the stage, microphone in one hand and a slip of card in the other looking very professional. She was chased by Summer, who was trying to snatch the slip of card away from her.

"Well look at this!" Aunt Carol announced to the crowd.

Summer was still jumping up and down trying to snatch the card out of her Aunt's grasp.

"I am proud to announce that my lovely niece, Summer Landers and Brad Anderson hereby announce their wedding, to take place on Easter Monday, in Kissing Bridge Mountain Church!"

Aunt Carol squealed with delight and the whole place erupted in cheering.

Dodie joined right along and Jason's face lit up with gladness.

Aunt Carol motioned for Brad and Summer to come up on stage.

"Well, we didn't want to overshadow the Ball," said Summer, "so we were going to wait until the very end, but it looks like you've outed us Aunt Carol!"

Summer leant back into Brad and he squeezed her shoulders. He took the mic. "Thanks everybody. I am the luckiest man in the world, right? Take one last look at Summer Landers because next time we are all together she will be Mrs. Brad Anderson!

The crowd clapped louder and louder.

Summer leaned into the mic,"Oh and you're all invited!"

Brad held up a bunch of invitations and the crowd went wild. He and Summer left the stage and went around and handed out the wedding invitations to everyone.

The romantic music cranked back up and everyone partied the night away, gazing into their partner's eyes and sinking into that gorgeous loving feeling.

"Well look at that," Aunt Carol said to her sister Ethel who had joined her onstage, turning the invitation over in her hand. "Looks like the Landers curse is well on the way to being broken for good Ethel."

Ethel hugged her big sister tight. She caught Earl beaming at them from the crowd and she smiled. "Maybe we should reframe this curse thing Carol."

Aunt Carol looked at her. "Whatever do you mean Ethel?"

"Well, if we were with the right men and we lost them, then that would be a curse. But what if were with the wrong men? What if God was looking out for us like we believe he does…might he not be saving us for our true love?"

Aunt Carol considered this. "So you are suggesting that perhaps it was more a case of the Landers' having luck then of the Lander's having a curse."

Ethel nodded emphatically. "Why not?"

Aunt Carol looked at how happy Summer and Brad looked as they made their way around the room accepting congratulations and passing out invitations. That had certainly worked out to be a case of Landers' luck. Against all odds and multiple states they had made their way back together. She saw Ethel waving to Earl and considered that perhaps her sister was right.

Now Earl was headed there way, and he had Old man Jennings with him. Old man Jennings was in a bright red shirt and bright red pants and he had the biggest grin on his face. His white hair stood out even more starkly against his bright attire. When he walked up onstage and stood next to Aunt Carol with her red dress and red hair it was almost too much, but also just perfect!

He grinned broadly at Aunt Carol as she looked at him like he was slightly deranged. "Why are you looking at me like that Jennings?"

Old man Jennings cleared his throat. "Well Carol seeing as you didn't bake anything for the auction, I also didn't buy anything."

Aunt Carol was not understanding. Earl nudged him to continue. Old man Jennings cleared his throat.

"What I'm saying Carol is, how about being my date for the night?"

Aunt Carol turned an even brighter shade of red then either of them had on, and for once was speechless. Old man Jennings was encouraged by her silence.

"I'll take that as a YES!"

And just like that Old man Jennings looped his arm around Aunt Carol and led her away toward the dance floor before she could utter a word.

Earl and Ethel broke into laughter like two conspirators.

Soon Jennings was whisking Aunt Carol about the room and Aunt Carol was smiling from ear to ear.

Brad came over to the table and handed Dodie her invitation and winked at his brother Jason.

Dodie opened up the beautiful wedding invitation and read it. She couldn't have been more at peace. All around her people were celebrating love. The warm glow of the feeling made Dodie feel happy all over. She couldn't believe this was all happening. Just a short time ago she was heartbroken and now she was sitting next to the man of her dreams. This town of good people and friends had saved her from herself. Given her hope, and now love again.

She was so glad for Brad and Summer, and the proof that true love really doesn't die. It was good to know that real love was still possible in this crazy world. Looking up at Jason, her heart bubbled over with joy. It wouldn't be easy for either of them to open up again, but in time she knew they would.

Brad and Summer's love was like a full bloomed flower, bright and eye-catching and wonderful. Her and Jason's were like a bud, just beginning to open.

Dodie smiled to herself, she couldn't wait to see how it bloomed.

The End

Chocolate
Kisses
and Love Filled Wishes
A Fabulous Feel Good Holiday Romance

Linda West

Chocolate Kisses and Loved Filled Wishes

A Fabulous Funny Feel Good Holiday Romance

BY
LINDA WEST

Dedicated to my Dad

#1
Best
Seller

Chapter 1

Pro Snowboarding Qualification
Grand Prix
Mammoth Mountain

Kacey Anderson, a 22-year-old all American cutie, eyed the scoreboard. The bright February sun shone off the white snow and lit up her beautiful sweet face sprinkled with a dusting of freckles across the nose and cheeks. Her strawberry blonde pigtails hung out on either side of her white snowcap, which was splashed with her sponsor's name, O'Neil. Her soft grey eyes shot up the mountain watching the next rider get in place.

The Grand Prix at Mammoth in California this year had been a free-for-all. With half of the usual winners out on the sidelines with injuries, the medals could go to anyone.

Her boyfriend, Brody Jenkins, had already secured first place in the Men's Slope Style and was almost assured to take first in the Big Air Event later. He had already scored an epic 9.8 on the first run and was way ahead of his contenders. He still had a second run to go.

Kacey screwed up her face as she looked at the conditions.

Horrible.

Another winter without enough snow on the west coast.

They had to make man-made snow and the mountainside was a dangerous mess of ice.

That's how she had ended up on the sidelines—watching.

Brody had told her not to try her latest trick when they were back in his hometown of Telluride, Co. The dangerous conditions were very similar and of course Kacey had not listened. If he could do it, she could do it.

Wrong.

She had fallen badly, and herniated a disc near her spine. She was under doctor's orders *not* to snowboard, and so her stormy grey eyes matched the clouds hanging above on this dreary February day.

Her biggest competition, Brittany Roberts, had just pulled out a new trick, and received a 9.3. This would put her in first place in the women's slopestyle and make her this year's Grand Prix Mammoth winner. She would be a top contender now for the Women's 2018 Olympics US team.

Kacey Anderson tried to think positive. She knew she could beat Brittany easily if she could just heal quicker and get back on the mountain to practice her new routine. Despite her youth and experience, she had come in 4th place, just under the medals two years ago in Sochi—beating out many well-known snowboarders. Her fluid style and courageous tricks had made her a fan favorite. Kacey was such a natural athlete; her tricks often rivaled the difficulty of the guys she trained with.

She had been such a hopeful for the 2018 Olympics but now all those dreams seemed to be going up in smoke.

She turned her attention to the Men's Big Air Event.

Brody was taking his place at the top of the hill, next in line. It was beginning to sleet, which was never good for the course. Off he went, with his perfect style and speed as he approached the jump.

Kacey couldn't help but to hold her breath.

Yes, he made it look easy like all the pros did—that was part of good style—but it was a dangerous sport.

Every jump you risked your life, or a horrible fall.

She knew first-hand on the latter, but her close friend had not been so lucky. A head injury had caused her death when she was only 13.

Brody hit the jump hard and spiraled into his signature 880 cab and hit the sweet spot.

A perfect jump!

The crowd went wild. Cheers of "Brody, Brody, Brody!" filled the air.

He continued down the hill and Kacey started working her way through the crowd to meet him.

She watched for the score. 9.8!

She shook her head and smiled.

No one had laid down the scores like Brody had in the last two years since taking the Gold in Sochi. He had come home with three gold medals and a famous face.

He was the American team's golden child and favorite poster child. Everyone expected a repeat performance in South Korea in 2018.

She made her way through the crowd, stopping to sign a couple of autographs along the way, until she reached Brody. He was surrounded by press as he pulled off his goggles and shook out his surfer blonde hair. He looked like a Norse god.

He had, in fact, been a surfer for much of his life before his parents had moved him to Breckenridge. For some reason he maintained that golden tanned skin, despite where he lived.

His green eyes sought hers and she waved and gave him the thumbs up. His smile spread from ear to ear.

Brody had truly missed his calling in the movies, but his sponsors made good use of his good looks plastering his face on everything from cereal boxes to action figures.

He was being thronged by fans and coaches and Kacey smiled as she watched Brody soak it all in. God, he loved attention. It always made her laugh, as she was just the opposite. The cameras and attention made her uncomfortable. But Brody reveled in it!

Without a doubt, he deserved all the credit owed for his amazing athletic ability and courage. It was a good thing be had that talent because he certainly wasn't winning any medals for his smarts.

In fact, he could be considered almost simple-minded.

He had never graduated from high school, could barely read a book and never kept up with current events.

Sure they were both involved in the "Save the Winter Campaigns" for climate change awareness, so he had a conscience at least. He meant well, but there was no denying it—he was just simple.

He was truly gorgeous and simply an

amazing snowboarder who scored consistent 9.8s!

To Brody's credit, he wasn't just a gorgeous boy toy—he was also very funny. It was he that had nicknamed himself '98' – after his typical snowboard score, and his inflated guestimate of his IQ. Whenever they took IQ tests on their iPhones, he seemed to score between 90 and 95, so they agreed to throw in an extra few. It had since become her favorite endearment for him.

Brody broke free of the horde and made his way over to Kacey. They embraced.

"Great job, 98!" She hugged him again. "I'm so proud of you!"

He beamed back at her. "Thanks, Babe. Sorry you couldn't be out there today."

Kacey winced.

It did hurt, but it didn't take away from being proud of her man.

"That was super air, honey, and you spun that like glass!"

Brody kissed her suddenly, looking at her with a depth and seriousness that wasn't usual for him.

She let him lead her away from the cheering crowd and press, wondering what was going on.

Brody usually wasn't one to cut off the press or his fans.

Kacey looked at him. "What's up, Honey?"

Brody's sea green eyes darted away, unable to hold her gaze. "I want you to take more time to rehab before—"

Kacey cut him off.

"I'm fine, Brody! The doctor said the threat is over. I just have to—"

"Listen."

He stopped her. "I know you want to get to the Olympics but it's not worth hurting yourself."

Kacey was indignant.

Easy for him to say—he already had *his* medals.

She had been a tomboy all her life, competing against her four brothers and half the town of Kissing Bridge. This was her chance. Kacey Anderson was tough—tough enough to make it work, despite all the obstacles thrown in her way. Brody knew that. Why was he being so serious? Why didn't he seem like himself?

He felt closed to her; hidden.

Not like her bouncy ball of child-like energy and joy that he usually was.

She steeled herself for his reaction.

"What—you don't want to train together? What about our trip to Vail?"

Brody shook his head.

"It's just too dangerous, Kacey."

All of a sudden, she didn't feel so tough anymore, having to blink back tears.

They had planned that trip to celebrate their anniversary of when and where they had met – in Vail, three years prior.

She was probably stupid to hope that Brody might ask her to marry him in Vail, but she couldn't help it. She knew he loved her, though he had never said it. Now he was acting as though their relationship meant nothing.

"But our special plans…"

"Look, the coaches are concerned too. They asked me to talk to you. They think you are working yourself too hard after such a big injury."

Kacey's mouth made a big O.

If this was coming from the higher-ups, then it wasn't a suggestion; it was an order.

"So this is coming from the coaches? I'm not sure what you're saying. Are they going to sideline me?"

Brody shrugged. "I don't know. I kinda got that."

"Oh, and they send you—like it's going to be any *easier* on me?"

"I agree with them, Kacey."

Kacey sniffed back her tears.

Darn it.

She wasn't going to cry like a little girl.

She'd learned that much, being the youngest sister of four brothers.

She'd suck it up.

No training.

No Vail.

Definitely no engagement surprise.

She did her best not to sniffle, though a bit did come out. "Maybe I'll go home for a while for some R and R?"

Brody grinned.

"Great idea."

She nodded.

If he didn't care to keep her with him, and the coaches wanted her gone, sure, she'd go home…

She'd go home to one of the best-kept secrets of Vermont, the Kissing Bridge Ski Mountain at Eagle's Peak.

Go home?

No problem.

Stop snowboarding?

No way.

Chapter 2

Brad held his cell phone hard to his ear to drone out the commotion of the Valentine's Ball.

"Hey little sis, what's up?" he asked. "Happy Valentine's day!"

Summer Landers, hometown super model, looked over and Brad motioned to the phone and pointed to the door. She nodded and blew him a kiss.

Brad stepped outside the door of the hall. It was a beautiful night.

The snow fell gently and the town glistened with the festive Valentine lights. Flowers were everywhere this special night. The beautiful colors making a lovely contrast against the clean white snow.

The flowers were strewn across the driveways of the homes where single women resided.

It was a lovely tradition for the single men of the town to secretly go out the night before Valentine's and sprinkle flower buds along the snow-laden walkway to their loved one's residence. Carnations meant new love, and baby roses meant *true* love.

"I'm so excited you're coming home!" Brad said into the phone. "Do you want to stay with me at the house until Summer and I get married? It's just little ole me."

Kacey's voice came across the phone more mature than Brad had ever heard her. She had left to tour with the Go-Pro Slope Team right out of high school. After three years away, she had grown up so much.

"I was hoping you could ask Earl if he had an extra room to rent at the at Eagle Peak's lodge for the next few months."

Brad waved at a happy couple as they walked by.

The young girl, Corrine, looked like a fairytale princess in her pink floaty dress.

"Sure, Kacey. A new friend of ours is up there renting a room there as well.

Her name's Dodie. I'll run it by Earl when I go inside."

"Okay, great. Can't wait to see you."

"Can't wait either, Sis. It's been way too long!"

As he put his phone away, he saw that Summer had come to meet him outside during the call. She still took his breath away.

Brad doubted he would ever get used to seeing her beauty so close up. For years he had stared at her modeling photos, wondering where the love of his life had gone, and *here she was*—back home and soon to be his bride.

He almost wanted to pinch himself to see if he were dreaming.

Brad smiled his happy smile.

His grey linen eyes with the flecks of blue crinkled with pure joy.

"Honey! You'll never guess who's coming home!"

Chapter 3

Eagle's Point Lodge was a beautiful building, situated at the bottom of the ski run. It was the quintessential log cabin, but on a grand scale, with beautiful large picture windows overlooking the mountain. A grand dining room, hall and bar graced the first floor, with fireplaces at each end that blazed all year round and lit up the place with a warm, dusty glow. Upstairs there were rooms aplenty for short-term and long-term visitors to Kissing Bridge Mountain.

Dodie Randall had recently moved into one of the apartment suites that sat at the back corner of the lodge. With its own fireplace, a gorgeous view of the mountain, and a beautiful bathroom—with a roll-top tub, perfect for taking long hot bubble baths after dashing in from the cold—she felt she couldn't ask for anything more.

Since coming to Kissing Bridge Mountain, her life had changed so much for the better. Each time she looked over the snowy beauty of the mountain, dotted with its stoic evergreens, she felt blessed. God didn't make mistakes. Against all odds, she had found happiness again—and hope.

Even love seemed to be beckoning her back into its warm embrace.

She smiled as she thought of Jason and how lucky she was to have him in her life. This town, and that man, had helped restore her faith, and that was a miracle in itself.

Dodie put a bright flower arrangement into a lovely vase, then placed it on the pedestal leading to the apartment suite across from hers.

Jason and Brad's little sister, Kacey Anderson, was coming to stay for a few months.

Dodie couldn't wait to meet this rising star of snowboarding—and possibly, if her dreams came true—her new sister in law! She was excited to have her as a close neighbor in the meantime. Who didn't need more girlfriends?

Earl came up the stairs with some fresh sheets and folded towels. He grinned at Dodie arranging the flowers. "Nice touch. Kacey will love those."

"Thanks, Uncle Earl," Dodie said, with a pretty smile.

"I'm looking forward to meeting her! Is it true she has a shot at making the Olympic team?"

Earl shook his head with a sad look.

"She did, but she had a bad fall. It's been touch-and-go ever since, with her recovery. Might be a sore subject."

Dodie nodded her head. "Of course. How sad."

Earl opened the door to Kacey's suite and Dodie peered in. It was a mirror image to her own, with the large picture window overlooking the mountain and the old-fashioned fireplace in between. The large four-poster bed was stacked with a fluffy mattress and white goose feather coverlets.

Earl placed the towels in the adjacent bathroom, then knelt down and pulled some small logs from the stack and got the fireplace going. In no time, it was beautiful. The warmth of the flames filled the room with a golden glow that set off the morning chill.

"Oh, Uncle Earl, it's so lovely."

"Just the same as yours," he chuckled.

Dodie grinned. "I hope she likes it,"

"Hope so. She's been through a tough time."

Earl smiled tenderly. "Like someone else I know."

Dodie nodded.

She was happy Kacey was coming, no matter what the reason.

It was a good place to heal.

Whatever ailed Jason and Brad's younger sister, Dodie felt that being up here at Eagle's Peak just might help.

Chapter 5

It was Sunday and the Landers ladies were brunching with hot cocoa and bourbon-infused maple scones. The movie *Breakfast at Tiffany's*, their all-time favorite, played in the background.

Ethel Landers, Summer's mom, put another log on the fire. Aunt Carol had just arrived and she was wearing a fetching new lavender frock that offset her large red beehive in a lovely gaudy way.

Ethel examined her sister's color combination and cocked her head.

Aunt Carol planted her hands on her hips. "Why are you looking at me like I have a rooster sticking out of my décolletage?"

Summer waved to her Aunt, then jumped up and hugged her. "Hi Aunt Carol. I have a cup waiting all ready for you!"

Aunt Carol took her coat off and sat down next to Summer.

"You look beautiful, Aunt Carol! Where are you going?"

"Oh, this little thing." Aunt Carol said. Her cheeks blushed, which just added another bizarre color to the whole off-red theme. "Just here with my favorite family to brunch and admire Audrey."

She studied the TV as if she couldn't be more interested in Audrey listening to *Moon River*.

Ethel and Summer looked at each other.

Ethel called bull. "Well if you have a date, then you might want to add a splash of white to break up that—brightness."

With that, she walked over and picked up a pretty white carnation bud that was in a bowl and pinned it to her sister's dress.

She stepped back to admire her work.

"Perfect. Just what you needed!"

Aunt Carol inspected the new development on her chest. "Hmmph," she said, which in Aunt Carol speak, meant it would pass.

"You just happened to have one handy?"

Summer sang out, "Someone left a trail of white carnations up our walk the other night."

Now it was Mom's turn to blush.

"Earl?" Aunt Carol said with a teasing grin.

Mom nodded.

"Well now, isn't that romantic?"

Carol hugged her sister, but Ethel pushed her away just as quickly.

"Ok," she said. "Now *you* fess up about your date with Old Man Jennings!"

Aunt Carol sat back down and turned her head to the side haughtily, her chin thrust up and her beehive bobbing down. "I'm sure I don't know what you're talking about."

Summer and her mom doubled over with laughter.

"Oh, you think you're the only one that can eavesdrop?" Ethel laughed. "I may need to be a whole lot closer to hear, but I also have talents and I—"

"She has Earl," Summer interrupted, grinning, "who told her that Old Man Jennings asked you out to dinner!"

Aunt Carol elbowed her sister good-naturedly. "Oh, you dickens. Don't you go honing in on my gifts!"

She arranged the folds of her lavender dress over her knees in a prissy, delicate way that was out of character.

"Besides, he prefers Jackson."

Summer spluttered. "Jackson?"

"I never knew he had another name!" Ethel said. "We've called him Old Man Jennings since he was in high school."

"He went white early, right?" Summer clarified.

"Yes," Aunt Carol said, quickly. "And there's nothing wrong with white. I, for one, think it looks distinguished."

Summer sat down beside her and squeezed her hand. "Well, you look absolutely beautiful, Aunt Carol. I'm sure he's going to be thrilled. I'm so happy for you."

Aunt Carol drank some more of her cocoa and squeezed her hand back. "You're a good girl, Summer."

Suddenly, Summer's smile faded away. She sighed deeply and took a deep gulp of her own cocoa. "I've got a problem."

Ethel and Aunt Carol were all ears.

Summer sucked her breath in. "My agent called me yesterday. She says I have to go back to LA to shoot the new *Sports Illustrated.* She says I can't get out of the contract. I'm stuck."

Aunt Carol twisted her lips.

Ethel got up and crossed the room to the cupboard. Retrieving a bottle of whiskey, she returned and poured a little in Summer's cocoa. She walked away until Aunt Carol cleared her throat *really* loudly.

Summer looked at her Aunt mournfully. "He's not going to take it well, is he, Aunt Carol?"

Aunt Carol shook her head and her red beehive swayed back and forth like a dizzy *Tower of Pisa*—if the *Tower of Pisa* were red.

"Bring the bottle back, Ethel. This is a conundrum."

Summer shook her head. "That's what I thought."

"The thing is," Summer continued, "I just don't know how to tell Brad. He already quit his job so we could commit to our life here and…" She trailed off. "Oh, I just don't think he's going to be happy about this."

Chapter 6

"What? When? Why did you wait to tell me?!"

Brad Anderson's grey eyes went stormy. Kacey had seen that look before. She was sure glad she wasn't on the other end of that glare! That was her older brother's *'I'm not happy'* posture.

She turned to look out the window and hoped everything would be okay.

"Look honey, let's talk about this when I get back later, okay? ... I know, I know... I love you too."

Kacey couldn't help but share a familiar smile with her brother Jason in the back seat. He flashed her his winning smile with the double dimples. One thing was certain; their big bro was still a pushover for Summer Landers.

Brad pulled up his Ram truck to the lodge and the full beauty of Eagle's Peak came into view.

Kacey couldn't take her eyes off of the mountain—it was so superb. It had been so long since she had been home to Kissing Bridge and her childhood friend, Eagle's Peak Mountain. After all the places she had been around the world, Eagle's Peak was still one of the most impressive ski mountains she knew.

She took a deep breath, breathing in the mountain air she loved so much.

It was perfect.

Here she could train the way she wanted to train—not the way the team physical therapists thought she should train.

She knew her own body.

She knew she was ready.

Her brother Brad had told her that they'd recently added some new snow slope features on the east mountain. It was simple, but it had everything she would need to train. She wouldn't be ready to make the next Grand Prix in Breckinridge and for sure would miss the Dew Competition. But if she trained hard, she could make the US Open and the last Grand Prix—which could make her a qualifier for the Olympic team.

She wished Brody could see Eagle's Peak. Only a fellow rider of his talent could understand how truly spectacular and special it really was.

She wondered what Brody was doing now—probably modeling for some underwear ad or men's cologne. She glanced at her phone. No messages.

As of late, Brody had blossomed into a big star (for a snowboarder). He wasn't only splashed all over ski wear and surf gear, but now mainstream commercial products wanted his California good looks and X Games raw charisma.

The retailers weren't the only ones who wanted a piece of Brody.

Everywhere they went together, he was thronged by women wanting his attention—or more. It wasn't easy for Kacey. She was a small-town girl with small-town values and he was a rising global sex symbol.

She knew they had a strong connection, and had been through a lot together.

They trained together, won together and traveled together.

They were "two peas in a pod," as their team members would call them, and they made a stunning couple for the press.

But the press liked winners, and for the last two months Kacey hadn't even been entered—let alone won anything.

Sometimes she feared Brody's fame might pull them apart.

She glanced down at her iPhone.

The mountain was notorious for bad reception, but Kacey hadn't heard from her boyfriend in a couple of days. She knew he spurned "technology" and could barely text (poor 98) but certainly he had to wonder how she was doing?

Or miss her…?

She let out a big sigh and a cold cloud formed—a symbol of her worry puffing out in the air.

She wanted to believe in love, but Brody had never said he loved her. That fact left her wondering what his true intentions were. Maybe he just wanted to be free? They *were* young, after all.

Kacey shook her head, like she could shake the thoughts right out of her mind.

All she wanted was to take a ride down the hill.

She had learned early on that the only thing that stops a worrying mind was a busy body.

She needed to get busy now.

Right now.

Brad and Jason each took a piece of luggage and Kacey followed them up into the lodge with her backpack. Earl and Dodie were just coming down the stairs when Jason held the door for her so she could step into the lobby.

Kacey lit up at the sight of the old lodge she loved and Earl, the lodge keeper—such a kind old man.

"There's our hometown golden girl! Great to have you back, sweetie!"

Kacey hugged Earl, grinning from ear to ear.

"Nice to see you, Earl! It's been a long time!"

"Let me look at you, all grown up," Earl said, holding her at arm's length. "I don't know why I still picture you as that pesky little tomboy that always wanted one last ride down the hill—keeping me working late." He winked.

"Ahh, Earl. And you always let me, even though you complained the whole time!"

He wagged his finger at her, pretending to be stern. "Hey, keep that soft spot side under wraps, Missy."

Jason cleared his throat as he came in, stamping the snow off his boots. "Hey, Dodie!"

Dodie smiled.

She looked beautiful in a blue and white polka dot dress and her hair pulled back with crystal-studded pins.

"Hi Jason. Hi Brad!" She swallowed hard to keep herself from smiling like an idiot.

Jason Anderson looked so handsome in his plaid lumberjack flannel shirt and blue jeans. Since being back home from the war he had relaxed, and if possible, had become even more handsome.

Dodie noted to herself that these Andersons certainly had it going on in the looks department! She caught herself imagining what her and Jason's children might look like. Then Jason stepped forward and took her hand, leading her over to Kacey, just like a true gentleman.

"Dodie Randall, this is our little sis, Kacey."

Kacey stuck her hand out and pumped Dodie's hand hard like the athlete she was.

"Nice to meet you, Dodie! Jason told me we're going to be neighbors." She smiled, all bright and full of young hope.

Dodie smiled. "I'm so glad you are home for a while, Kacey! I'm right across the hall."

Chapter 7

Dodie and Kacey met for breakfast the next morning on a big wooden table in front of a roaring fire. They gobbled up scrambled eggs with fresh herbs and little potatoes on the side. After a pot of coffee and enough food to hold them until dinner, they were fast friends.

Dodie was excited to share with Kacey her philanthropic desires and how she had loved working with the girls for Valentine's Day.

She had recently visited Burlington—a two-hour drive from Kissing Bridge—and had met with the head of a children's home that wanted to work together to help the kids and the planet. Since she took up writing to the soldiers from Kissing Bridge stationed abroad, she'd discovered how much helping others had eased her own pain. It seemed that whenever she could reach the heart of another, her own burdens lifted just a little.

Dodie chattered excitedly, telling Kacey that the kids might flourish with a ski event where they could learn to snowboard, and that she had been setting up a *Kissing Bridge Climate Awareness Day* to bring the children up to the experience the joy of the mountain. It was part of a larger event that was twinned with a documentary to bring awareness of climate change.

The guy in charge was a very handsome up-and-coming activist filmmaker, Tanner Williams.

Kacey cocked her head—she knew that name.

Her thoughts hovered on a tall, broad-shouldered, eagle-eyed man preaching about the effects of climate change around the world. Full of passion and the need to change the world, yes, she could almost hear his deep voice in her head.

Then it clicked – of course! *Tanner Williams!*

He was one of the stars of the documentary that really helped bring awareness to young people about getting involved – *Your World, Your Turn!*

She had met him at a climate change event sponsored by some of her snowboarding sponsors in Aspen. He was shockingly handsome.

"I've met him. Briefly. A very interesting and powerful guy for someone so young."

"Well, he'll be here on Saturday to help set it all up," Dodie continued.

"We'd be overjoyed if you'd want to be part of the event?"

Kacey didn't really have to think twice. "Of course!"

No competitions to enter.

No calls from her 'one and only.'

Why not help the world and some children too?

It had absolutely nothing to do with that gorgeous hunk of man, Tanner Williams.

Chapter 8

"Wow, so it's Kacey Anderson herself," Tanner Williams said. With his dark eyes so deep, Kacey felt she might get lost in them.

She withdrew her hand from their handshake quickly, trying not to acknowledge the tingle that played up and down her spine as she touched him.

"You follow snowboarding?" she asked, focusing on her shoes.

She had been in the lounge of Eagle's Peak Lodge, nursing a hot buttered rum in front of the fire, when Dodie and Tanner Williams walked in and Dodie had introduced them.

The truth was, that Kacey couldn't wait to get out on the slopes and away from this guy that made her feel like she was standing there naked. As she sat back down, she fixed all her attention on all her memories of Brody and how much he must be missing her. She looked down at her phone willing him to text or call. It had been another long span with no communication from Brody.

"Sure," Tanner said as he sat down, wide and powerful in his chair. His dark eyes flickered toward her, with an intensity belied by the small smile that turned up one corner of his lips. "I like all things mountain."

"Me, too," she said into her buttered rum, feeling an unexpected heat surge through her body.

Dodie, ever tuned-in to people's discomfort, took her own seat and leaned forward in it. "So what do you think the kids from the children's home will do?"

"Aha!" Tanner reached into his bag and drew out a piece of paper. "Well, I wanted to have shots of them reaching the summit. We could even make it like a metaphor, you know, like overcoming adversity and reaching new heights. Also, from the top, we can get a stunning 360 view. When people look out over things, they get a new perspective. Their eyes are opened to the world beyond theirs."

Dodie nodded. "Okay, so we could include a hike up the mountain… though I'm not sure all the kids could make it."

"No problem," Tanner said. "We can have the whole town make the hike, if they want to. Oh! And we can have some ride on the cable cars. I don't know of all the facilities here, but I want to have them using the mountain in every which way—

just as long as they look like they're enjoying themselves. I want everyone to be having an awesome time for the camera."

"That sounds good to me."

"I… I could teach them how to snowboard," Kacey offered.

A gorgeous, wide smile stretched across Tanner's face. "You can read my mind?"

Right then she was glad *he* couldn't read *hers.*

Brody, Brody, Brody, she kept repeating over and over in her head.

"I've got plenty of other celebrities

coming in," Tanner said. "Courtesy of..." He glanced down at his paper. "Aero Anderson. *Anderson.* Is that anything to do with you?"

"Oh no," Kacey said. "Those are my brothers! Brad used to be a pilot for American Airways, and Jason was in the military, but they both fly locally now."

He looked at her with such calm, interested respect that it made her feel uncomfortable. "So, so... so who have you got coming?"

Tanner tapped the side of his nose. "I like surprises."

Kacey didn't like surprises. They set her heart racing. Just like... *No.* Just like no one. No one but Brody.

"I think I'm gonna go out and train," Kacey announced, getting to her feet.

Dodie gestured towards her rum. "But you haven't—"

"Never mind," Kacey said, picking it up. "I'll just take it to the kitchen now. I'm getting awfully hot in here."

And she was gone.

Chapter 9

Up on the slopes, Kacey felt free. All her thoughts and worries disappeared somewhere into the cold air, as she switch nollied and busted a method air off a cornice.

How could she *not* snowboard? Sure, she understood that the doctors and coaches had to give her advice and were looking out for her, but she told herself they were being over-cautious to cover themselves. The last thing they wanted was a high-profile lawsuit from an Olympic athlete.

They didn't understand, though.

Sitting indoors, watching the snow fall and not getting a chance to feel it under the smooth board, to get the rush of hurtling down the mountain? No chance. It would feel like death itself.

She *had* to get the Olympics. If no one

else was going to help her, she'd have to help herself. Though she felt little strains and twinges in her back, where her disc had herniated, she convinced herself they were just psychological. She was just psyching herself out, and had to push through the twinges until she came out the other side. Her body wasn't used to her old level of training.

So she twisted, turned and nose grabbed. She twisted down the slope until she reached the bottom. There was no feeling so glorious in the whole world as busting some crazy tricks, then sliding down to the flat as if nothing had happened at all, with a nonchalant smile on her face—though her heart leapt inside.

But all that cool nonchalance was swept away as she caught sight of Tanner a little way off, watching her.

He had his legs parted wide in the snow, his hands on his hips, and a huge smile on his face.

"Wow," he said, walking over to her. "Now that was really something. You gunning for the Gold in South Korea?"

She fumbled with her bindings to unclip her feet. "Yep." She was surprised by how assured, how definite her voice sounded.

"Even with your injury?"

She blinked, then remembered it was all over the commentary. The fame was still hard to get used to.

"Yes. People say I shouldn't, but I know my body better than anyone else."

He nodded.

"The hard truth is that no one remembers a loser. You need to follow your heart, I say. If your heart says 'Olympics,' then don't ever let anyone stop you."

She had been so used to hearing people telling her to stop training, that his advice was like one huge gust of fresh air. If she hadn't found her heart almost palpitating around him, she might have reached out and given him a huge hug; that's what she normally would have done. But as soon as Tanner Williams stepped in, normality let itself out the back door, like they couldn't even exist in the same space. A shy, "Thanks," was all she could manage.

A buzzing in her puffy snowboarding jacket startled her.

"Oh, just one second."

"No problem," he said, stepping a little way back to give her some privacy and gaze up at the mountain.

Even as she got her cell out of her jacket pocket, pulling open the zip, she gazed at him. The wonder in his face as he stared up at the peak was almost mesmerizing.

She looked down at the screen. *Brody*. A feeling tugged at her heart, somewhere halfway between affection and guilt. Was it guilt for snowboarding, when she told him she wouldn't… or… something else?

"Hey, Babe," she said, kicking the snowboard up into her hand and walking away from Tanner.

"Hey, Babe," he said back. "Just calling to tell you I just got into Park City and the… Snow. Is. Epic."

She tried to find some enthusiasm. "That's great!"

The sound of girls giggling in the background made a lump rise in her throat.

"I hope you're having a good time."

"Sure I am," he said. She expected something else to come, like '*but it would be so much better with you here.*' Instead he asked, "What are you doing right now?"

"Oh… er… I'm just taking a walk around the bottom of the mountain," she lied—while the guilt multiplied and swelled in her chest.

"As long as you're not snowboarding. Take care of yourself, Kacey."

"I will."

A silence grew between them, and was filled with more feminine giggling.

"Well…" he said, and the discomfort in his voice made her feel awful. "I've gotta go."

"Okay."

And, despite everything, she waited, just as she did at the end of every call. Maybe this would be the time he would say those three small words that her heart craved.

"Well, bye, Babe."

Or not.

It looked like she'd be on her own again, the only one to go out on a limb and declare her feelings. "I love you," she said, in little more than a whisper.

A tiny silence, and then a series of three beeps that let her know he'd hung up. Had he heard her and hung up?

Or taken the phone away from his ear before that?

What did it matter anyway? He'd probably take up with some beautiful snowboarder—maybe even Brittany—and forget all about Kacey.

Blinking tears back, she headed over to tell Tanner she was going back up.

She needed another run down the mountain to get all the worry out of her mind.

But before she could speak, he did.

"Hey, you know it sure would be nice if you let me buy you dinner tonight."

"I'm in a relationship," she said quickly, though her pulse raced out of control.

He laughed a little, but gently.

"I just meant as friends."

Her mind grasped for excuses but found nothing.

"Oh… well, sure. Of course, friends, I don't even know what I was thinking. Friends. Dinner. Sure."

Chapter 10

Aside from Eagle's Peak Lodge, the *Old Cabin Café* was the place to eat in town. Since she'd been eating Earl's food morning, noon and night, she fancied a change. Somehow Tanner had read her mind and suggested it.

They sat at a table tucked into the corner. The dim flicker of the candle in the center of the table played over his face, making his eyes look more intense and magical than ever. Kacey felt uncomfortable.

Was she cheating?

She asked herself that throughout the night, and whenever she did, a twinge of guilt twisted in her gut.

She had felt guilty, as she'd stood in front of her wardrobe, way too long deciding what to wear. She had felt guilty when she'd spent ages fussing with her hair, straightening and curling and straightening it again, trying to work out what looked the best. She had felt guilty as he'd complimented her on how beautiful she looked and her stomach had fluttered with a thousand butterflies.

Friends, she reminded herself. He said "just friends."

"You seem really motivated by snowboarding," he said, leaning over the table toward her.

She noticed his eyelashes curled widely, softening his chiseled looks into something ever more gorgeous. She looked out of the window over at the streets of Kissing Bridge, flooded with golden lamplight.

"I just adore it," she said. "It makes me feel like there are no problems in the whole world."

"Wow." Tanner leaned back in his chair and looked at his hands. "I wish I had something like that, something that made me forget."

Her heart ached for him. She had heard that he had been orphaned early she could only imagine the pain he kept locked away. He looked so crestfallen.

She couldn't help but reach out and touch his hand in kindness.

"But at least you make a difference in the world. You don't run away, you face the problems head on."

He blew out a puff of air with a modest shrug. "I guess."

"You guess?" she said, laughing a little.

"You're one of the most inspirational people I know. You helped get so many people aware and interested in saving the earth. That's no small feat!"

He smiled then, staring at the wood grain of the table, though he was clearly trying not to. He looked up at her with troubled eyes and squeezed her hand tightly.

"Have you decided what you're having, Beautiful?"

Kacey studied his handsome face; so strong, so mature, so determined. The more time they spent together, the more she liked him. Not only was he achingly handsome, he was talented, passionate, and *modest,* too? So different from Brody with all his showboating.

"What are you having?" she asked.

Chapter 11

Climate Awareness Day – Kissing Bridge Mountain

The big day arrived, more dazzling and bright than Kacey had ever imagined. Tanner had called in a team to erect giant screens jutting up out of the slopes. Advertisements for *Billabong* and *Power Bar* and *Go Pro* flashed across them, then illuminated Tanner's handsome face.

Even zoomed in times a million, he was flawless. Those dark eyes seemed to reach out of the screen and into her very soul.

The event was to be simultaneously broadcast from the East and West coast events.

"Welcome!" he said, and the crowd around her burst into cheering. She caught sight of Dodie helping out with the kids from the children's home, and felt a warm glow surround her.

The whole of Kissing Bridge had turned out.

Tanner grinned; his smile so much larger than life. He sure knew how to work a crowd.

"Do you wanna change the world?"

The crowd cheered.

"I need you louder than that," Tanner said. "I need some passion! I need dedication! Now, do you wanna change the world?!" The crowd roared back at him and he burst into beautiful laughter. "Now that's more like it! There's a few other people who want to say a big hello to you all—people who would love to be here today."

The big screens suddenly were lit up and connected with the party from the West coast. The West coast party was a full-on red carpet event; filled with celebrities, producers and rich philanthropists. The California sun shone bright and cheerily, in direct contrast to Kissing Bridge's snowy mountains and parka-wearing crowd.

Summer Landers suddenly appeared on screen. She looked beautiful. She was in a silver, shimmering short dress that exposed her long tan legs and shoulders. Her blonde hair cascaded down her back and her blue eyes sparkled as she raised her sunglasses to address the crowd.

The reporter held a mic up to her and gushed, "Summer Landers, welcome!"

Brad had told Kacey, not too pleased, that Summer was away on a modeling job. He had not mentioned any star-studded events, but this, of course, was a great cause. Kacey glanced over to him by the VIP tent, escorting a couple toward the champagne. He froze and looked up at the screen at the sound of Summer's voice.

"Hey, Kissing Bridge!" Summer came through loud and clear on the speaker systems. "I so wish I could be there because there's nothing I love more than my hometown."

"It's Summer Landers!" Tanner said, his voice bursting with enthusiasm. "Tell us, Summer, can you see the crowd?"

"I sure can," Summer said, waving like

crazy. "Hi everyone! I'm coming to you from the *West Coast Climate Event*! It's a huge success and every star in Hollywood is here doing their part to combat climate change!"

The perky reporter chirped in next to her, "We've got good people here. People really care about the environment. About the world."

Summer smiled "I'm so proud to be a part of this."

All of a sudden, Drake Mason, movie star extraordinaire, jumped in the shot, topless and bronze, and all the young girls in the crowd went wild.

Kacey smiled at the big screen.

Wow, this was certainly turning into a star-studded event! She thought how wonderful the event was turning out to be, and helping climate change grow in awareness.

"Hey, Kissing Bridge." Drake drawled. His voice was undeniably sexy. "Miss you all." With that, he winked with a sly smile and squeezed Summer affectionately.

There were many giggles from the

ladies of Kissing Bridge who had gotten kisses from Drake under the mistletoe and felt on intimate terms with him.

"Whoah," Tanner said with a laugh. "Put a shirt on, Drake!"

Drake laughed. "It's hitting like a hundred degrees out here. I'm not putting on a thing."

With that, he squeezed Summer again. "Except maybe her."

The crowd cheered again.

Tanner cleared his throat.

"So, you guys have a message for all of us here?"

"Sure," Summer said. Drake draped his arm over her shoulder as she spoke. Summer pulled away discretely, obviously uncomfortable and forced a smile. Even from her place at the front of the crowd, Kacey could see Brad tense up as he stared at the screen.

"Remember that the earth is all we've got," Summer said. "We need to protect it for our children and our children's children. God bless you all for being part of this."

"That's right," Drake said, with a superstar nod.

The girls in the crowd squealed, but Kacey guessed they'd squeal if he snorted like a pig, or maybe even if he just stood there, breathing. *Wow, look at the way he inhales!*

"Well, thank you Summer Landers and Drake Mason!" Tanner said. "You guys go have a good time. We're going to keep this live stream going so we can all be a part of this sister event in California!"

The blond perky reporter from *Entertainment Tonight* was nodding to Tanner from her spot at the event, and bubbling and cooing over all the celebrities.

"Well, everyone's turned out for this event, Tanner! There's Ben and Jen... Sean Penn just came in with his lovely date..."

The blue Skype screen took over, showing the beautiful people of L.A. stardom—dappled with perfect tans and diamonds—milling about the red carpet event.

Suddenly, Kacey spotted a blonde god in the background.

She felt herself go weak.

It was Brody.

He was smiling from ear to ear, like he used to do whenever she said something funny.

Kacey felt a wave of sadness come over her.

Brody.

Her communication with Brody had become almost nil. She could blame his traveling, or the shoddy reception on the mountain, but the truth was, since her return to Kissing Bridge, she had been reluctant to talk to him. Each time they spoke, it seemed as if they fell further and further apart. Instead of the usual easy banter and comfortable warmth between them, it had become odd and filled with untruths.

Her untruths.

She cringed inwardly, recalling their last conversation.

She had had to lie to him about what her days were like. He thought she was home healing, and instead she was training harder then ever.

Kacey watched him on the screen

moving through the crowd like a lion with his golden mane. Kacey couldn't take her eyes off of him, but also dreaded seeing some beautiful girl draped over him, like Drake had been over Summer.

The reporter suddenly brightened to another perkier level, if that were possible.

"Oooooo.." She cooed, "I see superstar Gold Medalist, Brody Jenkins, in the crowd. Let's see if we can get him free from all his fans here to give us some words!"

"No, no, not yet!" Tanner said, charming as ever as he laughed.

"First, I wanted to bring the focus back here to Kissing Bridge and introduce a celebrity that we are blessed to havc within our midst at our *East Coast Climate Event*! I am pleased to introduce Olympian, and Gold Medalist hopeful, Kacey Anderson!"

All of a sudden, cameras were swinging around to point at Kacey, and her face was blown up to gigantic proportions on the big screen. She was in sky attire and had her goggles carelessly pushed off her face. She was still dusted with snow from riding and teaching the children earlier. Her grey eyes looked large and luminous on the big screen.

The crowds on both coasts were applauding and screaming. Kacey tried to control her shyness and pulled up her confidence. Her pulse hammering in her temples, she managed a small smile and a wave.

"Isn't she something," Tanner smiled. "I've only been here a few days but I've had the pleasure of personally witnessing some of Kacey's signature outrageous tricks and maneuvers. I'm betting on this little beauty from Kissing Bridge to take the 2018 Olympics by storm!"

The hometown crowd took up the cheer. "Kacey, Kacey, Kacey!"

Tanner, always one to know how to milk a moment, suddenly lit up with a great idea.

"Well, how about a little demonstration Kacey? Perhaps you could give the crowd a hint of that new big air trick you showed me that you've been working on to take the Gold?"

Kacey squirmed modestly, wishing he hadn't told everyone. Suddenly a voice boomed out of the speakers.

"WHAT?!!!"

Kacey froze.

She recognized that voice instantly.

Brody!

Suddenly, Brody's face flashed up on the big screen as he moved in to frame and everyone's attention was drawn back to the screen to see what had occurred.

Brody Jenkins was now standing next to the perky reporter looming over her small frame and looking tanned and angry. He glared at the screen and bore his green eyes straight into Kacey's straight through the camera as if there were not 4,000 miles between them.

Kaccy gulped.

This wasn't exactly the way she had planned to break the truth to Brody about her training.

In all fairness, she actually had not really come up with a plan for that yet. But this definitely was *not* it.

Tanner switched gears quickly to pander to the crowd.

"Oh, well hey there, Brody!" Tanner said, with a glare toward the technician tent, as they swung back to the screen with their cameras.

"It's Brody Jenkins, three-time Gold Medalist, folks!"

The crowd went wild. All the young girls, and old girls were swooning.

Tanner continued with a smooth smile. "So Brody, thank you so much for stepping up to do your part against climate change! Any words?"

Brody was frowning.

Kacey could see he wasn't happy at all.

Why would he be?

He had heard what Tanner had said about her snowboarding. Her untruths to him had come flying out—for all of America to know.

She looked into his eyes across the screen and hoped he could see she was sorry; hoped he could see that she loved him and only wanted to get better the way she knew how—by *training.*

He looked away from her on screen and Brody's eyes glazed and the practiced professional took over. He fixed his face into a smile and waved.

The crowd all cheered for him again. All the girls screamed, as if he were Elvis. Kacey wanted to remind them all he wasn't Elvis. He was soft-hearted, kind and super funny.

He was her loveable sweet '98'—if he was hers at all, anymore.

Brody moved away from the camera, and the rest of the celebrity screen appearances passed her by in a haze of worry. Soon she was caught up in a blaze of activities and helping the children learn. Still, the look in Brody's eyes shook her.

She wondered if she might have lost much more than her chance for the Olympics with that fateful fall.

Didn't he realize that without her being able to snowboard with him, they would drift apart? She was young, but even *she* knew that people had to be together to make a relationship work. His traveling the world without her would be a death knell to their union.

Tanner came over, grinning from ear to ear. "Did I do okay?" He sounded like he really cared.

"You were wonderful." Kacey assured him.

"Thank you." He gave a small bow, delightfully self-mocking, she thought. Then he slipped his strong hand into hers, and she felt her heart flutter out of control. "Come teach these kids how to snowboard and I'll get it all on camera." He nodded at his camera crew, who were standing by, waiting for his signal.

So she did.

Spending the afternoon watching the kids master the basics of getting on the slopes, filled her heart with gladness. There was nothing she liked more than being out in the cold mountain air with those who loved it just as much as she did.

The whole event was a massive success, with the residents of Kissing Bridge and surrounding areas enjoying themselves to the fullest. The celebrities were more than happy with their VIP flights, champagne and top-notch gourmet food served up by Earl. Of course, they were showered with an abundance of Tiffany-blue cookies, courtesy of Ethel Landers, Kissing Bridge's very own cookie queen.

"Mmm, delicious," Kacey had said when she'd first tried one. It was easy to believe Summer's mom had taken the crown.

Tanner had gotten plenty of footage and had retired back to his room and his Mac to work on it for the evening. The dismantling of the screens and the clean up would wait until tomorrow, when it was light again.

* * *

Kacey flopped back onto her bed with a huge smile. Earl had lit the fire for her when she was out finishing up with the kids and the room was warmed with its golden glow. Every part of her body ached and there was a niggling twinge in her back, but she couldn't remember the last time she'd felt so carefree

As she got up and unzipped her snow gear, she felt a new confidence burst around her body. She *would* make it to the Olympics. She was going to win. She was absolutely convinced of it.

She poured herself a hot bubble bath, ready to soak her aching body and breathe in the fragrance of the cinnamon candles that wafted their comforting scent around the bathroom.

Just as she padded back to the bedroom in the Eagle's Peak Lodge slippers, she caught sight of her cell. She'd left it there all day and had forgotten all about it.

12 missed calls, the screen read.

Uh oh!

They were all from Brody.

Her heart flipped. All those times she had looked at the phone willing it to ring, hoping to see his name and now here it was.

She rang him back right away.

"Yes?" Brody's voice was tight and cold as the mountain air.

"Oh my goodness, I'm so sorry," she said quickly. "I didn't even think to take my phone downstairs and the event has just been manic."

A pause. "So, I hear you're boarding?"

So he *had* heard Tanner.

"Just a little."

Kacey's heart but beating so loud she could barely hear her own voice.

A long silence hung in the air before Brody continued.

"Didn't sound like it. Sounds like you were putting on quite a show."

"Babe, it's nothing like that," Kacey assured him. "I just—it's just… I can't *not* board, babe. What am I supposed to do—sit around and not do anything? I'd go crazy! You know that already."

A long silence hung between them. Brody finally spoke.

"You said you wouldn't."

She flopped down on the bed, her heart in knots.

"I know. I know I said that."

She desperately wanted to fill the awkward space with reasons he could stop being mad at her, but she couldn't think of what to say.

In the end, it was Brody who spoke first.

"I want a break, Kacey."

Her heart beat faster. "What's a break?"

She dreaded the answer that was to come.

"It's a break… I don't know. Away time."

Kacey held back the tears. "You mean a break up. You want to break up with me, Brody?"

He let out a long, deep sigh but said nothing.

"I… I love you," she said.

Oh gosh darn it. Now she'd gone and blown it. The death knell. Saying, "I love you," before *he* says "I love you."

"I mean a break," he repeated. "I don't know how long. I'm sorry, Kacey."

Tears blurred her vision as she stared up at the rustic ceiling boards. "98." It hurt her heart to even call him by his nickname. Instead she cried, unable to hold back her feelings. Her hopes crumbling around her.

"It's not about me not caring about you, Kacey. It's about trust. You lied to me."

What could she say? She had kept the truth from him, which was the same as lying. This was all her fault.

"Goodbye, Kacey."

With that, he hung up and Brody was gone.

Chapter 12

Dodie and Kacey walked through the streets of Kissing Bridge, on the way to *Landers Home Baking* where Dodie worked.

"Come with me," Dodie had said, as she met Kacey in the hall of Eagle's Peak Lodge.

Even though all Kacey had wanted to do was dive back under the covers and hide from the world, she doubted it would help anything. The wonderful people of Kissing Bridge always lifted her spirits. Besides, she craved some comfort food and knew the bakery would be stocked full of sweet temptations.

* * *

"Wow, it's beautiful," she said when they got there, though her voice was flat and uninspired. She really *did* like the store though, with its baby blue coat, and modern black awning and lettering. It was the perfect mix between sweet and chic.

"Good morning, ladies," Ethel said when they stepped in. She stood behind the counter, kneading dough. "Welcome, welcome. Excuse my mess." She dusted off her hands with a little towel.

Kacey looked at the beautiful delicacies in the window display. Ethel smiled at her.

"Nice to have you back, Kacey! You'll be my son-in-law's sister when Brad and Summer get married. What does that make us?"

Kacey managed a smile. "I'm not sure."

Ethel smiled back. "We'll just stick with 'family' then. So which one strikes your fancy?"

Kacey breathed in the sweet, comforting smell of the baking, she could understand why Dodie liked working here.

Aunt Carol came in then, carrying a big Easter basket. "Morning, Dodie. Morning, Kacey."

"Good morning," Dodie said. "I take it I don't need to make any introductions then, huh?"

"Oh no introductions needed. We know Kacey," said Aunt Carol. "Since she was in diapers, actually."

Kacey smiled. "Nice to see you, Miss Landers."

Kissing Bridge was small enough for everyone to know everyone else. Aunt Carol cast her eyes over Kacey as she placed the basket on the counter. "But you're not looking your regular happy self."

Kacey sighed. "Relationship stuff."

Aunt Carol unpacked the basket and frowned.

"Some man break your heart?"

"Something like that."

Aunt Carol leant into the glass container, where doughnuts and cakes and cookies were presented in mouthwatering patterns. "First, have this," she said, picking up a ring doughnut with icing and sprinkles on the top. "I know we shouldn't comfort eat, but just once in a while a girl's gotta do what a girl's gotta do. Besides, you'll be up on those slopes burning it all off in no time."

Kacey took the doughnut. "Thanks."

"Secondly, listen to everything that Miss Dodie's got to tell you," Carol said. "Because she came here at Christmas looking a darn sight sorrier than you are and now look at her… beaming and happy and in love with your brother. Baked goods and small towns can do wonders for a woman's soul!"

Dodie chuckled as she put on her apron. "I think God just might have something to do with it, too."

Aunt Carol nodded. "Him, too."

"I think God has big plans for you too, Kacey," Dodie said. "Sometimes God has to break apart our old things so that we have space for the new things."

"That's so true," Ethel said. "You know my Summer was involved with that movie star, Drake Mason. I knew he was all wrong for her, but she wouldn't listen. Anyway, as soon as she broke up with him and came back home, she got back together with your brother. Now, most people would consider breaking off an engagement with Drake Mason as something like a tragedy—am I right?"

Kacey had a mouthful of doughnut so could only nod.

She had caught sight of a whole lot of Drake Mason on screen today and he was a stunning piece of work.

"But now they're both happier than they've ever been," Ethel continued. "Just hang on in there, Kacey, it's all happening for a reason."

The combination of the sweet baked goods and the sweet words of the ladies made Kacey feel a little better.

She'd planned to spend only a couple minutes there, then head back to the Lodge to hide from the world, but she decided to stay. "So, is there anything I can help with?"

"Sure," Aunt Carol said. "We're practicing with chocolate molds for Easter eggs."

"Does that mean melted chocolate?" Kacey asked, her mouth watering.

Dodie grinned and held out an apron toward her. "It sure does."

Kacey took the apron and grinned back. "I'm in."

Between the chocolate and restoration of faith, Kacey was feeling a little better.

Chapter 13

When things seemed overwhelming, Kacey took her broken heart out onto the mountain. Between her baking sessions and her boarding sessions, she was able to keep her mind off Brody for long enough that she didn't spend every day crying.

The worst times were in bed at night, where the loneliness wrapped around her in the darkness, and in the mornings when she remembered what had happened.

No more Kacey and Brody. Now it was just Kacey. Alone.

Ten days went by and she didn't hear a word from Brody. She tried to kid herself that every day got easier, but her heart still felt just as raw on the tenth day as it had the first. Maybe even more so.

This was seeming much more like a

'break-up' than just a 'break.' Kacey sighed.

On the other hand, her boarding was getting better.

Way better.

She was getting so much practice in, she was flying down the course with more style and precision than ever before. Somehow, her pain inspired her to get deeply into focus. It felt almost meditative as everything in the world disappeared except herself, the board and the slope.

She was feeling the twinge in her back much less frequently too, and she allowed herself to dream of the crowds at the Olympics, of the commentators calling out her name. She imagined getting on that podium and taking the Gold Medal, waving to the crowd as the national anthem swelled around her. All of Kissing Bridge would be so proud.

Her dream come true.

Except the part where Brody would be standing next to her...

Not hearing from Brody was becoming unbearable. The only thing that stopped her mind was to move her body. She began training harder then ever to squeeze out all the thoughts that tumbled over and over inside her. It had become her new habit to train all day, sun up until sun down. She knew she was pushing herself way too hard but she was determined to stay busy. That way she would be exhausted and able to fall asleep without thoughts of her and Brody bubbling up to consume her.

It was a beautiful day on the mountain. The new snow the night before had left it in perfect powder conditions. Breathing in deeply at the top, taking the cold mountain air into her lungs, Kacey committed to the toughest series of stunts she'd ever attempted. She had been working on a new trick when she had hurt herself and had not had the guts to try it again. Today was that day. After all, she had nothing to lose. She had already lost the love of her life.

Whoosh, she was off.

First, a front side lipslide. Done.

Then a Japan Air. Perfect, even if she did say so herself.

Next, a Backside Rodeo 720. *Yes!*

Power Method. Hit it perfectly.

Then a Cannonball, a Tailfish, a KB, then a mammoth backside Rodeo Flip off the jump at the bottom of the slope.

Yes! Yes! Yes! Her heart was beating like crazy as she drifted onto the flat. She'd never managed to perfect such a series before.

She felt exalted.

All her hard work, all her deceptions had been for *this*; this perfect moment, this perfect flow, and ultimate connection. It was what she was born for. She knew she was ready for the Olympics, right then and there.

As soon as showed the coaches how well she had healed, she'd be back on the circuit. That way Brody couldn't ignore her.

It had taken all her strength not to pick up the phone and call him, but she'd banned herself from doing so, just like she'd banned herself from saying 'I love you' first. *He'd* have to make the move if he was interested.

But there, standing next to him in the

Winners' Circle, he wouldn't be able to put her out of his mind.

She'd throw down the best new big air trick ever, and he'd remember why they were perfect for each other!

She jumped back on the lift to make one more trip down.

She was ready to try it. She felt in better shape then ever and she couldn't wait to bust this out on the snowboarding crowd. Her creative grab and the "Anderson Twist," as she called, it had never been seen before.

The difficulty was off the charts.

The first time she had done it was by sheer accident. Then it had become her dream, and nemesis. She had practiced it over and over.

It had, in fact, been what she was doing when she herniated her disk in that fateful fall.

But that wasn't stopping Kacey Anderson.

She had to get her signature flip perfected.

Then she'd be unbeatable.

Then she'd have everything she wanted.

Chapter 14

When she'd come down the third time – again, hitting the "*Anderson Twist*" perfect – she came face-to-face with Tanner.

He looked handsome in a black Patagonia ski coat and matching black cap. Kacey was taken aback by his presence. She had thought he had left yesterday with the rest of the camera crew.

"Hey, didn't think you'd still be hanging around Kissing Bridge."

Tanner eyed her mischievously.

"Are you trying to get rid of me?"

Kacey blushed. "No, I…just thought—"

He kissed her quickly it was as if it never happened.

"You're so cute. That was amazing! I wish I could have got that on camera. I thought you might be hungry after all that riding. You want to catch some lunch at the Lodge?" he asked her.

Kacey was still caught off guard by the kiss. She didn't know what to think about that, but her stomach was growling for certain.

She smiled shyly and conceded, "Okay. I am awfully hungry."

Soon they were by the fire, eating huge plates of meatballs and spaghetti—one of Earl's specialties. The fire light flickered off the walls and Tanner's deep dark eyes danced with the mirror images of the flames. Kacey was entranced by how deeply they drew her in. He leant forward and looked deeply into her grey eyes across from his.

"I'm so glad you are training Kacey. That trick was amazing. I see a great future ahead." he said. Although, by the intensity of his stare, she knew he was talking about something much deeper than that moment.

A fluttering in her heart made her look down at the plate, concentrating on cutting a meatball in half.

"Kacey, look into my eyes." His deep voice was gentle, but commanding.

She looked up into them and almost lost herself there. Her own voice sounded far away to her. "Yes?"

He glanced around to check that no one else was in the room. They were alone.

"I am falling in love with you, Kacey."

Suddenly everything in her mind was thrown out of orbit.

"I know we've just met, but I'm leaving Kissing Bridge so soon, and it made me realize I don't want to lose you," he said. "So I'm asking you to come with me."

"Wow," she said, leaning back in her seat.

Her mind was going a mile a minute and her heart fluttered at those three little words that he had just said. How much she had hoped Brody would say those words... She hadn't expected this.

"Where are you going?"

"To the Maldives," he said. "Filming more about climate change, and taking this thing to a whole new level. The

Maldives are the first casualty of the rising temps and we need to be on the forefront of how it's affecting the people on the ground."

"Wow," she said again. The Maldives had always been a place she'd wanted to go, but… "It's the middle of the season, Tanner. I can't just go off to an island right now. I'm training."

Suddenly, that passion that she so admired in him spilled out in his voice. He reached across the table and took her hands in his.

"I'm not a little boy like your other boyfriends, Kacey. I'm not looking to do underwear commercials to fill my pockets. I'm trying to change the world for the better."

She sucked her breath in with the reference to Brody.

Tanner looked at her with love.

"I believe in you, Kacey. I believe you can help me make that difference. There are really only two kinds of people in this world—those who care about making it a better planet, and those who care about themselves. Which one are you?"

Kacey's head was spinning.

She knew he was right.

In the end, history would look back and ask why her generation hadn't done more to help. She began to wonder if she had been going the wrong direction her entire life. Tanner seemed so sure of himself, so righteous, so empathetic. She had never met anyone quite like him. Maybe he *could* change the world.

He saw her confusion as her grey eyes went stormy with conflicted thoughts.

He softened his approach. Tanner lifted her hand to his lips and kissed it gently.

"Medal's are souvenirs. We're talking about our children's future here, Kacey."

"Children?" Kacey was taken aback. "Was that a *hypothetical* child, or are you—"

Tanner's eyes blazed. "I'm saying I want to save the world with you. I want us to be a team. Partners. In our work, and in our life. What do you say?"

Kacey looked down at her hands, her heart in a knot.

She loved snowboarding, and couldn't

imagine giving it up, even if it was for the beauty of the Maldives. She'd spent her life, it seemed, preparing for those medals, preparing for that Olympic moment. Maybe she could do both. Maybe she could have it all.

But…maybe she couldn't.

Maybe like Brody, if she didn't stay with Tanner, she might lose him—as she had lost the connection with Brody.

Tanner was talking *forever*. To save the planet, which truly needed help, to work together to change a dying world, and to do that for the good of all people… What a beautiful, important calling. She imagined herself flying around the world with their children, fighting against big business corruption. His words cut into her reverie.

"I want to marry you someday, Kacey."

This was so sudden. She wasn't even over Brody. But Tanner loved her. He loved the world and wanted to help. He didn't need a break.

"Will you come with me and think about it?"

Kacey gulped, then nodded.

Tanner wrapped his arms around her and kissed her tenderly.

Kacey hugged him back, and felt a surge of emotion fill her like never before.

She also felt divided.

She had loved Brody so much, but he had broken her heart.

Now God had sent her this wonderful man with this beautiful proposal for a new life. She should be jumping for joy.

After her horrible fall, and loss of love, it seemed like everything in her life might be turning for the better. The Olympics were a moment, but she and Tanner would be forever.

"I'm just going to compete in the US Open and then I'll go with you, Tanner. We'll fight this together, forever."

Chapter 15

Kacey felt a new lease on life, like the very air she breathed had a different taste. So what if she still had feelings for Brody? He obviously didn't hold any for her anymore. Maybe time away on a far-flung island with the world's most handsome and passionate activist would do her some good. There'd be nothing there to remind her of Brody and her heartbreak—no colossal mountains, no snow.

Once she'd got the US Open down, she'd be on a plane to a faraway place, where her heart could mend and she could leave the troubles of the past behind.

Of course, she'd have to face Brody there. She looked down at her marriage finger.

Tanner had promised her a ring but

had not picked it out yet. She was happy she wouldn't have to explain a ring to the press or to Brody—not that he'd care.

Kacey planned to put her full heart into training.

She might not be crazy in love, but she felt safe knowing that there was something on the other side for her. She didn't have to worry about her future anymore.

* * *

Kacey headed back to the slope early the next morning, determined to get her big final jump prepared. She knew her signature trick the "*Anderson Twist*" would be something so spectacular, that everyone would gasp. Being unique was the most coveted quality of a snowboarder. Kacey knew she had invented a move like nothing the world had ever seen before. Not only was the move insanely cool, but Kacey was likely the only boarder who had the athleticism to pull it off.

Okay, maybe Brody, she conceded.

She smiled at the thought of "98" she couldn't help but adore him. He really was an enigma—even to *himself.*

Kacey surveyed the run. It looked perfect. She stretched her arms above her head and twisted her body in a quick warm up. She felt good. She felt strong.

She set off down the shorter slope approaching the ridge, grinning, when she imagined Tanner's face when she showed off her perfected version to him.

And as soon as she hit the ledge, she tried to twist and turn in just the right way, but she couldn't hit it the way she wanted. Gosh darn it. Her body was not cooperating! Her back still wasn't healed all the way but she knew she could work around it. She had been training hard and doing yoga daily. She was supple and limber and ready.

Cursing herself as she skidded to a halt, she set off back to the top again, telling herself she just hadn't gotten enough momentum. The second time would be better, definitely.

The next try was a little better, the twisting just a bit more satisfying, but it wasn't at all what she'd imagined.

Darn it.

It was so frustrating having the perfect image in her head and not being able to match up to it.

It had been months now.

She should be back to top shape.

The third try, she told herself she'd do it.

Third time lucky and all that. *This is it,* she psyched herself up, as she stood at the top. She willed success to come her way. If she nailed this, it would be a sure sign she was ready to go back and start training with the team full time. They couldn't deny her ability when they saw this. Inside, she was full of hope that Brody would be impressed as well. He had always told her that the girls just couldn't meet the men in height and difficulty in big airs, and she meant to prove him wrong.

Zoom! She was off, and then she was in the air—twist, turn, twist, turn, twist, turn….she went for the board grab, but it slipped out of her hand. She tried to right herself, but it was too late.

Kacey fell from the sky in a tangled

mess of legs and boards and snow that sent her reeling in a topsy-turvy tumble down the hill at a dizzying height and speed.

"Oh no, no." Kacey thought as she fought to get her board under her for a safe landing. But to no avail. She fell hard.

There was a horrible snap.

Suddenly, everything went black.

Chapter 16

"Oh my goodness," Dodie whispered.

She looked back to see the horror on Jason's face, and her heart twisted with sick worry.

Tubes streaked in and out of Kacey's face and hand. One side of her head and face was black and blue. Her eyes were closed, and the doctors had told the family that she was unresponsive. She looked like a little girl—not like the tough snowboarding champ she was.

When she had found out from Jason that Kacey had been brought into the hospital from a fall, she had assumed it was a sprain or worse—a broken ankle. Looking at her now, she realized things were much worse.

The Anderson parents stood by her bedside, their faces clouded with concern. Dodie could not even begin to imagine what was raging in their hearts.

The Anderson family had another, perhaps much bigger, problem to worry about.

Jason's phone rang and he stepped out in the hallway to take it. He came back after a few seconds, his face white.

"Well, the VIP's checked in with Earl at the lodge two hours ago, but Brad still hasn't come back to home base. That's a ten-minute flight in good weather."

"What about *bad* weather?" Mrs. Anderson asked, clutching her husband.

Mr. Anderson asked for clarification. "So Jason, are you saying that Brad should have been back hours ago?"

Jason nodded. "I didn't want to worry you until he had time to make it back or until I heard from him."

Dodie's heart sank into her feet.

A sudden late blizzard front had started to move in to Kissing Bridge that morning and the whole mountain had been on stand by with extra provisions and supplies to wait it out. People had been warned to stay home and only emergency and state vehicles were allowed on the road. It had been all over the news. With Kacey in the hospital they all had been granted access.

"I've got to go look for him," Jason said.

Mrs. Anderson started to cry. It was all too much.

Jason comforted her. "Don't worry, Mom. I'm going to get the whole of Kissing Bridge out looking for him, if need be. At this point, we need a search team."

He shook his head in disbelief. "I know him. If he changed plans, he'd have called me."

Mrs. Anderson was beside herself. Mr. Anderson held her closely.

"It's a bad time, Annie, but we've gotten through bad times before. We'll get through this too."

He dried her tears. Mrs. Anderson nodded and kissed him sweetly on the cheek.

Dodie noticed how beautiful they were—still in love and now bonded in grief during this difficult time. She could tell theirs was a love that had endured many things.

Dodie spoke up. "The doctor said that with the sedatives they gave her for the pain, Kacey should sleep through the night. Why don't you all go and I'll stay a while longer, just in case she wakes up?"

Mrs. Anderson nodded. She stood up and gathered her belongings.

"Then I best make use of myself. I'll gather the women and we'll do what we can to get a ground plan together."

Jason leant in and kissed Dodie on the cheek.

"Thanks for being you."

Then Jason grabbed his coat and with that, the Anderson clan was out the door.

"God bless you," Dodie whispered, as she watched them rush down the hall and out into the oncoming blizzard.

Chapter 17

Summer finished her shoot on the Malibu pier and the crew was packing it up. It had been a long hot day in the California sun. They had posed the models on the pier, in the sand, on the rocks – and joyous to Summer – she had gotten to ride a couple waves on a surfboard for some 'authentic' surf shots.

They had planned to highlight her on the cover of *Sports Illustrated* and she secretly hoped they'd pick the surf picture instead of her biting her lips, rolling around in the waves.

She smiled to herself. Well, that was over!

She just needed to finish out her contract with Clairol and she was a free agent—or free *model*, in her case. That meant she was free to go where she wanted when she wanted. No more flying around the world at the drop of a dime. No more lonely nights in strange cities with no one but her cat 'Fluff' for company.

In fact, Fluff was a horrible companion to travel with. He always got ruffled after long flights and was extra huffy puffy. It was a version of male feline PMS and not even the super decadent kitty treats would soothe him. He certainly wasn't going to appreciate the gluten-free cat treats she had just bought to help him slim down.

She dried off her long blonde locks and looked at the blazing sun. It shone off her gold bikini, almost blinding her. She hadn't been back to California in a while and the hot sun felt good. But she missed Brad and the cold homeliness of Kissing Bridge. She put on her Gucci sunglasses and watched the waves roll in on Surfrider beach for a moment—wishing Brad was standing behind her, with his arms wrapped around her.

Missing him so badly that she had to hear his voice *right now,* she went back into the makeup truck and fished her iPhone out of her bag. Still no return call from Brad. That was strange.

She knew he was unhappy about her having to go back to work and leave their new life they were starting, but she hadn't any choice. They had argued briefly about it, but in the end Brad knew she was almost as distraught as he was about her having to leave and finish her contract.

He had planned to work on the house while she was away—they both wanted a pool in the sunroom so they could swim year round. It was an ultra extravagance but would be greatly used. She had to be gone for a month to finish off her contracted shoots, so she was excited to think the pool may be done when she got back.

In the meantime, he and Jason were building up their new business *'Aero Anderson'* that specialized in small group excursions to the mountain for skiers and other tourists. With Summer's contacts in the magazine and movie business, it had been easy for her to spread the word and advertise for a "secret special getaway for ski enthusiasts" and stressed out Los Angeles executives. The VIP service was perfect to help local businesses in Kissing Bridge, such as the cafés, the lodge and of course, their new private plane service.

It was working out so perfectly.

Even her having to come to L.A. had, in all actuality, helped build their new business. She had been networking and helping market their VIP service so she could stay home and have their children. She rubbed her flat stomach. Well, she chuckled to herself; she had certainly gotten her money's worth out of that!

She hoped to have it rounded out with a baby on the way by this time next year when she was "Mrs. Brad Anderson"!

Summer had decided to use her month away to engulf herself in networking and to focus on all the minutia for their wedding on Easter weekend. The color theme had been a no brainer—Tiffany blue.

The tables and the bridesmaids would both be sporting the Lander's favorite color. She hadn't broached Dodie yet, but she hoped she would stand up with Summer as her bridesmaid. It looked like she and Jason wouldn't be so far behind them at the altar and she relished having a sister—or sister-in-law—as sweet and loving as Dodie.

Summer smiled to herself. Her dream was coming true.

All those years of hoping and wondering what her life would have been like if she married Brad, and now here it was, just six weeks away.

She was still smiling when her phone rang and she saw it was her mother on the line.

"Hi, Mom! How are you?"

But her smile fell from her face as she listened to her mother's words.

Brad's plane had gone down in the mountains and there was still no sight of the plane, or communication from Brad.

Summer's head began to swim and she clutched the pier railing to steady herself.

Brad was lost.

Summer feared the Landers' curse had hit again.

The tears welled up and spilled from her eyes and rolled into the waves below.

Brad.

Chapter 18

Her Brad.
Lost.

Summer was in shock. She had thought their love could overcome the curse and now fate had stepped in to change the course of their lives.

"I'll get the next plane out," she said dully. She couldn't believe Brad was gone and she was 3,000 miles away.

"Impossible, Darling. I'm sorry," her mother said sadly.

"There is nothing you can do, Summer. All the flights are closed. We're in the middle of a full blizzard. Brad's the only one that would fly in this weather, which is why…"

Summer couldn't control herself and began to weep and shake.

"Mom, I love him. I have to do *something*!"

Ethel's heart swelled with feeling for her daughter, so far away.

"Have heart, Darling. The entire town of Kissing Bridge is scouring the mountain for him now. Jason has insisted on looking for him from above, despite the dangerous conditions. We'll find him, Honey."

"Oh, Mom," Summer sobbed. "Poor Brad. It's all my fault!"

Her mother shushed her on the other end of the line.

"You listen to me, Summer Landers. That curse has been lifted. Brad is going to be found. He's one of the biggest, toughest guys I've ever known, and one heck of a pilot. We're going to find him and bring him home. You are both going to bc happy and safe, and I won't hear anything but that."

Summer nodded on the other end, but nothing her mother said could soothe her heart.

The bright day suddenly fogged over. Summer couldn't think straight. Brad. *Brad!*

"I'm going to call a friend with a

private plane. Commercial flights may not be flying but—"

"Please Summer, please just be safe. Don't put yourself in danger, flying here now in this blizzard. It would be too much! They aren't even letting cars on the road—only emergency personnel and the search crew vehicles. I'll call you as soon as I hear anything. We've set up 'command central' at the bakery and it's open 24 hours with free refreshments for all the volunteers."

Summer held the phone to her ear, but all she heard was a dull drone under the thud of her heart pulsing.

"Have faith, Honey. We're all here and we all love Brad too. We're going to find him."

Summer hung up the phone in shock. She let the wet tears slide down her face.

Brad in danger.

Brad lost.

Gone.

Have faith.

It wasn't a case of the Lander's curse. Summer prayed it wasn't, anyway.

Chapter 19

Tanner paced back and forth in Kacey's hospital room on the phone. His hawk-like face was deep in thought as he listened on the phone and glanced at Kacey, asleep in the hospital bed. She looked beat up. Her face was bruised and she had various cords stuck all over her.

An annoying beep beep from the heart monitor machine taunted his nerves. He had driven the distance from Burlington to see her, and now she looked like she may not even wake up while he was there.

He finally got so anxious that he leaned over the bed and shook her slightly until her eyes fluttered.

"How are you doing, Champ?"

Kacey opened her eyes.

Tanner.

His serious concerned expression and

the worry in his deep brown eyes moved her. She had seen him look like that as he was trying to direct the shots for the documentary. His passion showed when he cared.

He took her hand.

She smiled weakly. "Well, I guess I blew it. My coaches…Brody… they all told me to wait, heal, and get stronger first."

He looked at all the tubes and contraptions all over her. "Did they diagnose you yet?"

"Basics. Broken hip, concussion, herniated disc—again."

Tanner looked dubious.

"Those are the basics?"

"Well, for a snowboarder, yeah. Injuries happen."

Tanner looked relieved.

Kacey was caught by how much she was beginning to rely on his intelligence and strength. Despite all of his business, he had made the two-hour hike to see her in horrible weather.

He behaved very unlike Brody, who had not bothered to call or text in over a month—which, even for him, was a record. The break they were on was turning out to be a break-up, after all. She guessed he just hadn't had the nerve to end it outright—string her on, let her down easy—she guessed. She swallowed hard. She couldn't think about Brody now. Tanner was her future.

Besides, Tanner was here. Tanner loved her. Tanner wanted to be her husband.

Still, Brody haunted her thoughts. She had thought about calling him when she first woke up out of the concussion. It had been Brody that came to her mind first, Brody that showed up in her dream, Brody; the first call she wanted to make.

She needed his lighthearted optimism, his lack of logic and depth of faith. Oddly, that combination had made him the extreme athlete he was. Even his partnership with her was extreme to the pro circuit, and everyone had warned him against it. *Don't get tied down... You're a star... Stay single—the young female fans like to think they have a chance... You're too young...* But they had stayed together anyway, despite all the naysayers.

They understood each other.

Kacey just wanted to call Brody now and hear his voice. She wanted to tell him how she was and what was happening in her life.

She wanted to say, "*Hey baby, I had a horrible fall but I made it. I need you.*"

But she hadn't called, and now it was Tanner who stood over her with a soft, caring look in his eyes.

Tanner Williams, the star activist, was dressed in a tie-dyed shirt that read *Save the Maldives*—his next endeavor. His dark wavy hair fell to his shoulders as he paced the room.

"I had hoped to have us on a flight to the Maldives next week," he said. "Do you have any idea how long until…?"

He knocked into Kacey's exposed foot by mistake. "Oh sorry, did that hurt?"

Kacey looked confused. "What hurt?"

"I just knocked into your leg. I didn't know if it hurt your hip or something."

Kacey screwed up her face. "I didn't feel anything."

Tanner's dark brows drew together.

He walked over and started massaging her foot. “Do you feel that?”

Kacey’s eyes dazed over with a worried look. “No.”

She tried to wiggle her legs.

Nothing.

A look of fear came over Tanner’s face.

“I’ll go get the doctor.”

Chapter 20

The following day the pin striper volunteer nurse, Justine, wheeled Kacey out of the hospital into the bright morning light. The brightness of the light off the snow hit Kacey's eyes hard and blinding.

"Sorry, Kacey," Justine said. "I should have brought you some sunglasses!"

"Oh, you're so sweet, Justine. It's okay. The light feels good on my face."

Kacey and Justine had grown up together in Kissing Bridge and attended the same high school.

"'Worst blizzard since '77' the news is saying…" Justine explained to Kacey. "Only emergency driving is allowed right now and all the stores are closed."

Any other day, the white-out conditions would have thrilled Kacey because that meant fresh snow on the mountain. Powder conditions on the way. She looked down at herself in the wheelchair and sighed heavily. She'd really done it this time.

She wondered about Tanner.

He had been a mess last night.

He'd been so worried. He had left abruptly when they couldn't locate a doctor to help get any straight answers.

Kacey found it odd that he hadn't called to find out what the doctors had determined was wrong with her legs.

She knew he was shocked but somehow she felt slighted.

She had spent the night lying awake, fearing the worst for her future and wishing she wasn't alone.

She could heal from broken bones, but if her spinal cord was affected in the fall, then her fate would be so much worse than she could imagine.

A possible lifetime in a wheelchair.

If she couldn't walk, she couldn't snowboard, and that would be worse than death. It had been the longest night of her life.

For some reason, she had wanted to

call Brody all that night. She wanted him to tell her that everything would be all right like he always did—bring her spirits up and remind her (in that goofy way he always did), *"You're Kacey Anderson, darn it!"*

Goodness knows they had each been through hospital stays and mends together before.

They had been through sleeping on friends' floors and having the bigwigs set them up in 5-star hotels.

They'd seen each other through the Gold and through the sadness of loss, when Brody's mother passed away. They had been each other's strengths. Boy, how Kacey needed that strength now.

She lay awake alone, staring at the ceiling, with that thought running through her head all night, until her doctor had arrived in the morning.

Now as she sat in the wheelchair with the snow falling all around her, as she waited to be picked up, she wondered why she had ever come home again.

The weather was some of the worst she had ever seen in the main town of

Kissing Bridge, nearly whiting out everything in sight. She shielded her eyes from the hurling sheets of white and caught sight of a blurry image coming through the snow toward her.

The image was coming closer, closer…

Out of the storm emerged Tanner.

Kacey smiled.

"You made it! I wasn't sure you Texas guys could drive in the snow," she joked.

The truth was she wasn't sure she'd ever see him again after the way he had looked at her in the hospital bed last night.

It had been the look of the owner of a prize race horse that had just broken its leg.

Sadly, Kacey thought, in a way it was *exactly* like that.

But here he was.

"You can count on me, Babe," Tanner said. The smile he gave her didn't quite make it to his eyes.

He looked her over in the wheelchair and cringed in a covert way.

She smiled weakly.

Kacey *hadn't* been able to count on him actually. She had been afraid—more afraid then she could ever admit—and he had gone home, without a word.

But he was here now. Looking at her uncomfortably.

She wasn't sure how she felt.

Tanner was acting strangely.

Kacey noticed he shied away from getting close to her, as if what she had might be contagious. Suddenly, his eye lit with a great idea and he rushed back to his car and pulled out his equipment bag. He ran back to them and pulled out his camera from his bag and started pointing it at Kacey in the wheelchair.

"What…what are you doing, Tanner?"

He clicked away photos.

"Smile, Honey," he chirped happily.

Click, click, click.

Kacey was agape.

Here she was in a wheelchair—broken and beaten—and he wanted to take shots of her? He wasn't going to ask how she was? What the doctor had said? If she was all right?

"Tanner, what are you doing? Please *stop* shooting pictures of me! I'd rather not have people see me like this."

But Tanner didn't stop. He kept shooting and ignored her pleas.

"Listen, Kacey ... I've been thinking about this all night. We might not have the life together as exploring partners I had hoped to have with you, but we can still use you for the movement as our poster child to garner sympathy! Cripples sell! We'll blame the fall on the bad weather conditions due to the climate change."

He zoomed in on the black and blue side of her face as if intrigued. He brought the camera in for an ultra close up.

Kacey was aghast.

"Did you just say 'cripples *sell*'?"

Tanner pulled back the video camera to get a full view of her entire face, now snarled in contempt.

"Yes. Give it to me, Kacey. Show your anger for what's happened to our world. The camera is *loving* you!"

Kacey felt disgusted.

It seemed that the camera was the *only* thing loving her at the moment.

She looked back at Justine, who shrugged her shoulders and looked completely confused.

Tanner continued on his 'save-the-world' rant.

"People have to know what lengths people are willing to go to help the environment! You are a star victim, Kacey. This is an exclusive! Would-Be-Olympic-Gold-Medalist crushed by climate change."

Tanner got in her face again with the camera—her now *angry* face. She was just this side of swatting it away when he pulled back and changed position.

Now he focused the camera on her unmoving legs covered by a plaid blanket. He panned the camera down her legs slowly, taking video of them.

Tanner narrated along with taking the video.

"Lost limbs—the first tiny victims of climate change left uncontrolled."

Justine reached around and pulled the blanket up over Kacey's legs protectively in the wheelchair as Tanner kept taping.

Tanner continued his sensuous narration.

"Olympic hopeful now lost of all hope. This is the future.

Inert.

Dead.

Just like poor Kacey Anderson's legs."

With that last bit of expose—extra heavy with fake emotion—he turned the camera on himself, and summoned up a look of empathy.

"We can stop this. We can make a difference. Help us. Help the children. Because we can't help Kacey."

With that last dialogue, he actually conjured up a fake tear and pulled the camera in extra close to follow its fall from tear duct to high cheekbone, down to chiseled jaw. He zoomed in with a long pause as the tear wavered on the side of his chin before dripping off his handsome face altogether, and he hit the 'off' button with finality.

He turned to them with a self-satisfied grin.

"That was Oscar-winning shit right there!"

He lifted a hand up to Kacey to high-five him.

"High-five, Kacey, that was great stuff!"

Kacey could not believe it.

She was certainly getting to see a side of Tanner she had never seen before!

He might care about the environment, but it appeared he could give a *fig* about people, or *her*! It looked like he cared more about his movie and being famous than anything else!

Tanner was too busy fiddling with the camera to notice what was going on inside Kacey's head—which happened to be a lot, despite the fall.

Now, Kacey Anderson might have been young, but she was not naive.

Having left Kissing Bridge Mountain at the age of 17, she had been around the world a couple of times in her career and met many kinds of people. Sadly, most of them were not like the good town folk of Kissing Bridge. But it had taught her much about the character of people—or lack of character, in this case.

She realized that she had come across Tanner's type of character before.

The faker.

The user.

The con artist.

They always hid so well, at first.

Acted so nice.

Appeared so handsome.

Told you they loved you and wanted to be with you always. Convinced you they loved you so much you believed them!

Ouch.

The truth was, they were great actors with nothing inside; soulless and heartless with only their egos being important.

Narcissists.

Kacey was forced to consider now that Tanner's entire courtship had merely been a sham to get closer to her fame—to use her for his cause.

All of those loving words of heartfelt feelings and having a future of serving and traveling the world together seemed to have flown out the window now that she appeared broken.

Now she was a just role model for his cause, but what did that mean for her heart? For their future?

She wasn't sure she could handle the truth about this relationship with Tanner. After all the pain she had felt over the loss of Brody, she thought that she had finally found her soul mate in Tanner. As he continued to shoot video of her so thoughtlessly, Kacey was forced to acknowledge how very wrong she had been, once again.

As the sun blared through the clouds, Kacey noticed for the first time the hardness around Tanner's eyes. The set of his lip curled in satisfaction as he got the video shots he wanted and manipulated them to mean whatever he chose. He was, in fact, everything that he hated about the 'establishment.'

A fake.

Tanner continued to shoot footage of the hospital and now close-ups of Justine as well, holding onto her wheelchair.

"Do you think you could wheel her around a bit for an action shot, Sweetheart?"

Before poor Justine could say anything, Kacey leaned to her side and whispered to her, "Just follow my lead, Justine." Justine nodded.

Now, Kacey Anderson had grown up the youngest of five children. She was the only girl and the baby of the family and so had had to endure life with four older brothers ruling the nest. Kacey learned a lot of things from her brothers.

She'd learned how to snowboard like a guy, how to hide the last cookie, pogo off the back of a truck, and how to play poker like a pro.

Late nights at the Anderson house would often find the five siblings seated around the fireplace playing poker with household chores as their chips.

Kacey would bet her laundry chores, Jason the floors, Jeremy the polishing, Jordan the dishes and Brad would bet his snowplowing the driveway. (Nobody wanted that one.) All in all, she had learned a lot from those late night poker games with her wily brothers, and one of those things she learned was how to bluff when you wanted someone to lie down their hand.

So ... Kacey decided to bluff.

"Tanner, my love," she said sweetly, "...Aren't you concerned about us traveling the world and you having to push me in this wheelchair? Won't it hold you back?"

Tanner struggled to keep a smile on his face.

He at least had the decency to put the camera down and knelt down beside her to deliver the bad news.

"You mean this…." He motioned to the wheelchair and her inert legs "… might be for good?"

Kacey bit her lip.

"It's possible…?"

Tanner looked blank.

Kacey pressed on.

"Does it make a difference in how you feel?'

Tanner tried to compose himself.

He looked around at Justine still holding the wheelchair. He cleared his throat loudly.

A few times.

"No, Baby, of course not. I love you for always. Just… I've been thinking about our engagement… and well, I've got places to go, things to do, and they involve legs and not really ... marriage."

Kacey got choked up, but it wasn't on tears.

She wanted to barf at his shallowness.

"You understand?" Tanner continued.

"Of course," Kacey smiled bravely, "Legs are good."

Tanner smiled broadly, now relieved. He packed up his camera equipment and prepared for a quick exit.

"So we'll keep in touch. I'll send you a text from the Maldives."

With that, he scrambled into his bright red mustang car and drove away in the snow storm (which was actually illegal during a white-out, but had been allowed, as he had come to pick up Kacey.)

Kacey watched as his flashy red mustang disappeared in the sheets of white and became a small red dot moving further and further away.

The girls didn't say anything for a long time until it was fully out of sight.

Kacey sighed. "I guess he forgot he was my ride home."

She felt like crying, but decided he really wasn't worth it.

Justine looked concerned. "I ... I'm so

sorry, Kacey. I'm not sure what just happened."

Kacey reassured her.

She had called Tanner's bluff and she had seen his real hand.

"It's okay, Justine. What happened was, he showed his true colors. His true *ugly* colors. I'm fine with it."

Oddly, she realized she *was*.

Tanner had been a great distraction for not dealing with her real feelings for Brody or for her career, but she didn't actually love Tanner.

She knew that now, without a doubt.

Justine was confused. "You could have just told him that the wheelchair was just for a couple of days and that your legs are just fine…"

"Yeah," Kacey smiled, "I could have..."

Then they looked at each other, and they broke out laughing.

Chapter 21

Dodie made her way down the slippery street in the Lander's Bakery delivery van, barely able to see through the blizzard. An officer stopped her and explained that no cars were allowed on the road due to the dangerous conditions.

It was Old Man Jennings' son, Kurt.

Kurt was a lively redhead with a sprinkle full of freckles across his face. He did not make a menacing presence as a policeman, but that fit Kissing Bridge just fine. There was rarely a need for a ticket, nor emergency call, in Kissing Bridge—save a cat in the tree or some other cat-strophe of that vile sort.

"Hey, Kurt! What's going on?" Dodie smiled.

"Hi Miss Dodie, sorry but there's a no-car ban going on right now. It's not safe to drive."

"Oh, I know, Kurt. I've got special permission. I'm on my way to get Kacey out of the hospital. Then we're going straight back to the bakery."

Kurt tipped his hat. "That's a valid reason! Send her my best then, and be careful! It's icy, on top of the bad visibility."

Dodie noticed a red Mustang that was parked by the side of the road. She saw Tanner in the front seat, looking angry. Dodie pointed over to him.

"What's going on with him?"

Kurt looked over to the sulking figure of Tanner.

"Driving violation. I have to give him a ticket. Like I said, no cars on the road except special reasons such as yours, Miss Dodie. Justine, from the hospital, was kind enough to give us a call and alert us about a speeding mustang."

Dodie raised an eyebrow.

Good for Justine.

She always had liked that girl since she had met her in cooking class. It had been Justine that called her from the hospital to ask her to pick up Kacey, and explained what had happened with Tanner leaving.

Dodie was happy to pick up Kacey, and kind of glad inside that he was gone. Tanner had seemed great at first, but ever since she'd met him in the flesh, she couldn't shake the feeling that he was one big phony. Of course, she'd given him the Christian benefit of the doubt, and treated him with kindness, but still, she wouldn't trust him as far as she could throw him.

As Dodie drove away, she saw Kurt writing out a ticket for Tanner and couldn't help but giggle.

When Dodie arrived at the hospital, it looked like an abandoned village.

Barely a car was in the parking lot.

Thc snow continued to fall harder then Dodie had ever seen. She pulled the bakery van right up to the front door.

Justine and Kacey came out when Dodie pulled up. Dodie and Justine helped Kacey into the van. The doctor had given Kacey a new metal hip, as she had fractured her own in the fall, and had managed to bring down the swelling on the unhealed disc that had been pinching her nerve. The pressure from the disc on the spine had caused the initial loss of movement in her legs. Luckily, the pressure had come down, and now all she needed was to stay off her feet for a while until her hip healed.

Her disc was another story. It looked like she had successfully screwed up her career for the rest of the year.

Justine folded up the wheelchair and put it in the back of the van. "Just a couple more days in that and we'll switch you out for some crutches!"

"Thanks for everything, Justine! You're a star."

"I'll bring by some crutches when the blizzard lets up. Best of luck with Brad!"

Kacey was confused, but waved at her as they drove away.

The snow was continuing to fall in crazy sheets of white, making it almost impossible to see. The entire town was snuggled in their homes keeping warm as the town was blanketed in snow. Little lights twinkled from inside windows and smoke billowed out with the smell of fireplaces burning fresh logs.

Theirs was the only car on the road, save for random emergency vehicle or large steel belted trucks trudging by on their way up the mountain.

"Lots of action going on up the hill for blizzard conditions," Kacey said. "That's odd. Hey, Dodie, we missed our turn off."

Dodie bit her lip and focused on the road.

Dodie wondered how best to tell her about Brad.

Kacey had been through a lot, poor kid, but she was going to have to broach the subject sooner than later, especially since she wasn't taking her back to the lodge.

Dodie drove past the turnout to go up the mountain and pulled into the small town village, eventually stopping in front of *Landers Home Baking.*

Kacey smiled. "Need some sweets before we make the hike up the mountain?" She looked around at the busy store with lots of people and big trucks, and her face clouded with confusion. "Looks like the whole town is here…"

Dodie turned to Kacey and took her hands in hers.

"Kacey, I'm sorry but I can't take you back up the mountain to the lodge right now. It's dangerous and it's closed. I've been spending the nights at the Landers in between shifts here…"

Kacey didn't understand why Dodie looked so distraught. "You're working long nights?"

Dodie shook her head. "It's your brother, Brad. His plane went down and he's lost in the mountains up there by Eagle's Peak, we think. We've set up a command post here. They're trying to get the National Guard in tomorrow, but the weather is inhibiting everyone."

Kacey swallowed, trying to digest the horrible news. "How long has he been missing?"

"Three days."

Chapter 22

Dodie and Kacey entered the bakery and the place was in a controlled chaos. Ethel and Carol Landers were busy baking and serving coffee, sweetbreads and sandwiches to the volunteers.

Many of the girls from the cooking classes—including Stephanie, Tassy and Carina—were also there, helping keep people fed and warm. In a corner, were blankets, cots and pillows that had been donated so people could sleep when needed. It was a 24-hour look-out post. Ham radio operators were in one corner. A big screen TV had been brought in to monitor the news and weather.

"I hope Earl is okay," Ethel said to Carol. Earl had the mountain command post up at the lodge where most of the men were gathered for warmth and sustenance between searching.

"Just keep praying," Aunt Carol said back, thrusting a pan of uncooked loaves into the oven.

Kacey watched them for a moment, but then the TV caught her attention. The news cut in showing footage of the blizzard conditions in the northeast, and then switched back to the normal programming. Suddenly a familiar face came onto the screen.

It was Tanner.

At the X-games event, live in Burlington, Vermont.

Kacey was agape. He must have zoomed all the way there in his Mustang! With all that had happened, Kacey had forgotten all about the X-games being so close by.

Tanner obviously had not. He was beginning to remind her of some cockroach that was impossible to get rid of—popping up in all kinds of unexpected places.

Kacey felt a million feelings flood through her at once.

Suddenly, the TV showed a shot of Brody—getting sprayed with Champagne and laden with first-place medals on the winners' podium.

Kacey felt a twinge in her heart as she watched "98." Of course, he was flanked by super models clinging onto him. Kacey felt jealous of each and every one of them. A voluptuous brunette grabbed his face and forced a deep, long lip lock on him. Kacey felt her heart flip over. She turned away from the TV—so as not to watch—but listened as the crowd cheered madly.

Kacey didn't know if she could hold back the tears. It had all been too much. Now Brody was so close, and yet still so far from her. She wanted to burst.

Dodie noticed Kacey's pain and her heart hurt for her. She, of all people, knew what it was like to have your heart broken. She came over and sat by Kacey and took her hand. Their looks at each other spoke all they felt with no words. The roar of the crowd from the TV drew them back. Kacey watched reluctantly.

The stupid brunette was *still* lip locked with her '98.' Ugh!!! Eventually Brody broke free from the supermodel and held up his medal for the press, grinning from ear to ear.

The camera zoomed in on the X-games Gold Medal around his neck before shooting back to the host of the games. With him was Tanner, beaming. Kacey couldn't believe she had ever found him attractive.

He looked so smug and egocentric, Kacey wanted to retch. The host continued, "Now for an inside exclusive by Director and Activist, *Tanner Williams*."

Suddenly, out rolled the inglorious footage of Kacey that Tanner had shot of her at the hospital—onto the big screen.

Tanner's voiceover told the grim tale of America's sweetheart, Kacey Anderson, paralyzed, and her brother, Brad, fiancé of supermodel, Summer Landers, lost in a blizzard."

The town folk had all quieted now and were staring up at the TV, showing video of Kacey at the hospital—earlier in her wheelchair—with snow pelting down, upon her pretty, bruised face. It was awful.

Perhaps the worst thing about it was Tanner's shallow commentary, which profiled her as a victim of climate change! He seemed to care nothing for Kacey or Brad's plight at all, except as it was useful to his platform.

Angry grumblings came from the gathered group at the bakery.

The TV cameras pulled back to show Tanner standing with the host looking intense.

"Kissing Bridge is running out of hope as the weather worsens," Tanner said dramatically. "Join the fight against climate change *NOW!*"

The bakery crowd was dead silent.

"Disgusting!" Aunt Carol finally declared loudly for all to hear, as she thrust a cup of hot cocoa in Kacey's hand.

"Darned if I ever sell that varmint another scone!"

The group cheered in agreement.

Aunt Carol bent down and whispered in Kacey's ear.

"I put a little something extra in that one for you, Sweetheart. Looks like you could use it."

Chapter 23

It was a brisk morning. The weather had actually worsened. People were calling it the worst blizzard in living memory. At least it gave credence to Tanner's documentary about the worsening weather conditions.

The bakery was still steeped in chaos, as the search for Brad continued. Kacey sat at a table in the wheelchair, with a cover quilt over her legs. She still had a little way to go before her legs felt better, but she was optimistic about her future. She bit into a slice of shoofly pie, praying for Brad.

She looked up at the door to watch the old group return from their search, their faces downcast, while the next batch headed out, determined that they would be the ones to find the beloved pilot of Kissing Bridge.

That was when she saw Brody.

He was standing at the door looking uncertain when she noticed him. He was surrounded by men bustling in and out and the commotion of the search.

"Brody!" Kacey called out, her heart suddenly full.

Their eyes locked full of emotion.

Brody ran to her and placed his hands on her legs, ever-so -gently. "I heard what happened," he said—his eyes flooded with concern—real tears cascading down onto his hands. "I am so sorry. I should never have let you leave."

Brody touched the wheelchair and looked up at Kacey. The look on his face told her all she had hoped was true. He still cared about her, even if it was becausc hc thought she was a cripple. She caught hold of his hand and tried to explain.

"It's not—"

Brody stopped her.

"I saw the news, Babe. I know what's up. I'm prepared to deal with whatever comes with you."

Kacey caught her breath.

He still thought the worst.

"Kacey, I know I needed time, but I never meant to hurt you. You hurt me too. You lied to me. I thought we were a team." He took a deep breath and looked at the wheelchair.

Kacey braced herself.

"I'm sorry Brody. You were right. I should have trusted you enough to share with you what was really going on with me. Now look what I've gone and done."

She shook her head. "I'm so stupid. I don't blame you for not wanting to be with me."

"What?!" Brody cocked his head and grabbed one of the wheels on her chair and spun it. "Is that why you think I came here—to breakup with you?"

Now the entire bakery was staring in their direction.

Kacey swallowed hard. "Well, I...I don't want to hold you back Brody. Things are different."

Brody searched her eyes then gently cupped her face in his hands. "I love you, Kacey."

Kacey was stunned.

Those three words! He had finally said them!

He'd never spoken so openly, so passionately. Kacey was incredulous.

"You…you love me?"

Brody looked up at her. "Of course I love you, Babe. You're my Kacey."

He hugged her gently and she couldn't help but bursting into tears.

"I thought you were breaking up with me. Oh, Brody, I love you too!"

The bakery crowd, really unable to not witness the whole event—looked at each other and then deciding applause was in order—broke into uproarious clapping and hooting.

Brady looked around the room and broke into his signature cocky sideways grin. "I let you go for too long already, Kacey. Whatever the future brings now, it's you and me, Babe. I'll roll you around and carry you like a backpack if I have to!"

Kacey caught her breath. She wanted to laugh and cry at the same time.

She wanted to thank God.

Right then, Brody dropped to his knees.

With that, he pulled out a big marquis-cut diamond ring with little diamonds all along the sides. It looked like a diamond snowboard. "I had it specially made." He smiled sheepishly.

Kacey stared at the ring.

The whole time she had thought Brody didn't love her, and he had just been attempting the biggest jump of his life!

The leap into a lifetime commitment.

She tried to jump up and hug him, but then winced back into the chair in visible pain.

"Yes, oh yes, Brody, of course!"

He hugged her tenderly.

"I'm afraid I don't want to hurt you by squeezing so hard."

She looked at him deeply, the love shining in his eyes.

"Oh, you're not going to hurt me, 98! I'm going to get better. *All of me* is going to get better."

Brody looked at her legs covered by the wool blanket. She stuck her stockings out and wiggled her toes and feet.

"I'm going to walk! This chair is only

temporary until my hip heals. Heck, I'm going to snowboard. With this bionic hip I might even be better!"

Brody looked confused.

"You... you mean you're not paralyzed like Tanner said, you're all right? I mean ... You're going to be okay?"

She grabbed his face and kissed him with the biggest smile she had ever worn.

"Yes, Sweetheart!"

Brody's smile spread from ear to ear and he jumped up with a hoot and holler.

"Gosh darn, I'm getting married!"

A cheer went up in the bakery. That was the best news the townspeople had heard all day.

Chapter 24

The odds for Brad being found alive were looking slim. The blizzard had continued to get worse and no government help was coming.

The town's men were exhausted after days of relentless searching with no sight of Brad. The rescue groups were all huddled together on this gloomy full moon night in the Lander's bakery and hope was running out. If they didn't find Brad soon, he wouldn't survive. Between the freezing conditions and the lack of food and water, no one could make it out alive.

Jason was leading the rescue group. After days of finding nothing, he had been going over and over in his head trying to guess what might have happened and what he might have missed. He knew about planes, and he knew about survival. Being a marine had taught him that with a strong mind and strong body, you could overcome even the toughest obstacles. It had been three and a half days since Brad's plane went down.

Jason's best guess was Brad was trying to avoid the heavy winds coming in from the west side, and tried to circle around the south side of the mountain to avoid the oncoming storm. He must have gotten caught, the storm front must have moved in to quickly. Between the blizzard winds and the snow falling heavily, the logistics of finding Brad was becoming tougher and tougher. The likelihood that he had taken the route, Jason surmised, meant his plane may have landed on the most southern severe drop side of Eagle's Peak.

It was so dangerous, they couldn't get any emergency equipment in there in normal conditions, let alone the blizzard ones currently happening. They had tried to get Jason's plane in but it had almost become another disaster with Jason having to abort the mission and barely making it back to home base.

Some mountaineers in the group had tried to repel down the mountain but the blizzard hadn't abated and they couldn't see further than a foot ahead of them. Fearing they would have more casualties, they too had had to return back.

A sense of hopelessness hung in the air, as the men refreshed themselves and warmed up by the fire. Finally, Jason stood up and declared, "I'm going to take a skidoo down the back of the south side and see what I can find."

He pointed to one of the mountaineers. "Duke said he was sure he saw a shot of red in the white drifts down below, and we all know nothing in nature is red in the winter."

The crowd nodded. That was just good sense.

"So I'm going to head in that direction and I'm hoping you'll all pray for me."

With that there was a dead silence, until Mrs. Anderson stood up.

She faced her son defiantly, hands on her hips.

"I will have none of it! I will not have

you risk your life, Jason Anderson! It's enough I have one son to worry about. We all know its suicide to attempt to go down that vertical slope on the south side with a skidoo."

The crowd bowed their heads to her. It was true. She had been the only one bold enough to say it. Taking a skidoo down that slope was a death wish.

"I could go on my snowboard." Brody blurted out.

Everyone turned and looked at the new-comer like he was nuts.

Go down the back hill of the mountain?

On a snowboard?

It was crazy.

Then they remembered.

He was Brody Jenkins.

He had done *crazy* before to the tune of three Gold Medals.

Even so, it was still life-risking.

The crowd erupted in chatter over what to do.

Brody stood up. "I'll go. I can get down that mountain where no other vehicle can. You said it yourself, you can't get in by air, you can't get in a snow vehicle—but I can get there on my snowboard."

The townspeople looked at him aghast.

But he was right. He might be their last chance.

As much as Kacey wanted to keep him away from the danger, she believed in him.

And she needed her big brother.

Brody insisted. "Look, I know you all don't know me, personally. But I'm not going to let someone die because I didn't try."

The bakery crowd looked at him in silence not knowing what to say.

It wasn't as if they had many options.

"So," Brody continued. "I'm going to try."

Kacey's voice trembled. When she spoke up.

"Brody...I know if anyone can do it, *you* can."

She turned to her brother Jason.

"Let him try, Jason."

Jason looked Brody up and down then

called him over to the table where they had maps out with likely spots the plane went down. He briefed Brody on what they knew.

"We usually go this pattern," he said, tracing his finger on the table, "and if he got caught in a weather pattern, it would be right here. It's the only place we haven't been able to get a crew to, and with the wind, we can't get a plane or helicopter in there either."

"I got it," Brody said.

"We need to find him. We don't have any time left to wait for the government emergency help."

* * *

As first light dawned, Brody stepped onto his snowboard, strapped with a backpack of food, water, blankets and an extra snowboard on his back. He took the lift up to the top of Eagle's Peak and made his way to the southern backside of the mountain that was a sheer drop off.

No riders were ever allowed on this side of the mountain. From here, it was straight down to certain death. Thanks be to God, the blizzard had subsided for the time being, and it looked like Brody had a lucky window of visibility.

Brody looked down the steep vertical slope slicked with ice. Taking deep breaths and praying, Brody secured his straps. He tried to psych himself up. It was just another run. Just another pro course with its own challenges. Don't think about it—just make it happen.

Jason had taken the ride up the lift with him and now stood peering down the ledge of the mountain with him. He encouraged him with some last words.

"Just look for the red. The plane is bright red, even if the tip is out of the snow, you will see it. We're all praying for you, Brody."

Brody nodded.

"You're our last hope."

Jason patted him on the back, not sure how to convey how much he felt. "…And thank you."

With that, Brody nodded, and then pushed off hard and headed down the perilous mountaintop in the blizzard, in search of Brad.

At first, Brody had some semblance of control. He zig-zagged back and forth down the vertical incline in an attempt to keep his speed down while he searched below for Brad's plane.

As he continued down the hill, it got steeper and steeper. He began to move faster and faster unable to slow himself down. Brody held his breath, realizing he was losing his ability to swerve. Soon it was a free for all, and he was shooting straight down the mountainside at a dizzying speed.

Brody looked for a flat edge to maneuver toward, but nothing was in sight. He was racing straight down the side now, in a pure vertical drop. Suddenly he started to lose hold onto the board. It started to slip out from underneath him. He grabbed hold of it, just as he was suddenly sent flying off the side of the cliff in a complete free fall without a landing in site.

Sailing over a sea of white snow.

At first Brody was filled with pure fright.

Then he was filled with adrenaline.

Then he went into X-game champ mode.

His pro snowboarding expertise came in handy as he searched for a landing. His eagle eyes spotted a flat patch below to the left.

Bingo.

First stop, left ledge three feet wide, 500 yards down.

He straightened out his stance trying to lengthen and stretch the jump and time it just right so he could make the ledge.

He landed with a hard fall.

Eureka!

He hit the mark he had aimed for. He skidded the board to a dead stop and had to make a quick grab for it as it threatened to careen over the side.

Yes, I'm alive.

Some snow let loose from the ledge and Brody had to step back as a bunch of snow broke off and hurtled down the side of the cliff.

Looking down the steep drop, Brody contemplated his next move, and suddenly he caught sight of something bright red standing out from the white snow. Brody squinted his eyes trying to make out what it was.

Yes, that was it!

Brad's plane!

Jason had described the red plane with the white *Aero Anderson* logo to him, and sure enough, there it was.

But it was further down from where he was, and he couldn't see a way to get down there—definitely *not* with his board.

Brody considered his options.

His board was all he knew.

His comfort zone. His area of expertise.

But it had to go.

He unstrapped his board from his feet and strapped it to his back with the other snowboard. The only way down to Brad was to climb. His hands shook and it felt like his heart raced a thousand beats per second, but everyone was counting on him.

He *had* to do it.

Brody climbed out onto a slim ledge of ice, and looked down to find somewhere to put his foot further down. He found somewhere and soon he had the hang of it—looking for places to put his hands and feet—knowing that a single misstep could cost him his life—and potentially *Brad's*.

At one point, his foot slipped and he felt a downward surge as it dangled free—threatening to take his whole body with it, plunging down into the depths—and to death. But he managed to get it back in place. After a long half hour of slow downward scaling, Brody had reached the wreck site.

He made his way over, stepping gingerly onto the plane's wing to peer into the cockpit.

Yes, there was Brad! Obscured by the plane door, but definitely there.

"Brad!" Brody called out, but there was no response.

He bent down and pried open the pilot's door.

Brad was in a heavy-duty snowsuit, with a hat covering his head and neck, and goggles covering his eyes. That was a good thing, as all of these would retain his body heat. On the cold of the slopes, the right clothes could save your life.

"Brad!" Brody tried to wake him, but to no avail. He was breathing shallow—but *alive.*

Brody realized he would have to drag him out, no easy feat, as Brad was a large man.

Brody tried to get a hold on Brad, but Brad was bigger than him, and it was a struggle. But Brody knew that he was everyone's last hope, and that gave him a strength he didn't even know he had. Pulling with all his might, he finally managed to get a limp Brad out onto the wing of the plane.

Next was the seemingly impossible task of getting him onto the larger shelf ledge a little lower down. That would be the only way to get them away from the tunneling wings that boomed through the mountains, bringing deluges of snow in its billows.

Brody scanned the mountain looking for a possible path.

After some quick thinking, Brody untied the extra snowboard and secured

Brad to it with the ropes. It was a makeshift solution, and not perfect by any means, but it looked like it would work for the moment. He strapped his own board back on, and began to make slow progress down toward the ledge, trying everything he could to keep their speed down. He knew that slow and steady was the way to go. One error could send them both flying off the ledge and find them buried in the thick snow—never to be seen again.

After a scary traverse of the snowy, steep mountain, they made it to the larger ridge. Brody breathed a sigh of victory and sent up a little prayer of thanks to God. He whipped out his phone, praying that the mountain reception wouldn't fail. Jason answered right away.

"I've got your brother."

He smiled as he heard Jason relay the news to everyone else at the Landers' Bakery and cheers of joy erupted. But it wasn't over yet. They didn't even know if Brad would regain consciousness.

Jason lowered his voice and asked, "How is he?"

Brody looked over at Brad.

"Dude, I think he's going to make it. I've seen guys stuck out in the winter conditions before that looked way worse, but he's unconscious."

Jason sucked in his breath hoping the extraction would be easier then he thought, and they could get Brad straight to the hospital.

"Where should we pick you up on the snowmobiles?"

Brody explained to Jason where the ledge was they were safely on—luckily close to the bottom, and easy access for the snow mobiles.

* * *

After a little while, the snowmobiles arrived.

Jason helped Brody lift Brad onto the back of one. He leaned over his brother and felt his face. Still warm; good sign. He checked his hands for snow burn but they were luckily encased in thick warm gloves, and thus unharmed. He breathed a sigh of relief.

Jason shook Brody's hand.

"You're a good man, Brody. We'll never forget what you did today. risking your life for our brother. You're a real hero."

Brody blushed for maybe the first time in his life, as they took off down the mountain, as fast as they could, to where ambulances waited for them.

Chapter 25

Brad woke up to find Summer bent over the hospital bed. "I took the first flight I could get out."

Brad shook his head, trying to clear his mind and remember what happened. He looked over the other side of his bed to see Kacey and Brody standing there, clutching each other's hands and smiling from ear to ear.

"Hey, Bro!" Kacey said. She reached out her hand to take his. His eyes focused in on the wheelchair.

"Don't worry. It's temporary. Just worry about yourself!"

Brad wanted to say more but he was weak.

"How did I get here? What happened?"

"Brody saved your life."

Summer leaned over him and pulled a

lone strand of hair off his face affectionately.

Brad rifled through his memories. The plane, the storm, the crashing descent. "Oh my gosh."

"I'm so glad you're all right," Summer cried all over him. "I love you *so* much."

"And I love you," Brad said, tears welling up in his eyes. It all seemed like a strange dream, but he knew life would never be the same again. It would be so much richer, so much fuller of the importance of family and love and everything that he loved about life.

"Thank you, Brody," he said. He wanted to say so much, more but the words caught in his throat. All he could do was cry right along with Summer and pull her close until they cried all over each other, their tears of relief and love mingling together until they were one stream.

Chapter 26

"You know, I really love Kissing Bridge," Brody said. "I can't believe I never wanted to come here before." Brody had been reluctant to do the whole meeting her family thing, but now, it was all he could talk about. They strolled through Kissing Bridge, gloved hand in gloved hand, beaming at each other. "I'd love to spend more time with you here."

"I love it too, and I never used to appreciate it," Kacey said. "Sometimes I think you need to be away from something for a while to appreciate how much you need it; how much you love it."

"Like you," said Brody, pausing to kiss her on the nose. "I knew I cared about you, but I really had no idea how much, until you were gone."

But then he said something that really surprised her.

"I'm thinking that it might be the right time to retire after the 2018 Korean Olympics."

"What? Really?"

"Yep," he said.

Kacey was floored. "I'd never thought I'd hear you say that. What's brought this on?"

He stopped, taking both her hands in his, and looking at her.

"You. Or this. This whole thing. These past few weeks. I've learned so much."

Kacey loved this change in him.

Not only was he his usual bouncy self, there seemed to be a new dimension to him. A deeper one, a smarter one.

"What did you learn?" she asked.

"I learned that I really want *this* kind of life," he said. "This place has a real sense of community. It just made me realize how empty all these crazy parties are. I'm bored with the whole snowboarding crowd; not the snowboarders themselves, but the whole thing that surrounds it."

Kacey instantly thought of the supermodels that fawned all over him. "I can agree with that."

"We've traveled the world already," he said. "And I know we want the medals. But why don't we just train together for the Olympics, and then call it a day with all the competitions?

I mean, it's nice to win, sure, but at the end of the day, it's a piece of metal hanging around your neck. That's all."

Kacey was so taken aback, she didn't know what to think, or say, but it didn't matter much, because Brody was on a roll.

"I mean, I was so mad at you when I found out you were training, but then I thought, how could I really blame you? When I was so focused on winning at all costs, and being so single minded—like snowboarding was all that mattered in the world. But to me, Baby, it doesn't matter if you ever snowboard again. If you want to, that's great, if you don't want to or you can't, that's totally cool… I guess what I'm trying to say, is that our relationship is about so much more than snowboarding. It goes deeper than that."

Wow. The words she'd always wanted to hear from him, pouring right out of his mouth. It felt like something close to a miracle.

"I do want to board again," she said. "I love it so much."

"I know you do, Babe. We both do."

"But I want to stay here, too. We can train up the mountain here until the Olympics. And after that, we can come back for good."

"That sounds awesome." Brody looked all around at the quaint small town and beamed from ear to ear. Kacey had never seen him so happy.

Suddenly, an idea popped into Brody's head and his eyes widened with excitement. "And we could open a snowboarding school!"

Kacey grinned and lifted her hand up. They slapped hands in a high-five. "That's what *I'm* talking about, 98."

Then he gathered her up in a kiss that made her feel like she was the only woman in the whole wide world.

"I love you, Brody Jenkins."

"And I love you, Kacey Anderson, though you won't be *that* for much longer."

Chapter 27

So came the day that so many had been waiting for—though none more eagerly than Brad and Summer—the day that Summer would finally put the Landers ladies' curse to rest; shedding her Landers name to become Summer Anderson.

Both Ethel and Aunt Carol had tears in their eyes as they linked their arms in with Summer's outside the church doors. Summer, however, was beaming from ear to ear—her heart fluttering with the promise of a bright future.

"I can't believe my baby's getting married," Ethel said.

"*Our* baby," Aunt Carol said, dabbing at her eyes.

Summer gave them both a hug, but then said, "You'd better believe it. By the end of today, I'm gonna be a married woman."

She turned around and flashed a smile at her bridesmaids, Dodie and Kacey. They both wore beautiful Tiffany Blue gowns.

Summer wore a beautiful white dress that made her resemble a Greek goddess. It was modern and classic all in one—just like the one Summer had always dreamed of—with a long tail and plunging neckline. Her golden hair was pulled up into an elegant bun and adorned with white roses and sprinkles of silver ice. She looked like a fairy tale princess.

Then the music started playing; the beautiful orchestral music Brad and Summer had picked out together.

"This is it!" Summer whispered, and the doors opened in front of them.

The church was packed to the brim with everyone from Kissing Bridge, all looking back toward her and smiling. Summer couldn't help but burst out into a happy laugh.

She began her walk down the aisle, flanked by her mom and Aunt Carol, who couldn't have looked any prouder.

Then she looked down the aisle and saw Brad.

Brad.

The man who still made her heart flutter; the man who she could truly be herself with. She couldn't wait for them to move in together into their beautiful new house. She was so glad they'd saved that pleasure for marriage. It would all mean so much more.

He looked so handsome in his black tux. His grey eyes soft, and full of love. He looked at her in such a tender way that she felt it, deep down in her heart. His father, Jason, his two other brothers, and Brody all stood up beside him.

She was moved by how much each of them meant so much to her.

Aunt Carol and Mom patted her arm and smiled down the aisle with her, and she felt she could never be happier than she was right then, surrounded by people who all loved her so much.

The town pastor stood at the front, smiling at all of them.

Soon all her beloved friends were lined up together awaiting her, the bride.

When Summer reached Brad, everyone else fell away.

She gazed deeply into his gray eyes.

"I love you," she whispered.

"I love you," he whispered back, gazing just as intently at her.

They were always meant to be together. This day would seal their love forever.

"The happy couple has chosen to compose their own vows," the pastor said.

"Summer, if you would like to go first."

Summer had memorized them by heart. "I love you with all I am, all I have ever been, and all I ever will be. I love you, Brad, with all my heart and soul, and now this is my proof."

Dodie handed her the ring; a heavy, thick band of gold.

"This ring is the offering of me to you, of my heart, my soul, my body, my health, my everything. All I have and all I will ever be blessed to have, is yours. I am yours and always will be yours."

With that, she slid the ring on his

finger, then wiped away the single tear that fell from his eye.

Jason handed Brad a matching gold ring, just a little bit more delicate.

"Brad, would you please make your vows," the pastor said.

"Summer, today I make the biggest promise one heart could ever make to another. I vow to be your constant support and your home, your place of calm and comfort, your respite from the trials of life and the world. My heart, my soul and everything I am belongs to you, and you alone. You are the most amazing woman I've ever known, Summer, and I pray to God that I can be the man you deserve, and make you feel like the queen that you are, every single day. I love you, Summer, with every fiber of my heart and my being. I am yours, forever."

"I now pronounce you husband and wife," the pastor said, as the church erupted into cheering. "You may now kiss the bride."

There was not a single dry eye in the church as Brad and Summer leant in to kiss each other. Aunt Carol was in floods of happy tears, and Ethel looked proudly on. Her little girl had finally come home and the Lander's curse was lifted after all.

* * *

The whole town was at the reception.

Aunt Carol and Mom had prepared it in an Easter theme, every table decorated with chocolate eggs emblazoned with silver and, of course, Tiffany blue. There were white roses on every table, too, and each name was carved into the chocolate eggs instead of place cards.

"It's lucky Kissing Bridge is so darn cold," more than one person joked. "Otherwise no one would know where they were sitting!"

Summer and Brad made the most exquisite couple. It might have been nearly impossible to have ever seen two people so happy. Brad beamed like he had won the Superbowl and Summer had a glow that only a new bride can have.

Mother caught site of Earl across the room, talking to Kacey and Brody. He winked at her and she blushed at having been caught eyeing him up. Aunt Carol bustled up to her with a smile so wide, you could barely see her cheeks anymore.

"Well, well, Ethel, this is a most glorious day. Plus the curse is officially finally lifted."

Ethel smiled back at her. "Yes, it is a glorious day, praise be to God. It's a great day for the Landers' ladies, Carol!"

Aunt Carol hugged her sister closely.

"Maybe you're the next Landers to go down the aisle?"

Ethel couldn't help but smile. "Certainly anything is possible after this last week of excitement!" Aunt Carol nodded, her red beehive bouncing back and forth in agreement, as she looked around the room at all the lovers. It had been one heck of a week, but love had won out in the end!

If it hadn't been for Brody's true love for Kacey, there would have been no saving Brad, and no wedding. If he hadn't shown up when he did to declare his feelings, then none of them would have had anything to celebrate.

Jason walked by and stopped to talk

to the ladies. He looked very handsome in his grey tux that matched those wonderful Anderson grey eyes. He gave each of the ladies a quick hug.

"Looks like we are officially family now."

Ethel beamed. "Yes. Lucky us!"

Aunt Carol smiled at Jason. It was nice to see him so at ease and rested. He had looked so worn out when he first got back home after years overseas as a Marine. He had seem defeated, sad and lonely. Now he was joyous and happy, and Aunt Carol guessed exactly why.

"Seems like maybe you might be the next one to consider settling down Jason," she tried to coerce him into telling his true feelings.

Jason leaned over and said into Aunt Carol's ear "You'll be the second to know." With that he sauntered away with a sly look on his face.

Aunt Carol looked after him suspiciously. Had her eavesdropping skills let her down? She had heard no inklings about town of any marriage rumours. Hmmmm.

She decided she best go take her ears about the room and see if she had missed anything, and off she went.

It was time to dance, with the lovers' classics playing, Brody helped Kacey to her feet. She was newly off her crutches and feeling much better. He pulled her closely on the dance floor and whispered in her ear. "If you can't manage, you just tell me, and we'll stop right away."

But Kacey didn't want to stop. She couldn't get enough of being close to Brody, of breathing in his smell, of feeling his stubble against her cheek. She closed her eyes and drifted away to the music, feeling wrapped up in romance.

Ethel watched all the young lovers dancing under the twinkling lights and thought how lucky she was. The beauty and the music and the love filled the room. She felt a warm arm go around her waist and turned to see Earl smiling at her tenderly.

"Would you do me the honor of a dance, beautiful lady?"

Meanwhile, Jason and Dodie were seated at the wedding table, surveying the guests all dancing. Jason took a bite out of his chocolate egg, chomping into his name iced on, in Tiffany blue writing. He glanced over at Dodie, thinking to himself how gorgeous she looked.

"Honey, take a bite out of your name tag egg. It's delicious."

Dodie laughed. "No babes, I'm going to save that." She ran her finger over the little bumps that formed her name.

"It's so cute!"

Jason laughed right along. "You're the cute one here. How are you going to save a chocolate egg?"

Dodie shrugged. "I don't know – in the freezer."

Jason hugged her.

"You are so adorable and old fashioned. I love that! Take a bite of yours, go on. Please. It's the best chocolate ever. Summer's mom made them up special at the bakery."

Dodie raised an eyebrow.

Nothing usually got by her at the bakery, as she was there most days helping out and/or teaching classes.

She shrugged and took a bite, curious

now. She chewed. Hmm, he was right. It *was* extra nice. She put the egg down and looked at Jason. "Delicious."

He nodded. "I especially liked the inner center."

Dodie picked up the egg to check out the special center, and a brilliant gleam came from inside the chocolaty depth. She picked it up and shook it out.

Much to her surprise, a beautiful diamond ring fell out onto the table.

Dodie gasped.

By the time she turned around, Jason was on his knees. Dodie thought she must be dreaming. She had thought she was going to spend her life with another man that had left her out in the cold at the last moment. There had been the promise of a ring that had never been delivered on. Now here she was, with this amazing man down on his knees, with a gleaming diamond in his hand. At that moment, she realized that God really *was* looking out for her. That a door never shuts without a window being opened. *Here* was her window.

"How about it, Dodie? Make an honest man out of me?"

Dodie threw her arms around Jason and hugged him, then kissed him, then hugged him.

He laughed and finally held her back to look into her big blue eyes. "Will you marry me, Dodie, and make me the happiest man in the world?"

Dodie's eyes filled with tears.

She had never thought she would be able to love again, and now she knew God had just been preparing her for her real true love, Jason—her whole life.

"Yes, darling. Oh *yes!*"

With that, he lifted her high into the sky and twirled her around for all to see.

Summer came over. "Is this what I think it is?" She looked down at the ring on Dodie's finger.

"You bet," Dodie said, grinning.

Summer whooped. "We're going to be *real* sister's now, Dodie! I am so happy for you both!" She motioned for Brad to join them.

Brad disengaged himself from a group of guests and appeared with the perma-grin from the chapel still on his face. He looked back and forth at the group, and then Dodie held up her hand. The engagement ring now on her finger glistened off the chandeliers.

Brad hugged his brother tightly, and then Dodie too. He slipped his arm around his new bride and looked at her like the sun looks at the flowers.

"I'm the luckiest man in the world. And if I never believed in miracles, standing here right now with all the people I love, I know I'm in the middle of one."

Suddenly a chorus of tinkling spoons to champagne glasses filled the room—the traditional calling for a kiss from the newly-married couple.

Brad scooped up Summer and kissed her tenderly. Summer swelled with joy.

Suddenly, he pulled back and looked at her with a big grin on his face.

She smiled back.

"Why are you looking at me like that, honey?"

Brad lifted his voice for the whole room to hear.

"Because, it just occurred to me, Mrs. Anderson, that the Landers' family curse has officially been lifted!"

A cheer rang out from the guests and

everyone clapped.

Summer threw herself so hard and so unexpectedly into Brad's arms, that they fell over in a tumble, knocking over a table, and landed with a thud on the floor.

The crowd went deadly quiet.

Then of course, cracked up laughing.

Aunt Carol and Mother attempted to help them up and untangle them from the yards of gossamer satin and lace of Summer's dress, and the tablecloth they were both wrapped up in—but to little avail.

Soon Mom and Aunt Carol were just as entangled in the mess—as Summer and Brad—and they all ended up together sprawled in a big heap on the floor, laughing.

Why shouldn't they?

Love was everywhere.

Brad and Summer were married.

The Landers' curse had been lifted.

It just might have been the happiest most wonderful Easter in Kissing Bridge ever!

The End

Firework
Kisses
and
Summertime Wishes
A Fabulous Feel Good Holiday Romance
Linda West

Firework Kisses and Summertime Wishes

A Fabulous Feel Good Holiday Romance

BY
LINDA WEST

Morningmayan.com Publishing

Dedicated to my Mother
Thanks Mom for being the best

If you haven't read the first three in the
#1 Best selling series
"Love on Kissing Bridge Mountain"
please check them out!

#1
Best
Seller

Chapter 1

"But I thought…I thought… you loved me…" Elle Saunders stammered trying to hold back the tears from falling from her big green eyes.

She looked around the fancy restaurant in Burlington that her boyfriend Todd had taken her to and realized what a fool she had been.

"When you said you wanted to have a serious talk, I thought you were going to ask me to marry you..."

She sucked back the tears that fought to flood down her freckled cheeks as she stared at the menu, not even seeing it. Her Irish red hair hung about her face and for once she had no inclination to pull it back as she usually did. Now it afforded her some kind of privacy, shielding her from Todd's staring.

Whoever thought that a public place was the appropriate spot to end a three year relationship was obviously not someone who had ever gotten their heart broken before!

She stared at the menu trying to look concerned about the dinner choices while holding back her tears.

Todd was unusually quiet for him.

She had never seen the break up coming.

The bouncy duo had been the most popular couple in Kissing Bridge High. They had started dating as freshmen when Elle was a cheerleader and Todd was the varsity quarterback. It had been love at first sight and Todd had chased her and courted her until she couldn't resist.

Elle, who had always been an awkward child, was overwhelmed by the attention of the class president and most popular boy in school. She could barely believe he liked her. Both his parents were prominent lawyers and the whole family was always in the papers at some exciting event or another.

They had the perfect family and they had let Elle be a part of it. She had found what it was like to have a real family for the first time.

She had always dreamed when she was young that her hero, her prince, her knight, would come and whisk her away to forever happiness.

Todd was that guy, her hero.

They had been a couple ever since.

After three years together everyone expected them to get engaged and despite the fact he had set his sights on an out of town college for his law degree she had never thought it would come between them.

Until this moment.

Todd cleared his throat across the table.

"Don't cry Elle. I just think we need to see other people we're young and we need experiences."

Elle couldn't look at him.

Couldn't let him see how much this devastated her. He seemed almost irritated now.

"Come on, Elle, you'll see you'll find someone awesome for you."

"I thought I had," she mumbled in disbelief. "You… you don't love me anymore...?" It squeaked out of her like a rusty hinge.

Todd looked around uncomfortably.

"I'll always love you, Elle, you know that. Heck, we practically grew up together. You're my best friend."

She lifted her eyes to meet his.

"Then why are you doing this, Todd? Maybe we just need a break for a minute, or a vacation away..."

She looked up into his eyes, daring to hope.

After a moment of looking like he was sitting in the dentist's chair, he leant forward and blurted out, "I'm in love with someone else Elle. I'm sorry."

The restaurant spun around. She clutched the sides of her chair and barely recognized the squeaking voice that came out of her.

"Who?"

He let out a loud sigh. "Buffy Adams."

Buffy Adams. A vision of long blonde hair and preppy perfectness popped into her head.

Elle had often seem them together on the college campus when she met Todd for lunch, but it had never occurred to her that Todd might be having romantic feelings for her!

Now she realized how naive she had been!

"We both got accepted at UB law school," he explained. "We're leaving tomorrow for freshmen orientation."

The floor dropped out from underneath Elle and she felt like she was falling through Alice's looking glass. This couldn't be happening. This was all a bad dream. She had thought they were getting engaged when instead he was in love with someone else.

Leaving with someone else.

How had this happened?

"You know it was just a hometown thing with us, Elle, you couldn't expect it to last forever." He gave her a pathetic shrug.

She swallowed hard facing the truth.

"Just say it, Todd. I have no pedigree for you to leapfrog off of. A future Senator needs connections. I've heard you say that a million times. "

He stared over his menu and whispered to her.

"It's different. She's different. I'm sorry Elle but I have to make the best choices for my future. The right wife is an important part of that."

Elle wiped a lone tear away quickly, and then looked through her purse for a hankie.

She caught sight of her nails as she did so. Darn it, she had forgotten to paint them before dinner! Working with the horses and helping at the diner was a tough combo on a girl's hands. The sight of them made her realize just how far away from each other they really were.

She glanced over at Todd's perfectly manicured man hands and felt kind of grossed out. No man's hands should look that unused, in her opinion.

But Todd wanted a girl with hands as pretty as his.

Elle recalled Buffy always had perfect nails.

Drat her!

Didn't that girl ever work in her life?

But of course Elle knew the answer to that. Buffy came from a rich and prominent family. She had never worked a day in her life.

They couldn't have been more different.

The perfect heiress bent on law school. The free spirited orphan that just longed to have a family.

She had thought that's what Todd wanted as well. But she was wrong.

Todd wanted Buffy.

Elle stood up and tossed her long beautiful red locks away from her face and collected her things to leave.

As she raised from the table her green eyes flashing she leaned in and whispered to him.

"I thought you were my hero. I would have loved you forever. You're going to regret this Todd Vanderling."

With that she swept out of the room, leaving him gaping behind her and not realizing the amazing acting job she had just pulled off.

As she strode toward the door she realized she didn't have her car with her.

She rummaged in her purse to find her phone, and then dialed the Inn.

Her grandpa Earl answered.

"Eagle's Point Inn. May I help you?"

All of Elle's bravado fell away when she heard his familiar loving voice.

"Grandpa, it's me…."

Earl's voice changed immediately at the sound of her voice.

"Murielle? You don't even sound like you. What's going on, darling?"

"I, I'm in Burlington. I don't have a ride home…" Her tears overcame her now she was alone and she sobbed, unafraid to be real with the one person who knew her best.

"Darn cell phones, Grandpa."

"Stay put, sweetheart. I'm coming to get you."

Chapter 2

Earl Elkins and Ethel Landers were soon in the car on their way to get Elle. Earl was unusually quiet and not his normal bouncy, happy self. Ethel could tell he was worried. When he had gotten off the phone and said he needed to go to Burlington right away she had just nodded and got in the car with him, no questions asked.

They drove a long way before he looked over at her and spoke in his soft, drawling way.

"It's Murielle. I've never heard her like this before. I'm worried, Ethel, real worried."

Ethel reached over and took Earl's gnarled hand and they shared a look of comfort.

Ethel Landers and Earl had just recently started dating at the ripe old ages of 62 and 63 respectively. Earl was a known figure around town as the lodge keeper and owner of Eagle's Peak. The Elkins' family had owned the lodge since the 1800's and Earl was much beloved amongst the townspeople. Everyone trusted his good sense and he was always the first to lend a hand if you needed a barn roof fixed or just a good breakfast.

Ethel Landers was a native of Kissing Bridge as well. She had grown up in Kissing Bridge and had always been a beauty. Her natural good looks had blossomed over the years into the stunningly handsome senior she was now.

The Landers ladies had always made their mark on Kissing Bridge. They were famous for their cookies, their bakery, and oddly for their family curse as well. The interesting family had had its share of unusual circumstances that had lent credence to the belief that the Lander's curse – that relationships could never work out for these ladies - was real.

But since Summer Landers, Ethel's daughter had married Brad Anderson, thus becoming Mrs. Anderson; they agreed the curse had been broken.

Now, for the first time in thirty years, Ethel had been open to the idea that maybe it wasn't too late to find love.

Earl felt comforted to have Ethel by his side. He had been alone along time now since his wife passed away. Raising Elle had taken up much of his time and energy so he hadn't missed love in his life. Still, as Earl looked at Ethel's sweet face and concerned look for Elle, he knew he was a lucky man. She understood being worried about the people you loved.

He shook his head.

"Darn cell phones."

Chapter 3

Once outside the restaurant, Elle broke down and cried as hard as she wanted. No use masking the truth to herself.

When she was happy she was happy.

People loved her.

Charisma they called it.

Laugher and joy filled the room whenever Elle showed up and she was rarely down.

But she was down now.

Usually she would berate herself for wallowing in low feelings but today she would be real at least with herself.

All her dreams had just broken apart

like a big pin pricking her beautiful red balloon.

She looked down at the lovely red dress she had bought just for the occasion, hugging her slim body.

Tonight she had thought she would become engaged.

Instead she had become single.

Without Todd she suddenly felt worthless.

Her hero prince was gone and her empire had toppled.

She was alone again with all her old insecurities.

She closed her eyes tight to stop all the old feelings from coming back.

Elle had had a tough time as a child. She had been an awkward child, overweight, short, with red hair and freckles.

Her mother's choice to name her after her great grand mum had not helped either. Murielle.

Born chubby, naturally clumsy and with a funny name. The cards had been stacked against her from the start.

But Elle had always had her parents to

love her and they had assured her she was wonderful.

She had the most beautiful laugh and people just seemed to adore her even if her classmates couldn't see her light yet.

When her mom and dad had died suddenly in a car wreck, leaving her orphaned at only seven years old, Murielle was beyond devastated. She felt like she had died right along with them, but somehow her body had gotten stuck.

She'd had to leave all she knew in her home in Florida and move to Kissing Bridge Mountain to live with her Grandpa Earl, who she had only met once before.

Earl was a nice man and overjoyed to have Murielle with him. It helped ease the loss of his daughter.

But Murielle refused to talk. For over a year she wouldn't say anything and Earl feared the loss of her parents might be something she would never be able to get over.

Then miraculously one special Christmas she had finally started to speak.

"Mistletoe," she had said as Earl had held her up underneath it.

He had never been so happy.

Brad Anderson had given her a peck on the cheek for her first mistletoe kiss ever and the smile that had spread over her face warmed Earl's heart.

It was the beginning of a change in her.

Earl owned and ran the Eagle's Peak Lodge, which also had stables and gardens.

Murielle had slowly found her solace and center in the horses. Although humans seemed to disappoint her, the horses never did.

They didn't judge her.

They just loved her back unconditionally.

As a young girl she would ride daily off into the mountains and leave all her loss behind. With the horses she could lose herself in the feeling of the union when they would gallop and the wind would whip her hair around and she felt God with her.

In time she became an expert

horsewoman with blue ribbons decorating her room.

By the time she entered high school she had sprouted into a tall slender beauty and shortened her name from Murielle, to Elle.

When she met Todd her freshman year and their love blossomed she finally felt like her life was good. She felt sure that together they would build the life she had always dreamed of but never had, and she would finally have her own real family.

So much for that.

Chapter 4

Jason Anderson sat across from his brother Brad at the kitchen table, looking over some business notes. It was Sunday morning at the Anderson house so as per usual, the large silver cooking pot was on the stove. The pot sat simmering with tomatoes and spices and meats in preparation for their traditional Sunday night dinner with the family.

It was the custom that the family would all start arriving early Sunday morning, each of them bringing something to add to the spaghetti sauce - fresh sausage, homemade meatballs, fresh garlic.

As the mixture simmered throughout the day the family would gather for conversation and then all go to mass before convening back at the Anderson house for dinner and the eating of the pasta and special sauce.

Grandma Christiano was full blown Italian and Mrs. Anderson had learned to make all her traditional specialties from Tuscany. She had grown up with the "Sunday Sauce" tradition.

Over time many a Kissing Bridge native had become privy to this information and would suddenly find themselves stopping by for a surprise Sunday visit, and dinner.

Of course they were always welcome at the Anderson house.

Mom came in from the garden carrying some fresh basil. It was June in Kissing Bridge. The snow had long cleared and the garden was full of fresh greens and vegetables and she intended to take full advantage of them.

She kissed both her boys on the cheek. "It's so nice to have you both here. Your brothers are on the way."

She couldn't help but give them each a big hug. Although all her other boys had stayed in Kissing Bridge, both Jason and Brad had just recently come home.

Brad had been a full time commercial pilot, with no real place to call home. But as fate would have it he had reunited with his high school love, Summer Landers, and they had married and made Kissing Bridge their home. Mrs. Anderson couldn't have been happier about it. Plus he had recently survived a harrowing plane accident where he nearly died.

It had been a wonderful but difficult time, but in the last few months she had never seen him happier.

Summer Landers was now her daughter in law and she and Brad had recently bought a beautiful house on the mountain and were planning a family.

Jason, her youngest son, had recently returned home after years of service in the military and gotten engaged to a lovely young woman named Dodie, who worked in the Landers Bakery. Together the boys had started their own airplane service that catered to Kissing Bridge. She couldn't be more overjoyed that her boys were both back home and happy.

Suddenly a light lit in her eyes as she remembered something. "Oh, Jason, I received a letter for you. I think it's a return card from the wedding invitations. It's from NY City. Do you know people there?"

Jason Anderson's gray eyes grew pensive. He looked at his mom and brother with the matching Anderson gray eyes and considered it. "Can't say I do, mom. That's strange."

"Well, here. Let me get it for you and maybe you can solve the mystery!"

Within moments she was back with a white envelope addressed to Jason. She handed it to him then went over to the counter to chop up the basil for the sauce.

Jason opened it up. It was a letter from his old friend Dayton Lowry.

"Wow, well, that's a surprise!" Jason exclaimed. "I'd lost track of him and had all my other letters returned."

"Who's that?" his brother inquired.

"It's my war buddy, Dayton Lowry. He's a full blow hero. Got a purple heart for running back into a mind field to save five men. You probably saw him all over TV. Actually stopped another hundred from sure death as well."

Brad nodded. "I think I have seen him. Young good looking guy, too. Impressive."

Jason shook his head. "Yes and no. I heard he was having a hard time. They've been tooting him around on all the news channels as an American hero but he hasn't been the same since the war. I heard he's been in counseling for PTSD."

Brad looked sympathetic. He would never know. He had lived a charmed life of an international pilot while his brother had gone into the armed services. "I'll say a prayer for him, bro. What's he got to say?"

"Says *congratulations. I'm thinking of coming.*"

Jason arched a brow. "Maybe Earl has an extra room at the Inn? That would be perfect for Dayton. I'm going to call him right now."

Momma Anderson's Authentic Tuscan Italian Long Simmering Sunday Sauce

- 2 lb. 80/20 ground beef
- 4 - 6 oz. can tomato paste
- 12 oz. water
- 2 - 24 oz. jar tomato puree
- 12 cloves garlic, minced
- 2 bay leaves
- ½ cup Olive Oil
- 2 cut carrots
- 2 onions chopped fine
- Full head of basil chopped
- ½ cup granulated sugar
- Pinch of dried oregano
- Pinch of onion powder
- Pinch of garlic powder
- Salt and pepper, to taste

Suggestions for guests to bring to add to the pot: Sausage, Meatballs, Chicken

In a large stockpot, sauté garlic until soft and fragrant in 2 tbsp. of olive oil, about 2 minutes.

Throw your meat in with the garlic and brown until meat has been thoroughly cooked through, about 5 minutes. Season with salt and pepper.

Pour in the tomato paste, tomato puree, and seasoning, including the fresh basil. Stir to mix well. With the 6 oz. can from the tomato paste, fill that with water and pour it in the stockpot as well.

Let mixture simmer, uncovered, for 3 or more hours (the longer the better, but minimum 2 hours), stirring occasionally.

Serve hot over fresh pasta.

Chapter 5

Dayton Lowry sat in his one room apartment in his only chair, staring out the window, as was usual during the day.

He was a strapping, nice looking young man with dark brown hair, and deep soulful brown eyes that had used to sparkle when he was happy. No one would have known that seeing him as he was now, though.

He couldn't remember what that felt like anymore.

He had long since ceased to take care of himself or his apartment.

Just didn't matter.

He had grown his hair long and his beard nearly reached his chest.

He rarely went out but when he did, people crossed the street like he might hurt them.

He always laughed at that.

But he understood why they crossed the street.

He was an unknown.

Unstable entity.

Unsafe.

Get away.

He had learned as a young child to spot guys just like him, and run the other way.

Dayton had had a tough upbringing, but his natural effusive personality had won him friends, despite his reticence to let anyone in too close. He kept up a good mask so no one would have ever guessed the life he had endured.

Now he couldn't even pretend anymore.

The war had left him a different man. Stronger, wiser but sadly even more broken.

A hero the President had called him as he pinned on his purple heart.

Dayton almost laughed.

Hero.

More like survivor.

He had survived, he had helped many others survive, but there had been the multitudes he couldn't help.

The memories of the cries of pain and the suffering moans of the dying still pierced his mind, shutting out any happiness he might have otherwise found.

In fact, each wonderful thing that happened in his life only seemed to magnify the pain in comparison. He had become a recluse after he'd left the Marines and his days were spent just the same.

Coffee,
staring out the window,
stomach growls, it's dinner,
time to eat.

Bed.

Oh, got to feed War Hero.

He had a dog now. A stray that had been abandoned and Dayton had found eating out of his garbage can in the alley.

Dayton had finally started to throw it scraps of his dinner instead but the dog stayed distant.

Finally one day the dog just showed up at his backdoor and stayed.

Dayton called him 'War Hero' because he had one eye poked out and a broken tail that jutted out like an L permanently. Half his fur was burned off. He wasn't pretty, but they understood each other.

Dayton was only twenty-two and his life was already over. His only friend was a stray dog and the pain from his hip wound wasn't getting any better.

He pulled out some pain pills and popped a couple with a glass of water.

He looked at the bottle.

Day after day.

Just waiting for the night to come so he could lie back down and not think about the horrors he had seen. At least when he slept the devils and the evils went away. Except when the nightmares came.

The phone rang and he saw Jason Anderson's name come up.

He smiled for the first time in months.

Jason Anderson had been the one man Dayton felt comfortable with.

His hometown values were the same as Dayton's and his soft reserved nature had allowed Dayton to open up to him.

Over time they had become best friends.

Unlike Jason's wonderful family, Dayton had joined the marines to escape his abusive upbringing.

His mom had died when he was young and with the loss of her he had lost his only protector against his alcoholic raging father. He had endured daily beatings from his father until the day he had run away and joined the armed forces to escape his life.

Dayton picked up the cell phone.

"Jason. How are you, man?" It was the first time in a long while he'd spoken to another person.

"Better when I see you! Dayton, I got you a room at the local inn that you're going to love. The wedding is next month and I could sure use my best man to make it here early to help me out."

Dayton stammered. "Best man?"

Jason softened at the sad tone in his friend's voice.

He still wasn't the same even a year after being home.

Jason had hoped the busy city of his hometown might help him heal where people could not. It seemed it was not so.

"Look, Dayton. It's beautiful here. The only time Kissing Bridge is prettier than summer is maybe Christmas. I was hoping you'd come stay a while and help an old friend get through the last of his pre marriage jitters."

There was a long silence.

Jason waited for a long while but Dayton didn't reply.

Jason lowered his voice and said, "Please come, Dayton. It would mean a lot to me."

Dayton squeezed his eyes tight.

Feelings of trepidation ran through him and he could feel another panic attack coming on. He mopped the sweat off his brow and reached for a pill case in his pocket.

He took out two pills and washed them down with water.

"Dayton, you there?"

Dayton stared at the pill case. He dumped out the whole bottle full into his hand and looked at them, contemplating.

It would be so quick and easy.

So painless.

No more pain, no more tears, just peaceful. Just dead.

He looked at the pictures of him smiling on his walls, getting honors and medals from the President and other dignitaries.

The photos only mocked him now. Some hero, he couldn't even get out of his room.

"Dayton," Jason said. "I love you man. Come down here and I promise things will be better. Miracles happen at Kissing Bridge. You deserve a miracle, buddy."

The tears flowed down Dayton's face as he looked at the pills in his hand.

Miracle.

He hadn't seen any miracle save all those men in Afghanistan.

He hadn't seen any miracle save his mother, or the small child from being beaten. No evidence in miracles.

Still he knew there was a God.

Maybe.

After.

He poured the pills back into the bottle and threw them across the room. He watched as the container hit the wall and all the little blue pills spilled out of the bottle and down the wall and across the floor.

He watched as they all rolled in separate directions…

"Dayton…are you there man."

Jason heard him breathing hard on the other line. He looked at Brad with a worried look and shook his head.

He tried one more time.

"You saved so many people," Jason said. "Maybe it's time to try and save yourself."

Dayton was shaking now.

Travel.

Go somewhere new.

Leave the safety of his one room.

He didn't think he could do it.

It was too much.

People might talk to him.

He might break down in the middle of the flight and freak out like the PTSD broken vet he was.

But somehow something in him moved.

Was it hope?

Did he still carry some vestige of faith even after all he'd seen?

That was laughable.

Still, he felt his heart open just a bit and then, before he knew what he was doing, he spoke.

"Yes." He whispered. "I'll come. Just don't tell anyone who I am, please. I just want to be your friend Dayton from NY."

Chapter 6

Brad and Summer sat at a long pine table looking out over the bright sunny morning through the picture window of the Eagle's Peak Lodge Inn Restaurant.

Brad was spooning down potatoes with his feta and broccoli omelet as if he'd never eaten before. Elle came over to refill their coffee cups.

Summer smiled at her. "Thanks, Elle!

Gosh, the Inn makes the best coffee on Kissing Bridge."

Elle smiled at Brad's face in his plate. "Looks like my grandpa's food isn't so bad either."

She and Summer shared a conspiratorial laugh.

To think that it had been young Elle, going by Murielle then, and that fateful Christmas mistletoe kiss, that had changed the course of her and Brad's life.

Back then Murielle had been a plump, awkward little girl with a mop of crazy red curls. Now she was 19 she had blossomed into a great beauty.

Summer surveyed her like a model scout - long legs, sea green eyes, lovely red hair, and a sprinkle of freckles. Oh, the modeling world would just eat her up.

But Elle had no love of fame of fortune. She knew that family was all that mattered. All that had ever mattered.

After losing her parents, everything had changed in her life. Grandpa Earl had always told her that God had saved her for a reason, and that was to be his shining example.

Elle had become just that.

She was a delight to everyone she met.

You would never have guessed the tragedy she had endured behind her easygoing personality. Before you fell under her mesmerizing green eyes you would most likely have fallen under the spell of her infectious laughter.

Joy just seemed to bubble out of Elle.

Her epic smile and easy laugh made her one of the most likeable people on Kissing Bride.

And goodness knows there are a lot of nice people on Kissing Bridge Mountain!

Still, Elle had that extra something that just made people feel good to be around her.

Summer noticed that Elle's smile didn't quite make it up to her eyes today. Something was wrong.

"So, besides your Grandpa working you to the bone here, what's new with you, Elle?"

Elle's green eyes clouded over, but she quickly shrugged it off and patted her hands absently on her apron, then retied the bow a couple times. "Nothing, really."

Summer knew it really was something, really. "How's that darling beau of yours?

Elle bit her lip and her face told the entire story. "I have to go make some more cornbread. You guys enjoy your breakfast."

With that she hurried away into the kitchen.

Summer looked after her with concern.

Just then Jason and Dodie came down the stairs into the main dining room. Dodie was stunning in a light blue dress that set off her china doll eyes perfectly. Her engagement ring sparkled off the morning light as she waved to them. Jason took her hand and led her over to Brad and Summer's table.

He pulled up a couple chairs next to them. Jason and Dodie were obviously very much in love. Just the way he looked at her with those famous Anderson gray eyes told it all! Summer was so happy that Dodie would soon be her sister in law.

"Hi guys!" Jason said. "We just finished setting up the room for Dayton.

Dodie picked the nicest flowers for him too!"

Jason squeezed her affectionately. She beamed back at him.

"I'm so excited he's coming in for the wedding!" he said.

Brad pushed his plate away and smiled broadly. "That's great news, bro! I've never met a real war hero before. The purple heart – how many people did he save to get that again?"

Jason's face clouded over and his grin faded. "Probably best not to bring it up. He's been having a hard time."

Dodie's hand reached out and she took Jason's tenderly. "I'm so glad he's coming here, darling. You came back and healed, so did I. Maybe Kissing Bridge Mountain is just what he needs."

Jason beamed and then grabbed his bride to be and gave her a big smooch. "Maybe you're just what I need!"

Dodie giggled and they stared at each other.

Brad turned to Summer. "Were we this bad?"

She laughed. "Worse."

Brad smiled back. "It's true. I'm a big wuss when it comes to you, Mrs. Anderson."

Summer tickled him. "Super, because I just adore wusses!"

They all had a good laugh.

"Hmm," Jason said. "It smells so good in here, I'm getting really hungry."

Summer noticed that Elle had not been out in the dining room for a while. "I'll go check on Elle."

Summer found Elle in the kitchen, making the dough for the corn bread. Ingredients were littered around her but nothing was in the bowl. Elle was just staring at it.

Summer grabbed an extra apron and tied it on. "Looks like you could use a little help."

"Yeah," Elle said, snapping out of her daze. "Corrine wasn't feeling well so I'm covering for both of us."

Summer started putting the flour, sugar and corn in the bowl from the recipe.

Elle was unusually quiet.

"You wanna talk?" Summer asked.

Elle threw in a cup of milk to the batter and the tears slid down her face. She turned her sad green eyes up at Summer. "Todd broke up with me. He's in love with someone else."

Summer threw the spatula down with a whack. "What?"

Elle nodded. "It's true. He left yesterday with her for college orientation. It's over."

Summer hugged her tight.

Elle was only 19! That was too young to have your heart broken.

"Look, Elle," Summer said. "I'm not going to say anything bad about Todd. You've been together years and I thought you were going to get married. But, you, Elle, you are amazing! You're a light in the darkness of this world! If Todd left then Todd isn't the one. He's not your guy. Your guy… your guy will never leave you! You have a great guy coming for you is what this all means."

Elle hugged her back.

It felt good to hug someone.

"I loved him, Summer," she said. "I feel broken. I don't want someone else. I always lose the people I love."

Summer held onto her tight. "I know, sweetheart. I know."

Summer's family had been through losses of their own throughout the years. But Summer knew if the Lander's curse could be broken, anything was possible.

Elle continued to cry softly. She was so thankful to let out her feelings instead of keeping up the false happy front she had worn like a mask since the breakup.

She cried as Summer held her close.

Summer was a good hugger.

She was the type that when you hugged her she held on a long time, as long as you needed. Most people let go.

Just can't go that emotional distance.

But Summer didn't let go, and oh how Elle needed someone not to let go.

Chapter 7

Jason landed the Cessna skillfully on the landing behind Eagle's Peak Lodge.

Dappled in sun specks the lodge looked beautiful and stately. The mountain was alight with the summer afternoon sun, which made the grass a special shade of green.

Dayton got out of the plane and smelled the clean pine smell of the air.

The sun felt warm and good on his face.

He closed his eyes to feel the peace of the moment. He had learned to cherish each of those fleeting moments of peace, if not happiness.

His reverie was broken by a low growling sound. "War Hero" had not been happy about his traveling case cage he had been forced into.

Jason came around the side of the plane holding the case at arm's length. "You got yourself a wild dog in here, Dayton!"

Dayton grunted. "We're stuck with each other. Both so cantankerous no one wants us. So here we are."

Jason laughed. "Well, we want you Dayton. You might scare the young girls with that beard, though," he joked good-naturedly.

Dayton's hand pulled at his grandpa like beard that hung down to his chest. No one would ever have guessed he was only 22.

He had seen more than his share of things in life and he came off as much older than he actually was.

Now, with his body looking too thin and clothes obviously a few days worn, it was unthinkable that a young vibrant man lived inside this outer shell of a man.

Jason couldn't help but feel worried at the sight of Dayton.

He had certainly wasted away since Jason had last seen him a year ago.

He hadn't sounded good on the phone, and he had heard that he had become a hermit, but he hadn't been prepared for the sight of him in this condition.

Jason hoped that in the days to come preceding the wedding that he might help Dayton back to himself again.

He'd been a scrapper. A survivor since childhood and the ultimate survivor in Afghanistan coming out as a hero and helping others survive.

If anyone could make it back it would be Dayton.

"Hey, maybe I can give you those flying lessons you were always bugging me about?"

Dayton nodded and Jason slapped him on the back. That was as enthusiastic as Jason had seen him since he picked him up.

Jason feared it was going to be a long road of healing ahead for his friend.

"In the meantime," Jason said as he handed Dayton the dog's travel case, "I'll let you do the honors of dealing with your wild animal in here. That is not a friendly dog."

Dayton took War Hero's case, "It's not a friendly world."

Chapter 8

Dayton sat down on the four-poster bed with the big white quilt, looking out of the large picturesque windows at Eagle's Peak mountain. It was incredibly beautiful. The sun was setting, the last rays of light dipping over the horizon.

On the bed table beside him was a vase filled with fresh yellow daffodils. The smell was heavenly and full of the essence of fun summer days. A small fire burned in the fireplace as the night was cold in the mountains, and it gave the room a cheery warmth and glow.

War Hero sat curled up deliciously in front of it. His broken tail jig sawed out to the side. Well, he was happy, Dayton thought to himself, and that was never an easy feat.

Dayton gazed at the natural beauty of the mountain and then around him again at the lovely place they had put him to stay in during his visit.

He thought how different this place was from his dingy dark and hoard filled one room apartment in NY.

Somehow in all its darkness and hopelessness the room matched him.

He felt the dinginess and unworthiness of himself even more in this beautiful love filled room.

Good people lived in places like this.

He didn't belong here.

He wasn't good.

He caught sight of his image in the mirror.

A shadow in the light.

He suddenly realized it had been days since he had showered and how he must have appeared to Jason.

He pulled off his shirt and grungy jeans and headed for the shower when something on the mountain caught his eye.

A red flamed object roaring down the mountain.

He watched it coming closer and closer toward the lodge.

Intrigued, he moved to the window and peered through the twilight.

Below he could see a man by the stable gathering hay while he conversed with an older gentleman. It looked to be Earl the lodge keeper that he had met when he first came in. Nice guy. Straight forward. Big heart.

Dayton had learned to pick up people's real self and pin a person straight away as part of his survival skills.

Each day growing up at his home was like walking on eggshells to see which side of his father's personality would show up. Thc drunk, thc sober, the angry, the beater?

He had learned early on to read the subtle cues. He knew when to hide and wait out the storm when he saw one coming.

Just like in the war.

They never saw the enemy coming, but Dayton had.

He'd been training his whole life.

When he was able to stop the rest of the troops from falling into the trap it had just come second nature.

NO. DON'T GO. NOT SAFE.

The land mines had started exploding like the fireworks on the fourth of July. But he had turned around and gone back in anyway.

It was a death wish.

He should never have made it out.

But he did, and he pulled out five wounded and saved hundreds more their lives.

They gave him medals. Now he was a hero. Life was really funny.

The red rocket burst into view now and in the last of the golden dawn Dayton saw it was a woman on a horse.

The horse was outstanding. A bold black thoroughbred full of spirit and galloping hard toward the barn.

But the woman riding the stallion was even more breathtaking!

She was laughing and smiling and her red hair was flying out in the wind behind her like a mad hatter.

An extremely beautiful mad hatter.

She pulled the horse to a stop but it continued to prance and pull up onto its two feet full Zorro style. She handled him flawlessly, leaning into him with her weight to push him down and all the while laughing.

Dayton was amazed at her bravery!

He would have been scared to bits if a horse ever acted like that when he was on it!

Some big hero.

Earl obviously felt the same way and came over to help the girl with the horse. He grabbed the reins and pulled the horse's head down until he calmed him down. Then he led him quietly toward the stable.

The redheaded girl slid off the horse effortlessly and walked alongside Earl into the stable, still smiling!

Earl didn't seem so happy about it.

Suddenly, as if drawn by his stare, she turned and looked right up at Dayton in the window. Her flashing green eyes seemed to look right into his dead brown orbs.

Dayton pulled away from the window as if he'd been caught.

He sucked in his breath.

He thought he had never been quite so impressed by any other woman.

Chapter 9

It was Wednesday at the Eagle's Peak Lodge Inn Restaurant and Elle was hiding in the kitchen wringing her hands. Darn her Grandpa Earl making her work for him. Of all the days!

Today was Euchre day and all the seniors in Kissing Bridge came to the Eagle's Peak Lodge for their weekly Wednesday game and lunch. Euchre meant Todd's parents. They were fiercely competitive when it came to Euchre and they never missed a Euchre Wednesday.

She couldn't be angry with her Grandpa for anything, let alone covering for him so he could take Ms. Landers out for a picnic. Goodness knows she was thrilled that they had found love at their age when at nineteen she was not doing so well.

But she had forgotten it was Wednesday!

She just wasn't ready to face Todd's parents.

Buzzy and Lulu Vanderling.

They always dressed alike.

Often in pale pastels. They both were both very elegant and tall and had matching platinum blonde hair. They were quite the couple.

She had thought they would be her family some day. In fact, the family holidays and events she had shared with Todd and his family almost made it feel like she had one of her own.

She had Grandpa Earl and God knows she loved him more than anything, but she still found herself longing for a big family.

She still yearned for the family she lost and siblings she never knew. For a while that wish had been filled by the Vanderling family adopting her like one of their own.

There had been the camping vacations. The late night scavenger hunts. Teaching the twins to ski – that had been a trying event! And of course the Fourth of July fireworks celebration.

The Vanderlings were in charge of the most explosive event of the year. The Fourth of July fireworks in Kissing Bridge.

Fireworks on Kissing Bridge were a huge event. The festivities started early in the day at a big cookout on top of the mountain. The Eagle's Peak Lodge always hosted a big clambake and everyone in town brought a dish to share. By sundown everyone would gather to sit down and watch the fireworks together.

The Vanderlings were in charge of the firework presentation every year, and every year they sought to outdo themselves.

They really did a fabulous job and the family put a lot of time and effort into finding just the perfect ones.

The Vanderlings loved to travel the world and they did so often. While on their travels they would search out the most unusual and spectacular fireworks and then bring them back for the Fourth of July extravaganza.

Every one always looked forward to see what type of fireworks the Vanderlings would bring next.

Last year the finale had exploded into a complete zoo – there had been bright red monkeys, yellow parrots, orange giraffes and even a purple elephant.

The group of thirty Euchre players had arrived and Elle could see that Lulu and Buzzy Vanderling were seated smack in the center of the table.

She couldn't keep hiding back in the kitchen forever, unfortunately. She was going to have to make an appearance and, worse yet, take their order. There was no way around talking to Todd's parents.

Elle checked her teeth to make sure nothing was in them and raised her head high. Todd's parents adored her, she reminded herself. Todd's future bride or not, they would still think of her as another daughter. Surely?

She came around the corner with a fake, bright smile on her face. The Vanderlings did not meet her gaze. She swallowed hard and started at the end of the table and took the first person's order.

Egg Salad for Madge.

Tuna on Rye for Stan.

Dolores wanted a ham sandwich minus the ham with extra cheese no mayo.

Why weren't the Vanderlings looking at her?

Old man Jennings and Carol Landers were now dating and as new lovers do, wanted to share everything, fruit plate with cottage cheese with an extra plate.

Joe will have the Rueben.

Why weren't Todd's parents even acknowledging her?

Now she was in front of them. She managed a light smile hoping they wouldn't mention Todd or the breakup.

She needn't have worried.

"Hi, Mr. and Mrs. Vanderling," she said, trying to make her voice as cheerful as was humanly possible. "It's so nice to see you!" She smiled as sincerely as she could manage, hoping they wouldn't see how hurt she was. How much she just wanted to be back as part of the family again.

Losing Todd had been hard but not having a connection with the adopted family she had come to love would be unlivable for her. At least she still had them.

But they just kept talking to other people like she never said a word.

Were they shunning her?

No, they just must have not heard her.

She summoned up her courage with even more gaiety. "Hi, Mr. and Mrs. Vanderling!"

NO REPLY.

Oh, goodness! They *were* shunning her purposely.

Elle thought her heart might just plop right out of her body and onto the table right then.

She wondered if they would say anything to her if her heart actually did suddenly plunk down onto they're butter plates and slither around the white tablecloth.

Would they talk to her then?

Elle took a deep breath and tried again. "Ahh okay, anyway, do either of you want to order?"

Lulu was acting like a real diva jerk and just pointed to her husband Buzzy without even looking at Elle.

Buzzy finally blurted out, "We'll both have the beef on weck." Then just as abruptly dismissed her with a flick of the hand and started a conversation with Carol Landers.

Carol Landers at least had the heart to notice how rude Buzzy was being and she stopped him mid-sentence and turned her attention to Elle. A softness of understanding filled her eyes and she looked deeply into Elle's green ones.

"Thanks for filling in today for your Grandpa, sweetheart. My sister Ethel was thrilled about going on a picnic today with him. You're a good granddaughter. And I like your hair."

Elle self-consciously reached for her hair and then realized Carol was joking, being a fiery red head herself.

Carol winked at her and adjusted her signature large red beehive.

Elle found herself laughing and thanked God for Carol Landers saving her from falling through the cracks of the lodge floor in complete embarrassment.

After what seemed like a lifetime to take the Euchre club order, Elle put the ticket in for the cooks.

Joe the cook looked at her oddly. "What's up with you today, Elle?"

She shook her head. If she started talking she just might start crying again.

She put her hands on her head, defeated, and sat down on the chair in the back by the door looking glum.

This was turning out to be one of the worst days ever.

What was she supposed to think?

Why should they be angry with her when Todd was the one who broke her heart?

What was wrong with the world lately why did everything seem so upside down?

She considered smoking. Smokers always had a smoke at a moment like this. They just pulled out a smoke and by the end of it they had everything figured out. Cool and precise one cigarette solution.

Of course she would never take up smoking because she was a health nut. Still it was nice to think about.

A thin man with a weird beard walked into the restaurant and looked around, unsure and hesitant.

Elle didn't recognize him. Not a local. Maybe day worker? Definitely different.

"Hello, I'm Elle," she said in her best server voice. "Sit anywhere you want. Menus are on the table." She motioned to the open booths.

He looked right at her but he didn't say anything. He just walked away without a word and sat down at a corner booth far away from the other customers and the frenzied euchre players.

Great, Elle thought. I'm batting zero today in the popularity department. Was 'hello' too much to ask for these days?

Those darn cell phones!

She laughed in spite of herself.

Her Grandpa Earl always blamed everything on cell phones. It was like a get out of jail free card but with cell phones.

"It was all better *before* cell phones," he always said.

"We didn't have these new world problems *before* cell phones," he said.

Because of cell phones we had no morality, and worse yet, no mystery.

Now he would randomly blame every calamity on cell phones!

Electricity is out. Cell phones did it.

Late storms breaking. Cell phones did it.

Todd broke up with me and now his parents won't even look at me. Cell phones did it.

Gosh darn it.

Ouch. Getting slighted by the Vanderlings really hurt.

Elle felt like just going up to her room and just hiding away from the world, but she had to go take the order from the strange weirdo guy with the long beard.

This was just not turning out to be her day.

Chapter 10

By the time Earl came back to relieve her of her duties, Elle was ready to run for the hills. She pulled on her boots, tossed her waitressing sneakers under the desk and headed for the door.

"Do not ride Lightning, Elle," Earl said sternly. "Sal says he's had a demon in him lately. Nearly broke his nose this morning trying to get a bridle on him."

"Okay Grandpa, don't worry."

Elle went down to the stable and saddled up Tomico, a beautiful Arabian who was her favorite horse. She loved to ride Tomico and run off, leaving the world behind.

Galloping through the countryside always made the world drop away.

By the time she and Tomico made it back to the barn the sun was going down and her mood had lifted.

When Elle pulled into the pen to unsaddle Tomico she found the weirdo guy with the beard from the café looking at the horses.

She got off her horse and led her over to get some water.

The guy with the long beard said nothing as he watched the horses.

He really seemed to enjoy them.

Elle pulled out a piece of a carrot from her pocket to give to Tomico as a treat.

"Good boy. Good boy."

Weirdo guy watched silently as the horse nibbled the treat from Elle's hands and she petted him affectionately.

She noticed him staring and tried to be nice.

"Do you want to feed him one?" She offered.

He looked startled to be spoken to, then just backed away quickly and walked away without a word.

Elle didn't know what had happened.

She called after him. "Okay well maybe next time. You can come whenever you want.

Elle sighed.

Weirdo guy.

Chapter 11

The next morning, Elle went down to the stables to get a ride in before her breakfast shift at the Inn.

She was surprised to see the weird guy from the day before back at the stable again so early.

She smiled, remembering how she had been when she first fell in love with the horses. Everyday she'd suffer through her classes with thoughts of galloping in her mind. While all the other girls had begun to fuss with their hair and nails to attract the boys, Elle had been just fine with the horses. She was a natural tomboy at heart and jeans and a flannel suited her more than Chanel.

That had always been a bone of contention with Todd, she found herself thinking, fighting back the bad memories. He had always wanted her to dress up, to be more feminine, more refined.

And she had become that for him.

Changed for him.

Not that any of that had mattered.

She made a mental note to burn anything that had a designer label in her closet.

Elle pulled out the bucket of brushes and tools to clean the horses. The strange man watched her every move carefully all the while saying nothing.

"Would you like to try brushing one?" she offered.

He shook his head.

"You like animals?" she asked.

There was such a long pause that she thought he wasn't going to respond at all, but then he quietly said, "I have a dog. He's around her somewhere. War Hero, his name is."

As if on cue, War Hero came out of the brush looking crazy with his burnt fur and crooked tail. Elle backed up.

War Hero growled at her.

The man reached out and grabbed his collar. "Don't pay him no mind. He hates everyone."

The dog eyed her up with his one eye and continued to growl.

Elle pulled out a snack from her pocket and reached out a hand through the pen gate to offer it to the dog. She was great with animals.

War Hero showed his teeth. She pulled her hand back.

"Wow, you weren't fooling," she said. "That's one ornery animal!"

The man tied up War Hero by the stable and wandered back over to the ring.

She followed him a little way. "So what's your name?"

"Dayton," he said. "Yours?"

"Elle."

They talked no further, but instead leant against the ring and watched the horses. Elle gazed lovingly as they ran around the ring. So simple and beautiful. This had been her meditation for so long. Watching the horses move and run and toss their manes and tails. Happy.

Dayton noticed the love in her eyes. "You're good with them," he said.

She smiled at him. She was happy to know he wasn't a mute as she had suspected. "They helped me when I lost everyone. They allowed me to find peace. I guess you can say I healed being with them."

She looked at him as he nodded, and found her eyes lingering. He was a shell of a man that could barely converse, hiding behind a bushel of hair, with a hateful angry dog.

Her heart went out to him.

Those eyes.

The hiding.

It reminded her of herself.

The one she had fought hard to leave behind. Maybe that's why he was drawn to the horses just as she was.

Chapter 12

Elle was waiting on tables on a busy Sunday morning. Sunday brunch at the Inn was always a popular event in Kissing Bridge and there was always a line to get in.

Elle noticed the hostess seat a single guy in her section. The hostess shrugged and whispered, “Sorry, he wanted your section.”

Elle sighed and went over to the take the weird guy’s order.

He was staying at the lodge so he had been coming in daily for meals all week besides hanging around the stables.

She was getting used to his weirdness at least.

He had been kind of scary at first. Manson-ish looking. But he had been so sweet and loving with the horses that Elle knew he had to have a good heart. How people treated an animal said a lot about them.

Still, he was an odd one, so sullen and somber with that odd beard.

Today he looked, well, better. His normal long scraggly hair was under a baseball cap that said Yankees on it. Suddenly his large luminous brown eyes were apparent. He also had a clean white t-shirt on and she could see that he was quite muscular, with long lean muscles. She realized he was much younger than she had first thought.

She caught herself staring at his tanned, muscled arms. And when she looked up, he was staring at her in that weirdo way he always did.

She avoided his eyes and hurriedly reached over to pick up his plate and utensils, but suddenly accidentally hit a fork. The pressure boomeranged the fork and sent it suddenly sailing straight toward Dayton's chest at high speed.

Dayton instinctively grabbed the fork midair between both hands, just a mega bit from impaling him right in the heart.

Elle sucked in her breath.

Oh my goodness! I almost just killed the weird guy with a fork!

They stood, eyes locked. He still held the fork weapon between his hands, as if in shock.

He looked intensely at her as if she had meant to hurt him.

What could she say?

"Nice catch?"

With that, he broke out laughing. A warm deep-dish filled apple pie kind of laugh. The kind that makes you want to laugh as well.

Elle cracked a smile.

Well, who would of thought? Weirdo guy actually did have a sense of humor.

They both laughed and Elle thought maybe weirdo guy was okay after all. Though he did seem to stare at her a lot.

"What's this?" Jason Anderson approached the table with a big smile on his face to see his friend laughing. "Having a good time without me." He leaned into the table and gave his pal a hug. "How's it going, Dayton? I see you've met our girl, Elle. Lucky you."

Dayton blushed under his beard and croaked out a short, "Yeah."

"Hey Jason," Elle said, surprised. "So how do you guys know each other?'

"We were…" Jason began, but then his eyes flickered over to Dayton, who looked uncomfortable. "Well, more importantly, he's going to be my Best Man at the wedding."

Elle quirked a brow at this news. Weirdo guy was friends with Jason Anderson? Go figure.

She couldn't quite see how the two of them were buddies but here they were. Well, at least now it made sense how he fit in at Kissing Bridge.

She smiled. "That's wonderful news, Jason. I'm so happy for you and Dodie."

Jason smiled. "Yeah! I'm a blessed guy and I know it." He turned to Dayton. "How about that flying lesson I promised you, bro?"

Dayton nodded and they both got up from the table.

On the way out, Jason stopped Elle and spoke with her sincerely. 'Thanks for being nice to my friend. He's had a tough time. I haven't seen him laugh like that since I met him."

Elle blushed now. "Wait a sec." She dashed into the kitchen and returned a couple of seconds later with a little doggie bag. She handed it to him. "That's for his evil dog. Filet mignon. I never met an animal I couldn't win over."

Jason cocked a brow and smiled on the way out the door.

Chapter 13

It was early morning. Elle had time before her shift at the restaurant to get a ride in. She walked down to the stables, breathing in the fresh new day and wondering what Todd was doing. Probably not thinking of her, she guessed. It had been a tough night of continuous nightmares featuring Todd leaving her.

She had to shake lose from these feelings.

The best way she knew to leave feelings behind was to run as fast as you could in the other direction.

Today she would ride Lightning, the wild black stallion.

She knew she shouldn't. Her grandpa Earl had pleaded with her to not ride him. They had rescued him from the racetrack circuit when he had broken his leg and been left to die. Elle had nursed him back to health, and some would say he was better than ever. But he was a wild card, not used to trail riding and the critters of the forest. In all honesty she knew he was skitterish and unfit to ride.

Perfect for her mood that day, though, she decided.

She may not get what she wanted in her love life, but no one could stop her from sailing away on her favorite horse.

At least while Grandpa was sleeping!

When Elle approached the stables she saw that someone was up even earlier then her. She hoped Grandpa hadn't figured out what she was up to. She moved closer. She heard the sounds of hay being bailed and a soft voice talking to the horses inside. Must be Sal the groundskeeper, but it was too early for him to be here.

When she entered the stable Elle was surprised to see not Sal, but the weirdo guy! Dayton.

He had his long hair pulled back and he looked a little less scary than normal.

She was surprised to see anyone up earlier than her. "Wow, you're up early. If you want more to do you could clean the stalls too!"

She laughed, looking around at all the work he had done.

He looked shy and answered apologetically. "I have a lot of energy. Thought I'd help out." He mumbled under his breath.

Elle felt a surge of compassion for him. She watched as he tentatively reached out and patted one of the horse's necks. She recognized that look on his face because the horses had done the same thing for her. Drawn her in.

Offered to love her when no one else would.

Accepted her just the way she was.

Simple.

She had learned that you could count on animals where you couldn't count on people.

Elle really didn't want to interact with anyone. She just wanted to gallop the thoughts out of her head. But she saw something of herself in this strange unkempt man and she felt her heart tug.

She pushed back her urge to leap on Lightning and run away and instead reached out one more time to the strange young man. "Would you like to help me brush them today?"

Today Dayton nodded.

Elle led out the four horses in the stables and tethered them outside in the morning sun. She pulled out the brushes and hoof cleaning tools.

Dayton watched her intensely. She picked up a brush and handed it to him. She lifted his hand to show him the technique.

"Strong and forceful. We need to stimulate the coat and they really like the extra massage."

Together they brushed each of the horses.

Elle loved to see how the horses reacted to him. He had a natural way with them. His gentle speech and mannerism were calming and Elle found herself liking him in spite of his weirdness. She knew he must have a story.

She decided to share hers. "When my parents died when I was a child the only thing that would get me out of the house was coming to see these guys."

Dayton looked at her deeply. She could see her pain echoed in his eyes.

"I'm sorry," he said.

She looked away.

"Yeah, well it was a long time ago. These guys became my family. Spent more time with them then people for a lot of years." She grinned and shook it off. "Anyway. They are very special creatures and you can always count on them to be there."

Dayton nodded as if he understood. "I was always a city kid," he said. "Horses scared the heck out of me."

"Well, they certainly seem to like you."

Dayton almost smiled.

She watched him as he carefully yet skillfully worked with the horses. Seemed to sense when they needed to move or wait. Patient. Smart. Weirdo guy.

Those dark eyes seemed to have seen too much.

She gathered her thoughts together.

She wasn't in the place to save someone else.

She was barely making it through each day with her heartbreak. She was like a drowning victim trying to save someone else. The ocean would take them both down if she let it.

She needed to take care of her own broken heart.

With that, she swung herself up on the back of the black steed Lightning and gave him a little kick with her boot and off they shot.

She laughed in her lovely free spirited way as she bolted off on the horse with her wild red hair billowing out behind her leaving the world, weirdo guy, and her feelings behind.

Chapter 14

Elle and Dayton began a routine of meeting at sunrise and cleaning the stalls in the early morning.

They never talked about it.

Each morning she had come down to find Dayton waiting for her at the stables.

At first she wasn't sure about this stranger and his intrusion on her private time.

Her meditation was being with the horses.

Now she had a weirdo guy here every morning.

Still, she had grown to like and respect him, even if he was a bit strange. He was a smart and quick learner and she had already taught him how to bridle a horse, feed it, saddle it and unsaddle it and even clean its hooves.

Elle watched Dayton as he silently brushed the horse next to her. He had trimmed his beard and had on a fresh flannel shirt and jeans.

She was happy to have him here that morning. It had been another difficult night of nightmares about Todd and Buffy and her left out in the cold crying.

She had come to find solace in the horses and realized that despite the fact she would never get over Todd, at least she could be friends with someone.

She realized that she was happy to have company after the ghosts of last night's agony.

She needed a ride bad. She pulled Lightning out of his stall and leapt on him bareback like a wild Indian Princess. She was in a rare mood. "I'm going for a ride, Dayton."

He looked up at her. She saw his look. "What? I'll be fine."

Without a word he went over to the saddle rack and grabbed a blanket and saddle.

He picked out the quietest of the horses, Sunshine, a palomino, and slowly put the saddle on. "I'm going with you."

A big smile spread over Elle's face at his bravery. She knew he was afraid of the horses though he never admitted it. "Okay then, cowboy, let's ride!"

Chapter 15

That was the beginning of Dayton's love affair with horses and Elle.

As the sun rose each morning they silently met for a ride to greet the day.

Each day had seen Dayton open up and talk more as he learned the paces of the horse.

Soon Elle found herself looking forward to seeing him each morning. If felt good to have a friend.

Being around Dayton somehow made the loss of Todd less difficult. At least if she couldn't stop the nightmares she could awake to chase them away with a friend by her side.

Little by little Dayton had become a

better rider and his confidence increased as his horsemanship improved. He had gradually opened up to Elle about his own troubled childhood and they realized they shared many of the same hopes and dreams.

Neither of them had had the family life they had hoped for. Elle knew she would get that family life one day. That Todd would have to realize he loved her. It would only be a matter of time now.

She worried about Dayton though. Who could love this odd young man that looked like a homeless person and stared at one so intensely? Although Elle had to admit, it seemed like he only stared at her that way.

Probably never had a date, she guessed.

It never occurred to her that he might be falling in love with her.

Chapter 16

Elle's favorite horse Lightning seemed extra high spirited that day. It matched Elle's mood exactly. She had had a horrible run in with Mrs. Vanderling and when she had asked her about her shunning she had learned that Todd had asked them not to talk to her anymore! He thought they should have a clean break to avoid entanglements!

Elle had been heartbroken.

Mrs. Vanderling had been lovely about it, but supportive of her son. "I'm so sorry, darling. You know we love you. It's not about you."

But it *was* about her.

She should have tried harder to look like a future Senator's wife. Not been so headstrong and tomboyish.

The loss of her longtime boyfriend was one thing, but now to lose her pseudo adoptive family was too much.

Dayton watched Elle as she yanked the brush through the horses' hair and remained silent. He of all people knew what it was like to have pain and sadness.

He could tell she was sad now. If she didn't want to speak he would be with her in her pain in the silence.

He brushed the horse he had taken to named Sunshine, and watched quietly under his lids as Elle finished cleaning the horse and threw the brush with a whack into the bucket.

Within moments she was on the horse and flying out the door.

Dayton looked after her with admiration. She was an amazing woman. Her natural power and connectedness made her so unique. Like a light in the darkness of shallow people.

He could see her. He could see her pain.

He never worried about her riding. He knew she could handle any thing that came her way. Her spirit was strong.

Still today, when she had insisted on riding Lightning, Dayton had a bad feeling. He had survived with those instincts and learned not to ask why, but to just act.

He tossed a saddle on Tomico, Elle's usual choice for a ride. Tomico was a white Arabian that would be considered too much horse for a newbie like him.

He jumped up on the horse anyway and prayed he wouldn't be thrown off. He petted Tomico who was snorting and throwing her head.

Tomico could tell that Dayton didn't have the experience. The horse whinnied and lifted up in the air, testing him. Dayton leaned his weight, bearing down on her and forcing her to settle.

Still, he would take the risk.

Tomico was the only horse that could keep Lightning in its sight on a full run. He knew Elle didn't want company that day, but he would follow at a distance at least. Just in case.

Chapter 17

Elle was galloping faster than she ever had before. The trees and the branches flew by at frightening speed but she didn't want to stop.

The tears were blinding her by then and she just kept pressing on, forward and forward and forward.

Suddenly a rabbit jumped onto the path and Lightning skittered to a stop, then went straight back on his hind legs.

Elle wasn't prepared for the change in direction and nearly fell right off his back.

She struggled to entangle her foot that was stuck up in the stirrup.

Lightning bolted back and started

running full speed in the other direction. She grabbed the saddle to hold on and reached for the reins but she couldn't get a hold on them.

Lying off the back of the saddle she attempted to right herself without falling off at quantum speed, her heart racing faster than Lightning's hooves.

Lightning bolted straight toward the mountain ledge, casting twigs and stones off the path that hit her and blinded her sight.

She struggled to grab the reins as the edge of the cliff came into sight.

"No, Lightning, no!"

Her foot was wrapped around the stirrup strap and she couldn't free herself.

Suddenly she heard someone yelling her name.

"Elle! Elle!"

Dayton! It was Dayton.

She screamed out to him. "Dayton! Help me!"

Dayton spotted the Lightning through the trees, running wild, with Elle struggling to hold on. He knew he *had* to stop it.

He kicked Tomico as hard as he could to head Lightning off at the path.

Tomico bolted ahead and Dayton urged him on. "Yes! Let's do this!"

They met each other at the edge of the cliff and Dayton positioned Tomico as a buttress, squeezing his eyes shut and praying to any God that would listen that all their lives would be spared.

But as he looked over at Lighting, he saw it darted to the side, intent on running straight past the human horse barricade.

Dayton caught the wild look in the horses eyes and without thinking, dove off his horse and barreled into Elle, freeing her leg and sending them both flying onto the ground.

Elle's head hit thc ground hard. The horse stopped just before the edge and then with a wild eyed look darted back toward the barn.

Dayton bent over Elle, feeling shaken up. This wasn't Afghanistan. Of all the people he had saved he never knew them. Not their heart and soul like he knew Elle. If they had died he would have been sad and disappointed, of course. But if anything happened to Elle he would have been devastated. It would feel like all the hope had been sucked out of the world.

He would have gladly killed himself to stop her from being hurt and going over the edge.

He took a big sigh.

He already was over the edge.

He had fallen in love with Elle.

It was the most afraid he had ever felt.

* * *

When Elle woke up Dayton was leaning over her, wiping her red hair away from her face.

Her eyes focused on his dark brown ones, full of concern.

She rubbed the bump on her head. "What, what happened?"

"You took a hard fall. I'm sorry I couldn't think of any other way."

Elle shook her head, trying to clear her thoughts. 'Lightning..?"

"He's okay. He didn't go over. I think he ran back to the barn."

"Oh my gosh. This is all my fault. I could have killed us both. My Grandpa told me not to ride him."

Dayton put his arms around her instinctively and tried to calm her. He hugged her close and whispered to her softly, "It's not your fault, Elle. He's messed up inside it was bound to happen."

The fact that she could have been died finally sank in for her. Dayton had saved her life. The man who had been afraid of horses had fearlessly thrown himself at high-speed toward a galloping wild horse.

As he held her crying in his arms he realized he loved her. He wanted to protect her. Take her home and take care of her.

He held her for a long time until her breathing became easy.

She pressed away from him. Shaken. "Thank you. You. You saved my life, Dayton."

He looked away. The emotions were too much. "It's time we got back," he said.

Chapter 18

All night long Elle had gone over the events of that day, as she had done for many previous nights. The horse running crazy. The ravine getting closer. Dayton throwing himself into harms way to save her.

She lay down staring at the ceiling, thinking of his arms around her and how tight he held her as she cried tears of relief and fear and finally safety.

It had been a few days since the event with Lightning and she just couldn't bring herself to go back to see the horses.

She felt like she had failed. She knew that horse. Knew he was capable of anything but she had urged him on in her own thoughtlessness.

For some reason she hadn't been able to face Dayton either. She saw him outside the lodge each morning brushing the horses but she just couldn't bring herself to join him.

Today she watched him out of the corner of her eye from a cozy booth in the restaurant. Earl came up and put his hands on his granddaughter's shoulders as she drank her coffee, staring out the window.

"Oh, Elle. You can't change an animal's temperament, just like you can't change a leopard's spots."

She continued to stare out the window with a heavy heart.

"You learned a tough lesson but you're not supposed to get stuck on it," Earl continued. "You're supposed to learn and move on. So move on."

She turned to look at her beloved wise Grandpa and gave him a smile. "Darn cell phones, Grandpa."

He shook his head in agreement. “Darn cell phones.”

* * *

Elle finished her coffee and wandered out to the barn. She heard the dog barking and wondered if she should fear for her life. As if on cue, Dayton came around the bend with a smile on his face and a basket in his hand. War Hero was bouncing at his heels.

That crazy dog saw her first and started growling.

Dayton turned to see what was the trouble and saw Elle standing there. He lit up.

“I was hoping you’d miss us,” he said. The dog growled low and ominous at her. “Oh, be quiet War Hero. I meant miss the horses. I knew you couldn’t stay away too long.”

Elle barely recognized his new strong confident voice. She took in his new look.

His hair had been cut shorter and his beard was trimmed to a normal size. She could almost make out a chiseled chin and strong jaw underneath it all, though he still kept a moustache.

The sight of him cheered her up. A warm glow and big smile spread over her as he approached her.

She was surprised at the way her heart leapt at the sight of him. Here she had thought she was safe from feeling anything, but her heartbeat's rhythm told her otherwise. She was definitely feeling something.

They saddled up Sunshine and Tomico, and then rode for a long while just enjoying the clear day.

She was glad that Dayton wasn't a jabberwocky that needed to talk all the time.

Todd was always pontificating about this or that and never just enjoying the moment.

It was then Elle realized she hadn't thought about Todd all morning. She breathed a sigh of relief. Maybe she was getting over him.

She looked over at Dayton who shot her a big smile. "Let's pull over here," he said. "I have a surprise for you."

Elle was intrigued. She loved to see Dayton smile. She had only caught that grin on his face a couple times but now it seemed permaplastered on his face. He certainly was in a good mood.

When they stopped, Dayton spread out a red and white checkered cloth on the ground, then pulled out fresh fruit, mini sandwiches and her favorite, kale salad.

Elle was taken aback. "Wow, you brought all this? Where did you get a kale salad from for Pete's sake!" She couldn't help but laugh.

She thought she was the only one on Kissing Bridge Mountain who ate anything green!

She always had the gluten free this and the organic that and the rest of the town's folk thought she was just food crazy.

But he had brought her crazy.

She looked up to see him looking at her for approval. "Do you like it?"

She instinctively reached out and hugged him.

"It's just what I needed. Thank you."

The feel of his strong body next to hers made her feel safe. She leaned into his strength and he held her tighter. She realized she didn't want to let go.

He pulled away and looked at her with love in his eyes. For once she didn't pull her gaze away from his.

He leaned over and kissed her gently and it felt something close to heaven itself. "I know you could have any guy you want, Elle. But I'd like to put my resume in to be your guy, your hero, your prince." There was no sense of awkwardness about him anymore, and that surprised her. "I want to be all those things for you, Elle."

Elle could hear her heart beating all the way up in her temples. What beautiful words! But yet…

"I never thought I would say that to anyone," he said, and now he sounded shy.

Elle took his hand and looked at him. "Oh, Dayton, that was so nice. Really it was. But I'm not… I'm not sure I'm ready."

"Oh," he said. "Well, I should have never said anything, but—"

"No, it's okay," she interrupted. "I'm just, not really over my ex. But don't give up on me. Please. Maybe I'll get there soon."

"Okay." There was a twinge of disappointment in his voice but he was evidently trying to sound brave. That alone did something to her soul.

When he looked deeply into her eyes, Elle knew without a doubt that this man would never leave her. He loved her just the way she was. Broken nails, tangled hair and the smell of horses.

It felt so, so good to be seen. Intoxicating, even. To be loved for just being her. To not have to *try* to be something she was never meant to be. But… what about Todd? Instead of tying herself up in knots, she decided to drop that thought and try to savor the moment. That rare moment of being completely and utterly accepted for who she was.

As they walked their horses back toward the stables, Elle felt a wonderful calm inside. "It's pizza and wings night at the Inn. Want to come?"

"If you're there, I'm coming."

Elle beamed at him. "You'll have to catch me first." And with that, she and Tomico dashed inside the stables.

Chapter 19

They were both out of breath and laughing like kids when they came racing into the barn area.

Suddenly Elle looked like she saw a ghost. The smile fell off Dayton's face as he followed her gaze.

Todd. At the gate. With flowers.

Todd looked back and forth between the two of them suspiciously but managed a big grin. "Hi."

Elle could barely talk. "Todd. What are you doing here?"

Todd cleared his throat and thrust the flowers toward her. "These are for you. I was hoping we could talk."

Elle was in shock. She looked at Dayton for strength.

Todd.

Back.

He knew how hard this must be for her.

Dayton jumped off Sunshine and grabbed hold of Elle's horse, then led them both back toward the barn.

"Alone, Elle," Todd said, a bit louder.

Dayton turned back to him with a look of disgust. "Don't yell at her. You left her, man. You don't get a second chance. If a girl like Elle loved me I would never leave her."

Todd rolls his eyes. "You're kidding me, right? Who is this guy and why is he acting like an authority on you, Elle?"

Dayton's voice was hot with indignation. "Because I love—"

"We are just friends," Elle interrupted quickly. She tried not to notice Dayton wincing in the corner of her eye.

Todd folded his arms across his chest and stuck his chin up. "Well, if you're friends, then tell your *friend* to shut the heck up and stay out of out business."

Dayton threw down the reins of the horses and walked toward Todd, manly and in charge. "Listen, buddy. You don't deserve her. You never deserved her and you don't get to get her back just because you come waltzing back into her life."

Todd backed up, pretending to be scared, and yelled to Elle, "Get your rabid dog away from me, Elle!"

Elle ran toward the arguing men. "Stop it! Just stop it!"

By the time she got to them they both had their fists raised, ready to fight. Dayton watched her, and dropped his fists.

Elle stared at Todd, waiting for him to do the same, but instead, he lunged forward with a massive swinging sucker punch.

But Dayton was ready. He surprised Todd by catching his punch mid swing.

Elle was afraid Dayton would hit him back, and she couldn't stand when people fought, but Dayton instead held Todd's arm firm. Todd tried to wriggle away but his strength was no match for Dayton. Dayton's eyes were like steel.

Finally Todd seemed to give up the struggle. That was when Dayton tossed his arm away.

"You don't deserve her," Dayton spat out.

Todd nursed his sore wrist and shot Elle a dirty look. "I'm outta here."

With that he ran out of the stables. The sound of his car roaring away sounded far too loud in Elle's ears.

She threw up her hands. "What the heck was that?!"

"I was trying to help!"

Elle felt like the ground was opening up beneath her. All her hope of a family, of the family she and Todd would build together, of the big family he had that had welcomed her, seemed to be falling into some dark, chasmic hole, never to see the light of day again. "I don't need your help!"

"What?" Dayton said. "I was trying to protect you from that jerk. To help you! He doesn't love you, Elle."

"What do you know about love!?"

He stopped, like Elle had slapped him. Her words seemed to reverberate around them. All his indignation faded away. When he spoke again his voice was heavy with depression.

"Nothing," he said.

"Right, nothing!" Elle replied. "I won't let you ruin my relationship!" She burst into tears and sunk down onto a hay bale. Dayton's declaration of love, and the wonderful way she had felt about it, now seemed so utterly ridiculous. "You don't know even me, Dayton! What gives you the right to get involved in my life?"

Dayton stared at her, and when she looked up at him angrily it seemed his dark eyes blazed into her very core. He looked more serious and fierce than she'd ever seen him before.

She stared back at him through her tears.

"I do know you, Elle," he said. "We're just alike, you and me."

"No, we're not."

"Yes, we are," he said, with a lot of force in his voice. "We both need a real love. I love you just like you are."

She stared at him, dumbfounded.

Love?

How had this happened?

Why had Todd come here?

Why now?

Dayton saying he loved her?

Had the world gone crazy?

Those darn cell phones.

Elle's eyes clouded over. "I don't want to hear that. Just leave me alone! I never want to see you again!" Elle picked up her purse and ran away from him up to the lodge, but he followed her.

"Please, Elle!"

She stopped and turned to him, her chest heaving up and down with the emotion of it all. "I'm going to marry Todd. I'm sorry."

Dayton watched her beautiful red hair flowing out behind her as her image got smaller and smaller.

Chapter 20

The Vanderling mansion had never looked so imposing, but Elle was on a mission. She was going to get her fairy tale reunion. She was going to reinstate herself into that wonderful big family, and cement her place in it by having Todd's children. Then she would live happily ever after, she was sure of it.

It wasn't until she got to the massive mahogany entrance doors that she remembered what she looked like. Her hair was everywhere, having been whipped by the winds out on the mountain. Her nails were dirty from looking after the horses. Even she could take the smell of the stables on her clothing. She was far from the elegant vision she knew Todd wanted her to be, but she'd been in such a hurry there had been no time to change.

She turned to Earl in the car and waved. "Wish me luck, Grandpa," she whispered, before she knocked on the door. Even though she knew he couldn't hear her, it was comforting just to say the words.

It was one of the housekeeping staff who opened the door, Rosie.

"Hey, Rosie," Elle said urgently. She'd met her many times. "Is Todd here?"

"Sure, Elle," Rosie said, though she looked wary. "I'm not sure… I don't know if he'll want to see you."

Elle felt like her heart were breaking right there and then on the polished marble step. "I know. But I really need to speak to him. I have great news."

"Okay," Rosie said, and let Elle in. "I'll just buzz him on the intercom."

She leaned over to the control panel in the wall and pressed a button. Soon it crackled into life with Todd's irritated voice. "Yes?"

"Elle is here to see you and she says she has good news," Rosie said. "Shall I---"

"Send her up," Todd interrupted.

Rosie gave Elle a thumbs up, and Elle grinned back nervously. Then she began to mount the huge grand staircase as quickly as she could, feeling so out of place amongst the luxury finishes and soft gold lighting.

Todd's bedroom, or rather his set of rooms, as he had his own study, living room, huge bathroom and dining area, was up two flights of stairs. It was like a hotel suite, and with the housekeeping staff there to cater to his every need, he never had to lift a finger.

As Elle ran up the second flight of stairs she tried to hand comb her hair into submission. At least if she'd had a hairband she could have made a bun or a pony, but her wrists were bare. She smoothed the top and tugged it into a tight braid, hoping it wouldn't unravel itself. There was nothing she could do about her clothes or her nails or her smell. But if he truly loved her, as she knew he did, he would be able to overlook those things for just one day.

"Elle!" Todd said, standing outside his room on the landing. He looked overjoyed.

"Todd!" Elle ran up the steps toward him and dove into his arms.

"My little orphan tomboy," he said, hugging her for a moment. He soon extracted himself from their hug, wrinkling his nose. "You smell like horse."

"Sorry, sorry," Elle gabbled. "Well, you know, I didn't have time to—"

"I missed you, Elle," he interrupted. "You always made me feel so good."

He clearly steeled himself before hugging her again. She had guessed she would have been melting into his arms by that point, but instead a nagging feeling tugged at her.

Wait, back up.

Did he just wrinkle his nose like that at her and tell her she was an orphan that smelled of horse? None of what he said sounded like a joke. It sounded like a boatload of disrespect, though.

But before she could say anything, he popped a ring box out of his pocket.

Her heart skipped a beat and she had to catch her breath. The moment she had always been waiting for!

Disrespect? He had only been making jokes. Sweet jokes that only lovers could share. Like when she playfully called him an idiot and punched him on the arm, that sort of thing.

"Oh, Todd!"

Todd got down on one knee and looked her in the eyes.

"Elle, will you marry me?"

And there it was, what she had always wanted! The opportunity to become a part of a family!

Chapter 21

His counselor had told him not to get in a relationship. That the ups and downs might be too much for him as he was adjusting into normal life.

That made sense. But talk to the heart. Guess the heart had its own agenda.

In any case, Dayton cursed himself for being such a fool to open up and hope for love in his life.

Ever since he was a child he had wondered why he wasn't worthy of love. Why was he so bad that everyone that was supposed to love him never did?

Not that Elle owed him anything. It

wasn't her fault he came and got a mad schoolboy crush on her and expected her to change his life by loving him.

But he had fallen in love with her. And she loved someone else. That was the truth, and there was no avoiding it.

Back in his room at the Lodge, Dayton looked at his pain pills and considered for the first time in a long time, taking too many.

At least not caring was a dull spirit kill but losing the glimmers of true love and a real life was too much for him to take.

He looked at the open suitcase on the bed, and then at the pills again.

War hero growled and there was a knock on the door. He heaved himself off the bed and dragged himself to the go see who it was.

Elle.

"Hey," she said.

He didn't have the energy to answer.

She looked past him into the room and saw the suitcase on the bed. War hero was in the corner but for once didn't growl when she came in.

She held up a little doggie bag. "Fresh

turkey breast." She motioned toward War Hero, who immediately started to growl again. "For the beast." She offered a small smile, which he did not return.

Dayton took the bag from her hands and then stared at her, waiting for her to say something. Anything.

"I just wanted to make sure we were cool before the wedding tomorrow," she said, looking down at her feet, then facing him with that smile. "We're going to be at the same table and all and I just want Jason and Dodie to have the wedding they deserve. So, are we all good right?"

"Yep, good." His tone was cold as ice.

She gave him the fake smile, the one that didn't light up her eyes. "It looks like you are packing up. Arc you going?"

"I have nothing to stay for."

She breathed out. "I'm sorry, Dayton. I shouldn't have gotten mad at you."

He looked at her seriously. He wanted to be angry but it felt more like devastation. He loved her. He had to try. If he let true love get out of his reach then he was a coward.

He summoned all his courage one more time to confess his truth. "I forgive you, Elle. I love you. I wanted to have a family with you. The one neither one of us had."

Elle stopped him. "Listen Dayton, I know Todd didn't act like the hero I know he is but… But, he and I belong together. He's perfect. Perfect family. Perfect hair. When I'm with him I think I might have a chance to be perfect too. Have that fairytale ending. You want that for me, right?"

Dayton mumbled. "He's no hero."

Elle continued softly. "That may be. But you and I, Dayton, we would never work. We're both broken. Two broken parts will never make a perfect whole family."

Dayton struggled to hold back his emotions.

"I don't believe that, Elle. And neither do you!"

"Yes, I do," Elle said firmly.

But Dayton was nowhere near done. "We understand each other. You were more real with me than you could ever be with Mr. Perfect. I see you. All the parts. The broken and the whole and I love all of them. I love all of you."

She looked back at him, her eyes glazing over with tears.

He knew he would sound desperate but did not care. He had to take that last chance. "Please pick me. I promise I'll make you happy the rest of your life. I'll do everything I can."

She shook her head sadly but let him draw her close into an embrace and didn't pull away.

She could hear his heart thumping hard in his chest. He felt so good next to her. So safe. Most of all, so sincere. So like home.

Everything he said was what she had always dreamed of hearing. The offer of true love and a real family of her own.

She couldn't tear her eyes away from him now, and confusion clouded her thoughts.

The thought of him leaving and not being there to greet her at the stables every morning was unthinkable. He had become part of her ritual. Somehow worked his way into her heart.

But she was engaged to Todd. Her hero.

All she had wanted was for Todd to come back to her and now she felt so conflicted.

Todd had never said those things to her.

Todd had left her once already.

She tore her gaze away from Dayton and looked down at the sparkling ring on her finger.

Dayton followed her gaze. Todd's engagement ring.

Elle saw him stiffen. He drew back and sucked in a deep breath.

She pulled her hand back instinctively but the damage had been done.

His warm eyes were cold and glassed over now. Dismissing her. "You'd better go. You're engaged, Elle. You have what you wanted. Your husband your family, I'm happy for you."

Then he closed the door on Elle forever.

Chapter 22

Jason opened the door at the Anderson house.

He didn't have a smile for Elle that day.

Elle swallowed hard.

He was obviously upset and she had never seen Jason upset. She bet it had something to do with Dayton.

That guy was always screwing up everything, she told herself. Just a big screw up. He was a loose bolt rattling around her life. He had almost screwed up her and Todd. She wondered how Jason and he had ever even ended up friends.

Elle took a deep breath and forced a smile. "I'm here to meet Dodie and Summer, but by the look of your face I guess there is something you're not happy about."

Jason stared at Elle hard. Then he straightened up and sucked in his breath.

"I don't expect anyone to love someone they don't. But you don't know Dayton like I do. He's one of the greatest men I know and I just… well, I hope you will just leave him alone now if you don't want to be with him."

Elle was angry now. She had been nice to Dayton. She had taught him how to ride and embrace life again, and yes, possibly love too.

But it wasn't her fault if he had fallen for her. She had just been being nice. Nothing more.

She remembered the picnic they shared and how her heart had leapt to hear her dreams echoed in his words.

She had felt something.

When he kissed her she wasn't thinking about Todd, she was…

No, she could not afford to think

about that now. She looked down at the rock on her finger and straightened up.

"Sure, Jason. I was just being friendly. I didn't mean to hurt anyone."

Jason nodded.

Dodie appeared in the doorway with Summer in tow, ready to go. Dodie looked at their faces.

"Is everything okay?"

Elle nodded. "Just those darn cell phones."

Dodie arched a brow and figured she'd get the whole story later on the way out of town.

Dodie drove the 4x4 through the mountains and chattered on happy, as could be. It was the day before her wedding and she was positively bubbling with excitement.

On the other hand, Elle was quiet most of the way. So many thoughts were warring in her head.

"So I thought we might all get manicures and pedicures before the wedding as a treat from me!" Dodie said.

Summer squealed and Elle forced herself to squeal right along with her, although her heart felt like a stone.

They ended up at a lovely town just outside Burlington at a place called *Tips and Toes.*

Elle tried to rouse some excitement as she got out of the vehicle. After all, her new manicure would show off her gorgeous ring. The ring that had all the promise of family and happily ever after.

She usually kept them short and unpainted because she worked with the horses. But after an hour of pampering and painting in 'Tips and Toes' she was looking like a real lady.

Elle looked down at her red painted nails and her engagement ring and sighed. They didn't even look like her hands. Perfect. Coifed. Just the way Todd liked her, just the way she wasn't.

The ladies were paying for their services when in walked a stunning blonde pastel laden prep girl.

Elle gasped beneath her breath. It was Buffy Adams, the girl Todd had left her for.

Elle felt like someone had hit her in the stomach just at the sight of her and the pain of the loss she had felt. This was one more thing she didn't want to deal with.

Elle put on her sunglass and attempted to sneak by Buffy unnoticed. But to no avail. Eagle-eyed Buffy caught site of her immediately, and in all fairness Elle was with Summer Landers who was a famous super model and hard to not notice!

Buffy made a beeline straight to Elle and her eyes glazed over when she took in the large two-carat diamond on her newly manicured hand.

Elle steeled herself for the confrontation. She should be mad at Buffy but she couldn't blame everything on her. Todd had made a choice. But in the end he had chose her.

She wasn't sure how Buffy was feeling about it but she was pretty sure she was about to find out.

"Well, look at you, Elle. You finally got the ring?'

Elle looked around uncomfortably.

Buffy didn't seem upset at all about breaking up with Todd and his giving her a ring!

She didn't know what to expect but she hadn't expected this.

"Ahh thanks Buffy. I wasn't sure you would be upset..."

"Why would I ever be upset, darling?" She laughed, a tinkling irritating sound. "I'm here to get ready for the biggest event of my life. Tonight is my father's VIP connection event. It's the best one yet, with people flying in from all over. Daddy says he's going to seal some important deals that will send my great great great great grandchildren to college." She laughed again.

"That's great," said Elle.

"And the most handsome man in the area is going to be hanging off my arm," Buffy said. She looked directly at Elle then. "So glad we worked all of this out."

Elle had no idea what she was talking about, but was in no hurry to find out. "Yeah, me too. So glad."

Buffy then turned to the nail staff. "Now, I know this is a little bit embarrassing, so you're going to have to be sensitive. My boyfriend, he usually gets his grooming done at home, but since we were out for lunch I told him to come with me. You'll take him straight in a back room, right, and do it all in private?"

"Oh, sure, sure, of course," one the nail staff said.

"Perfect," Buffy said, "just a minute while I go get him." She giggled. "He's hiding in the limo right now."

Dodie stepped up to the counter to pay. She was beaming from ear to ear, her French tips gleaming in the sparkling lights of the salon.

Summer rolled her eyes at Elle. "Wonder which idiot has fallen under her curse now."

When the door opened and Buffy strode in with her beau, Elle's mouth fell opcn.

It was Todd.

As soon as he saw Elle, he turned to leave, his face stripped of color, but Buffy huffed, grabbed his arm and dragged him inside. "He's so shy. Honestly, babe, there's no shame in this. All decent men get groomed properly these days."

Elle looked down at her ring, then up at them both, too stunned to speak. Summer and Dodie both stared at Elle in shock.

After Buffy had finished jabbering away to the nail staff about the treatments she wanted for Todd, she turned to them. "What are you all staring at?"

Then Elle found her voice. "Todd, what's going on?"

Buffy looked back and forth between the two with a baffled look and slipped her arm around Todd protectively.

Buffy said. "I don't see what business it is of yours Elle. You've got your own fiancé now. Leave us alone."

Elle crossed her arms and stared at Todd.

She put on a tough exterior but inside it felt the whole world was closing in on her.

Her voice started out as a squeak until she toughened it up.

"Todd, tell us. What is going on?"

Todd didn't have a whole lot to say it seemed.

He just stood there looking rather stupid with his mouth hanging open.

Buffy was getting angry now. "I told you—"

But Summer was angrier. "Is your name Todd?!"

Buffy screwed her lips up and said nothing.

"All right," Elle said shakily. "Since you're not going to say anything, I'll just tell Buffy."

She thrust her hand out, to show Buffy the ring. "This is what Todd gave me a couple nights ago when he asked me to marry him."

Buffy gasped, then looked at Todd.

He could not meet her eyes.

"You're lying!" she said, though Elle could tell she was panicking.

"It's true," Elle said.

Buffy stared at Todd. "Todd? Tell her she's a liar!"

Todd disengaged himself from Buffy's grasp and he walked over to Elle and took her hands in his.

"Please, babe," he said. "You gotta understand. I was going to break up with her after her father's VIP event."

"You what?" Buffy said.

But Todd ignored her.

He looked deep into Elle's eyes. "I choose you, Elle. I choose you. I meant it when I said I wanted us to be a family together."

Elle listened to him saying the sweet words she had so longed to hear. It was the first time he'd ever spoken such tender words to her. She had waited so long for that moment, that precious moment when he'd gaze deeply into her soul and utter just how much they were meant to be together. How they were made for each other. How their family was written in the stars.

Now as she gazed back and forth between Buffy's tear stained eyes and Todd's indifference she felt sick. Here they were in this awkward situation and his words only felt hollow and fake.

"Please, Elle." He pleaded with her to understand. "I needed the connections from her father's party. That was all."

Elle believed what Todd said about his reasons for being with Buffy and lying to her.

She truly did.

Behind his shoulder she saw how sad and confused Buffy looked.

Poor Buffy, Elle thought.

She had never seen Todd's betrayal coming.

Though she had never guessed it would happen, Elle found herself in Buffy's corner.

Now what Todd had done to them both became clear.

"So you'd just humiliate Buffy like that? Make her think there's a future between the two of you just to use her?"

Todd didn't like where this was going, he drew up his lips and furrowed his brow, disbelief all over his face. "What do you care?"

"The question is Todd, why don't you care?"

He shrugged, and then took on a romantic expression as he looked down at her nails, and took in her neat hairstyle. "Elle you look more beautiful than I've ever seen you before. Let's just put this behind us and think of our future."

Elle followed his gaze to her hand with her perfectly done nails and her diamond ring.

She realized that she barely recognized her own hands.

In that instant Elle knew that Todd wasn't her hero at all. He was a louse and a liar and a cheat. His promises of love had proved hollow before.

She wanted more. Not just a ring and promise of a family, but real love. Love with a man who was capable of loving her with all her horse smells and her tangled hair and unpainted nails.

She looked at Buffy's sad face and the crowd of onlookers at the salon taking in the scene. She wondered how long Todd would have kept them both on the line lying to them both to get what he needed?

Elle felt disgusted, and she had thought him her hero.

It became crystal clear to Elle that God had sent her in to get a manicure the one time she needed it most.

She took a deep breath and slipped her engagement ring off and handed it to Buffy.

"I don't know what Todd is thinking, Buffy, but if you're willing to give him another chance you should have this."

Buffy took the ring, looking confused.

"But I wouldn't, if I were you," Elle added. "I think you can do a lot better."

Summer looked at Todd and opened her mouth as if to say something. Instead she took Elle's shivering perfectly manicured; now ring less hand, and led her out the door.

"I'm so sorry," Summer whispered on their way to the car.

Elle shook her head. "It's over. I'm glad I found out the truth."

The loss wore heavy on their shoulders as the ladies got in the car to drive back home. They rode in silence for a long time because sometimes loss just needs to be quiet.

Chapter 23

The wedding was upon them before anyone knew what was happening. Jason and Dayton both stood in their marine uniforms in front of the blue and white striped gazebo. They were both dressed in their service whites for the ceremony.

Elle was surprised to see Dayton next to Jason in uniform. He had never mentioned that was how they knew each other.

Dayton looked so handsome Elle felt her heart lurch.

She tried to catch his eye, but he would not even look at her.

Elle sat in the pew with her Grandpa and the Landers ladies, all admiring how beautifully everything had been set up in the Lodge's large grounds. Thick and glossy red white and blue ribbons twirled themselves around the gazebo corners and fluttered their ends into the cooling breeze. Bunting was strung up from tree to tree, the first red and white striped, the second blue with stars, then alternating in the same pattern throughout.

The aisle was what got everyone talking though, the perfectly mown grass having been sprayed with stencils until it glowed with perfect white stars.

Elle was dressed in a lovely bright blue dress that made her eyes go more blue green. She had hoped Dayton would think she looked beautiful in it.

She looked down at her hand as Dodie and Jason spoke their beautiful vows, which they had composed themselves. She had taken off the red nail polish as well as the ring.

It had been a difficult night of owning up to the truth that the illusion she had created was gone.

But maybe, just maybe, a beautiful reality could take its place.

Summer reached over and took her hand as if reading her thoughts.

Brad was standing tall next to Dayton.

Elle was bursting to run up the starry aisle and tell Dayton just how wrong she had been.

The service concluded and Dodie and Jason were kissing now. She rose with the rest of the crowd to shower them with rice and laughter and cheers as they passed by the guests.

The happy couple practically danced down the aisle way and the wedding party followed behind, throwing confetti of red, white and blue stars along with the rice.

Elle waited for Dayton to look at her as he passed, but he stared straight ahead as if she was invisible.

For the first time Elle could really see him fully.

He had cut his hair short, military style. His beard and moustache too were shaved and gone. For the first time she realized he was actually handsome!

He had a strong jaw and full lips and now that his mop of hair was gone she could really see his eyes. Those eyes that had told her he loved her and meant it.

She smiled to herself, thinking back on all the times she had fantasized cutting off all that beard and long hair.

And here he was in all his shorn beauty.

So handsome.

So familiar.

Elle gasped as she suddenly recognized Dayton from being on TV!

Now that he was standing in all his glory. Shaved, haircut, white military uniform with the purple heart pinned on the lapel.

She had never even seen the real him underneath all the hurt and hair.

Oh my goodness, Elle thought as it dawned on her.

Dayton. Dayton Lowry the purple heart recipient. A true modern day hero.

Elle recalled the news spots showing President Obama giving Dayton the medal of honor, and the interview she had seen him on with Barbara Walters about what actually happened that fateful day on the war field.

He was a true national hero.

A decorated war hero.

And she had compared stupid Todd to a hero, and had called Dayton weak.

What a fool she had been!

Elle wanted to fall through the floor.

Dayton had saved so many people.

Elle realized he had tried to save her too.

He had actually saved her the day with Lightning.

She swallowed hard. He had tried to save her from Todd as well.

He had seen right through Todd. Saw Todd for the shallow, callous career climber he was.

Dayton had offered her his heart and the promise of a real family. She had shot him down. Killed his love just as sure as his friends had been lost with those land mines.

What had she been thinking?

She had been chasing and mooning over Todd when all the while ignoring what was right in front of her.

Todd had never understood her passion. Todd had always tried to tame and squelch her wild free nature. Dayton loved her because of it.

She had been a fool for not seeing the truth.

Now she feared it may be too late.

She turned to Summer with dismay. "Oh, Summer, I've made such a huge mistake. I was horrible to Dayton and he loved me. I turned him down and broke his heart and now I've lost him."

Summer put her arm around Elle and looked at her with sympathy. She had certainly been through a lot in the last couple days.

"There's always time to make things right Elle. He's still here. If you truly love him, then tell him. It's not too late."

Chapter 24

The wedding reception had been set up in another part of the Lodge grounds, the part that Elle had always thought was the most beautiful.

There was a wide but shallow rocky pond, which she had enjoyed wading in as a little kid, and a tall willow that bent over the top of it and tickled the surface with the wisps at the end of its branches when the breeze blew.

Usually it was so calm and serene, but today it was bursting with energy and life. The vibrancy made Elle smile.

There were circular tables set up with sweet gingham tablecloths and it gave the whole scene a homely, good old times feel. Little metallic pinwheels spun in the breeze, flashing their patriotic colors everywhere.

There were even white and red striped picnic rugs laid out over the lawn, with an American flag sticking up at each corner and patriotic pillows stacked on them. The kids of Kissing Bridge gathered upon them and smiled and laughed as they ate their party food.

Under the lovely white gazebo, now strung with garlands and ribbons, the dinner buffet had been arranged.

Earl and the Landers' ladies had spent days together in the Lodge kitchen preparing the many special succulent dishes for the momentous occasion.

The buffet was now laid out with a sumptuous feast. There were aromatic smoked ribs with dry rub, Southern fried chicken and boiled lobsters for the main course. The side dishes were delectable and featured tasty poppy seed coleslaw, German potato salad, spiced black eyed peas, peach cobbler, grilled sweet potatoes, grilled corn, zucchini rolls, mash potatoes, and of course some good old home made biscuits to sop the gravy up with!

In the corner was the beautiful wedding cake. It was in the shape of a flag and had been made by the girls at the bakery. On top of the cake were the little figurines of the bride and groom and written in silver frosting on top, "Congratulations Mr. and Mrs. Anderson."

Though everyone was eating his or her heart out, Elle could only pick at her food. She had hoped to talk to Dayton by now but he had stayed distant and busy with his best man duties.

Toward the end of the meal, nearly time for dancing and music, a tinkling of a glass sounded and everyone looked toward the wedding table.

It was Jason, looking happier than Elle had ever seen him, who had tapped on a champagne glass.

Dodie whispered to Jason, then rose with a champagne glass in her hand. "A toast to my new family and friends in Kissing Bridge!"

The crowd cheered.

She threw a kiss to Kacey and Brody who had made it in for the wedding and were sitting with the Anderson family.

"I wanted to say thank you all so much for coming today and making a stranger to your town feel like I had a home here." She smiled lovingly at Jason.

"I oddly also want to thank my ex fiancé Peter for breaking up with me or none of this would have been possible!"

The crowd clapped and laughed.

Diode looked directly at Elle now and directed her heartfelt words to her. "Because I know now deep in my heart, that God had a great love planned for me. Today I am evidence that God did have the right man for me all along."

She winked at Elle and turned to her husband with love in her eyes.

"I love you, Jason, with all my heart."

With that Jason rose to his feet and kissed her deeply, making the crowd cheer.

Jason picked his new bride up in his arms and whisked her away onto the dance floor.

Dusk was beginning to set and little

delicate white lights now lit up the dance area.

The band played *Wonderful Wonderful* and the couple danced staring lovingly into each other's eyes.

Elle found herself looking for Dayton.

Dodie's words had not been lost on her.

Yes, God had taken Todd away.

It had hurt.

She had broken.

But the truth was Todd wasn't worth it.

She had seen his true light and it was not attractive. Todd seemed like a shallow child's crush now compared to what she had shared with Dayton.

Dayton had vowed that he would never leave her. Now she couldn't even get him to look at her.

She spotted Dayton sitting over at the Anderson table conversing with Brad and Kacey.

Buoyed with the love she had seen Dodie and Jason share, she summoned up all her courage and went over to the table.

"Dayton," she said, trying to make her voice not shake. "Will you dance with me?"

Dayton avoided her eyes and just shook his head no. Elle's heart sank. But Brad would have none of it.

"Go dance Dayton," Brad urged. "It's a wedding, bro, there's no escaping it! Run when they start the chicken dance, though. That's my two cents."

Summer pinched him affectionately. "You always dance the chicken dance with me."

"Exactly!" Brad laughed, "Which is why I'm advising him to run for the hills when they start playing it. I feel like an idiot shaking all my stuff."

They all started laughing and Dayton stood.

He took Elle's hand silently and led her onto the dance floor. Elle's heart skipped a beat, but his eyes seemed so glazed over and foreign she felt her hope fall. His touch now was distant and detached as he took her in his arms to dance.

She gazed at his face. So open and

unhidden now without the beard and the hair. She cleared her throat.

"Dayton," she started softly, as they danced. "I've been thinking. I was wrong."

She could feel him go stiff and cold with her words.

"We don't need to talk about this, Elle. I'm moving on."

Elle continued. "I broke up with Todd."

He paused in the dance for a moment, but did not reply.

"Dayton I was a fool for not seeing what was right in front of me. I told you I wanted a hero and all along you were the only real hero I've ever known."

She longed for him to look at her but he just stared straight ahead as if turned to stone. Elle continued.

"You were right, Dayton," she said. "Two broken parts won't ever make a right whole."

Elle looked up at him, forcing his eyes to hers like a magnet.

"Look at me, Dayton."

He reluctantly met her gaze.

"We can start new," Elle pleaded. "New today Dayton! The pastor always says grace can happen in an instant… I hope this is that instant."

All the hope she felt died as she felt him pull away coldly. He looked at her sadly and she realized he was already gone. All the warmth and glow of love that his eyes used to hold for her had melted away into nothing.

He stopped dancing and carefully detangled his hands from hers.

"I'm sorry, Elle. I just can't do this."

With that he turned his back to her and walked off the dance floor and headed back toward the lodge.

Chapter 25

Elle was crying when Summer found her in the ladies room. Elle looked up at her through her tears. "Well, that didn't go so well."

Summer hugged her. "I'm so sorry, honey."

"I tried but he didn't care."

Summer rubbed her back. Dear Elle with her big heart and her optimism.

"Love isn't easy for some people honey. Give him time."

Elle continued to cry softly. "But we don't have time! He's leaving back to go back home to New York and who knows if he'll…" Elle looked up in terror.

"Oh my gosh, he's leaving!"

She jumped up and checked her face quickly in the mirror. She wiped off her mascara that was running down her face and straightened her dress.

"I gotta go!"

The fireworks were due to begin soon, and everyone was beginning to find seats on the open field to watch the show. Elle ran outside and through the party looking for Dayton but he was nowhere outside to be found.

She ran back inside the lodge to look for him and bounded up the stairs two at a time with her fancy dress hiked above her knees. She was determined to talk to Dayton. She refused to let her future walk out of her life without fighting for it. He was strong, but she was strong in the ways where he was weak.

This was one of those areas.

She spotted his room at the end of the hall and noticed the door was ajar. She breathed a sigh of relief as she hurried toward the open door with her heart beating wildly.

"Dayton?" she looked inside his

room, and she gasped. Dayton's room was completely cleaned out.

The sheets turned down.

All of Dayton gone.

That nasty dog too.

Elle felt sick to her stomach.

By the time Elle ran back outside, darkness had fallen and the place was lit up with ethereal lamps dotted all over the lawn. She didn't have time to take in its beauty. She scoured the wedding guests, looking for her grandfather, and eventually found him sitting with Ethel sipping on lemonade waiting for the fireworks to start.

"Grandpa!" Elle called out desperately. Earl got up quickly and ran over to her.

"What's up, sweetheart? Why are you breathing so hard?"

"Grandpa, did Dayton check out? I can't find him?"

"Settle down, honey. He paid up about fifteen minutes ago and was headed to Burlington to catch a plane or train, I can't remember. He's fine."

"No, no! It's anything but fine!"

She began to pace, her head in her hands.

"Why? What's going on, honey?"

"I love him, Grandpa! I can't let him leave."

Earl pointed at the cell phone in her hand.

"Not answering that thing?"

Elle shook her head.

Earl threw his hands up and in unison they said. "Darn cell phones."

Earl sighed. "Well then only one thing to do."

He pulled his car keys out of his pocket and threw them to Elle.

"You better take my car, honey, and good luck!"

"Thanks Grandpa but it's too late. I won't make it in time! He'll be hitting the valley by now. If I could only go the short way over the hill…"

A thought came to her and she lit up.

Grandpa Earl looked uncertain. "I don't like that look in your eye, Elle."

But she was already running toward the stables. He sighed. There was no stopping a girl in love.

Within moments Elle had Lightning saddled and was flying over the mountain in her blue ball gown.

If Dayton could risk opening his heart to her, she could risk riding Lighting for him.

The moon glowed silver in the dark sky and the fireworks, which had just started as she'd left the barn, lit the sky up like day.

Elle had a clearly lit path and a strong will.

"Don't fail me now," she whispered to Lightning, and off they went.

She rounded the top of the mountain in no time and spotted the red rental car Grandpa had described. It was the only one leaving the mountain. Everyone else was home or at the wedding celebrating the Fourth of July.

Elle bolted down the hill now at high speed, bent on heading Dayton's car off at the turn.

"Yes, yes!" she encouraged the horse. "Good boy! We can do this! We can do this!"

Just as they got to the side of the road,

and Elle thought her heart might burst she spotted the red rental car up ahead.

She pulled up to the side just as the headlights of the red car turned the bend. She could see the surprise in Dayton's eyes as he slowed the car down upon seeing them, and she smiled.

Suddenly, there was a loud series of firework bangs that frightened the horse and Lightning reared up onto his back legs pawing at the air.

Elle struggled to stay on in her ball dress and bare feet and tried to calm the horse down. "Easy boy, easy."

Lightning pranced around scared and unsure on his hind legs as Elle urged him back to all fours.

Dayton slammed on the brakes.

He couldn't believe what he was seeing.

Dayton got out of the car and ran over to them. "Elle are you crazy! What are you doing?!" Dayton exclaimed.

"Please don't be mad," she said. "I had to come try and I knew only Lightning would be fast enough."

He shook his head. "Are you trying to

get yourself killed? Get off that horse right now!"

He came over and grabbed hold of Lightning's bridle with a worried look in his eyes.

"Gosh darn it Elle what were you thinking riding him?"

Elle slid off of Lightening's back and watched as Dayton talked softly to the horse and held his bridal tight. All the love she felt for him doubled as she watched his kind way with the scared horse.

"I can't lose you Dayton." She whispered. "You risked opening your heart to me and so I risked…"

Dayton stopped her and suddenly stiffened.

"I can't do this Elle. I'm sorry."

He handed her the reins and turned back to the car to leave. Fireworks filled the air again bursting open with a red white and blue flag to the tune of "God Bless America." Lightning bolted up again prancing around scared and agitated.

Dayton glanced back at Elle looking

so fragile in her pretty blue dress and bare feet trying to calm the frightened horse.

He shook his head and went over to help her with him again. He tried not to look at how beautiful she looked in the moonlight and the falling tendrils of fading firework streams.

Her green eyes locked with his and he couldn't pull his gaze away. Elle took his hand in hers.

"Give me a chance, Dayton, please. No, give *us* a chance. Give us a chance."

He stared into her beautiful green eyes now fully taking her in. He loved her. He knew he had loved her from the moment he had seen her. She had been the one he had always dreamed of. The promise of a life worth living. The warmth of real love and family.

If only it could be real.

A flash from the previous night stuck him. He had sat in his chair in the unlit room and had stared down the bottle of pain pills begging to be taken. He had contemplated how easy it would be for him to take too many and to forget and not feel hurt ever again. He had been so close to death so many times and cheated it, but last night he had almost lost. He wasn't sure he could make it back again from that ledge if he let his heart be vulnerable again. After hours of contemplation Dayton had come to a choice. When the sun finally peeked over the horizon he had won his hardest fight yet. He dumped out the bottle of pain medication and decided to walk away from the pills, and Elle, forever.

He was a survivor after all.

Somehow through all the loss and pain, he had still chosen life. Kissing Bridge had given him hope and he had changed by his connection with Elle and the horses. He had had a glimpse of real love and joy. But he didn't trust himself to be strong with Elle.

He slowly shook his head. "I have to get home."

Elle was encouraged by the glimmer of love shining from his eyes he was unable to hide. "What home Dayton? Your one room apartment you told me you hate so much? Staring at the walls.

Avoiding life. Avoiding love. Avoiding me?"

"Elle. Stop. I can't do this. You were right. I am broken. You deserve a happy normal life. The home and family you always wanted. I've never had that. An old dog can't learn new tricks, I guess."

Elle shook her head trying to hold back the tears. She didn't know what she would do without him. He had hardened his heart to her and she didn't have the magic to melt it again.

The fireworks were magnificent as they shot colors into the sky. The Vanderlings had outdone themselves this year but Elle took no solace in the beauty of the fireworks as she usually did.

Dayton looked over at the prancing horse. "You're not getting back on that horse, Elle. Get in the car I'm taking you back to the lodge. I know your horses can all get back to the barn themselves."

Elle nodded.

She watched him as he unsaddled the horse and pulled if off his back. He looped his reins around a tree.

Elle got into passenger seat of the car, downcast.

So much for that idea. She looked down at her dress that had been ripped along the wild ride and at her bare feet that were now caked with dirt.

She looked like Cinderella after midnight.

She sighed sadly.

Dayton was putting the saddle in the trunk when Elle heard a low mean growl behind her.

She spun around quickly to see War Hero glaring at her and baring his teeth from the back seat.

She frowned. Good grief! As if things weren't bad enough! Now she had to deal with a dog that didn't want anything to do with her either!

She wanted to cry. It was hopeless. She started to pray.

Suddenly, an idea occurred to Elle, and a smile came slowly came over her face.

The sky was exploding now in all its fourth of July splendor. Dayton couldn't help but be impressed by the display. Kissing Bridge Mountain certainly took its holidays to heart! Dayton went over to

Lightning and stroked his neck and untied him from the tree. He turned him toward the barn and with a pat on the butt said, "Get on home now boy."

The black stallion took off toward the barn at top speed, as usual.

Dayton breathed a big sigh.

Today he had watched his only friend marry the woman he loved. He knew they would find happiness. It seemed living in Kissing Bridge it was inevitable that happiness would find you.

He wished he was as brave as everyone thought he was, but he knew the truth. He was a coward. He was running away from the only place he had ever felt good. He was going home to a life he hated, because he feared death by heartbreak even more.

A girl like Elle could never stay with someone like him. He was too ornery and angry, bristled and broken, just like War Hero.

Broken heroes who were better off not messing up other people's perfect lives.

He walked back to the car with a

heavy heart to take Elle back home.

When he opened the door he saw Elle sitting in the front seat grinning from ear to ear.

Dayton looked at her quizzically. She pointed at her lap. The sky alit with more fireworks and Dayton looked down to see War Hero sitting in her lap, happy as a lamb, eating out of her hand.

Dayton stared in disbelief.

Elle smiled mischievously. "What was that about an old dog…?"

He looked at them, amazed. "I can't believe it! He hates everyone!

Dayton smiled now too. "Well look at that old dog, he finally came around!"

Elle pulled out a piece of fried chicken from her pocket and waved it.

"What's that?" he asked.

"Undeniable bait," Elle said. "That's what Ms. Landers said."

War Hero was a mush ball in Elle's lap now settling in for a nap. Dayton reached over and tried to move him but he wouldn't budge.

Dayton couldn't help but double over laughing now as he watched Elle petting him as if he weren't the evil dog they both knew him to be.

Watching the two of them together tugged at his heart. War Hero being happy made him feel truly hopeful, for the first time in a long time. If that old dog could open up and let someone close to him, maybe anything was possible. If War Hero could change, maybe he could too. Maybe, just maybe, they could be a real family.

"You really love me?" Dayton asked still incredulous.

Elle looked him in the eye.

"I really love you Dayton."

Just then, War Hero licked Elle's face like she was his best friend. The sight of them together melted any resolve he still held.

"Now what?" he said laughing.

"Now we go back to Kissing Bridge, and you stay?" Elle said hopefully.

Dayton reached over and took her into his arms.

Which was not an easy thing to do now that War Hero was glued to her lap and refused to leave.

He kissed her tenderly and looked into her sea green eyes.

"I will stay Elle, but only on one condition."

Elle raised a brow and guessed.

"No more riding Lightning?"

He shook his head.

"No more being single."

Elle looked deeply into his dark brown eyes.

"I want you to marry me, Elle. I might not be the best guy but I will try my best for you and our family every day. I promise."

Elle's eyes alit almost as bright as the exploding fireworks around them and she squealed with delight.

"Marry you?!"

She kissed his face over and over and over.

They embraced as the fireworks finale went off behind them in the shape of a heart with two silver wedding rings. The Vanderlings had bought them special just in honor of Dodie and Jason's wedding.

Now, as the beautiful firework rings shone in the sky above them, Elle knew it was the perfect symbol of the beginning of a new life for them as well.

"Yes, darling! Yes, I will marry you. Yes!"

The End

Thank you for coming along to
our wonderful little town!

Linda is currently working on the last
two books in this series.

Christmas Wishes and Paris Kisses –
Available now!

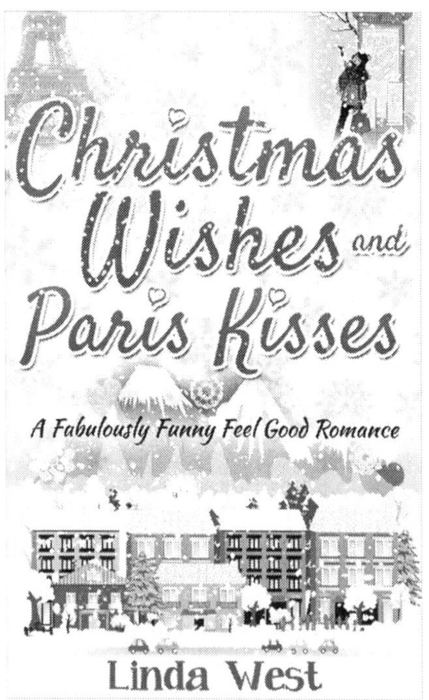

She promises to keep all of your
favourite inhabitants around!

And
The final in the series-
Christmas Belles and Mistletoe
Due out in November of 2016

Thanks for reading my books I had a great time writing them for you!!!

Linda West

Final Thoughts

When you turn the page, Amazon will give you the opportunity to rate this book and share your thoughts through an automatic feed to your Facebook and Twitter accounts.

If you believe your friends would get some joy from reading this book, I would be honored if you told them about your thoughts.

Amazon reviews help other people find great books!

Press here to go to review page ☺

Thank you for reading
Morningmayan.com books

Please write us at:
morningmayan@gmail.com
and we'll send you the first book in our best-selling series
'PRINCESS WANTED'
as a
FREE GIFT
to say thank you for reading our books

MORNINGMAYAN
PUBLISHING

Made in the USA
Las Vegas, NV
02 January 2022

40053753R00385